HELD FOR RANSOM

by Russell Atkinson

Foreword

This book is fiction. The events, characters, and dialogue on the following pages are the product of my imagination. But make no mistake about it: the story is real. The case is modeled in large part on real crimes that occurred when I was an FBI agent in the 1990s. If you want to know what it is like to be an FBI agent, or what it is like to be the victim, or family member of a victim, of a terrifying crime of violence, read on. For obvious reasons, I have invented investigative techniques and omitted others, but the greater story itself, what it is like to be an FBI Agent responsible for the life of a ransom victim, is all too chillingly real.

Characters in works of fiction generally are more villainous, heroic, treacherous, or good-looking than the real human beings around us, and this book is no exception. The people in this book are larger-than-life. None are real. Ample literary license has been taken. Even so, the truth is that the criminals in real life are, if anything, even more reprehensible than portrayed here. It is also true that my coworkers in the FBI were the finest group of people I have ever known. The quirks and foibles I present here are concocted from whole cloth or Bureau lore, and do not represent the actions of any real individuals who were involved in the cases mentioned or any other matter. Occasional media portrayals of FBI agents as dishonest or arrogant notwithstanding, the reality is that FBI agents and support personnel are scrupulously honest, underpaid, and dedicated to protecting the public. Nothing I have ever done, or will ever do, could give me more pride than my 25 years as a Special Agent of the FBI.

I have occasionally been asked by friends what they should do if they, or family members, were ever kidnapped. There are too many variables to be able to answer that question in general terms, but this story can serve as something of a roadmap, showing some dos and some don'ts, either of which can be fatal – or life-saving. No one plans to be kidnapped, but anyone reading this book will be better prepared to face that day.

Movies, crime novels, and TV "detective" shows usually show the main investigators working either alone or in pairs, and they do virtually all the work themselves, fighting the bureaucracy along the way. This works well for dramatic purposes. In reality a major kidnap case, in the FBI at least, involves hundreds of FBI agents and other personnel. It is a true team effort – a very large team. I have managed to pare this down to dozens for improved readability, but it is still a lot of people to remember. For this reason I am including lists of main characters as well as acronyms and FBI terms.

Terms and Acronyms

302 (or FD-302)--The FBI form used to report investigation

ADIC -- Assistant Director in Charge

ASAC -- Assistant (or Associate) Special Agent in Charge

Bucar -- Bureau car

Bulletbird -- Fictional FBI software to locate a cell phone

CHP -- California Highway Patrol

CII -- Criminal Information Index, California's crimes database

CLETS -- California Law Enforcement Teletype System

CP -- Command Post

DAD -- Deputy Associate Director

DOJ -- United States Department of Justice

ERT -- Evidence Response Team (crime scene specialists)

FBI -- Federal Bureau of Investigation

FCI -- Foreign Counterintelligence

FSI -- Forcign Scrvicc Institutc (run by Statc Department)

FOA -- First Office Agent, i.e., a new, relatively inexperienced FBI agent

Legat -- Legal Attache, an FBI agent assigned to a foreign consulate

MIOG -- Manual of Investigative Operations Guidelines

NCIC -- National Crime Information Center, FBI's official crimes database

OIG -- Office of the Inspector General, DOJ

QSI -- Quality Step Increase, a merit raise given to a federal employee

RA -- Resident Agency, a smaller office within a Field Division

Relief -- Relief Supervisor, agent who runs a squad for an absent supervisor

SAC -- Special Agent in Charge (of a Field Division)

SJRA -- San Jose Resident Agency

SOG -- Special Operations Group (a squad specializing in surveillance)

SWAT -- Special Weapons and Tactics

VCMO -- Violent Crimes and Major Offenders

VMC -- Valley Medical Center

List of major characters

Carl Fischer -- Kidnap victim, President and COO of Claritiva Software

Francine Fischer -- Wife of Carl Fischer

Pam Fischer -- Daughter of Carl and Francine Fischer

Carlos -- Kidnapper, gunman

Miguel -- Kidnapper, weightlifter

Cliff Knowles -- Special Agent, acting case agent

Peter Stroaker -- SAC, San Francisco Division

Ben Olson -- Supervisor, Violent Crime squad, San Jose Resident Agency

Tim Rothman -- Special Agent, pilot, close friend of Cliff Knowles

Don Zwolinski ("Z-man") -- VCMO coordinator for San Francisco Division

Robert Carmody -- CEO of Claritiva Software, close friend of Carl Fischer

Mitzi Carmody -- Wife of Carmody and close friend of Francine Fischer

Carlotta -- Fischer's secretary

Ron Jemperson -- Agent on the SOG, tech agent assigned to San Jose

Nick Lark -- Case agent, vacationing in Disneyland during most of the action

Harry Rice -- Agent, trained as hostage negotiator

Kim -- Squad secretary for the VCMO squad, San Jose

Belinda -- Office Services Manager for SJRA

Ralph Tobin -- Lead Technical Agent for the division

Mo Morales -- Supervisor of the SOG

Matt Nguyen -- First office agent on the VCMO squad, San Jose

Gina Torres -- First office agent on the VCMO squad, San Jose

Quincy Allen ("Q-Ball") -- Agent in the SJRA

Chet Murray -- Agent on the Evidence Response Team

Antoinette Bertinetti (Toni, "AB", "The Awful Brafull") -- Stroaker's secretary

Buzz -- Agent and helicopter pilot

Hank LaPointe -- Agent and SWAT leader

Claude Becker -- Agent on SWAT team

Louellen Murphy -- Agent trained in psychological profiling

Luciana Malarna -- ("Lucy") First Office Agent on the VCMO squad, San Jose

Randy Finkman -- Agent on the SOG

Ichiro Tsuruda -- Witness (son is Martin Tsuruda)
Brad Williams -- ASAC of the San Francisco Division
Terry Izawa -- Agent on the SWAT team
Mike Bean -- Chief Radio Technician
Wei-jun Lee -- Chief Engineer at Broadcoast Cellular

Day 1
Tuesday

Silicon Valley
The 1990's

Chapter 1

Graceful and powerful, the sports car glided effortlessly over U.S. 101 toward Shoreline Amphitheater. The mustachioed man behind the wheel hummed cheerily as the May sun warmed his body and his spirits. The V-12 engine, despite its 367 horsepower, was almost noiseless. The combination of quietude and spring weather tempted the driver to turn on his CD player. He selected the Pachelbel Canon and adjusted the volume up a bit. His hearing was not quite as good as it used to be.

He had waited six months for this Mercedes and paid six figures for it, expensive even by Silicon Valley standards. This sum, however, meant little to him, as he was one of the wealthiest of technocrats in this yuppie-infested quarter. His picture had recently appeared on the pages of the *San Jose Mercury News* business section as one of the 50 richest men in the valley. He was now thoroughly enjoying the trappings of his success. The car's exterior was a rich, lustrous shade uninformatively named Alexandrite Green by the marketers at Daimler Benz, and it was unquestionably a beautiful and superbly crafted machine.

It was difficult not to be in a good mood, although Carl Fischer's perfectionism caused him always to be at least a bit obsessed with what could go wrong. Software was a volatile and tricky business. But the data format for Claritiva's latest release had just been named as the industry standard for digital acoustic information transfer, beating out several competing technologies. This guaranteed a healthy revenue stream for at least five years, until the chameleon industry adopted yet another standard. He was already wealthy, but this ensured his children and grandchildren would all be comfortable, and his life's work, his company, would provide prosperity for his employees and co-founder for many years to come.

Fischer made a right turn onto Charleston Road and continued eastbound. When he passed the two-story metallic stick figure that passed for statuary in this part of the world, he turned into the parking lot and maneuvered into one of the too-narrow spots clearly labeled "Customers Only." He was no customer, but nobody told the company president where to park. Except for the blue-painted handicap slots, this was the closest parking place to the door, and he had a bad leg, weakened by a circulatory problem.

The building before him was typical of Silicon Valley corporate architecture: a concrete tilt-up two-story box. It had been recently painted, and nicely landscaped in the drought-resistant style required by local ordinance. This attempt to bring a bit of cheer to the campus merely served to elevate the overall impression from depressing to bland.

Claritiva leased the two buildings nearest Charleston, but there were three others in the complex, situated back a hundred yards. The current occupants of those buildings were Sun Microsystems and Alza, representing computer hardware and pharmaceuticals, respectively, in the valley's technological olio. Those corporate neighbors were older and larger than Claritiva, and these particular units were merely overflow space for them, sites that had been grabbed for their convenient location, but still far enough away from corporate center to create difficulties for their Facilities and Security departments.

As Fischer emerged from his understated luxury, one could see he was larger than the average American male. Tall and thickly built, he could have been a formidable figure despite his 62 years. However, his elegant gray handlebar mustache and apple cheeks gave observers an impression more of a Santa-like joviality than power or ruthlessness. Indeed, his employees knew him to be brilliant, friendly, and caring, the antithesis of the more notorious examples of high-tech capitalists which abounded in nearby industrial parks. Like most local executives, he followed the casual corporate style of dress that was the hallmark of this high-tech Mecca. Today he wore slacks, loafers, and a polo shirt with the company logo on the left breast. He carried his Italian leather briefcase in his right hand.

As he moved his Nokia cell phone from the car seat to his pants pocket, he turned it off. At that moment a grey Ford Taurus pulled into the handicap space next to him. The driver was a muscular young man with a surly expression, staring straight ahead. The passenger, however, quickly emerged. He was dark-complected, with black ringlets of hair curling over his ears. He wore a sports coat and carried himself erect. Young women might have thought him handsome. Immediately he hailed the executive.

"Excuse me. Can you help us?" he called out, somewhat nervously. He held in his hand a large, creased piece of paper which seemed to be a map or driving directions. He sounded well-educated but had a slight accent.

"What do you need?"

"We are looking for InfraTech. It is supposed to be here," the passenger said, pointing to the paper. He seemed hopelessly confused.

The executive had not heard of InfraTech, but, incorrigible altruist that he was, came over to see the paper in hope of providing some assistance. He approached the passenger side of the Taurus and stood next to the younger man. With a sudden, sharp jerk the passenger pulled down the paper to reveal a 9 mm semiautomatic handgun pointed directly at the older man's gut. His finger was firmly on the trigger.

"Get in the car. Now, or I'll kill you."

The young man pressed the barrel of the weapon forward, hard, until it met rib. His other hand opened the rear door. Then with both his free hand and the gun barrel, he gave the older man a shove toward the open door. The executive was both dumbstruck and immobilized by a fear he had never before experienced, or even imagined. He gave no resistance, letting himself be pushed inside the vehicle. The gunman followed him into the rear seat and closed the door behind him. He pulled a pair of sunglasses from his jacket pocket and slipped them on the captive.

"Look away. If you look at me I'll shoot you," he declared calmly. He continued to hold the gun against the older man's ribs. With his left hand he pulled two large cotton pads from his other pocket. Fischer, however, could not see this, as he was looking to the left, away from the gunman as ordered. He could see the back of the driver's head as the Taurus began backing out of the space. The driver was darker than the gunman and had a cruder, more menacing, appearance.

"Close your eyes."

The executive did so.

The gunman then removed the sunglasses and placed the cotton balls over the eyes of the hostage. He quickly replaced the sunglasses. These were the cheap, super-dark sunglasses one gets after a dilation at an eye exam. They were thick on the sides to protect against sunlight even from the peripheral vision areas. In this instance, however, they were for the sole purpose of preventing a casual observer from noticing the cotton ball blindfold.

The Taurus pulled out of the parking lot onto Charleston, then made a slow right onto Shoreline. The driver continued scowling as he merged into Highway 101 southbound, and muttered under his breath at the glut of traffic. He watched his speedometer nervously, making sure to stay at or under the 65 speed limit. This required him to stay in the far right lane, since the rush hour was nearly over and he was heading the counter-commute direction; traffic was moving at 70 or 80 in the other lanes. Within minutes the Taurus left Mountain View and crossed into Sunnyvale.

U.S. 101 was better known locally as the Bayshore Freeway. At one time it had been the main north-south route on the west coast, and most of it ran along the route that was once El Camino Real, the King's Highway, under Spanish rule. Its northern terminus was in Puget Sound, and it continued south through Los Angeles, where it merged with I-5, ending at the Mexican border.

Fischer could feel the sunlight on his right cheek and nose. He was already somewhat disoriented, but thought they had merged onto the freeway. Highway 101 southbound bent eastward in this particular stretch, resuming its southerly course in San Jose. As he thought this through, the executive reasoned that the car must be heading east, meaning south, on the Bayshore. Toward Mexico, he thought.

"What do you want from me?" he asked.

"Just do like I tell you and you'll be safe," the gunman responded. "We will not hurt you unless you force us to. When we get to the place where we are going, you will find out."

"You can have my wallet. I don't carry much cash, but my ATM card is there. I'll give you my PIN." Even as he said it, Fischer wondered whether that was a smart tactical move. He had almost $200 in cash in his wallet, which to him was only the pettiest of cash, but to the robbers, as he thought of them, it might seem like a lot. If they realized $200 was not much to him, it might encourage them to ask for a lot more. But he was hoping to get them to an ATM where their picture could be taken, or where he might somehow be able to signal for help.

The gunman just grunted and told him to be quiet.

Fischer could not see, but he moved his legs around. His knees seemed to have plenty of room. Since he was well over six feet tall, this meant the driver's seat must be forward more than average. That meant the driver was probably not very tall. This was one more fact to tuck away for when he was asked for a description.

Fischer still had his cell phone in his pants pocket. He had not been searched. He hoped it wouldn't ring, as it would surely be taken away; then he remembered he had turned it off. He felt it would be impossible to take it out and use it with the blindfold in place, and he was unwilling to risk trying to dial 911 surreptitiously. Better to wait. Didn't he read somewhere that a cell phone's location could be tracked if it was turned on? God, oh God, he hoped so. Maybe he could find a way to turn it on without them noticing. But he could still feel the gun in his ribs.

They drove for what seemed like two or three hours, but time was hard to judge under such conditions. The gunman questioned him as they rode, asking about his family, his finances, his cars. After awhile, the Taurus pulled into a driveway, and the sound of gravel could be heard under the wheels.

"We are going to stop here for the night. Don't give us any trouble or we will kill you. If you yell or try to run, you'll never see your wife or children again. We have someone watching your house."

At these words Fischer felt stomach acid rise in his gut. The burning sensation was sharp and real. He knew this was no ordinary robbery. These men knew who he was and where he lived. They had something more sinister in mind.

The passenger got out of the car and pulled a Giants baseball cap low over his face. He walked slowly to the small office of what turned out to be a cheap motel. The car license plate number he listed on the registration slip was intentionally written one digit off. He told the clerk that they had a sick friend who needed to rest undisturbed. He asked for an end unit in the back where no one would come by the front of the room. He asked also that no telephone calls be put through. After ten minutes or so, he returned to the car. They moved the car closer to their room, and the hostage was led inside. One of the men turned the television on loud. Fischer could not see, since his blindfold was still on, but he recognized the program from the dialogue and sound track. It was the movie *Ghost*. They had tuned in right where Patrick Swayze's character was about to die.

Chapter 2

Cliff Knowles sat watching the news when he heard the phone ring. His wife Rickie was passing through the kitchen and picked it up first. Immediately she called out, "It's the Z-man for you."

Don Zwolinski, the Violent Crimes and Major Offenders, or VCMO, Coordinator for the division was universally called the Z-man. Knowles wondered what was going on. The Z-man didn't have much reason to call him these days. Knowles and Z-man had served together doing foreign counterintelligence, or FCI, in the Palo Alto Resident Agency for a few years. There had been the occasional calls at home in the evening for work purposes then, and sometimes for social events. But a year ago Knowles, at his own request, had transferred to the San Jose RA to do criminal work, since FCI work had become humiliatingly irrelevant after the fall of the Soviet empire. Z-man, a supervisor from FBI Headquarters, only recently had transferred up to San Francisco to take over as the VCMO squad supervisor and Program Coordinator. In rank, he was now equivalent to Knowles's supervisor, Ben Olson, and usually dealt directly with Olson for any case-related matters. Z-man usually left operational matters to his agents, since he still knew little about VCMO work.

"Hey, Z-man, what's up?" Knowles answered as he took the phone.

"There's been a kidnapping. Get some paper and I'll give you the details. I paged Olson, but he didn't answer." Knowles, as Principal Relief Supervisor, was number two in charge of the squad.

"Hang on." Knowles pulled the telephone message pad close, and took the pen from his pocket. He always had a pen handy, a long-ingrained habit after 15 years as an investigator. "Go ahead."

"At 7:12 PM we got a call from a Robert Carmody, CEO of Claritiva Software reporting that his business partner, Carl M. Fischer, is missing." He paused to let Knowles write things down, and he spelled the proper names. "Carmody received a call from Mrs. Fischer, first name Francine, saying she received a ransom call at about 12:30 this afternoon. The call came in to their home number, which is unlisted. The caller said they took him to Mexico. They want $650,000." He gave Knowles the phone number. Knowles recognized it as a Los Altos prefix. The Fischers apparently were almost his neighbors. "You need to call her and interview her right away. This can't wait until morning. You need to establish a command post in the RA and do a teletype to the Bu tonight."

"OK. Where are you calling from...home?"

"No, I'm in the office. I'll stay here, or I'll be on the radio."

"Why didn't Mrs. Fischer call herself?" Knowles was already starting to analyze the situation. Normally the victim's family calls law enforcement directly and immediately upon receiving information of an abduction. He also wondered why call the FBI - most people called 911, which would connect them with local police. The FBI normally got kidnapping complaints from the police after they had worked the case for a few hours, when the federal statute, the Little Lindbergh Law, was getting close to taking effect.

"I don't know."

"How'd the call come in?" Typically major corporations had security managers who had established liaison with the FBI and other law enforcement, and they would call their contact. It was odd to have a CEO call the FBI himself.

"Direct to the public switchboard number," the Z-man answered. "If you want to call Carmody back I can give you his number."

"Yeah, I will. I want to get the story from him before I call the wife." He took the number. "I'll let you know what's going on after I talk to him. Who took the call, the night supervisor?"

"No, Communications." This meant the clerk in the Communications Unit.

This was the answer Knowles had hoped for, because the clerks answer the phones most of time, and are very experienced at assessing complaints. The night supervisor is an agent, not of supervisory rank despite the name, but typically clueless compared to the clerks. In some divisions the night supervisor is a post traditionally filled by whichever agent has been unofficially dubbed the next squad supervisor, and this spot is used as a resume filler for when the career board convenes to look over the candidates. In San Francisco, however, it had always been filled by whoever didn't like working cases and enjoyed the premium shift pay and regular hours. All they had to do was sit there and watch TV unless an urgent teletype or phone call from the Bureau came in. The clerks did most of the work. Of course, if something bad happened at night, their ass was on the line. Some of them had been good, solid investigators, but most had not.

"Let me talk to him," Knowles asked.

"I'm not at switchboard; I'm in my office. I'm not sure how this goddam phone works. Why don't you just call back to switchboard."

"OK. I'll talk to you in a bit."

They both hung up. Typical Z-man performance, thought Knowles. He didn't even know how to transfer a phone call, and, like always, sprinkled profanity into every conversation. On the other hand, Knowles was somewhat impressed. The Z-man had been in that position for less than 90 days and had probably not handled a kidnap call before. He obviously had to look up the procedures, but he got them right, and he called Knowles quickly when he couldn't reach Olson. Z-man was decisive and definitely among the top ten percentile in IQ among Bureau agents, probably the top one percentile among management. He had perceived immediately why Knowles had asked how the call came in, without having it explained to him, and given the efficient, useful reply. Knowles thought it ironic that the Z-man, a true believer in FCI work, was trying so hard to be credible in his new role as VCMO supervisor. In a sort of reverse sycophancy, he had begun mimicking the agents on his criminal squad in putting down the FCI agents, making remarks about being on a real working squad now, and joking about no longer having time to go to the gym, not that he had seen the inside of a gym in years. It was a tradition that criminal agents thought of FCI agents as some sort of pansies who sat around reading newspapers, while FCI agents thought of criminal agents, especially the self-anointed "heavies" on VCMO, as goons who couldn't read a newspaper if they tried.

Knowles called back to the public switchboard number and talked to the clerk who had taken the original complaint call from Carmody. The clerk said the caller sounded well-spoken and calm. He had answered all the clerk's questions quickly, and without complaint, including those about his own identifying information. Some people objected when asked their date of birth, full name, and so forth. Other than that, the clerk had little to say about the call. He had taken the information down, then relayed it to the night supervisor, who told him to give to the VCMO coordinator, who happened to still be in his office. The clerk had detected nothing suspicious or unusual about the call, other than the fact that kidnap for ransom calls are uncommon.

He told Knowles that Carmody was expecting to be recontacted. Knowles thanked him and hung up.

"Rickie," Knowles called out. "I'm going to have to go out on a kidnapping. I need to make some calls first." Rickie's real name was Frederica, but her parents had mercifully given her a nickname with which she could survive the schoolyard. She hated her legal name, and even refused to tell anyone what it was, except when she had to for legal reasons. She was unruffled by this bit of news, since she had by now become used to the irregular hours of her husband since he had switched to reactive work. She still used the old term "reactive" which she had heard agents use many times, since she was not current on all the latest FBI acronyms, of which VCMO was a relatively recent example. She knew that Cliff's squad handled most of the kinds of cases that required immediate response, like bank robberies and fugitives. She had even learned, as he had, that kidnap cases nearly always turned out to be nothing.

"How long do you expect to be gone?" she asked.

"I don't know. I don't even know how long it'll take me to finish the calls."

Knowles tried calling Ben Olson's pager first and waited about five minutes for a call back. Olson was notorious for not being around. No one even knew where Olson lived. He'd get in late one morning complaining of an overturned big rig, which Knowles knew to be south of San Jose, on the route in from Santa Cruz. Then a week later it would be the same thing, but the bottleneck would be north, toward Pleasanton. Did this guy have girlfriends all over the map or what, Knowles often wondered. Knowles knew he couldn't sit there waiting for a call back. He had to get going on the case calls, so he gave up on keeping his phone line free.

He got out a legal pad and called the number the clerk had given him for Robert Carmody. Knowles worked a lot of high-tech cases, like chip thefts, and knew Claritiva Software by reputation. However, he had never heard of Carmody. This was unsurprising, since he had never worked a case there, and most high tech executives were engineers with fairly low profiles, at least compared to traditional industries, although there were some notable exceptions.

One of Carmody's children answered the phone. So this must be the home number, not the office, Knowles thought. He asked for Robert Carmody. A man came on the line.

"Mr. Carmody, this is Special Agent Cliff Knowles of the FBI. I'd like to talk to you about your call reporting a kidnapping."

"Yes. Thank you for calling back. We're not sure what to do next."

"Don't worry; someone will meet with you tonight. But first I'd like to get some additional details."

Knowles knew the clerk would have all the personal information on Carmody in his complaint form, but he had no way to access that right now, so he asked for it all again: full name, aliases, date and place of birth, all telephone numbers, address, job title, work address, and so forth not only for himself but for the Fischers as well. Carmody patiently gave it all again. He, too, had a Los Altos address. This was getting cozy. Knowles was the only active FBI agent who lived in Los Altos. Most of the town was very expensive real estate, populated by executives and stock-optionaires. The address Carmody gave was in the northwest part of town, in the foothills, where homes all cost well over a million dollars.

"Can you tell me what happened?" Knowles was experienced and knew not to ask a question that presumed any facts or suggested the FBI had already reached a conclusion. A rookie agent might ask something like, "I understand there was a kidnapping. Can you tell me how it happened?" If it turned out to be a hoax, which was most of the time, the reporting party would know they already had the hook set and would be encouraged to continue.

Carmody said he had first heard that Carl was missing in the morning when one of the secretaries had asked if he had seen Carl. She had said Carl's wife, Fran, had called him about 10:00 AM to discuss a party they were going to in the evening, and he was not in. Fran had thought this was odd, because she knew he had called in that morning to see if he had any appointments, and had been told by his secretary that he did not. Carl had dressed casual when he had received that answer. He was planning to be in catching up with paperwork all day, he had told Fran. Fran had asked Carlotta, the secretary, when he was due back in his office, and she said she had not seen him all morning. Fran became concerned and asked Carlotta to check around to see if he was there somewhere. Carlotta had gone out to the parking lot and seen Carl's car, then made a quick pass through the building, but had found no one who had seen him. Carmody had not thought much of it at the time, since he and Carl were on very independent schedules. Carmody was the CEO, and Carl was the President and COO. They were good friends and co-founders, but didn't keep track of each other's schedules.

Knowles let him talk, but had to slow him down in places to catch up with his note-taking. This fellow was telling him things he needed to know, so there was no point in interrupting him.

Carmody then became slightly hesitant in his account. He said Fran had come by the office herself around 11:00 and looked at Carl's car to verify he had arrived. She had left complaining that something was wrong and seemed upset. Carmody had been in a meeting at the time and had not talked to Fran, but when he heard about it afterward, he became somewhat concerned himself. Then, about 12:30, Fran had called him on his personal line and reported that she had to meet him. She was whispering, and said she did not have much time to talk. She asked him to meet her at the Andronico's Market on Foothill at 1:30. She had hung up before he could ask any details, but he assumed it had something to do with Carl's disappearance. Carmody paused again, fumbling for words.

This story was getting a bit screwy, Knowles thought, and he sensed that Carmody was aware that it would sound strange. "Did you meet her there?"

"Yes. Well, I went there, but she didn't show up right away. She got there about 2:15, and was all out of breath. I had called her house a few minutes earlier, and her housekeeper said she had gone out a little before 1:00. It only takes maybe five minutes to drive to that market from her house, so I had been almost ready to give up and go back to the office. But I gave it a few more minutes, and she showed up. She said she'd walked."

Knowles knew the route. It was almost four miles from the Fischer home to Andronico's. The route was hilly, but there wasn't much traffic in midday, as it was mostly a rich suburban residential neighborhood. It might take 10 minutes to drive if traffic was heavy, but no more. Walking, however, was another matter. There were no sidewalks in most of Los Altos, an affectation codified into the local building ordinances to give it a rural look. The only straight route was down Foothill Expressway, which had been cut through the hills on a beeline years earlier for a now-defunct railroad, and later paved over. Foothill, though, did not allow pedestrian traffic. The residential streets meandered around the hillsides. It could easily be five or six miles on foot if one didn't know the shortcuts. He figured Francine Fischer's age at close to 60. An hour and twenty-five minutes was about right for that walk, for someone her age. But why would she walk? And why wouldn't she leave a lot earlier if she did? This wasn't getting any less bizarre.

"When she caught her breath," Carmody continued, "she handed me a note she had written. She was afraid people were watching her; that's why she walked to the store. She told me Carl had been kidnapped, and there was a call to the house demanding ransom. She was in a panic and didn't know what to do."

"Do you still have the note?"

"Yeah, I've got it here at my home. I figured you'd want it."

"OK, hang onto it. Someone will get it from you. How can I reach her? I've got to talk to her right away."

"I gave you the home number already. She'll be there, but you'd better call soon because she works at the TV station twice a week. That's the station at Foothill Junior College. She's a volunteer producer. She said she was going to keep up her schedule so no one watching her would get suspicious. And I think she said she had to bake a cake."

Bake a cake? Your husband is kidnapped, so you bake a cake? Knowles jotted this down, but this whole thing did not sound right to him. "Let me ask you for a frank opinion, Mr. Carmody. Do you think Mr. Fischer was really kidnapped? I have to ask. If something else is going on, it's better to stop it before this gets too far."

"Well, I can understand it might sound a little odd to you. But I don't think Fran is making this up. Carl's car arrived at work, but he never showed up. He's definitely missing. You're the FBI; what do you think? How common are these things?"

"It's too early to draw any conclusions. I need to talk to her first, and do some other investigation. Kidnappings for ransom are very uncommon. Most kidnap cases are juveniles who are taken for family custody, sexual, or other reasons. Of course, there's a case right now in New Jersey of an oil executive missing, and someone is demanding ransom. You've probably seen that in the papers. That might have inspired a copycat."

"No. I hadn't heard about that. How about in Silicon Valley? No one ever told me about any risk like this. Is my family safe?" These were good questions, and not surprising to Knowles. Corporate executives almost never put any priority on security until disaster struck. Security Directors or Managers usually answer to technocrats like Facilities or Human Resources vice presidents. Most of them have never even had an opportunity to discuss security with a CEO or COO. Claritiva didn't even have a Security Manager.

"This is the first case I've heard of in Silicon Valley of a corporate executive. Kidnapping someone for ransom is very rare because it's very rarely successful. It's a low-percentage crime. The victim is usually released or rescued unharmed, and the criminals almost always get caught. Even when they get away with the money, they can't use it for long, because it's marked and recorded in every way possible. Of course, there are no guarantees. It's a dangerous situation, and some end in tragedy. But I've never known of a kidnap situation where the kidnappers came back after another executive or family member. Usually the last place they want to be is around the scene of the crime - or associated locations." These assurances came out calmly and were truthful, but they did little to assuage the turmoil Carmody was feeling.

"Would she have any reason to make up this story?" Knowles asked. It was a delicate question, but experience had proven that it had to be asked. At least 90% of reported kidnaps turned out to be runaways, hoaxes, or unfounded for some other reason.

"Well, uh...Fran has medical problems."

Uh-oh. Why say anything about her medical history unless it reflected poorly on her credibility. "Something that would cause her to ..." delicate phrasing was needed, Knowles realized, "... perceive something that might not be true?"

"No, no, nothing like that," Carmody said too quickly. "She's on medication, that's all. I just thought you should know. You'd better call her before she leaves. I'll expect to hear from one of your other agents, then."

"All right, thank you. Someone will be back in touch."

Super, thought Knowles. The complainant suggests the victim's wife is unstable, maybe, if that's what he was hinting at, then takes it back. You can't put it in a report, but if something goes haywire he'd say he told the FBI. Knowles called the number for the Fischer residence. A woman, not Mrs. Fischer, answered. She said Fran had already left for the TV station. Knowles was able to get the woman to give him that telephone number, saying it was an urgent medical matter, but he didn't have to identify himself as FBI. When he called the station, someone Knowles visualized as pimple-covered answered "Yeah?"

"Is Fran Fischer there, please?"

"She's here. Just a minute."

Fran Fischer came on the line. Knowles introduced himself. Mrs. Fischer said she couldn't talk right then; people were within earshot. Knowles tried to get some of the basic facts there on the phone, but she was rushed and insisted she couldn't talk. She whispered that the caller had told her they were watching her and that if she told anyone about it her husband would be killed. If she didn't do her routine activities, they would know she was doing something, she feared. After the TV session, she had to go to a party because she had already confirmed, and people were expecting her. She had promised to bring a strawberry cake. She was absolutely determined; she was not going to miss her scheduled events.

"Mrs. Fischer," Knowles said firmly, "you absolutely must meet with me. It's essential we get our investigation started, and we can't do that without finding out everything you know about it. You're the one who talked to the caller. You can tell the hostess that you aren't feeling well. I don't believe the kidnappers are watching you - that's just something they always say so you won't call the police. But even if they are, saying you aren't feeling well and staying home from a party are things they would understand someone in your position would do. You don't have to tell anyone you're meeting with the FBI."

This seemed to sway her. Knowles could be very convincing; he was self-assured and calm. He worked on her a little more, and she agreed to cancel attending the party, and meet with him instead. But she insisted on finishing her stint at the studio. They agreed to meet at the college right after the broadcast at 9:00 PM. Knowles would not tell anyone he was FBI, and she would introduce him as a family friend if necessary.

Knowles called back to the San Francisco office and talked to the Z-man. He told him he was going to meet Mrs. Fischer and gave him a thumbnail of what Carmody had told him. Z-man told him that Olson had called in and found out what was going on. Olson was on his way to the San Jose office. Agents always called it the RA, for Resident Agency. Knowles thanked him and hung up.

Knowles called Olson on his direct line, but he wasn't in yet. He left a voice mail message saying he was going to interview the victim's wife up at Foothill College and would be available on radio. He then called back to the RA main switchboard number, hoping someone would pick up. The clerks who answer the phone go home at

5:00 and a recording comes on telling emergency callers to call the San Francisco main number which is manned around the clock. Usually, there are agents working in the RA at almost all hours, but they don't like to pick up the main line after the clerk leaves. They stay late to get their own work done, not take messages or complaint calls. Sure enough, no one picked up. There could be a boatload of agents working there late, but even another agent has no easy way to contact them, even during a kidnapping.

Knowles checked the RA standby list. Every day of the year someone was on duty for emergency after-hour calls. As Relief Supervisor for the VCMO squad, he often needed to know who that was, so he could send them out to cover a late-breaking bank robbery, or other inconveniently-timed crime, so he kept a copy of the list at home. The name on the list was Quincy Allen, better known as Q-ball. Allen was nearly totally bald with a pasty white complexion. He worked applicant cases - background investigations for federal appointees and applicants for sensitive positions. He took his turn on RA standby like everybody else, but he did not regularly work VCMO cases. Allen answered the phone himself.

"Q-ball, it's Cliff. Hey, has anybody called you about a kidnap case?"

"No, this is the first I've heard."

"Typical," Knowles said. "The office never calls the standby agent, they always drag us reactive guys out first."

"You need me to roll?" Allen asked.

"Nah, stay put for now. Olson's already on his way in. He'll want our squad to handle it. I'm headed out to interview the victim's wife. You should stay available, though. If this turns out to be real, there'll be a whole slew of people needed."

"I'm on standby anyway. Call me if you need me." He put a major emphasis on the last four words. It went without saying that Q-ball didn't volunteer for anything. He'd been around 25 years, and his cynicism was legendary. He'd be content to let the young guys handle the hot stuff. Cliff Knowles was a "young guy" at 40, by Q-ball's standards. They hung up.

Chapter 3

Ben Olson was sipping a bourbon and soda at The Binnacle, a touristy little bar in Capitola, a small town on the Monterey Bay seashore southwest of San Jose. His date was his current girlfriend, whose name was forgettable and would soon be forgotten. Olson moved from woman to woman with a depressing regularity, but never let the Bureau people know who or where they were. He believed in the old police adage, "Don't shit where you eat." The only female he truly cared about deeply was his daughter, at 13 already a precocious singer, dancer, and stage performer. She had won her daddy's heart long ago, and knew it. She skipped in and out of the San Jose RA like it was her backyard, without regard to security rules, escorts, and other trivialities beneath her notice.

Olson's pager started beeping, and a senior citizen couple in the next booth cast a disdainful look his way. Suddenly he remembered that he had been paged once before, on the way here, and had forgotten to return it. He scrolled back to the previous page; it was the same number. He recognized the number as the Z-man's office phone. He had to call it often enough himself during regular hours. If the Z-man was calling him twice, he'd better return the page. He excused himself and walked to the pay phone. Cell phones were coming into vogue among the technorati, but were still something of an expensive toy, and not yet ubiquitous. Cell coverage was still quite spotty and this area was a dead spot, he knew from experience. He didn't really mind that he was being called away from his lady friend. It made him look important and would probably turn out to be nothing, he figured.

He was wrong. He listened with interest to the full account of what had been reported. A kidnap for ransom was pretty rare. Kidnap reports usually involved juveniles, not wealthy adults. He knew he would have to go in on this one. The SAC, Special Agent in Charge, would expect him to. In fact, Pete Stroaker would probably call him within the next hour to get an assessment. Olson told Z-man he was heading to the RA. He threw a tip on the table, said goodbye to Nameless Girl, and jumped in his Bucar. He'd had two and a half stiff ones, but he could hold his liquor, and he had his Get Out of Jail Free card, he thought, as he patted his pocket to verify his badge and credentials were safely tucked away.

As a squad supervisor, he got the pick of the new cars that his squad was allocated each year. He was driving a Pontiac Grand Am this time around, cherry red. He drove fast, but not recklessly, as he pulled the mike off the dashboard. He radioed the San Francisco office to begin calling agents to come in. He had a cell phone but didn't have the agents' home numbers programmed in. He also didn't want to be trying to use it to dial while driving with a couple of drinks in him. He already knew Knowles was responding; the Z-man had told him. So he asked the clerk to call agents Rothman and Lark. They were senior agents and relief supervisors who had good judgment. They would come in without complaint and give good advice.

He asked the clerk to keep calling as necessary to get both Rothman and Lark into the RA. By the time he was done with the conversation he was starting up the hill over Highway 17, more popularly, if tritely, called Blood Alley for its treacherous curves. He took it at 15 miles over the speed limit. His pager went off again. The number was a 650 area code, so it was probably either Knowles or Stroaker. He radioed the office again and asked for the telephone number of the SAC. It didn't match, so it wasn't Stroaker. He should have known Knowles's home number, but he didn't. Still, he had no doubt that was who it was trying to reach him. He couldn't dial Knowles on his cell while driving this road, and cellular coverage was non-existent anyway until he got over the mountain. He'd call him when he got into the RA.

Tim Rothman was at home doing e-mail on his computer when he got the call from the office. He didn't ask any questions. He just put on his suit, holstered his gun, and headed to the RA. He assumed this would be routine. There hadn't been a real kidnapping on the squad in about three years, and that had been a teenaged girl snatched by an ex-boyfriend who didn't want to be ex- anything. Kidnap cases just didn't turn out to be real, in his experience, and he'd been doing VCMO for over four years. He hoped it wasn't real because he was the squad pilot, and would draw airborne surveillance duty. That meant drilling doughnuts in the sky for hours. Boring.

He lived in San Jose, closer than Lark or Olson, so he arrived first of the three. There were a couple of drug squad agents working late on some undercover operation, but he would be alone and in the dark until Olson arrived. He called the Communications Clerk in San Francisco to get an update. He learned that Knowles was already out at the victim's doing an interview, and that Olson had called in Nick

Lark. That surprised him, since Lark, a close friend, was scheduled to leave early the next morning for a family vacation. Olson would have had to pre-approve the vacation, and should have known Lark wasn't available. Olson had probably forgotten, he concluded. He made some notes of the names and phone numbers involved in the kidnap and other basic facts provided by the clerk. Then he tried to call Knowles. The line was busy. So he sat at his desk and caught up on his paperwork waiting for Olson.

Nick Lark was not happy about being called in late right before leaving for vacation. He started to argue with the clerk, but he knew the clerk was just passing on orders from Olson, so he decided to cut him some slack. Lark himself had started his Bureau career as a clerk, and knew how much grief they took over things they couldn't control and didn't initiate. With this empathy for the clerk, he hung up and called Olson on his cell phone. Out of the coverage area. Damn, those Santa Cruz Mountains always killed communications. He went out to his Bucar, and tried his radio. He got a garbled response, so he knew Olson received the transmission, but reception was too bad to communicate, so he decided just to go on in. It would be another hoax, and he would get out of there for his vacation in the morning.

For Lark, this meant driving 70 miles each way. He was the Senior Resident Agent in the Monterey Resident Agency, the southernmost RA in the division. This officially made him the administrative head of that office, but, since the MRA was too small to warrant its own squad supervisor and he handled violent crimes, he reported to Olson in San Jose. He jumped in his Ford Crown Victoria - vintage by FBI standards, but the biggest car on the squad he liked to point out - and headed north for San Jose. He routinely drove at least 85, and tonight was no exception. He would be in the office in less than an hour.

Olson arrived in the RA about 8:30, and Lark arrived shortly thereafter. Olson, Rothman and Lark listened in on speaker phone while the Z-man filled them in on what he knew. It was agreed that Rothman and Lark would contact Carmody and get him to meet them at the Claritiva site so they could look at the car and the scene. Olson would stay in the RA and coordinate for now. After they got some assessment of the situation, they would plan further action. They had to notify the SAC and the Tech Squad. If they were going to have to trace or record incoming calls, they needed the Tech Squad to contact Pacific Bell and do any technical work on the receiving line.

The FBI Manual of Investigative and Operational Guidelines, or MIOG, contained a set protocol for handling and investigating every type of crime within FBI jurisdiction. For most classifications, the MIOG gave little guidance beyond the copy count and reporting frequency for any paperwork. For kidnap cases, however, it was quite a bit more specific. If the initial report included a witnessed abduction or a ransom call or note, then the SAC must be notified. If the abduction was verified, the SAC must take personal control of a case. Local law enforcement must also be notified if they have not been already. Olson wasn't quite sure this applied yet, since the reporting party, Carmody, never got any ransom call, and was only passing on hearsay from Mrs. Fischer. Callers often exaggerated the facts either out of excitement or, more often, because they were trying to the get the FBI to do something for their own personal reasons, such as impressing a girl, intimidating a business rival, and so forth. Until Knowles could talk to Mrs. Fischer and Olson could talk to Knowles, they wouldn't really know what they had, if even then.

Olson decided to call Pete Stroaker. Stroaker was an aberration among SACs in his friendliness and "warm and fuzzy" approach to management. He wouldn't give Olson a hard time for disturbing him in the evening. Most SACs were egomaniacs who would take the head off an agent for interrupting him at home for any matter less significant than a call from the Director. Olson tried Stroaker's home phone, but it was busy, so he tried his pager next. This telephone tag was getting to be irritating. He looked over at Lark, who was on the phone to Carmody. Lark was giving him the thumbs up, indicating Carmody was willing to meet with them. At least that was going right.

Olson next called Knowles, hoping to catch him before he left to interview Mrs. Fischer, but he was too late. Rickie said Cliff had left about 15 minutes earlier. It was now 9:03. Olson's phone rang. It was Stroaker calling him back. He gave the SAC what information he had, and said he was sending agents out to interview Carmody as well as Mrs. Fischer. Stroaker seemed satisfied and said to keep him updated. He, too, knew these things almost always turned out not to be real.

Lark and Rothman headed out to meet Carmody at Claritiva headquarters in Mountain View. Olson thought about trying to get Knowles on the radio, but figured that would be hopeless. He would be in the middle of, no, make that the very beginning of, his interview with Mrs. Fischer. Knowles'll call in when he has something, he decided. Knowles was a solid performer, if not a long-time VCMO agent. Olson still thought of him as an FCI guy, but had been very pleased with his work on the squad. Knowles, as Principal Relief, handled a lot of the paperwork on the squad while Olson was out doing police liaison and other things he enjoyed more. Olson had lucked out in drawing Knowles as his Principal, and he knew it.

Rothman and Lark left for their interview with Carmody, and Knowles would be a while with the wife, so there wasn't much to do just yet. Olson turned on the handy-talkie in his office so he could hear the radio chatter, and pulled out a cigarette. Smoking was now illegal in federal office buildings, but there was no one around to complain. He lit up and waited for something to happen.

Chapter 4

Cliff Knowles pulled into the parking lot of Foothill Junior College. Nestled among white oak and manzanita covered hillsides, it was in a beautiful setting. The home sites in nearby Los Altos Hills were even more expensive than in Los Altos, with vacant lots going for millions of dollars if they had a view of the valley. The college was also deceptively good academically for a junior college. Many of the local kids were children of Stanford professors or Silicon Valley engineers, but some were too immature to start at a university despite good grades. Then, of course, there were the many Asian immigrants, some of them borderline poverty cases. Some decided to take advantage of the nearly free college education the State of California bestowed upon its residents, coming here for a couple of years, and later transferring to Berkeley or UCLA. For these reasons, the scholastic competition at Foothill was stiff, and the amenities reflected the wealthy community. Not many junior colleges had their own TV stations.

He pulled his brown Dodge Diplomat sedan into the section of parking lot farthest from the buildings. His car looked like the cliché cop car from every TV crime drama on the air. He didn't want passers by to realize he was law enforcement. He had intentionally not worn his suit for that reason. He had on jeans, flannel shirt, and a jacket long enough to cover his holster and gun. These days almost all agents were allowed to take Bureau cars, always called Bucars, home for just such occasions. In San Francisco Division this was more of an employee perquisite than a real operational need for most agents, since very few were doing work that needed frequent call-outs. Housing was so expensive here that the government pay rates, even with locality adjustments, simply could not offset those costs, so cars were used as a way to keep new agents or transferees from quitting when they got sticker shock during house-hunting. But for VCMO agents, these emergency calls after hours were pretty regular business, and having the car at home was a significant emergency response advantage. You just can't use your personal car for some things, like a high-speed chase, radio communications, or transporting prisoners. He was glad he didn't have to go back to the office to get a car, the way he used to when he was first-office.

Knowles was not an impressive-looking figure. Of average height, he was just a tad pudgy, with a thick midsection. He worked out with weights regularly and was deceptively strong, but his full face made him look heavier than he was. In addition, his thick glasses gave him the stereotypical appearance of an accountant or computer geek. In reality Knowles was an attorney, but he had in fact studied accounting and computers in his undergraduate years. He was one of the best-educated agents in the FBI, but he didn't look like the well-chiseled stud the public came to expect in their G-men from movies and television. The Bureau wanted to convey the image of a Dick Tracy, but as for comic strip characters, Knowles looked more like Dilbert, with glasses, bad hair, and a tendency toward chubbiness. This worked against him more often than he would have believed, keeping him from winning supervisor slots because he did not "look the part" or "project the right image." At the moment, however, it was an advantage. As long as they did not see his Bucar, he would not be recognized as a fed.

He strolled casually into the campus building area and looked for the TV studio. Mrs. Fischer had told him where it was, but he still had some difficulty because it was dark, and the redwood signs were impossible to read in this lighting. Soon, he found it and went in. The show was over, and the crew was discussing the things that had gone well - or not so well. He recognized Fran Fischer immediately from the description she had given of herself. She was the only middle-aged woman there and she wore the green slacks and tan sweater she had mentioned. Despite her wealth, she was unostentatious in her clothes and makeup. Women in California just didn't dress the way they did in New York or Washington, D.C., Knowles noted silently. Fran Fischer had a model's figure: slim and youthful. She looked like those sporty women in the ads for osteoporosis products, the ones who play tennis and go boating because they pop the right pills.

"Hi, Fran," he called to her, waving. He wanted to get this show on the road and was not inclined to wait for the conversation to finish.

She waved at him to come on over, and introduced him to her fellow volunteer editor simply as Cliff, an old family friend. Knowles was gratified she remembered his name, so he wouldn't have to fake another name. She excused herself from the crew and walked outside with Knowles. He steered her toward his car. He let her in and explained that he had to get some of the facts down before they could do any investigation. He pulled out his notepad and started to write, careful to keep eye contact with her, and tried to seem comforting.

Mrs. Fischer seemed pleasant and unfazed. She began to tell him her day, beginning when Carl had gotten ready in the morning. In great detail she described what he wore, what their conversation had been, what they had eaten for breakfast. She mentioned that he had called his secretary at the office to find out if he had any interviews or major business meetings. The secretary had said no, so he had decided to wear the polo shirt and slacks. He had told Fran he would be in the office all day. She had told him that she might call later to discuss the party they were going to tonight. He had said fine, call around 10:30 to 11:00. Knowles had to slow her down once or twice to catch up with his note taking. Carl had seemed normal and had said nothing to suggest he might have to leave suddenly. He had left for work in his Mercedes, which she described in detail.

Then she began to tell about her morning, and all the social plans she had. After Carl had gone, she had baked a cake for the party, but still had to get some berries to put on it. Knowles glanced at his watch. He had to move this along, as the people at the office would want to get the basics so they could get started with whatever investigation was to be done, or go home. He decided to interrupt.

"Mrs. Fischer," he said, "could we skip to the ransom call? There are certain things I need to know so we can take immediate action to save your husband."

She looked at him quite sternly, apparently flustered and annoyed. "Well, I'm getting to that," she said. "I need to tell you what was going through my head so you'll understand." She started back on the choice of berries she had been contemplating, then said she had called Carl about 10:20 to discuss it. He had not been in. She had tried again a few minutes later, and he still had not been in.

Knowles was getting impatient. He had been writing for over 20 minutes and they still hadn't gotten to the meat of the case. There would be several agents waiting for word from him. He tried again.

"Please, Mrs. Fischer, let me just ask you one or two questions. What telephone number did the ransom call come in to?"

"Our home number," she replied curtly. "I'm going to tell you about the call in a minute. Can't you just listen to what I have to say?" She launched into the berries story again.

This was not going well. She didn't even tell him what the telephone number was, and he was losing his rapport with her. There could be another ransom call any minute, and they needed to get a trace on that line. There could be more than one number at the house; he needed to have an exact number for Pac Bell to put the trace on. If this was real, that is. Why wouldn't she answer his questions? She was beginning to sound like she was having trouble speaking, as well. Could she be drunk? It didn't seem likely, considering she had just come from the studio, and she had no odor of alcohol. The medication Carmody had referred to, perhaps?

As Knowles considered this, his pager went off. The number was a 650 area code number he didn't recognize. That area code covered the peninsula between San Jose and San Francisco, which included Los Altos, but neither one of those larger cities. That was odd. The only FBI office on the Peninsula was the Palo Alto office, and this was not one of their numbers. It wasn't his home number, so it wasn't Rickie. Who else had his pager number besides the office and his wife? He stopped Mrs. Fischer once more, apologizing profusely to prevent her further annoyance, but saying this was a very important message from the FBI office. He didn't have a cell phone; the FBI was too cheap to give them to all agents. He tried to reach the office on the Bureau radio but could only get static. The public was used to hearing perfect, clear transmissions on TV cop shows, but real life was very different. Even local cops were scornful of the bad communications the FBI had. But the budget for radio communications for the entire San Francisco Division, stretching from the Oregon border to just north of San Luis Obispo, a distance of about 500 miles, was one-tenth the radio budget for the San Jose Police Department, which covered just one city. If the FBI could put a repeater on every hilltop in their jurisdiction like the city departments, they could get good reception, too. FBI agents in the field could only communicate well about 50% of the time.

Knowles was getting riled, but tried not to show it. He needed to let the office know that this was going slowly, and do it discreetly without Mrs. Fischer being insulted. He couldn't reach anybody by radio and had no phone. He asked Mrs. Fischer if she had a cell phone. She said no. Wouldn't you know it; he had to be with the only high-tech multimillionaire in the valley who didn't carry one. He considered getting out of the car and looking for a pay phone at the college, but he was afraid Mrs. Fischer would feel affronted and leave. He decided to just gut out the interview. Whoever it was that was paging him would just have to wait.

"I'm having radio problems. Why don't we just try to finish the basic story quickly, then I'll go and return this call. You were telling me that you called your husband, and he wasn't in. So then you went to the company offices, is that right?"

This ploy worked. Mrs. Fischer didn't start up again with the cake. "That's right. When he didn't call me back, I had Carlotta look for him. She said his car was in the lot, but she couldn't find him. I got worried, so I drove down there. I looked all over, but I couldn't find him, either. I left a note on his desk to call me." She seemed to be breathing hard now, and concentrating on something. "I talked to Bob, and he said he would let Carl know I was looking for him. He said there was nothing that should have taken Carl out on a sudden trip, so far as he knew. I moved Carl's car away from the front around to the back parking lot so that he couldn't come back and just leave in it. He would have to go ask someone where his car was, and we would find him. I told Bob this."

Knowles could see now that she was straining to hold back tears. This woman was very, very frightened. Talking about the moment when she realized her husband was missing was obviously bringing her close to the reality of the situation. She had been able to keep it together when she was talking about the cake and the party, but now it was getting hard for her. That was why she didn't want to be rushed to the phone call. She just had a hard time dealing with it. He decided they should take a break before she got too upset to continue.

"All right, I need to return this call. Is there someplace we can go to talk where there's a phone? I want to get the rest of your information, but we can't stay here all evening. We shouldn't go back to your house, since you said someone may be watching you there." Knowles did not believe for a minute that the kidnapper was hanging around her house, but it was remotely possible. His main purpose was to make sure she remained available to him. If they went to her house, she might just collapse, go to bed, take a stiff drink, or who knew what. She couldn't throw him out of any place besides her own home.

"Yes, okay," she responded with relief. It was clear she wanted the break, too. "We can go to Bob and Mitzi's." This was a reference to the Carmody residence. Knowles did not want her to drive in her condition, but mainly he wanted to be in control of where she went, so he suggested that he drive and continue the interview while he did so. Someone could get her car later. She could navigate for him, since he didn't know how to get there. She agreed and seemed further relieved not to have to drive. It didn't bother her at all to leave a brand new Cadillac in the unguarded parking lot.

Knowles prompted her to continue the story, but he was not able to concentrate much on the story while driving, since the streets were narrow, winding, unlighted, and unfamiliar. Fortunately she was just discussing more of her morning routine after her return from the company. They were heading into a hilly part of north Los Altos Knowles had never entered. The houses were getting bigger, and the yards had gates. It took less than ten minutes to get to the Carmody home. It was on a heavily wooded cul-de-sac. Just as they pulled up, she finally began to tell him about the ransom call. Perfect timing. Knowles picked up his notepad and began writing furiously, trying to get every word. His pager went off again, but he ignored it. He couldn't interrupt this now that she was finally telling him the guts of it.

She said the caller had been male and had a slight accent. She wasn't sure what kind. He spoke harshly and demanded she do as he said or her husband would be killed. He wanted her to get $650,000 dollars in cash ready by the day after tomorrow. He would give her instructions on how to deliver it then. She should not call the police. If she told anybody about this call her husband would be killed. They had people watching her every move. She should get the cash herself and tell nobody. The police couldn't help her because her husband was now in Mexico. He told her not to fuck with him. She paused slightly at the word, showing some slight discomfiture. It was obvious that term was not in her normal vocabulary, but she continued unembarrassed, sensing that it was important to get it all as accurate and complete as possible. She could not remember any noises in the background or anything else useful. Knowles thanked her and said it was time to go inside.

They walked to the front door and rang the bell. A tall, gangly teenage boy answered the ring. He obviously knew Fran Fischer and invited them in. Bob Carmody appeared, shook Cliff's hand and invited them into the living room. Knowles realized his own house could almost fit in this living room. The house was huge - at least 8000 square feet, maybe twice that. Through the windows Knowles could see an enormous yard with a swimming pool Olympians could use for practice, and a tennis court. We may both be Los Altans,

Knowles thought, but we aren't in the same neighborhood in any other respect.

Carmody, however, was all graciousness and muted bonhomie. He was so glad the FBI was here and could take charge. "I just met with two agents down at the company office. They looked at Carl's car. They said they were going back to the FBI office in San Jose."

"Do you have their names?" Knowles asked.

"It was an agent Rothman and agent Lark. They said another agent, Harry Rice, would be coming here later."

Knowles took this in with mixed feelings. It was good that Carmody had been contacted. Knowles already felt like the least-informed person there. He didn't know who had been called in to do what. He felt comfortable with Rothman and Lark working on the case, since both were close friends and good agents. Rice, however, was another matter. Harry Rice was a fifth-generation Texan, as he liked to let people know, a direct descendant of the Rice University Rices. He worked in the Hayward RA, another small RA without a supervisor. Rice was the Senior Resident Agent of the Hayward RA, the counterpart of Nick Lark's position in Monterey. Since Rice worked violent crimes, he, too, reported to a VCMO supervisory agent - Ben Olson. The only problem was that Harry Rice never solved anything. He was the type who had a resume a mile long but never actually did any work. He loved schools and wangled his way into every Bureau school he could, flying to the FBI Academy in Quantico, Virginia with a transfer of planes in Dallas-Fort Worth, where he would hold over a day or two and visit his relatives and buddies. He was, on paper at least, a hostage negotiator, a firearms instructor, and a kidnap specialist. However, he had never actually negotiated with any hostage holders, was usually too busy to instruct at firearms qualifications, and unlike Knowles and Olson, had never worked a real kidnap case. Rice was just never around to do any work. Knowles had been obliged to drive up to Hayward to cover robberies for him on more than one occasion.

Knowles sat down with Carmody and Mrs. Fischer. Mitzi Carmody entered the room at the same time. Knowles stood and shook her hand. She efficiently kicked the teenager out of the room and turned off the television. The three friends all started talking simultaneously. As soon as Fran began to tell Mitzi about the call, she choked up and began to cry. Mitzi shifted closer and gave her a hug.

Mrs. Fischer was soon consumed with wracking sobs. Knowles looked at his watch. It was 10:45. Over and hour and half just to get the basic call details, and he still had lots to ask - did Carl have any enemies, had there been any threats or suspicious incidents lately, what about finances, marital problems, depression, wanderlust, the walk to the grocery store and the note, and on and on. He needed to get on the phone to Olson and let him know what they had so far. He also wanted to find out what the rest of the squad had on their end.

He asked Carmody if he could use the phone, and quickly excused himself when shown to a private den he could use. He looked at his pager to see the last saved number. It was Olson's direct number in the RA. Good, that was who he wanted to call anyway. He dialed. Olson answered on the first ring.

"Cliff, what'd you do, drop off the earth? We've been trying to reach you."

"I know, Ben. I was up at Foothill College and there was no radio reception. Neither of us had a cell phone. I couldn't break off the interview just to call you. She's very linear in her thinking. Every time I'd interrupt her she'd start over at the beginning. I had to let her go through. In fact, I still have to cover a lot more. All I've got to so far is the ransom call. I still don't know what the hell the walk to the store was all about."

"Stroaker has been trying to reach you. Did you call him back?"

"So that's who that other page was. Stroaker's home number. I didn't think of that. You told him about this case already? We don't know if it's legit yet."

"Yeah, he'd be royally pissed if it was, and we hadn't told him right away. So what do you think; is it real?" Olson was the first to pop the big question. This is what they wanted to know. They wanted to either go home or call out the whole squad and get moving.

Knowles took a big breath. This was the first big judgment call he'd had to make since becoming the number two man on the squad. He wished he'd heard more about what Carmody told Lark and Rothman. If he got it wrong either way, a lot of people would be on his head. He stalled. "Not sure yet. What did Tim and Nick learn?"

Olson didn't press Knowles. "Lark thinks it's a hoax or a domestic quarrel. The wife's story just doesn't wash. The CEO told him that the wife has been traveling in Hong Kong for the last two weeks. As soon as she gets back, he disappears. She doesn't call the cops, she bakes a cake. This doesn't sound normal. No one saw the car arrive. She could have driven it there after..." the words tailed off. He didn't say what he thought happened before the "after."

"He thinks she did this? I don't think so. She's stressed out and not making some good judgments, but her story rings true to me. I don't think she's faking her fear. If she is, she's a better actress than I've seen in a long time. Did Carmody say anything to suggest she's behind this? What does Rothman think?"

"He's on the fence. What about you?" He wouldn't let Knowles go that easily.

Knowles took the plunge. "I think it's real. He's rich as Croesus, and the business is solid from what I hear. He's a prime target for this type of thing, and there's that one with the oil exec back in New Jersey. This could be a copycat. I'm the one who interviewed her, and I think she's just an emotional wreck from the fear. And the car didn't get to Claritiva by itself."

"Okay," Olson replied. "You're the man on the spot. I'll accept your judgment - for now. I'm sending Rothman over to help with the interviews. I've already sent Rice to help you out. I'll stay here until I hear more from you. Now call the boss."

Knowles realized there were mixed motives in Olson's response. Olson did trust his judgment, but he was also happy to have someone to shoulder the responsibility with him. If it turned out to be a wild goose chase, he could say he was backing up his agent, that's all. If things went the wrong way, well, he hadn't been there, it was his Principal Relief. It would be easy for him to distance himself. Not so easy for Knowles.

He dialed the other number still in his pager. It was Pete Stroaker, the SAC. Agents from other federal law enforcement agencies also used the term Special Agent in Charge, but they pronounced the acronym SAC as "sack." FBI agents always spelled it out S-A-C. You could always tell whether someone was FBI by how he said this one term. He remembered the day in training school when his class was briefed on Bureau terminology. The instructor had said, "How would you like to spend your whole career struggling to the top, only to be called a 'sack'? Sad Sack? Sack of shit? No, we call them S-A-C, Ess Ay See." He had drawn out the syllables.

Stroaker didn't much care what his agents called him. He preferred just to be called Pete. He was friendly to all the employees and disdained the terms "boss" or "big guy" used frequently by the suck-ups. He pronounced his last name 'Strawker', rhymes with Walker, but almost everybody got it wrong the first time because of the spelling, which might have been one reason he preferred first names. Of course he couldn't be unaware of the sniggering, never to his face, over the similarity in sound to "peter stroker," which was probably another reason for the unintuitive pronunciation.

"Cliff, thanks for calling." He made no mention of the fact it took Knowles an hour to return the page.

"Sure, Pete. I'm sorry it took me so long. I tried to radio, but I couldn't get through and we didn't have a phone. I didn't want to break off the interview. If I'd known it was you..." He realized he shouldn't be apologizing for something Stroaker didn't take him to task for. He was starting on the defensive. That was bad, he told himself. Stroaker was actually a nice guy who liked him personally, at least so he thought. The SAC had called him into his office more than once when he was the Principal Relief on an FCI squad in San Francisco a few years back, mainly to discuss FCI priorities and problems. He seemed to have a high opinion of Knowles's analytical abilities.

"Cliff, what is your assessment of this kidnap report?"

Right to the bottom line, thought Knowles. "I think it's for real. I believe he was snatched." No waffling. If you're going to give your opinion, don't hedge. He's going to hold you to it anyway, and it sounds a lot better if you sound self assured.

"Did you know Mrs. Fischer is on mind-altering drugs?" Stroaker asked.

Jesus, where did that come from? Neither Carmody nor Mrs. Fischer, or even Olson, had said anything about mind-altering drugs. Well, he didn't want to sound too ignorant. "Well, Carmody said she was on medication, that's all. He didn't describe what it was." The long pause from Stroaker seemed to Knowles to mean, "And you didn't bother to ask?" Knowles added, "I asked him if she was unstable, and he said no. Besides, the car ended up at Claritiva. It didn't drive itself."

"She could have driven it there. She came to his work and moved it later."

Stroaker was arguing with him, not listening to his opinion. Still not good, he thought. "Maybe so, but I still think it's real. I've talked to her. I think she's just really upset. She seems truly afraid for her husband."

"Have you seen the note she passed to Carmody at the store?"

"No." Shit, Stroaker knew more than he did about this case.

"That's what I like about you, Cliff. You give me a straight answer. Okay, we'll treat this as real. I'll have the Tech Squad put a tap on the home line. Get her consent ... in writing. And I want you to go to the house and look around. See if there is any evidence ... that might show what happened."

To the house looking for evidence? The kidnap must have happened in the parking lot at Claritiva, not at the house. This could only mean one thing. Stroaker was asking him to look for signs of violence. He thinks Mrs. Fischer bumped off her husband and staged the kidnap. Either that or he thinks they had a violent row and the husband took off for parts unknown. Knowles began to sweat. This was going to be dicey. Stroaker was telling him that he was taking his word for it, but he didn't really believe him.

Knowles called Olson back and told him what the SAC had said. Olson said nothing at first. Then he told Knowles to break off the interview. Rice would finish up when he got there. Get over to the house like Stroaker had said. Olson would send a couple of agents to help him search.

Knowles went back out to the living room. He quickly told Mrs. Fischer that they would like to put a recorder on the home telephone lines. The kidnappers could call back at any moment. They needed to have the recording and the trace going as soon as possible if they wanted to have the best chance at saving her husband's life. She could hardly say no in front of her friends. She consented readily. Knowles did not have the preprinted form for consensual wiretap in his briefcase, but he did have a general Consent to Search form. He filled it in with her address and said he had to have her sign this to make sure the recording would be legal. He avoided using the term "admissible in court" because he did not want to alert her to the possibility of a trial. That might make her think twice.

While she was signing the form the front doorbell rang. When Bob Carmody answered it, Harry Rice and Tim Rothman entered. Rice introduced himself and made a beeline for Mrs. Fischer. He immediately launched into a series of questions that were obviously right out of some training material on how to interview a kidnap victim. Rice had kept his notes from that school, apparently. Some of the questions were pretty good, Knowles realized, but Mrs. Fischer seemed put off by his abrupt manner. Knowles could see her stiffen, and only with difficulty repressed a desire to intervene. He had his orders, after all. He pulled Rothman aside. "Tim, try to keep Harry from pissing her off too much. She's wound pretty tight. I have to go over to her house."

Rothman agreed to do what he could, but warned Knowles that Stroaker wanted Rice to do the interview because he was qualified in the Bureau school as a kidnap specialist.

"Only an SAC would believe that certification crap," Knowles whispered. "You know a four-day school doesn't teach you how to work cases, especially something you've never worked before. Rice hasn't handled a real kidnapping, hell, a real case of any kind, in the year I've been on the squad."

"I know that, and you know that, but the SAC doesn't know that," was Rothman's only reply.

Knowles then motioned Bob Carmody aside and asked him about the medication, telling him what the SAC had said about the mind-altering drugs. Carmody said it was some prescription pain-killer she used for post-surgical pain. That was why she had come back from Hong Kong. She had needed some surgery to remove a cyst, and had only been out of the hospital a day. She was taking the medication, and was zonked out from the jet lag as well. She was exhausted, in pain, and probably her hormones were affected by the surgery, too, he said. He was dismayed to hear that the SAC had described the medicine as mind-altering drugs. He certainly had not used that term, he told Knowles. He had told agent Lark the name of the drug, but that's all. The SAC had the wrong impression. She was not psychotic or hallucinating, just in really bad shape from the surgery, the trip, and the stress. He had only mentioned the medication because Carl had told him it gave her some difficulty in concentrating, and when it first kicked in, made her sound drunk. "He was sort of laughing about it, but I could tell he was a little embarrassed about it, and wanted me to know in case I heard her on the phone. She hardly touches liquor. I just wanted you to know so you wouldn't think she was an alcoholic when you talked to her." He stammered, "I guess I should have explained it better. She loved her husband, and their marriage is solid. They're both devout Catholics. There's no way she made this up, or Carl took off." Carmody shook his head convincingly and even muttered "Oh dear" a couple of times.

Knowles thanked him. This made sense. The SAC's wife was a nurse, he had heard. Stroaker had probably looked up the drug in some reference book, or had his wife do it, and read that it had some potential bad side effects. Carmody's attempt to ensure that the FBI did not misjudge her credibility had ended up having just the opposite of its intended effect. Knowles gritted his teeth silently. Why don't people just tell the FBI the whole story right up front? Hiding things just leads to confusion and suspicion.

They both went back in the living room. He could read body language, and Mrs. Fischer was sending out vibes that would lift the ceiling pretty soon. Rice wasn't even looking at her. He was reading from a list of questions he had written down.

"Mrs. Fischer," Knowles interjected. "One more thing. I need to go to your house right now to set up the phone recording. Do you have a key I could use?" He wasn't about to tell her the man in charge of the division thought she was a homicidal maniac. She gave him the combination to a security panel on the side of the house and explained how to use it. He could get in without a key.

He left - to go look for a body in the bathtub that he knew wouldn't be there.

Day 2
Wednesday

Chapter 5

It was just after midnight when Knowles reached the Fischer home. He drove by once, just to see if there was anyone looking out a window or watching from nearby. He saw nothing unusual. The home was a faux Tudor with a beautifully manicured lawn and garden. And it was large - very large. Knowles was once again reminded of the Fitzgerald line about the very rich – they were indeed different from you and me. He drove around the corner and parked on a side street, then walked up the driveway to the side door. He had no trouble letting himself in with the combination.

Mrs. Fischer had told him the housekeeper would be gone and that there should be no one in the house. Her children were all grown and gone, although her youngest son, a sophomore at Notre Dame, was finishing up finals and would be home in two weeks. Just in case, he called out 'hi' a few times. No response. The house was dark and unoccupied. The only light came from a small spotlight shining on the oil portrait of a jolly-looking man in a business suit - probably Mr. Fischer. This was getting creepy, he thought. If it this had been a movie, this is where the strings would start building in a rapid, rhythmic dissonance. The hairs on the back of his neck and arms prickled. He half expected to open a closet door and have a body fall on him as the music reached a sudden crescendo. Still, he didn't pull out his gun. He didn't want to shoot some relative or servant Mrs. Fischer had forgotten to mention.

He made one quick pass through the house looking for anything obvious. He was leery of turning on too many lights, just in case someone was watching. He found nothing out of the ordinary, unless you thought five bedrooms and five baths were out of the ordinary. He went back downstairs. Carl Fischer's home office was on the basement level. As he descended to the last step he felt around for a light switch, without success. He went over to the desk, which he could only feel, not see, because of the near total darkness. There was an overhead lamp, but it was hanging from the ceiling, not sitting on the desk. Damn. That meant it probably worked off a wall switch somewhere. He explored the fixture with his fingers, but it was obvious there was no switch on the lamp itself. Why hadn't he brought his flashlight from the car, he chastised himself. Because I thought I could just turn on the lights, that's why, he answered himself. Don't beat yourself up over something you can't change and didn't have any reason to anticipate.

He walked upstairs and turned on all the lights in the living room. This would throw additional light into the lower room through the stairwell. He returned and began a methodical search of the walls, but still could not find a switch. He walked back upstairs to see if the switch was at the top of the stairs. There was a switchplate there, but it only worked the lights over the wet bar. He tried to reason it out. This home was too high-class not to have a switch in a convenient location. Obviously Fischer couldn't use that room without the overhead light. It must be there somewhere. It would normally be on the right, just by the door as you enter. He went back down the stairs, and looked at the wall on the right of the bottom step. It was a floor-to-ceiling bookcase, filled with books. There was nothing but bare wall before the bookcase. Then it struck him that the bookcase looked like it was custom-built, not part of the original house. If there had been a light switch, it would be right where the bookcase was now. Maybe they didn't move it; maybe they just built around it. He stood directly in front of the rightmost column of bookshelves - containing an eclectic and G-rated selection of reading material, he noted. Sure enough, there was the switch between two books in a space just barely wide enough for his hand to fit. He flipped in on.

He scanned the desktop with a practiced eye. He had done many searches in his fifteen years in the FBI. Nothing struck him as significant. There were masses of paperwork, too much to review tonight. He saw credit card invoices and receipts, checking account statements, periodicals, travel brochures, and routine items found in most American homes.

There was a desktop calendar - the kind with a new flip page for every day, with a Garfield cartoon on the left leaf, and the date and blanks for appointments on the right. The top page was turned to today's date - actually the previous day's since it was now after midnight. But this meant Carl Fischer had looked at his calendar before leaving that morning. That, or perhaps Mrs. Fischer had come down here to see if there was any explanation for Carl's disappearance. But she had told Knowles she never went down into Carl's office; he got mad if she touched anything there. Possibly someone else had wanted to see if Carl had any plans besides going to work that day. That would mean someone with access to the household was involved. There was only one entry on the calendar for that day: "Delis early" it looked like. The writing was faint and hard to make out. Something about delicatessens? They were going to a party that night. Maybe he was going to pick something up for the party. But that didn't make much sense - his wife was baking a cake, and he wouldn't buy perishable food in the morning for a party that started at 9 PM. The word 'early' might have some significance, since he had disappeared early in the day. Cliff remembered seeing a small home copier to his left. He didn't want to take the whole calendar or rip out that one page, as Mrs. Fischer might become upset if she noticed. He popped open the metal rings and slipped that page out. He moved to the copier. It seemed to take forever for the contraption to warm up. Finally he made his copy and slipped it into his briefcase. He returned the original to its place and snapped the calendar closed.

He finished up in the office, finding nothing more worth pursuing. He returned to the kitchen and looked it over more carefully. There was a frosted cake sitting on the sideboard. He peeked in the refrigerator. Sure enough, there was a bowl of fresh strawberries ready to be cut up and placed on the pristine white surface. His mouth began to water. He usually had dessert around 9:00, but he had missed it tonight. He wondered if he could sneak a bite of something. It was after 12:30, and he hadn't eaten for almost 6 hours. He had never been good at controlling his appetite. Naww, he thought, better not. Suddenly the doorbell chimed. Knowles could feel his heart race. He realized he was a lot more on edge than he should be. Who could it be at this time of night? The chord echoed hollowly in the empty house. Of course! It was the other agents Olson had promised. He went to the door and let in Gina Torres and Matt Nguyen. They were both first-office agents without major case experience. Torres, tall, broad-shouldered, and sporting long, luxuriant black tresses, was a former varsity volleyball player. Nguyen, perhaps a smidgen shorter than Torres and no heavier, was the son of a South Vietnamese general who had been driven out during the fall of Saigon. His language ability had already proven very helpful working the Southeast Asian gangs in the Valley. Both were single, which was increasingly common since married agents now often quit or wangled transfers because they could not afford to live in Silicon Valley.

Knowles brought them up to speed. He told them he had done a quick search, and mentioned the calendar page. Torres took a look at it. "That might be 'Delia' not 'Delis'," she offered. "That's a woman's name in Spanish." Knowles was slightly irked that he had not already considered that. Of course he knew Delia was a woman's name, but he hadn't thought of it when he had looked at the writing. He still thought it looked like "Delis." Torres continued, "I heard this guy might be having an affair since his wife was loony. Maybe this is a girlfriend, and he staged this whole thing to find a way out." Knowles was genuinely concerned now that the mindset was already developing that this was not a real kidnapping. Mrs. Fischer was not crazy, just suffering from an unbearable load of pain, stress, and jet lag, exacerbated by some prescription medicine. She was actually an attractive, charming woman, and Carmody had told him the Fischers were still madly in love after 32 years of marriage. All her actions had been logical from her point of view, believing that her husband would be killed if the spies around her detected that she was reporting the kidnapping.

Knowles could feel in his gut that this was real, and he respected Carmody's judgment on this as well. Carmody had been Fischer's friend and co-worker for over 18 years, since long before Claritiva Carmody was CEO of Claritiva because of his intellect and his ability to judge people. If he said this was real, Knowles would trust him.

"Don't rush to judgment. I think this is real," Knowles said to Torres. "We need to check the place out and find out how many telephone lines they have. Check for fax, modem, and security system lines, as well. You never know how the kidnappers are going to try to contact her next."

Knowles saw Torres and Nguyen exchange a glance. Obviously this was not the line they had been given back at the RA. They would be in a tough position if their supervisor, Olson, had told them to do one thing and the Principal Relief, who also signed their paperwork and assigned them cases, told them something else. They nodded noncommittally.

Knowles sent Nguyen out to the yard to look for anything relevant. The fog was beginning to roll in, and a slight breeze had come up. It was pitch black, and with the fog it was impossible to see anything in the yard. Nguyen tripped over a patio chair he couldn't see and barked his shin. Torres and Knowles continued through the house doing a more thorough search of the rooms that had only received a quick look on the first pass. While they were at it, the doorbell rang again. It turned out to be Ron Jemperson, an agent from the Tech Squad. Jemperson hauled with him two enormous black plastic cases. It was a good thing Jemperson was a jumbo-sized guy. The equipment was probably over 100 lbs., and the walkway to the door was long and uphill. Knowles let him in.

Jemperson was the only black agent in the SJRA, and the only technically trained agent, as well. He got a lot of jokes about *Mission Impossible*. Agents would sometimes start to hum the theme music from the 1970's TV series when he showed up with his plastic cases. The humor of it all had worn off for him long ago, but he never said anything to anyone about it. The first thing he did was ask to see the consent form. Knowles showed it to him.

"This is *not* a consensual monitoring form, this is a consent to search form," Jemperson protested. The two forms have different formats, and he recognized this one without having to read it. He wasn't about to place a recording device on a phone without a proper consent form or a court order. Government-haters thought that the FBI did such things regularly and cavalierly. The truth was exactly the opposite. Recordings on phones were rare, and viewed as risky. They carried all kinds of administrative requirements and potential liability for the agents who did them. It was hard to convince the tech agents to do one even when it was perfectly legal. Defense attorneys and other scum apologists, as Knowles thought of them, were winning this particular battle.

"I didn't have a consensual monitoring form, Ron, so I had to use this," Knowles replied calmly. He pointed out where he had hand-written in the 'Place to be searched' space the words "all telephone numbers at residence to be recorded." Jemperson looked it over carefully. "I'm the Legal Advisor," Knowles continued. "This is valid. Take my word for it. You can ask her consent yourself when she gets here if you want. You have four witnesses." There was confidence in Knowles's voice.

"OK. You da man. But next time use an FD-396." Jemperson began to unpack his gear. He remembered Knowles giving the lecture on electronic surveillance at the last annual legal instruction. Knowles should know if anyone did. This was one of the reasons Knowles had become an FBI Legal Advisor - people who were otherwise undecided or unmotivated would often do what he told them simply because he was their lawyer. It's not that they thought his interpretation of the law would always win out in court. They knew better than that; it was that they had someone to take the blame if it went wrong. Jemperson had already checked with Pac Bell, the local phone company, and gotten a list of telephone numbers at the address. There were only two: the regular voice number and the fax/modem line in Carl Fischer's office. Both were unpublished. In order to get the numbers, Jemperson's squad supervisor had been required to certify in writing that this was a life-and-death emergency. Even with that Pac Bell would require a court order or consent form within 48 hours or inform the U.S. District Court that the FBI was conducting an illegal wiretap. Jemperson knew he had to produce that consent form for his supervisor or he'd get an earful. He asked Knowles for a copy of it. The original would go in the case file 1A section of the file at the VCMO rotor in San Jose. Knowles had already made him one on the copier downstairs, and handed it over.

Jemperson quickly located the phone drop and determined the routing of the lines. He pointed out that he was going to have to bring an extension of the fax line upstairs. During any ransom call they needed to be able to call out to Pac Bell on a separate line to start the trace. That meant they had to have another line in the same room. Sometimes a cell phone would work, but the signal was not good enough here. They could lose communication right in the middle of the call, or, worse, right before the call. They needed a land line to be on the safe side.

The only room that had both lines was the office downstairs, which was too small, dark and far from the center of activity. Fortunately, the phone company had not run a separate line for the fax. They had just used the second pair in the original cable. Most telephone lines brought into a typical home contain four separate wires. Any two, called a pair, can be used to make a complete circuit, what the consumer thinks of as one line. The advantage of this for Jemperson was that he could just wire a connector to the non-voice pair in the box on the family room wall, and then make sure that pair was connected to the equivalent pair from the downstairs fax where that came in at the phone drop. He didn't actually have to run a wire up from downstairs. He could just jack an FBI handset into the new connector and use the existing cable. He did the necessary wiring on the wall jack in a matter of minutes. Connecting at the phone drop on the outside, however, was a little trickier. The box was low and on the side of the building, but, even so, a person working there would be visible from the street. There was no decent lighting, so he would probably not be noticed. There was no one walking around this street at 1:00 A.M. The problem was that it was really difficult to see the tiny wires and identify the right colors of the wire in the dim glow of a penlight. Someone would have to hold a real flashlight for him as he worked. He couldn't do it the *Mission Impossible* way, with the penlight held in his mouth, as he dangled upside down. He enlisted Nguyen to help him, and they went outside to complete the connection. They just had to hope no neighbors, or kidnappers, noticed two guys snooping around the phone box.

While they were at work, Fran Fischer arrived home. Two of the Carmody children had been sent to retrieve her car, and one had driven it back to Carmody's house. She had driven herself home.

She seemed in a bad mood when she came in, and asked why there were so many people there. Knowles explained that it was necessary to complete the phone monitoring. Jemperson returned at that moment, and Knowles introduced Fran Fischer to all of the agents. She greeted them warmly but briefly, and excused herself to go upstairs. Jemperson connected a new handset to the jack in the family room just off the kitchen. Next he connected a small cassette recorder to the regular voice line using a phone patch between the handset and the telephone itself. He explained to Knowles that there should be an agent to work the recorder when the call came in. The victim would be too busy listening or talking, and thinking of what to say, to remember to push the buttons on the device. Like most cassette models, this one required that the user press both the Play and Record buttons at the same time in order to record. One started the tape moving, and the other connected the recording head to the live input source. Many an agent had lost valuable evidence because he or she had pressed only Record. Most made that mistake only once. For this reason the standard methodology was to press both Play and Record, then Pause during setup. When the call came, Pause was to be released.

Jemperson asked if one of the agents was staying overnight. They all looked at each other and waited for someone to say something. Apparently no one had been assigned to do that, and no one was volunteering. They didn't even have consent to do that. Jemperson said in that case he would have to show Mrs. Fischer how to press the Pause button in case the call came in the middle of the night.

Knowles wondered whether Mrs. Fischer had gone to bed already, but he needed to get her down to explain this. He called up the stairs to the bedroom area. She came down in response. She still seemed to be cross and curt in her replies. Jemperson led her to the recorder and started to explain how it worked.

"We can't have this," she exclaimed. "The housekeeper or gardener could see it. They'll both be here tomorrow. The man said they were watching the house. It could be them. I think he had a Spanish accent. We don't know who's in on it." She was starting to sound screechy now.

Jemperson hadn't known about this aspect and had not tried to make the recording covert. Fortunately, he was a quick thinker. He placed the recorder under a sofa pillow, with the line continuing out to the Princess-style phone on the cushion. The new handset he pushed behind the sofa. Both were detectable if you searched, but they weren't immediately visible.

Knowles took note of the mention of a Spanish accent. She had mentioned the accent before, but wouldn't be pinned down as to what kind. He presumed the gardener and housekeeper were Hispanics, since about 90% of domestics in this area were. That might be why she was so fearful of being overheard in the house, and could explain why she was being so covert in her movements. She was afraid of her own servants. That was perhaps not unreasonable, either, Knowles thought. He knew of several kidnappings where workers, either domestic help, or at the factory or office, had indeed been involved. They needed to be careful. However, she seemed mollified by this current telephone arrangement. It was also good that she had committed to what kind of accent. That might help.

Jemperson moved to the wall jack in the kitchen. He put an extra long cord on the kitchen counter phone. Mrs. Fischer looked at him with suspicion. This was getting to be a lot of hardware.

"This one is necessary so we can have someone listen in on your line when the call comes in. We'll be taking notes and giving you directions on what to say," Jemperson started to instruct Mrs. Fischer. "This will stretch from the kitchen to here. You don't have to explain this to the housekeeper. If she notices it, which I doubt, you can just say you wanted a longer cord. This way you won't be alone when the call comes. Someone can sit right next to you and listen in."

Mrs. Fischer picked up the phone receiver in the family room. She held it to her ear a moment, and then put it down.

"What have you done to my phone?" She asked severely. "It doesn't even work now."

Knowles could see her clenching and unclenching her jaw muscles. What the hell was going on? He walked over to the same phone she had just used and picked up the receiver. Dead silence - no dial tone, nothing. He pushed down the receiver button a couple of times, but still got nothing. He looked up at Jemperson. "She's right. The line is dead. You must've disconnected something."

Jemperson seemed astounded. He picked up the extension in the kitchen where he had just placed the long cord. It was dead, too.

All of a sudden Mrs. Fischer commanded, "Get out. All of you, get out. I don't know what you're doing but you aren't being honest with me."

Knowles stayed calm, and attempted to reason with her. It was critical that they pinpoint the problem with the line, he explained to her. The kidnapper could call back any minute, and would not be able to get through. It was just some technical glitch that could be easily remedied. She continued yelling that she wanted everybody out. At that exact moment a man's figure appeared at the sliding glass door between the patio and the family room. Fran Fischer screamed.

Knowles had been standing with his back to that door. He turned instantly and reached for his gun. Then he recognized the tall, rotund silhouette of Harry Rice outlined by the dim patio light. Harry pounded on the glass and mouthed "Let me in."

Fran Fischer kept up her screaming. "Don't let him in! Don't let that man in. I don't want him in here. This is my house and you can't just come in here and take over."

Knowles tried to keep his voice calm and reassuring. "It's just agent Rice, ma'am. He must have come to finalize some details. He's not anybody to worry about." Knowles moved toward the door.

Fran Fischer screamed at maximum lung capacity "I told you not to let him in! I don't like that man and I won't have him in my house. Get out, all of you, now, or I'll call the police."

Knowles kept trying, but every time he moved toward the door to let Harry in, Mrs. Fischer became hysterical. Rice was getting more irritated each time, too, he realized. The fog was really rolling in now, and a bone-chilling wind had come up. Rice started making shivering motions to indicate he was getting cold and to please open the door. Knowles was torn as to what to do.

Fran Fischer started to rip at the phone cords. "Get this stuff out of here. I'm withdrawing my consent. I don't want you spying on me." She started sobbing. Jemperson hovered over the wires as close as he dared. He was afraid she was going to wreck the equipment. Knowles made a snap decision.

"All right, we're leaving. Let the agent disassemble the wires; he'll take off any equipment. If you don't want us here, we'll go. But please reconsider in the morning. We have to have a trace going on that phone line when you get the next call. Please, Mrs. Fischer, your husband's life is at stake."

Knowles motioned to the agents to get ready to go. He told them he was going to find a phone he could use; since Mrs. Fischer had withdrawn her consent to use hers. They started packing their notepads into briefcases. Jemperson started taking out the recording equipment. It was a lot faster coming out than going in. Rice was still standing in the cold with his face pressed against the glass trying to figure out what was taking so long. Knowles went to the door and opened it. Mrs. Fischer started screaming again not to let that man in. Rice was mystified and downright churlish for being kept waiting. He had not been able to hear what was going on inside because of the wind chimes by the door. He tried to step inside and was cursing under his breath at Knowles for keeping him in the cold so long. Knowles told him Mrs. Fischer had just withdrawn her consent and didn't want him in her house. "Just go home, Harry. We'll regroup in the morning. I have to get to a phone and call Ben." He left Rice standing there, and the others still inside packing up. Right now, the most important thing was to show Mrs. Fischer they would not run roughshod over her. They were powerless without her consent. They had to find a way to get her trust back, and clearing out was the only thing that might work. After they all had some rest, they could start again the next day. Tomorrow they would call the Carmodys to help.

It was now after 1:30. Knowles tore down Foothill Expressway until he came to the nearest shopping center and swung the car into the lot. It was the one with Andronico's Market, the same one Mrs. Fischer had walked to earlier to meet with Carmody. There was a gas station at one end. Sure enough there was a pay phone. Knowles called Olson at the RA. He gave a quick thumbnail, trying to minimize the hysteria as much as he could. He made it sound like Mrs. Fischer was just too upset to know what she wanted to do and had withdrawn her consent to monitor. But he also knew that the other agents would tell the story with all the gory details, so he finally added that she was pretty much out of control. He explained what Carmody had said regarding the medication and suggested that she had just had a bad reaction to that. He asked Olson to try to reach the Carmodys in order to get them to intervene. Olson said he couldn't. Rothman had just come back to the RA and said they were all exhausted and were going to bed. They had asked to wait until morning to do any more. Tim Rothman had just been sent home. Olson said he was about to send Nick Lark home, too, but in view of this incident, he'd better have Lark meet him. He asked where Knowles was, and said he would radio Lark to meet him.

"I'm making Nick the case agent on this," Olson informed him flatly. "I want him to have all the details. He'll make notes and then write it up when he comes back from Disneyland."

So that was it. Olson didn't believe him either. He was convinced Lark was right that this was some kind of hoax or argument, not a real kidnapping. Knowles could taste the bitterness in his mouth. Normally the first agent to respond is designated the case agent, except in really big cases, where the most experienced and senior agents will get the case. Knowles was both the first responder and the most senior. The case should have been his. This had to be happening because Olson and Stroaker thought he'd made the wrong call and couldn't be trusted. They would think he hadn't returned their pages, he was taking the side of the crazy woman, and he was an FCI agent without the street experience of Nick Lark even though he had more time in. As bad as it felt to be dealt this blow after all he'd been through that night, he was more concerned about what was going to happen to the victim. How can you assign a kidnapping to somebody who's going to be 400 miles away on vacation while it's in progress?

"Ben, you gotta listen to me. This is real, I'm telling you. She may have had a bad night, but Mrs. Fischer did not make this up. The car was driven over to Mountain View. Carmody is sure Fischer is happily married. He's a multi-gazillionaire, for Christ's sake. He's exactly the kind of target a kidnapper would pick. We have to see the wife gets medical help and get her consent in the morning."

"Okay, okay," Olson said. "We will. If it turns out you're right, we'll get the call traced and recorded." He sounded patronizing.

"Talk to Nick and then go home and get some rest. I'm going home now myself." They exchanged goodbyes and hung up.

Knowles slumped in the car seat. He was exhausted emotionally as well as physically, and just wanted to go home. Now he had to talk to Nick Lark. He was getting cold with the fog enveloping the car. He tried the good-time radio, but couldn't find anything worth listening to. He gave Nick a call on the Bureau radio. Lark was already en route. One good thing about Lark's driving was that when you were waiting for him, it didn't take long. Lark pulled up next to him. Knowles got into Lark's car since it was bigger and warmer.

"Cliff, my man. What a night, huh?" Lark laughed with his usual infectious Arkansas lilt.

"Not my finest experience in the Bu, Nick." Knowles grinned at him. He was upset that Lark had contradicted his judgment and had been given the case by Olson, but he didn't hold it against Lark personally. Lark was a good investigator who happened to have a different opinion.

"Nick," he went on, "I know the wife is not behaving rationally, but I think this is for real. You can't just leave in the middle. Not if you're going to be case agent."

"Don't worry. Ben told me that if it turns out to be real he'll assign it to you. If that's what happens, it couldn't be in better hands. I have prepaid tickets to Disneyland, and they're non-refundable. I'm going, come hell or high water; I lost my deposit last year when Olson canceled my leave, and my wife won't let me forget it. Take my word for it, when the sun comes up tomorrow morning and they do a real search out in the backyard, they're going to find a hand sticking up out of the garden. This'll be a homicide, and you can turn it over to the locals."

"No. You're just talking though your wallet. You don't want to have to cancel your vacation and stay to work it, so you've convinced yourself, and Olson, that it's bogus."

"And Stroaker, and Nguyen and Torres, too. You're the only one who thinks this woman isn't a lunatic. She either killed him or he took off to get away from her." He said it with the caustic black humor of a seasoned violent-crimes investigator. Then he became more serious in his tone. "Maybe you're right. Heck, the chances are 50-50, probably, but I have to go with my instincts. This story about Mexico is nuts. If she's telling the truth, the call came in at 12:30. He couldn't have been snatched before 9:30. You can't drive to Mexico in three hours. What'd they do, fly him on their own private jet?"

"Actually, we shouldn't rule that out. Kidnappings of rich executives are pretty common in Mexico right now. They could be branching out northward. Or maybe they're locals who just said that to keep her from calling the police."

"Why? That just makes it FBI jurisdiction if he was taken across state lines. You think the kidnappers would *try* to make it an FBI case? That doesn't wash. What about the $650,000? Nobody asks for $650,000. Why not a million or half a million? And the deal with the note at the grocery store? That's bizarre." He opened his briefcase and handed Knowles the note. It was on a long, narrow piece of paper with "To do or buy" preprinted at the top. He remembered seeing a notepad like that in the kitchen of the Fischer home. The writing was in black felt-tip ink hastily written in block letters. It read:

> *Bob I got a call from man said Carl is kidnap. $650,000 in hundreds day after tomorrow. I will be at party tonite see you there. I have to do cake strawberry OK? Otherwise they can see me. Carl will be killed if we tell. I don't know what to do. What do you say? I have no time - must walk Alicia not suspicious.*

Knowles didn't try to analyze it. He already knew Mrs. Fischer had to have scrawled it while keeping her housekeeper from seeing it, or knowing what she was doing. He guessed that Alicia was the housekeeper's name. She probably used the grocery list paper to make it look like a regular errand list she was preparing, and the run-on sentences and cryptic wording were probably the result of the narrow paper and lack of space, along with her hurried manner. The note didn't change much for him, but the incident at the house had given him pause. Even if was a reaction to the medicine, she was capable of a violent reaction. Lark didn't even know about the tantrum yet. Knowles told him what happened with the consensual monitoring. Lark just grinned with an I-told-you-so expression.

"I'll bet you my next paycheck this is no kidnapping. She killed him or he's on a beach in the Caribbean somewhere. Me, I'm going to Disneyland. See ya, buddy."

Knowles got out of Lark's car, and could only muster, "We'll see. Have a good trip. Say hi to Jayne and the kids." They both waved, and Lark headed out of the parking lot for the long trip back to Monterey.

Knowles drove home and entered as quietly as he could. His watch read 2:18. He fetched the kitchen timer and set it to go off at 6:30, a half hour later than he usually got up. Four hours sleep would have to do tonight. He curled up on the couch so as not to wake Rickie and went to sleep.

Chapter 6

Carl Fischer woke. He was being shaken by one of his captors. It was the short burly one - the driver. Fischer had slept surprisingly well under the circumstances. They had all watched, or, in his case, listened to, movies on the cable TV for hours the previous day. Though blindfolded, he was able to hear the two men coming and going. They didn't tell him where they were going or why, but around dinner time they had brought him some food. It was a McDonald's meal - a Quarter Pounder, fries, and a Coke. He had been famished and had eaten it greedily. Then he had been told to go to sleep. He wasn't sure what time that was, but it could not have been more than an hour after they ate. The local news had just ended. It was a San Francisco station, so they must be in the Bay Area, or close to it. There was no mention on the news of him being missing or kidnapped. That was good, he thought. The kidnappers wouldn't panic.

He could tell it was still dark outside. He still had the cotton balls over his eyes, but he could open his lids enough to see whether it was night or day. He could even catch glimpses of the men's shoes. One of them had white tennis shoes, but he couldn't recognize the logo.

He tried to move his arms and realized they were tied together with rope of some kind. Oh yes, he remembered now. They had tied his hands together the prior evening and tied the other end of the rope to the bed. He judged the knots as being rather unprofessional, and considered trying to get untied. But he could hear the men moving around at all times and figured they were watching him always. Even if he got loose, what would he do? They were armed, and he wasn't. He had no car keys, and his bad leg meant he couldn't outrun them. He had decided to cooperate, at least for now.

He felt the rope being untied from the bed frame, but his hands remained bound together. As he rolled over on the bed, he realized they still had not found his cell phone. It was in his left front pants pocket. The lump had been uncomfortable at times while he was trying to get to sleep, but he had said nothing to the captors. He just hoped he would have a chance to turn it on. He couldn't reach into his pocket with his hands tied.

Fischer sat up on the bed. He rubbed his hands against his eyes and said, "I need to go to the bathroom. Can you untie my hands?"

"No! You can do it with hands tied." It was the driver who replied.

"I have to ... sit," Fischer lied. "You'll have to wipe me."

"Just a minute." The driver was obviously not the decision-maker of the two. The other man had apparently gone out to the car briefly. He came back in within a few seconds. The driver whispered something to the other man.

"All right, we will untie your hands. But don't try anything. I have my gun, and we will stand in the open door." He sent the driver to the bathroom to make sure there were no razors or other objects that could be used as weapons. The driver indicated it was clear.

Fischer's hands were untied slowly. Both men stood close to him, one in front, one in back. He could see the shoes of the man in front - brown loafers. From the voice he knew it was the gunman who had been in the passenger seat yesterday. That meant the white tennis shoes must be the driver, unless there were more than two of them. He was led into the bathroom. He pulled down his pants without assistance. He couldn't see whether they were watching him, since they had not removed the blindfold. As he sat on the toilet, he decided to chance it. He reached down to his pants, around his ankles, and put his hands in both pockets. He felt the cell phone, and fumbled for the on switch.

"What are you doing?" called out the gunman.

"Just getting my comb. I must look like a mess." Fischer found the button at that moment and gave it a push. He wasn't sure if he had held it down long enough to power on, but he couldn't keep his hand there. He withdrew his hand as casually as he could, pulling his comb out from his front pocket at the same time. He began to run it through his hair. "Here it is," he said. With his other hand he flushed the toilet. He wanted the noise to cover the beep the phone emits when it handshakes with the cell site. He couldn't hear the beep himself, so he felt he was safe from them hearing. But he wasn't sure if it was because he had failed to activate the phone or because the sound was masked by the flush. He kept combing his hair.

"Never mind that. Just finish your business and let's go." Fischer 'finished his business' and stood up. He took care to pull up his pants carefully, so they wouldn't accidentally fall to the floor with a telltale clunk. He buckled his belt and said he was ready.

The gunman tied his hands once again, and draped a towel over the wrists so the ropes wouldn't show. He grabbed Fischer by the back of his collar and shoved the gun against his spine. "Now we are going to leave. Don't try to run or resist. I will kill you if you try anything." He pushed the older man out the door to the car, which had been pulled up to within a few feet, motor running. Once again they entered the back seat just as they had at the Claritiva parking lot, Fischer behind the driver, gunman to his right. Fischer could tell from the chill air and the quiet that it was still very early morning. The rush hour around here started by 5:00 AM. If they were within three hours driving distance of Silicon Valley, as he estimated, there would be heavier traffic than this by 5:00. Fischer figured it was probably between 3:00 and 4:00 in the morning, but he had no way to verify it.

They drove for an hour, maybe two. Fischer couldn't tell. And he couldn't tell direction without the sun shining on him. He had become disoriented the previous day when they had first pulled into this lot and driven in circles, backed up, and gone forward again. He could tell they were turning right as they pulled out of the motel parking lot, but he didn't know what direction that was. They could be headed back to Mountain View for all he knew. But since they had started out going south yesterday, he guessed they would continue that general direction.

Fischer tried to calculate how far they could be from their starting point. He figured they couldn't have driven more than four hours the previous day, at the absolute most. It was probably more like two hours. He had heard the gunman tell the driver to keep within the speed limit, so that meant they could not have covered much more than 150 - 180 miles, maybe a lot less. If he was right about it being to the south, that would put the motel somewhere from Salinas to King City or thereabouts. The motel had carried a San Francisco news station on the cable TV, so that was consistent, he thought. He wasn't sure how far down the state the cable systems would carry Bay Area stations. If they had headed eastward, they could be in the Central Valley by now, but he was pretty sure they had been going south most of the time yesterday. The Central Valley motels would carry Sacramento, Fresno, or Stockton TV stations, probably. He decided his working hypothesis should be King City. This morning they had driven another hour or two, long enough that they could possibly have made it to San Luis Obispo.

A car horn blared right next to him. He sat bolt upright, and quickly felt the warmth of the sun on his left temple. He realized he had dozed off. They were no longer on the freeway. The car was moving too slowly and was obviously stopping at stop lights or stop signs. He felt the gun muzzle poke hard against his right side. Apparently the gunman had noticed his sudden movement and was warning him not to do anything to draw attention. He sat back and relaxed a little. How long had he been asleep? The sun on his left meant they were still headed south, if it was early morning, that is. What if it was noon already? That would mean they were going west. He wanted to peek at his watch, but his hands were still tied and the towel was still over his wrists. Any attempt would be noticed. It was May, he reasoned, so the sun came up in the northeast and rose high quickly. He could tell by moving his head around a little that the sun's angle was below the level of the window top. It had to be shortly after sunrise. So they were headed south or maybe southeast. But they could have turned any direction while he had slept. Even as he mulled that over, they turned a corner then turned another one. They could be almost anywhere.

Fischer felt the road get rougher. The car bumped badly, and they were taking some spots exceptionally slowly. It was probably a rural area, he decided. There were no major metropolitan areas he was familiar with locally that had potholes this bad for this long a stretch. Besides, the traffic noise had died away. He wondered what the coverage area was for his cell phone. Even if he had managed to turn it on, would he still be on the network? He simply had no way of knowing.

The car came to a stop. The driver's door slammed and Fischer could hear footsteps receding from the car. Then came the bang of a screen door. The gunman told him to get out. He slid across the rear seat as instructed, and inadvertently smacked his head hard on the upper doorsill. He mouthed a silent oath, but knew he'd be threatened, or worse, if he cried out. He hoped his head had bled; at least then there would be forensic evidence to match him to the car. He was led inside.

Initial impressions of a location are usually formed from visual images. In Carl Fischer's case, he could see nothing of this new location other than a few glimpses of old linoleum flooring. His other senses, however, told him quite a bit. The place was sparsely furnished, if at all, and not carpeted. Noises from his own movements echoed off the walls and floors in a way not consistent with large volumes of fabric and carpet. There was a slight odor of garbage mixed with a strong smell of cleaning agents. The garbage smell had been stronger as they entered, but faded as they moved into the interior. They had probably entered through a back or side door by the garbage can. The room temperature varied widely as they moved through the space, and he could see some brightness through the cotton in the warmer areas. This told him curtains were non-existent or, perhaps, pulled wide open. He heard a toilet flush, and the water ran noisily. Always the engineer, he recognized the sound as the continuous gushing made when the pull chain loops under the flapper, preventing a proper seal. It was going to keep running until someone jiggled the handle. For some reason this irritated him more than anything else he could recall during this whole frightening misadventure. Why couldn't they just jiggle the handle? They were wasting water while California was in a drought. His captors seemed not to notice.

After considerable clanking and clattering, Fischer felt himself being guided to another room. At least, he had thought it was a room until he bumped into some coat hangers. This was obviously a closet, probably in a bedroom, but the floor felt soft and spongy.

"My name is Carlos," said the voice he knew to be the gunman's. "The same name as you in Spanish. That should be easy for you to remember. My friend is Miguel. He is a dangerous man, Miguel is, and very good with a knife. But if you do as we say, you will not be harmed. You will stay in here. Do not try to leave, even to come out of the closet a little. And be quiet. If you need to go to the bathroom, ask us. Please sit down on the mattress."

"What do you want from me?" Fischer asked, never having received his answer from the first time he had asked, the day before.

"You are being held for ransom. Your family will pay if they want to see you again. Now sit down."

Fischer sat. He remained motionless and compliant as he felt chains being wrapped around his ankles and heard the ratcheting sound of the links being pulled through a metal bracket of some kind. Then he heard the distinct sound of a padlock being snapped shut. Finally, his hands were untied. The relief was fleeting, however, as metal handcuffs were immediately snapped on his wrists. So this closet would be his abode until who-knew-when. He sickened at the thought. This would take days, even if Fran could raise the money.

And then what - would they let him live? A shudder shook his frame as his predicament became clear to him. He had seen the gunman's face briefly, but not that of the driver. Carlos and Miguel; at least now he had names to use, although he knew better than to believe those were their real names. He determined not to look at either of them if he got another chance. It would give them a motive for killing him when this was over. At least his hands were more comfortable in the cuffs than tied, and they were in front, not behind. If only they would stop that infernal toilet from running.

"Keep your eyes closed. I'm going to remove the glasses," Carlos instructed. Fischer did as he was told. The dark glasses slipped off his nose, and the cotton balls were gently removed. Moments later he could feel the cotton being pressed against his eyes once more, then a mask of some sort was wrapped around his head, with elastic in back. This was a more traditional blindfold, covering the eyes snugly; in fact, he was fairly sure it was a sleeping mask. Apparently Carlos did not trust the glasses to hold the cotton balls in place.

"Give me your wallet." Fischer tried to comply with Carlos's request, but could not reach his rear pocket with his hands cuffed in front. He told Carlos to pull it out for him, which Carlos did gingerly.

Carlos took considerable time going through the contents of the wallet. Fischer could hear the click of the plastic credit and ATM cards being dropped or placed on the floor or a table.

"Are these your children?" Carlos asked. "Which one is the girl with the cat?"

Fischer had to think about the photos in his wallet, since he could not see them. Oh yes, the Christmas photo where Pam had given their cat a new collar. That snapshot had turned out particularly well, and he had kept a copy in his wallet. He gave brief consideration to lying about the names, but he couldn't see the advantage of doing so. Carlos probably knew his children's names, and certainly had their photos now, so Fischer would do little to protect them by lying, and he would just hurt his credibility. "That's Pam."

"And the boy?"

"Patrick."

"How many cars do you have at the house?"

"Three - the Mercedes, the Cadillac, and the Jaguar my wife uses." He intentionally left out the children's cars. They did not live with their parents, except for Patrick, who was attending graduate school right now, and would be coming home from Notre Dame soon for summer break. Eileen was married and living in Southern California, but Pam was still a frequent visitor to the house, and Fischer did not want Carlos to know or recognize her car. She could be the next victim.

"Who drives the Cadillac?"

"My wife and I both use it when we want a bigger car. She uses it mostly. The Jaguar is a convertible. It's too small for grocery shopping." Fischer could hear the faint scratching of pen on paper. Carlos was taking notes.

"What about your oldest daughter?"

Fischer swallowed hard, or tried to, but his throat was incredibly dry. "She lives out of the area, and doesn't drive here. She and her husband usually rent a car when they come, or we pick them up at the airport." He had given Carlos no information about where his daughter and son-in-law lived or what their car looked like, he thought with some small satisfaction. He hadn't even given her name.

As if reading Fischer's thoughts, Carlos asked, "What is her name?"

"Eileen," he replied, barely able to force the name through his lips.

"Patrick? What does he drive?"

"Sometimes he drives the Cadillac or the Jaguar when he's home. He has his own car at school, but he doesn't bring it home."

"What does Pam drive?"

"She doesn't have her own car," he lied. "She usually rides with her roommate or boyfriend."

"Where does she work?"

"At an advertising agency in San Francisco. She's a copy writer." He hoped Carlos would drop this questioning about his family, but he had a feeling it would not be that easy.

"Where does she live?"

"In Berkeley."

"How does she get to work without a car?" asked Carlos, unwilling to drop the subject.

"She takes BART." BART was the subway system, Bay Area Rapid Transit.

"Bullshit. You are lying to me. You're rich; your Mercedes costs $127,000. She would not live and work without a car. She has to have a car to get food and other things, and you would buy her one.

We are watching the house. Don't lie to me. If we find her driving a car you didn't tell us about, we'll kill her."

Suddenly Miguel's voice cut in, "That fucker is lying. You ought to blow up his fucking house."

Oh God, Fischer thought, don't do anything foolish. Pam won't be coming by anyway, probably. Better just to tell the truth. "Okay. I was just trying to protect her. She drives a Volkswagen Beetle. But I was telling the truth about the other two. They don't drive their own cars here any more."

"That's better. Don't lie to me no more." Carlos was back in charge.

"I won't." Fischer's heart was racing again, and he felt faint from the fear engendered by the probing and threats to his family. Why did Carlos care so much about the cars?

Carlos continued the questioning for almost an hour, asking about finances, daily routines of family members, and the hired help. It was essentially the same line of questions as the previous day in the car, but much more detailed, and this time Carlos was taking notes. He asked very detailed questions about the Mercedes, and he seemed to know already the exact specifications of that model. When the questioning stopped, Fischer could hear the sharp snap of a plastic lid or housing, but he was not certain what the device was until Carlos spoke. "You are going to record a message. I will tell you what to say. Memorize what I say to you." He began reading off a paper, Fischer could tell, from the sound of paper rustling and the fluency of the speech changing. Apparently Carlos didn't want Fischer to take off the mask to read the message for fear of risking identification.

> *Hello, Fran. This is Carl. I love you very much. I'm sick. At the moment, I'm okay. I'm being treated well. The people who have me are very serious. You should follow their directions. Please don't report to the authorities. Our lives could be in danger. They're watching the house.*

Carlos had him go over the message several times until he felt comfortable Fischer had the gist of it down. Then he told Fischer that they were ready to record it, and to make sure he did not try to put any secret messages into it. Fischer recited it as best as he could remember. He stumbled over a word or two, but Carlos seemed satisfied. He stopped after one take and played it back. Fischer heard his own voice, and, like most people hearing their own voices recorded, hated it. Did he really sound like that? He realized he had inadvertently tacked on an extra "I love you very much" at the end, but Carlos did not mention it.

Carlos let him use the bathroom and promised they would bring him some food soon. Then he chained Fischer in the closet once more and shut the closet door. Fischer was left in the dark - in every sense of the word.

Chapter 7

Knowles heard the timer go off and forced himself to open his eyes. Oh, how good another couple of hours of sleep would feel. He put his feet on the floor before he allowed that temptation to insinuate itself further into his thoughts. He dragged himself through his morning routine. Rickie was just getting up as he was tying his necktie. She chastised him roundly for not taking better care of himself, but was too good a Bureau wife to get mad about the hours. This kind of thing happened too often for that, and she would never have married an FBI agent if she hadn't been prepared for that aspect of Bureau life. She didn't even ask about the kidnap case - she just assumed it was yet another false report. He kissed her and left without telling her. There was no point in taking a stand on this one with her - it would just be one more person to look foolish to if he turned out to be wrong.

He arrived at his desk at 7:30, later than usual. A couple of other squad members were there before him. He didn't like that; he prided himself on setting an example for the younger agents. He pulled out his notes from the night before to write up his FD-302s. He wanted the computer before his office mate, Tim Rothman, came in, since they had to share one between them.

Olson showed up shortly before 8:00. "Cliff, I'm going to call the Carmodys to get them to talk to Mrs. Fischer. They have to get her to let us put a recorder on that home line. If she refuses, I'm going to have to report this whole thing to the locals as a missing person case and close it."

Knowles wanted to call Carmody himself, to let him know the seriousness of what happened the previous evening, but was not about to try to force his supervisor's hand. He was in a bad enough spot now. He nodded and kept writing his 302s. As he reviewed his notes, he struggled to read his own handwriting; it was as bad as anybody's he'd ever seen. That could be a good thing - defense lawyers were entitled to view an agent's rough notes during pre-trial discovery, and it wasn't pleasant to be questioned under oath on every word you wrote months or years earlier. He was intentionally cryptic and illegible so no one else could read his notes.

He had not been able to take a lot of notes during the search, so he had to re-create a lot of that from memory. Fortunately, nothing of any significance had been found, so the 302 would be irrelevant later. He did one 302 for the telephone interview of Carmody, one for the interview of Mrs. Fischer, one for the consent to search, and one for the results of the search. Technically he should do a separate 302 of the information Carmody provided at the house about Mrs. Fischer's operation and medication, but he decided not to. If it turned out there were no more ransom calls, the case would be closed and nothing further would ever come of the case - on the FBI side, anyway. If there was another call, it would show Mrs. Fischer was telling the truth and he didn't want to cast doubt on the credibility of someone who would be a star witness, especially one who had suffered so badly. He didn't want to make her subject to a grueling and possibly mortifying cross-examination.

Rothman came in, sat down at his desk, and asked Knowles how he was doing. They bantered good-naturedly for a few minutes about what a crazy job it was sometimes. Then Rothman inquired under his breath, "So, I hear you think it's a real snatch?"

"Yeah, I do. Mrs. Fischer wasn't faking the terror - that part's real. I've been fooled before by professional crooks - con men - but she's not in that category."

"I agree with you. I saw her at Carmody's; that panic was real. I also saw the car out at the company. How did it get there? Olson said she could have driven it, but how could she drive her own car and the Mercedes? Did she drive it out and take the bus back? Walk eight miles through rush hour traffic? If she did it, there has to be someone else involved."

"And she did it her first day out of the hospital," Knowles added, relieved to have some support.

"Exactly my point. How could she have planned this while she was in Hong Kong or under the knife? She weighs half what her husband does; how could she overpower him, kill him, and move him somewhere, leaving no signs of a struggle."

Knowles smiled. He could count on Tim to back him up. Rothman was a good friend, but that wouldn't color his judgment on this case. His observations were all good, professional, investigative conclusions. Of course, they weren't really proof, either. It was still possible Fischer himself planned it, skipping out for some reason and arranging for someone to make the ransom call to make it look real. Knowles knew also that you could never really think of all the possible things a criminal might do, or understand the reasons for the things they did do. Nevertheless, he was gratified to have an ally. "You're pretty smart for an airborne taxi driver."

"Don't remind me. I have to do flight instructor duty this afternoon. I have four hours to do starting at 3:00. This is going to be a long day."

The FBI had some full-time pilots, but most of the agents who flew did so as an additional duty to their regular case work. It was a good deal for both them and the FBI. The government got an extra 25 or 30 hours a week of work out of them for no extra pay, since all agents max out on the overtime just from their case work anyway. The agents get to fly at government expense, and have the benefit of top-notch instructors and equipment. They upgrade their ratings, get in required hours, and get their flight physicals at Bureau expense on top of that. If they weren't flying on government time, they'd be doing it on their own time and at their own expense. Some squad supervisors didn't like the drain on their agents' time, but Rothman kept Olson happy, so Olson let him fly.

Rothman was also a good source. Since he split his time between the San Jose RA and the Special Operations Group, or SOG, the squad that specialized in surveillances and technical work like Jemperson's, he mixed with other part-time pilots from other squads. He was always coming back with juicy tidbits of gossip that otherwise might not have made it to the RA circuit - like who just got promoted to FBIHQ, who got stopped by the local police for drunk driving, and, most popular of all, who was banging whom. The best agents learned it was more important to cultivate informants among other FBI employees than it was to recruit the street-variety snitches.

His latest morsel involved 'Mo' Morales, sometimes referred to as Slow Mo, the SOG supervisor, who had rear-ended a little old lady with his Bureau car on his way home the previous night about 8:00. Knowles asked if Mo had been drinking, since it was well-known he liked to tip a few after work. Drinking so much as a jot of alcohol and then driving a Bureau car was absolutely forbidden, and grounds for dismissal. Of course, that didn't mean it never happened.

"Blinded by the rays of the setting sun," was Rothman's only reply. They both laughed. That apocryphal phrase was code in the FBI for an imaginative excuse put on the form a driver had to fill in if he or she was involved in a collision. Knowles had read many such write-ups in his day, since Legal Advisors had the unpleasant duty of handling civil claims and lawsuits against the FBI, such as those from people involved in collisions with FBI cars. Like Rothman, his second 'hat' got him no extra pay, just extra work, but it gave him a little variety and kept his hand in an activity that might come in handy during a second career some day. Knowles had gone into the FBI right out of law school, and he always felt just a tinge of regret about not practicing law full time.

Knowles finished up his typing, and turned the computer over to Rothman. Knowles walked out to the network printer by Kim's desk. Kim was the squad secretary, and, competent though she was, she was better known among the males as the sweetest eye candy the office had to offer. The FBI paid only civil service wages for support personnel and could not compete with private industry for most clerical spots, so it was sometimes hard to attract competent support, especially those who met the appearance standards top executives demand. But a little-known competitive advantage of the FBI over the other bureaucratic backwaters was that FBI agents were mostly male, young, athletic, and high-status. In a word, studs. Not all of them of course, but enough so that many attractive young ladies thought they could do a lot worse than marry a G-man. They entered FBI service with stars in their eyes and Wonderbras on their bodies. When Knowles had first started, in the prehistoric days before sexual harassment lawsuits were *de rigueur* and there was no such thing as a personal computer, all paperwork was done by dictating to a steno. The Chief Steno in his first office would actually assign only single girls to take dictation from the young, single, male agents. The skirts were so short that the girls needed the steno pad for strategic placement. It was hard to concentrate on your dictation back then, Knowles thought, whenever the topic came up, but today he was middle-aged, married, and very un-studlike. He just liked Kim because she was a dynamite secretary ... not that he didn't notice her assets. He chatted with her a bit about the case while the 302 was printing out.

"Don't tell Ben I said this," she whispered conspiratorially, "but I wouldn't take Nick's word on this. He was so primed to get out of here he would have said anything to keep his leave from being canceled. He missed his vacation last year because of that biker gang trial. His wife would have killed him if he had to do it again. He had prepaid, non-refundable tickets." Her voice trailed off as Ben Olson emerged from his office. Officially, she was Olson's personal secretary, but in reality, she served as the secretary for the whole squad. She wouldn't take shorthand - those days were long gone for all but the oldest clerical veterans - but she would type dictation from recorded tapes for the agents she liked. There was one part-time typist for the RA, but a good agent knew his or her work would get done faster and better by the squad secretary. "Hi, Ben," she said with a bit of forced cheer as Olson walked in, "Cliff was just telling me about the kidnapping."

"Or whatever it is," Olson finished the sentence. "I just got off the phone with Carmody. His wife went over to see how Mrs. Fischer was doing. I guess she's better now, and very embarrassed about what happened. Carmody says her reaction was because she had been unable to take her pain pill on time last night. First she talked to you so long, then she went over to their house, and didn't get back to her own house until she was way overdue for her pill. She was so upset and in pain that she had three glasses of wine at Carmody's. That's about two and half over her normal limit. When she got home, she popped another pain pill, forgetting that you aren't supposed to mix them with alcohol. The result was a paranoid episode, one of the known side effects of the drug. She's already talked to her doctor about it, and got a scolding. Anyway, he says she's willing to give her consent again and have the phone monitored."

"Good news," Knowles said.

"Yeah. Let's get up on this line and resolve this. Go talk to Jemperson and see if he got that line problem figured out. It won't do us any good to go up on the line and not have it working."

Knowles paged the tech agent. Jemperson called back from his home, obviously just out of bed. Knowles told him they had consent again, and needed him back over at the house. Jemperson cursed more than a little, and said okay, he was on his way. "And I'm bringing my own consensual monitoring form this time," he said sarcastically.

Knowles was never one to shy away from a fight. "Good idea. Should I bring my own recording equipment, too, or do you think you can get it right this time?"

"Okay, okay, touché. I figured it out as soon as I pulled it off the line. It was a bad recorder. We have this goddam crap to work with. The friggin' agents sign out the recorders, and if they work, they squirrel them away somewhere for their own use instead of returning them to the tech room. This was the only one left, and I recognized it as the piece of shit I sent back to the Bureau for repair a month ago.

It's still a piece of shit; they didn't even fix it right. I'll find another one - a good one."

Olson came into Knowles's office to inform him that he was also sending Louellen Murphy to the Fischer house to be with Mrs. Fischer when the call came. Knowles was surprised by this, since Louellen was on another squad, all the way in the North Bay. It wasn't easy getting her, or any agent, to drop everything on an hour's notice and drive 80 miles to sit all day waiting for something to happen on another squad's case. Stroaker must have ordered it. Knowles didn't take long to figure out why.

"To do a psychological assessment of Mrs. Fischer?" he asked. Louellen was a very experienced agent with a master's degree in psychology. She had trained with the psychological profiling unit at Quantico on some one-week in-service classes, although she was not qualified as an expert witness or a real profiler in a legal sense. She was, however, the best trained person in the division to determine if someone was a murderer or psychotic criminal, and her assignment to this case could only be interpreted as Stroaker trying to get her view as to whether or not Mrs. Fischer was a psychopath. Olson would never admit this, though.

"To help guide her as to what to say in case the call comes in," Olson replied.

Knowles noticed he did not say "when the call comes in." Knowles wasn't upset about Louellen being brought in to second guess him. She was among the top talent in the division, and would do a good job. She had excellent people skills, and Mrs. Fischer wouldn't have to face any of the agents from the night before, except for Jemperson. Knowles was sure Louellen would vindicate his judgment, and he would be assigned the case. Besides, someone had to be there, and after last night, he didn't want to sit all day waiting for a call that might not come today - or ever.

"Also, Pete called the Los Altos P.D. and told the chief about the case. She's taking the department managers to some kind of group hug retreat down in Asilomar for the next four days, so she said for us just to handle it however we see fit." Olson was matter of fact about it, but this was not so routine. Los Altos had the only woman police chief in the Bay Area and was therefore the subject of much derision by the old line male managers. Olson obviously was pleased she had not chosen to get into a territorial dispute over this case, as many department heads would over a reported kidnapping. Most local cops, male ones anyway, hated to give up jurisdiction to the feds on any case that had potential for good publicity. The testosterone was flowing only on one side in this case.

"Los Altos?" Knowles inquired. "The car was found in Mountain View, at Claritiva. Why didn't he call MVPD?" He already knew the reason, but he wanted to hear what Olson would say.

"Well, that's where Fischer was last seen alive, and that's where the reporting party and the victim's wife are both located. It's the logical jurisdiction."

"Not if the crime took place in Mountain View, it isn't. Besides, Mountain View is a bigger department and it's better equipped to handle a case like this. They'll want to have their own detective present during the investigation to follow it if it turns out to be a local prosecution." Which is exactly why Stroaker told Los Altos instead of Mountain View, Knowles figured, although he might still believe this was a homicide at the house. Olson just shrugged and returned to his own office.

Knowles turned to Rothman. "You done with your 302?"

"Yeah, why?"

"You want to head over to Claritiva and show me the car? You guys didn't have a chance to interview the office staff or see the car in daylight."

"Good idea. Let's do it. We can go for a jog afterward."

They grabbed their guns from their desks and headed out before Olson gave them some paperwork to do. This was a godsend having Olson in the office doing his own inbox for a change, something that Knowles routinely had to do. They jumped in Cliff's Bucar, which was marginally nicer than Rothman's. When they pulled into the Claritiva parking lot, Knowles looked at the oversized statue of a man leaning over the sidewalk and gave Rothman a quizzical look. It resembled a giant Tinker Toy stick figure leaning over a rail.

"Don't look at me," Rothman said. "I didn't build it. Carmody says the employees call it The Barfing Man. The city zoning laws require public artwork to get a building permit, so this is what you get. At least it's easy to recognize the right building. The car's over there." He pointed to a row of cars under The Barfing Man.

They cruised by the Mercedes. Knowles parked as close as he could get, and they both walked over to it. No obvious signs of a struggle. The doors were locked. They took care not to touch it, but they got as close to it as they could and looked in the windows.

"What's that?" Knowles said, pointing to the console area.

"What? I don't see anything."

"That pink thing sticking up. Slipped down between the passenger seat and the gear shift."

"I can barely see it. It looks like there's some printing on the top. A receipt maybe?"

"Could be. Let's ask inside to see if anybody has a key." Knowles oozed enthusiasm.

"Whoa, Cliff. We're not the Evidence Response Team. Only ERT can process physical evidence. That's an iron-clad rule."

"We aren't going to process it, just look at the piece of paper. We can read can't we?"

They went to the receptionist and, identifying themselves only by name, asked to talk to Bob Carmody. The receptionist asked if they had an appointment, and was surprised when they said no. No one came to see the CEO without an appointment. She was even more surprised when she called up to Carmody's secretary and received an affirmative response. The secretary was down in the lobby in thirty seconds to escort them up. They started up the stairs without visitor badges, to the great consternation of the receptionist.

They asked Carmody if he had a key to Fischer's Mercedes. He said he did not, but maybe Fischer's administrative assistant did. She might move his car once in awhile, or keep a spare in case he needed something that was locked in the car. They discussed the pros and cons of letting one more person know about the ransom call. Carmody pointed out that Carlotta had been with the company since its inception four years earlier, and her stock options were worth over $3,000,000 once they all vested. He said he'd trust her with his life. She had no need of money. He called her in and introduced her to the agents. They impressed upon her the need to keep confidential the fact that Mr. Fischer was missing and might have been kidnapped. This was life and death - not idle office gossip. Then they asked if she had a spare key to the Mercedes.

"Yes, I do. He has me keep it in case he locks his set in the car or something. He's always losing keys. I have a bunch for his office door, too."

"Carlotta, can you tell us exactly what happened yesterday morning when Mrs. Fischer first contacted you?" Knowles asked.

"Sure. Fran called around 10:30 or so asking for Carl. He hadn't been in all morning. I thought that was odd myself because he told me Monday that he'd be in. If he gets sick or something he always calls me. So I told Fran, and she got worried. She asked me to go look around for him, so I did. I can't find him anywhere, see, so I went down front where he likes to park to see if his car is there. It's right there where it always is. Locked. It looked normal to me, so I figured he came to work, then met with another person to go off to a meeting at another company and just forgot to tell me. I didn't see his cell phone in the car seat, so I tried to call him on it, but I just got that message it was off or out of the area."

Knowles and Rothman both looked up simultaneously from their note-taking. "He has a cell phone?" they gasped almost in unison. "Which cellular provider?" Knowles continued.

"Hold on, I'll check," she replied. "My cubicle is right around the corner. I'll be right back. And I'll get the car key, too." She walked out and returned in less than a minute. She was holding a car key in one hand. Knowles noticed she had a cellular phone in the other.

"Is that his cell phone?" he asked.

"No, it's mine. I have his number programmed into it since I contact him so much on it. I don't have it memorized, since I just have to hit the button. It displays the number when you dial it. I figure you can look up which company he uses from the number. I don't do his expense report - Sally does that." As she said this her thumb pushed a button. "Hey, it's ringing now."

Knowles leaped from his chair and lunged at her hand. "Don't dial him! Oh god, turn it off," he shouted. He grabbed her hand and wrenched the phone from her. He could hear the ringing even without putting the phone to his ear. Hell, where was the off button? These cell phones had so many damn buttons. "Where's the 'off' on this thing?" Knowles croaked. Carlotta, astonished and highly displeased to be so roughly treated, pointed. Knowles stabbed the indicated button, but nothing happened.

"You have to hold it down a few seconds before it turns off," Carlotta offered.

Knowles heard one more ring before the power off finally kicked in. "I'm sorry, Carlotta, but if the kidnappers heard it ring, and turned it off, that could be the end of our chances to find out where he is." He turned to Carmody. "Do you use one cellular provider for all company cell phones?"

"No, each employee buys his own instrument and service, then puts it on his monthly expense report. Sally takes care of that for all the upper management."

"Find out from Sally what cellular provider Carl uses - now!" Knowles ordered. Carmody immediately dialed Sally's number.

"I'm sorry, I didn't know..." Carlotta whimpered, trying to hold back tears. "I was just trying to get the number to display for you. Uh … it was off yesterday... I didn't think..." Her lower lip began to tremble. "Oh god, oh god I've killed him."

"No, no, you haven't. Don't blame yourself. You had no way of knowing." Rothman said sympathetically. Good looking, superbly fit, and well-dressed, he was always good with women. He put his arm around her shoulders as she cried and gave her a little squeeze. She seemed not to mind. Knowles caught her glancing at Rothman's left hand. Rothman wore no wedding ring since his divorce. Carlotta didn't either, he noticed.

Carmody was able to reach Sally immediately - it helped to be the CEO - and got the name of the cellular company. He gave it to Knowles. Knowles used Carlotta's cell phone to dial Olson's direct line. Kim answered and said Olson was on the other line. He told her to never mind, just get him Jemperson's pager number. She looked it up in the RA phone directory and gave it to him. Even the tech agent didn't have a cell phone, just a pager. Those cheapskates at FBIHQ were going to end up killing somebody, he grumbled to himself. He dialed the number, but when it rang and prompted him to punch in the number, he realized he didn't know the telephone number of the phone he was calling from. "Quick, what's the number here?" he asked to no one in particular. Carmody gave him his personal line. Knowles punched in the numbers, then '*' for a space, then 911 to signal this was urgent.

Jemperson called back almost immediately. "Yeah," was all he said, since he didn't recognize the number and didn't want to identify himself until he knew who was paging him. With Carmody's permission Knowles had answered, and responded, "It's me, Cliff. I just found out Fischer is carrying a cell phone, and it's turned on. Yeah, someone dialed it by accident and it rang. It's a Broadcoast Cellular number. Can you Bulletbird it?" Bulletbird was the code name for the technique of locating a cell phone by how strong its signal was on various cell sites, using triangulation.

"Shit, why didn't they tell us about this yesterday?"

"No time for that. The kidnappers might have heard it ringing and could turn it off any second. Can you do it?"

"I don't know. I'll try, but that requires a lot of prep time for the cell company security people. I haven't done it with Broadcoast. I don't know if they even have the capability. Did the call get answered? If it did, the billing log will have the cell site location it connected to. That might be easier."

"No. It rang three times, maybe four, with no answer. We can't risk it again. If the kidnapper answers, or even hears it, he'll probably figure someone is trying to locate Fischer. Besides, that will only tell us the one cell site. We need to triangulate with three to get an exact location. It's got to be Bulletbird or nothing."

"Or maybe Fischer will answer and tell us it's all a big mistake. I don't know if Stroaker will approve Bulletbird for this. It's controversial, and I don't think he believes this is a real kidnapping."

"Jesus, a man's life is at stake! It doesn't even take a warrant to do it. Why not just do it. Don't ask Stroaker."

"Let me get back to you. I'll page you. I'm at the house now, by the way. We're up on the line, and everything's working fine. If another call comes in, we'll record it. Mrs. Fischer is really being nice. She gave Louellen and me some strawberry cake. That woman can cook." Jemperson hung up.

Chapter 8

Rothman and Knowles decided they might as well look inside Fischer's car while they were waiting. They told Carmody where they were going to be in case a call came through to his phone. They tried to cheer up Carlotta, but she was still punishing herself over the cell phone call. They decided it would be a good idea to have her with them anyway, in case anybody saw them looking in Fischer's car. Many of the employees probably knew it by sight and would be suspicious of strangers. She came downstairs with them at their request. She walked next to Rothman the whole way.

Knowles went to his Bucar and opened the trunk. He always kept various supplies there for just such occasions. He pulled out a pair of cotton gloves from his search bag. TV shows always depicted cops using rubber gloves, but in reality that is only for cases requiring waterproof protection, such as where there are chemicals or blood evidence. Cotton was better for preventing fingerprints from being smeared - or new ones left. He slipped the gloves on, then walked over to Fischer's car. No one was in the parking lot except the three of them. Carlotta was giggling at Rothman's witticisms. She seemed to be in a good mood now, Knowles observed. Rothman wasn't exactly depressed, either. Maybe the three million in stock options helped enhance this young lady's other admirable attributes just a tad.

Knowles placed the key in the passenger-side door lock and turned. The lock knob popped up. Keeping the key turned, he pulled outward. This opened the door, rather than withdrawing the key, since the lock mechanism was engaged when in the turned position. This allowed Knowles to open the door without having to touch the handle and ruin any fingerprints that might be on it. He carefully looked at the seat before touching it. He could see no evidence on the seat, although, of course, there could be fiber evidence. He placed one gloved hand on the seat to brace himself, and reached over to pull out the pink object he had spied earlier. He called out to Rothman.

"Look at this. This is the thing on the calendar!" His voice was animated. The paper was a dry cleaning receipt for Delia's Cleaners, dated the previous day. In the back seat Knowles could see something dark lying across the leather upholstery. A necktie - a school tie of some kind. Cal Tech, it looked like, once Knowles moved his head 90 degrees to read it. Fischer must have gone to the cleaners to pick up his tie. Mrs. Fischer hadn't mentioned it in the morning routine yesterday, and she had covered every minute. Carl must have seen it on his calendar in his home office, and just done it on his way to work without telling her.

Rothman hadn't been at the Fischer house, and didn't know about the calendar entry. Knowles explained it to him. He had thought it was "Delis," while Torres had thought it was "Delia." They had both been almost right. Rothman contributed his own observation that Delia's was a large chain in the Bay Area. Which outlet was it, he inquired.

"Here's the address, Tim. It's on El Camino in Mountain View. It's right on the route he would take to get here. We should be able to get a clerk to identify him."

"We've got to let Olson know about this," Rothman said. "Gimme the keys and I'll radio it in."

"No, not the Buradio. The kidnappers could be monitoring the channel. We need to use a land line. Or at least a cell phone." He looked at Carlotta. She got the hint and offered hers back to Rothman, holding it up with two hands, like a ring bearer at a wedding. He took it from her - much more gently than Knowles had upstairs.

Rothman made the call to Olson and got through. He told him about the cell phone being on and about the receipt. Knowles could only hear one end of the conversation, but it was obvious Olson was asking a lot of questions and was very interested in the answers. Finally, Rothman finished the conversation. "Olson's on board. He says if we can get the clerk to ID Fischer from the receipt, and he was by himself, he'll push for the full treatment - ERT processing the car, Bulletbird, everything. But if Mrs. Fischer picked up the tie - well, ..." The rest was left unsaid.

"Let's go." Knowles practically sprinted toward his old Dodge Diplomat that squatted among the BMWs and Saabs like a toad in a flower garden. Rothman, who could normally run circles around Knowles, had trouble keeping up.

When they got to the cleaners there were two customers in line. Knowles tried to get the clerk's attention, but she just ignored him. Apparently too many people tried to cut in, and this was her coping mechanism. The number two customer, a hefty Mexican woman, glared at Knowles menacingly, afraid her priority was about to be usurped. Exasperated, Knowles held up his credentials and called out in his Official Fed voice "FBI. This is urgent police business. I must talk to the manager - NOW!"

The clerk at the register appeared cowed. She backed away slowly at first, then turning rapidly, she tripped and almost fell. She hurried to the back of the store, and within seconds an older woman, appearing to be a Pacific Islander, emerged from between the racks of garments hanging in filmy bags. The clerk resumed her service of the customers, and the Mexican woman seem content now that she could see she was not going to lose her spot in line.

"Can we go in back or some place more private?" Knowles asked.

"Follow me." The woman stepped expertly between the rows, while Knowles and Rothman tried to follow, negotiating with difficulty the maze of hangers and bags. When they stopped, it was in a cramped, dark corner of the rear section of the store. There was a desk cluttered with financial records, bills, and typical small retail store documentation. There was posted on the wall right above the desk a sign with large red lettering that read "NO SMOKING - FLAMMABLE MATERIALS". A municipal code section was cited, apparently applicable because of the cleaning chemicals pervading the atmosphere. Directly below the sign was an ashtray full of butts.

"Can you tell me what time this pickup was made yesterday, and who picked it up?" Knowles handed her the receipt.

The woman didn't even glance at it. "No."

"Why not?" Knowles was not in a mood to stomach attitude. What now, the woman was going to claim customer privacy rights as to when they pick up ties?

"I don't work the desk. Maybe Julia can tell you. If she remember." The woman made no effort to read the slip or take them back to the front. She just sat there and reached for a cigarette from the pack on the desk.

"Well could you maybe look in your records and see if you can tell whether it came early in the day, or verify which clerk handled the transaction?"

The woman grunted and looked over to the desk. She poked around among the miscellany until she found what she had been looking for, a small bundle with a rubber band around it. She finally looked at the slip Knowles had handed her, and then started flipping through the slips of paper in the bundle. It took her several minutes, but eventually she stopped and compared the pink slip to some yellow clone in the bundle. "Dis one," she uttered.

"What can you tell us about it? Please, this is very important." Knowles was turning on his most charming smile, although he knew he couldn't match Rothman's.

"Hmm, it's almost to the bottom. Must have been early. We open at 8:30, so maybe 9 or 9:30. No way to tell. Depends on how busy. I don't work the desk." She took a long drag on the cigarette.

"Who was at the front desk yesterday morning?"

"Julia. Same girl as now. Go ask her. She maybe could remember."

They both tried a few more questions, but the woman seemed tapped out. She just kept telling them to ask Julia, and sat there smoking. They decided to retreat before the whole place burst into a Death Star-grade fireball. They returned to the front of the store and tapped Julia on the shoulder. The Mexican woman was having her transaction rung up now, and there was someone waiting behind her, a young blonde woman with two bawling brats tugging on her shorts. Both women stared venomously at the interlopers in suits. Knowles just held up his badge so they could see it, and wiggled a finger at Julia to step over and talk to them. She dutifully dropped what she was doing and turned to Knowles. He showed her the slip.

"Do you remember this pickup?" Knowles asked.

"I don't know, we get a lot of ties," she managed, after some apparent effort.

"It was in the morning, pretty early. It was a college tie."

"What's a college tie?"

Knowles had to stifle an impulse to unload on her with a sarcastic comment. How could someone not know what a college tie was, especially someone who handles ties all day long? But, he realized she was only about 18 years old, and had grown up at a time when nobody wore ties to college any more, especially in Silicon Valley. Even the lawyers in the corporate law firms in Palo Alto didn't wear ties unless they were going to court. She probably had never seen a college tie, other than this one.

"It's a dark blue tie with red and white stripes at an angle. It has a small crest on it, and there's embroidered words saying California Institute of Technology in a circle."

She took another long look at the receipt. "Is that the big tipper one? Fincher - yeah I think that's him."

Knowles looked at the slip again himself. The customer name was misspelled 'Fincher.' Knowles could tell that wasn't Carl Fischer's writing on the slip, so the clerk had probably filled it in when the tie was brought in.

"Julia, this is very important. Who picked up the tie yesterday; do you remember?"

"It was him, Mr. Fincher. He gave me a dollar tip. No one ever tips me. He was really nice." She said "No one ever tips me" extra loud, loud enough so the customers up front could overhear.

"How do you know it was him? Is he a regular customer of yours?"

"I've seen him before, I think. I mean I never ask for identification, you know? As long as they have the claim slip. You know, like you don't need a driver's license to pick up a tie. Know what I mean?"

"What did he look like? Can you describe him?"

"Old. At least 50. Older than my dad. Tall, and he had a big mustache."

Bingo. Knowles started to thank her and leave, but Rothman had one more question. "Was there anyone else with him?"

"Well, I think there was a woman in the store then. We usually have several customers at once. I don't really ... ya know ... pay much attention when they come in. You know. They could have been together, I guess. But I think she was, like, just another customer. You know?" Rothman tried to get a description of the woman, but all Julia could manage was "she looked like a housewife."

They left the store, with the Mexican woman planting little cartoon daggers in their backs with her eyes. Knowles was elated. Rothman was more temperate. "That woman in the store could have been Mrs. Fischer, you know. That means she still could have done something - put a gun in his back right after they got to the car. Whatever."

"I suppose, ... but it wasn't her. Mrs. Fischer is for real. Olson told us he'd go full court press on this if we got a confirmation it was him picking up the tie. We did."

"He said 'if it was Fischer by himself,' Cliff . We don't know he was by himself yet - not really."

"Tim, Tim. Don't be so negative. Do you think Mrs. Fischer would go to the trouble of taking him all the way to a dry cleaners in Mountain View at gunpoint to make his routine look normal, and then forget to tell us about it? She could have just taken the receipt from the car when she moved it if she was trying to conceal it. None of that makes sense. This is exactly what it seems to be - he went to work, by himself, picked up his tie en route, and got snatched in the parking lot."

"I think you're right, but I'm not sure Stroaker'll buy it. He's really into this medicine thing. He pulled the PDR right off the shelf and read us a complete description of the drug after Nick told him what the drug name was that Carmody gave us. There were half a page of side effects. He started to define for us what 'delusional psychosis' was. He thinks the wife was turned into some kind of man-eating zombie and bumped the man off, then staged a cover up."

"Bull. We tell Olson the clerk identified Fischer - the *male* Fischer. We need Bulletbird, and we're going to get it. If she buried him, she buried him with his cell phone on. Let's find out where it is." He called Olson himself and told him the clerk described Fischer to a T. Olson promised him he'd get the cell phone trace started, and get the Crime Scene Team out to do the car, but they'd have to drive it somewhere else more discreet. They couldn't process it in the lot or the whole employee population would know what was going on. Knowles agreed. Olson also promised to send another agent out to the residence to help with the call. Louellen would need more help if this was for real. He said he would send Luciana Malarna, the newest agent on the squad.

"He's sending Lucy to help out at the house," Knowles informed Rothman. Malarna was a kitten-cute Filipina four weeks out of New Agent class. She spoke fluent Spanish and Tagalog. The Spanish could come in handy if it turned out Fischer had really been taken by Mexicans. She was also impossible to dislike, which would add to the comfort level at the house. "Mrs. Fischer also has her daughter there now. Her name is Pam. Pam is taking the calls, apparently at Louellen's request. Mrs. F isn't sure she can handle another ransom call."

Knowles decided to return to Claritiva and talk to Carmody again. Now that the victim's car and phone lines were being handled, he could concentrate on the mainline investigative work - interviews.

They were ushered into Carmody's office once more, but they didn't mention to him the cleaning receipt. They had warned Carlotta not to say anything, but they figured she had probably told Carmody.

Still, better just to follow the need-to-know principle. Carmody didn't need to know.

They asked him why he originally called the FBI instead of the police. He said he had discussed the situation with the company chief counsel, an attorney who specialized in software licensing. She had told him that since the kidnappers said they had taken Fischer to Mexico, that was across a state line, and required FBI jurisdiction. The agents didn't tell Carmody that kidnapping someone is really only a violation of state law, and should be reported to the local police in any event. It is only the interstate transportation after the kidnap that was a violation of federal law - an anomaly forced by the interstate commerce clause of the Constitution. The relevant federal statute, known as the Little Lindbergh Law, since it was passed as a result of the kidnapping of Charles Lindbergh's baby - contained a provision requiring a binding presumption that if a person was missing more than 24 hours after an abduction, that person was taken across state lines. It might be a legal fiction, but it got the FBI into the case after 24 hours. In this case, it was proper to ignore the 24-hour rule and report it directly to the FBI because there was specific evidence - the mention of Mexico in the phone call - to indicate interstate transportation. Knowles wondered whether the company lawyer was smart enough to recognize the advantages of having FBI jurisdiction, and had recommended reporting it there first for that reason. He doubted it. She had probably just relied on her basic knowledge of statutory and constitutional criminal law from law school. She most likely had no idea whether it was better to have the case investigated by local police or the FBI.

They questioned Carmody, then Carlotta as well, about Fischer's cell phone use. It seemed that he only kept it on when in the car or traveling, never when at the office. He thought it was too distracting to have it ring when he was in meetings or on the phone with someone else. He also liked to have Carlotta screen his calls, which she could only do with the regular office line. So his normal routine was to turn on the cell phone as he walked to the car, then place it on the front passenger seat, where it was easily accessible. When he got out, he would turn it off and put it in his pocket. Since they had just looked in the car, they knew the phone was not there. Since Carlotta had called it with no answer Tuesday morning, Fischer had probably followed his normal routine in getting out of the car. But since it was now on, or at least had been an hour earlier, someone had taken the trouble to turn it on. That someone was probably Fischer. Conceivably, the kidnappers might be foolish enough to turn it on to place a call at Fischer's expense, but they would have to be idiots not to know that the call would be recorded for billing purposes. The point of origin of any call could be determined, at least to the cell site. But if Fischer had enough access to the phone to turn it on, why not dial 911 and summon the police? Possibly it had been on the whole time, but moved out of the coverage area, then back in. Maybe the kidnappers had discovered it and sent it with a conspirator to some remote location to send the cops off the track. But if they had discovered it, and assumed the police were monitoring it, then why not use it to place the call to the house? They could use it while in motion, making it harder to locate than if they used a land line. Rothman suggested that maybe they did in fact use the cell phone for yesterday's call. Jemperson should check with the carrier to see when and where the phone was used last.

As if on cue, Cliff's pager beeped melodiously. The number in the display was the Fischer house fax line. Only Jemperson would be using that number.

Chapter 9

Louellen Murphy chatted breezily with Pam Fischer as they sipped coffee in the family room. Fran Fischer had retired to her quarters upstairs with Mrs. Carmody to keep her company. She had recovered from the effects of the alcohol-drug combination of the night before, but really did not want to have the responsibility for taking the next call. She was terrified that she would do something to cause her husband's death. The housekeeper and gardener had been given the day off, with pay, a state of affairs about which they were quite pleased. They had not made any attempt to hang around.

Pam Fischer and Louellen Murphy both lived in Berkeley, and they were comparing their favorite eating spots on both sides of the bay. The Fischer phone rang once, then a second time. Luciana Malarna and Ron Jemperson both sprang to attention. Jemperson picked up the spare instrument that he had wired to the fax line and dialed a special Pac Bell security number. He whispered "Lucy" to Malarna, pointing to the recorder, then he signaled to Pam with his finger. Murphy picked up the second phone, the one with extra long cord, at the same moment Pam lifted the receiver of the house phone. Malarna released the Pause button on the recorder, allowing the recording to resume, while Jemperson watched the tape to make sure it was moving.

Murphy heard a man's voice, speaking English with a slight foreign accent. She made a hand sign to Jemperson to indicate it was the ransom caller. Jemperson in turn began whispering to the security agent on the other end to begin the trace. Jemperson sat in the far corner of the room so he could talk without his voice being heard by the caller.

During the previous hour Murphy had briefed Pam Fischer on what to say and do, and what to avoid. She had even written out a sort of script to try to follow. She pushed this in front of Pam now. Pam followed it like a seasoned actor.

The FBI transcript of the call, later to be attached to an FD-302, read as follows:

MALE -- Yes, may I speak to Fran, please?

FISCHER -- Um, I'm sorry, she's sick right now. Can I take a message?

MALE -- It's urgent. I have to speak to her.

FISCHER -- Uh, may I ask who's calling?

MALE -- Just tell her it's regarding her husband.

FISCHER -- Well, I'm sorry but she's sick. She's practically in the hospital. This is her daughter, Pam.

MALE -- Okay, good. Listen you tell your mom, do not do anything stupid.

FISCHER -- Don't do anything stupid.

MALE -- We know everything about you and your brother Patrick. You're being watched. We know everything about you people. Anything stupid, your dad will die. You understand?

FISCHER -- Yes, I do, but we fully understand, uh intend, to do...

MALE -- Do you understand?

FISCHER -- Yes.

MALE -- Good. I have a mess-- a record-- Listen. I have a recorded message from your dad. I want you to listen very carefully.

[The text of the message Carl Fischer had recorded was inserted in the typed text.]

FISCHER -- Is my dad safe?

MALE -- Yes. Did you hear that?

FISCHER -- Yes, I did, but my dad ...

MALE -- Good. Now listen to me very carefully. We're watching you twenty-four hours a day. We know everything about you. Any stupid move, you'll have your dad back in pieces. You understand? Now -

FISCHER -- Yes.

MALE -- I told your mom yesterday what we need is six hundred fifty thousand dollars in one hundred dollar bills. The money must be circulated and marked and traced. You should have it by one week from today. That will give you five business days.

FISCHER -- Um, can we give it to you earlier? I mean, not tomorrow, like.

MALE -- Fine. You can give it if you have it earlier. I'll contact you on Friday.

FISCHER -- Um, can, ca... is there any way we can get him back earlier? If I have the money by tomorrow?

MALE -- If you have the money tomorrow, we'll contact you tomorrow.

FISCHER -- Well, how do I know you're going to call tomorrow?

MALE -- I'll call tomorrow. Now listen..

FISCHER -- What time?

MALE -- I'm gonna give... listen. Just listen. You will be at your dad's house. You stay at your mom's house. I'll call you tomorrow evening. If you have the money, fine. You will make the drop for me. You're going to use your mom's Jaguar. Do you understand?

FISCHER -- Okay.

MALE -- Make sure nobody knows. If anything happens...

FISCHER -- Who's gonna know, except for me, you and my mother?

MALE -- Good. Good. I don't want your brother in Illinois to find out, or your sister, either. I am serious. You're all being watched. If anything happens you're all gonna be sorry.

FISCHER -- Well, we intend to fully comply with your instructions.

MALE -- What?

FISCHER -- We, imply, uh, I mean... we'll do anything you want us to do.

MALE -- Good, Pam. Good. Now your mom seems very naive to me, so I want you to make the drop for me once you have the money. I will call you tomorrow.

FISCHER -- Can I talk to my dad?

MALE -- No. He's in a safe place. He's outside the state.

FISCHER -- He's where?

MALE -- Not in California. We've taken him to another state. Once we have the money, he'll be released after twelve hours.

FISCHER -- Well, can I just talk to him?

MALE -- You can't. Understand? You can't. He's not in the state. I'll call tomorrow.

OPERATOR -- Please deposit ten cents.

MALE -- I'll talk to you tomorrow.

END OF CONVERSATION

As soon as the call ended, Murphy praised Pam effusively for the great job and gave her hand a squeeze. She then called Olson at the SJRA. He was out, so she left word with Kim to page him and tell him a second ransom call just came in. Jemperson was just hanging up with the Pac Bell security rep. Murphy looked at him expectantly.

"GTE trunk line," the tech agent intoned. "It didn't come from a Pac Bell number. The call came from a GTE trunk line off the Morgan Hill switch. They can't trace it back any further; only GTE can do that. They gave me the number of the GTE security rep who covers that area. I'll have my supe work that angle. We need to get ready in case the caller calls back. Keep that line open."

"I tried to reach Olson," Murphy said. "He was out. Who did you say the case agent was?"

"Cliff Knowles."

"Page him to call us on that number."

Jemperson paged Knowles, punching in the fax line of the Fischer home for call back. It took about a minute for the page to go out and for Knowles to call back. "Cliffie boy, you were right," Jemperson told him. "A ransom call just came in. It comes back to a GTE trunk line in Morgan Hill. Pac Bell can't trace it, but GTE should be able to find it. I didn't listen to the call myself, so let me put Louellen on." He handed the phone to Louellen without waiting for Knowles to reply.

"Hi, Cliff, Louellen Murphy out at the Fischer home. I guess you're the case agent on this kidnapping."

Knowles hesitated a moment. Actually he had not been assigned the case, Nick Lark had, but he decided there was no point in explaining to her that a breaking life-and-death case was assigned to an agent who was probably climbing on the Pirates of the Caribbean ride 500 miles away right about now. "Yeah, can you describe the call?"

"Sure. We got it recorded. Ron is switching tapes now so we can get the next one. It was a male speaking English. Slight accent, not sure what kind - maybe Spanish. He demanded $650,000 in hundreds, and, get this, he asked for them to be marked and traced."

"You're kidding."

"No."

"Well, let's oblige him then. We'll mark those babies with everything known to man. Any proof the hostage is okay?"

"He played a tape recording of Mr. Fischer reading a prepared message. It basically just said these people are serious, do what they say."

"Any threats to life?"

"Yes. They said if anything happened, Fischer would come back in pieces."

"Did he give payoff day and place?"

"He said a week from today. No place. He'll call tomorrow."

"A week? That's unusually long. And the 650K is for real, too, huh? That's an oddball amount. I wonder what's going on there. Do your profiler buddies analyze that kind of thing?"

"In fact, they do," Murphy said with a touch of smugness. "I'll send them a lead as soon as we get the tape transcribed."

"Great, thanks. How's the family?"

"Mrs. Fischer is upstairs. Pam just went up to tell her about the call. Pam did a super job on the phone. She pressed to get the payoff done sooner, and when she tried to follow my script to tell the caller she would 'comply with his instructions', he didn't understand, so she was smart enough to rephrase it in ordinary language. That was my fault. I shouldn't have written it in legalese. It sounded like something an FBI agent would write - it could have tipped off the kidnapper. Anyway, she hung in there and carried it off. The caller says he'll call again tomorrow with more instructions."

"Good job. Thanks for being there, Louellen. Does Olson know?"

"Not yet, ... at least I don't think so. Ron just left a message with the squad secretary to page him with the news. Look, Ron is signaling me to hurry up. He needs to use this line to make some calls."

"Okay, I'll let you go. Thanks again."

Louellen hung up. Jemperson was showing Malarna how to label the cassette tape for evidence. When he saw Louellen get off the line, he called his supervisor, Ralph Tobin, with the information about the call and the need to trace through GTE, and to ask about the Bulletbird request.

"The caller must be in Morgan Hill or Los Gatos," Tobin opined, "since those are the only two towns near here served by GTE. Their trunk drop's in Morgan Hill."

"Not necessarily," Jemperson corrected. "The call ended with an operator request for ten cents. That means a pay phone, which could be anywhere. GTE puts those all over, even areas where they don't serve residential customers."

"You're right, then. But ten cents is the FCC rate for local long distance only. It would have been a quarter if it was any farther. The call must have been placed within 100 miles or so - probably less. This changes things."

"Did you call Broadcoast about the Bulletbird on the cell phone?"

"Yeah, but I probably didn't make it sound as high priority as I should've. Stroaker said this was probably a false alarm, you know. Now that we know it's real, and probably the guy is being held close by, we need to do that NOW."

"So do it, man," Jemperson replied.

"I'll get all over their ass. I know they have the software, but they've never used it in the field in a real case. They told me they were doing tests, but it didn't always work right. I'll take care of the GTE trace, too. You just hang there and make sure everything is working right. You having any problems with the lines or the equipment?"

"No, we got it recorded okay. I played the tape back. It's clear. It would be good to have some backup equipment, though, now we know we're going to be getting more calls here. I'd like a replacement for every single piece we got - you never know what's gonna fail. That's the phone patch, the recorder, the long extension cord, the duplicate handset. We have plenty of blank tapes and evidence labels. And get me a goddam cell phone, will ya? We have to keep the main landline open for the kidnapper, and we have a house full of people trying to use one fax line for voice."

"You got it." They hung up.

In the FBI, priorities change once it becomes clear to everyone that a life hangs in the balance. Tobin's reaction was just one of many ways this truth manifests itself. Suddenly equipment, manpower, and management attention are showered on a case. Sometimes agents become bitter or cynical when they see resources appear magically right after they had tried, unsuccessfully, to get such things. The resources "weren't available"; now they see they are available. But the truth is that the resources come at a price that can only be paid for special cases. If backup equipment is needed, it may be yanked off another case, and certainly agent manpower is taken off other matters to work on life-and-death cases. There will be drug deals that go unrecorded, or meetings with informants that get postponed. That's life in any organization. It really can't be done in every case.

Tobin called GTE to talk to his security liaison contact. He got voicemail, so he left a brief message, then called the emergency pager number given in the voice mail greeting. The security agent called back within 30 seconds. Tobin explained the situation in detail. These people could be trusted not to reveal the information. The need-to-know principle applied, and GTE Security needed to know. The GTE agent said that if he had been told to put a trace on while the call was in progress, he could have done so, but once the call ended, there was no way to trace it. However, since this was a toll call from a pay phone, the automated computer system would update the billing database overnight, and the call could be located by the destination phone number. The originating number would be shown. But that information wouldn't be accessible until the next morning. This was the answer Tobin expected. Now he realized he should have requested a trace from GTE as well as Pac Bell, but there had been no way to anticipate this yesterday. There were too many different phone providers to put them all on alert. Pac Bell was the destination number; you had to start there and work back. He requested the security agent be prepared for a trace tomorrow, the day the next call was expected. What time, the agent asked. Tobin couldn't say, since the kidnapper hadn't committed. Tobin guessed that the caller would give Pam enough time to find out about the money, so he would probably not call until late in the day, or evening. If only the crooks would be more accommodating; didn't they know there's a lot of preparation to be done? The GTE agent was uncomplaining. He said he'd work a late shift and handle it himself.

Tobin then called Broadcoast Cellular again. The security representative was unable to help him personally, since Bulletbird was a new software based program he didn't understand. He put Tobin in touch with the chief engineer, Wei-jun Lee. Lee was working on the request already, since Tobin had called it in an hour earlier.

After introductions, Tobin asked him, "How is it going? Any success yet?"

"When I checked it about twenty minutes ago, the MIN was active." MIN stood for mobile identification number, a number assigned by the carrier to a specific instrument. The instrument itself had a number known as the ESN, or electronic serial number, programmed into it. "That could be a clone phone, of course. Is this a drug case? Clones are pretty common in those, I hear."

Tobin realized that he had not told the security rep what the nature of the case was; he'd only asked him if it could be done. The request had been passed on to the engineer, probably as another routine drug matter. The engineer didn't really need to know what kind of case it was in order to operate the software program, but Tobin knew that in the outside world, just as in the FBI, people's priorities change when they know a life is in the balance. If that knowledge made the difference between the engineer getting it done now, or fiddling around, then he had a need to know. Tobin made a snap judgment call.

"The owner of this phone is being held hostage by people who have threatened to kill him. If we don't find him in time, he could be murdered. We think there's a good chance he intentionally turned on the phone in order to be located. Bulletbird could save his life. If word of this leaks out, to the press, for example, that could mean his death."

"Hmm. In that case," said Lee, "I will initiate it now. The problem is that the version provided to us requires that we place the software in our startup routine in order to synchronize it to our system clock. It's like your personal computer, like having to reboot. That will kick everybody off the system. We have over 25,000 users in our region, and there are hundreds of calls in progress at any given time during a busy work day. Reloading the system will dump them all off in mid-call. I was planning to wait until the call volume came down some, but under the circumstances, I'll do it now. You know, this program is experimental, and may not even work. After I reload, I still have to run the application, and locate the MIN. It should take about five minutes."

"I'll wait," said Tobin.

Chapter 10

Carl Fischer was lying on the lumpy mattress, cuffed hands on his chest, when he heard his cell phone ring. He flushed angrily at the stupidity of someone calling him on that line, but he reasoned that it was probably someone who didn't know his predicament. When he heard the first tone, he realized that whoever was watching him might be able to hear it, too. He tried to roll over from supine to prone, in order to block the sound with his own body mass and clothing, but the chains on his ankles made this awkward. He came to an abrupt halt halfway over, on his right side, with his back to the open closet door. He tried to scrunch down towards his feet so as to get enough slack to roll the rest of the way over, and to get the phone farther from the open doorway, which was near his head.

"What is that?" It was Miguel asking.

Fischer didn't answer. He wasn't sure whether it was better to tell the truth and get punished for having the phone, or to lie and possibly get even worse for the deception. Miguel had threatened to blow up his family for lying about Pam's car.

"I said, what is that? Something made a noise." Miguel scooted close to Fischer and grabbed his collar roughly. He gave Fischer a hard yank, rolling him back over onto his back and up toward the doorway.

Fischer weighed over 230 lbs. Yet this guy tossed him around like a rag doll. Miguel wasn't very tall, but he must be strong for his size - remarkably strong - Fischer thought. "It's my cell phone," he said, since the game was obviously up. "Someone must be calling me. It's in my pocket. It must be my wife trying to confirm that I'm okay. You should answer it and tell her not to worry, that I'm okay."

Miguel looked panicky. He began to rip furiously at Fischer's pants pocket until he was able to get the phone out. It finished the third ring, then stopped just as he managed to extract the device. Fischer couldn't see what was going on, but it was obvious Miguel wasn't answering the phone. Fischer just lay still, not wanting to incur his wrath any more than he had already. Had Miguel turned the phone off? He didn't know, but he could hear Miguel pacing around in the same room, just a few feet from his head.

"You should leave that on in case Carlos needs to contact my family. Using other phones is risky. They can trace those. No one can trace a cell phone, because it moves everywhere, and my family would know you really have me if you have this phone."

"Shut up! Shut up, you goddam mother-fucker. You should have told us you had a cell phone. I should chop you up right now!" Miguel was barely able to get the words out, either from anger or panic. "What else you got that you didn't tell us? He should have searched you."

Miguel kicked Fischer in the left shoulder. Fischer realized the kick wasn't that hard, that Miguel was trying to put on a show but wasn't sure how to react. He could feel Miguel tug at his belt and then pull his pants toward his feet. Soon, though, it was apparent that the pants would not come off over the chains. Miguel rifled through the pants and pulled out Fischer's keys, comb, a pen, and some loose change. There was nothing else in the pants. Carlos had removed the wallet earlier. Miguel left the pants around Fischer's ankles and moved away. Fischer could hear steps retreat from the room. Then he heard the screen door slam. He assumed Miguel had gone out to get Carlos from outside. He hadn't heard Carlos for at least the last fifteen minutes.

Fischer knew the room was light. He lifted his hands to his face and felt the sleeping mask. It covered his eyes snugly, but was secured only by the elastic band. The handcuffs did not prevent him from moving the mask. Believing Miguel to be outside, he decided to risk a test. He slipped his thumbs under the lower edge of the mask. Despite the cotton balls still in place, the brightness startled him. He took a few seconds to allow his eyes time to adjust. Then he tried to move the cotton ball on his left eye. He discovered that it had been taped on with adhesive tape in an X pattern. He hadn't even realized that at the time he was being blindfolded. Still, it was easy enough to loosen one leg of the X and pull the pad partially away from his cheek and eyelid. He caught a glimpse of the room.

The first thing to strike him was the peeling linoleum floor, a black and white speckled pattern intended as imitation granite. There was no carpet or furniture, except for a folding chair and card table placed between the door to the hall and the closet door. If that was where Miguel sat to guard him, he would be able to see Fischer at all times, and he would also serve to block the view of anyone coming down the hall. The rest of the tiny room was bare. He could see his own briefcase on the floor next to the card table. From his angle near the floor he was unable to see what was on the table, if anything. He inspected the chains on his feet. They were padlocked to a ring bolt screwed to the closet floor. There was no way the chains could be broken or the ring bolt loosened, but the chains themselves were just wrapped around his ankles. Unlike the handcuffs, there was no device - stocks, manacles, legcuffs - designed to hold the ankles. The chains had been wrapped tightly, but there were several loops, which allowed for some slack. He considered the possibility that with enough work he could slip one of the loops over one heel, which would release the whole thing. It would take some thrashing and clanking, and it obviously could not be done while he was being watched, but at least there was a chance to escape if he were left unguarded. With considerable effort, he pulled up his pants and flipped over onto his hands and knees, then raised his head almost to the level of the card table surface. There was something on top of the table. He couldn't quite make out whether his cell phone was there. The sound of footsteps reverberated through the hallway door. Quickly he let the blindfold slip back into place and lay back down on the mattress.

Miguel re-entered the room and headed straight for Fischer. "Carlos will be back soon. He is calling your wife now. He will decide whether to kill you for this. I will tell him you should have your balls cut off."

"I didn't lie to you, Miguel," Fischer said as calmly as he could. "I didn't even think of the phone. It's been in my pocket since you... since we left the company parking lot. If you had asked me about it, I would have told you the truth. You should use that phone. It's safer than a pay phone."

"Be quiet. You are not in charge here," Miguel intoned sarcastically.

You obviously aren't either, Fischer thought. So this guy is just a thug. It's Carlos I need to work on. Still, Fischer considered, he did not know if Miguel had turned the phone off, or where he had put it. If he could free himself momentarily, would he be able to find the phone and use it?

The phone had been on for several hours, ever since they left the motel in the early darkness. If the phone could be traced or located by the authorities, why hadn't they been found by now? They had been at the same location for at least two hours. Were the police surrounding the place even now? Did they even know he had a cell phone? Someone had called him. Who? How long would the battery last? These questions tormented Carl Fischer as he lay on the mattress.

After an hour or so, Carlos returned, banging the telltale screen door as he entered. Fischer could just make out some animated conversation in a far room. It sounded like they were talking under their breath to prevent him from overhearing. Miguel was obviously furious, probably telling Carlos about the cell phone. Carlos, in turn, sounded unconcerned. Soon, Carlos entered the room.

"I talked to your daughter Pam. She will be the one to pay us. She says she will, anyway. You better hope she does or you'll be floating in the bay."

At first Fischer was actually encouraged by this remark, although he felt a stab of surprise at the mention of Pam's name. The mention of the bay was probably a good sign. The only likely bays he could be referring to were San Francisco Bay or Monterey Bay. He was pretty sure they had not traveled far enough to be in the Los Angeles area, and there were no bays eastward - inland. Fischer decided they were still within close driving distance of the San Francisco Bay, as it was primarily Bay Area residents who used that term. The closer he was to the Bay Area, the closer he was to his home turf, and the better chance he had of being found - or so it seemed to him. As for the ransom, he knew his family would pay whatever was asked. He had no worries about that. What if his family had notified law enforcement, though? What if there was a shootout, or the payoff failed? Would Miguel kill him? Would these men grab Pam? Fischer considered all of these scenarios and began to feel a dark, oppressive foreboding. Then he did what he had always done when confronted with his most difficult worries: he began to pray.

"How will your daughter get the money?" Carlos interrupted his thoughts. "Does she have access to your bank accounts?"

"No, my wife will have to get it. My daughter doesn't have that kind of money. Fran'll have to get it from our stockbroker and bank accounts, like I told you yesterday."

Fischer had discussed his financial situation with Carlos at great length the previous day. Carlos had wanted to ask for a million dollars, and was intent on finding out how long it would take to get together that much cash. Fischer felt that it was probable his wife could get that much cash together, maybe even twice that; but it would take a week. Even so, being a sharp businessman, he was not about to tell Carlos that. He patiently explained that most of his wealth was in the form of unvested stock options. As President of Claritiva, he had hundreds of thousands of shares of options at various strike prices. Some were vested, but some would not be exercisable for up to four years. Even the vested ones could not be exercised by his wife, as they were in his name. He was also an insider under SEC rules - the ultimate insider in fact - and therefore due to securities trading laws could not exercise even vested options except during non-blackout periods, such as right after financial results were announced.   He already owned millions of shares of Claritiva outright, but Fran couldn't even sell those shares due to the blackout rules imposed by securities regulators. They owned real estate, of course - their house and a vacation condo on Maui - but these could not be sold, or even used to negotiate a loan, in a week.

He had explained this to Carlos, and Carlos had understood it all, even getting ahead of him and asking sophisticated questions about when the blackout rules went into effect, and when they would be lifted. Of course there were other assets - IRA's, 401K's, oil and gas leases, the cars - but his wife did not have signature authority over these. It would take both signatures, or just his alone, for most transactions involving the big-ticket assets. Fran would be limited to the money in their checking and savings accounts, the money market fund account, and the "ordinary" unrestricted stocks and bonds in their brokerage account. He tried to minimize the amounts in each of these. Fischer was consistent throughout the interrogation in claiming the amounts available to his wife could not be more than $300,000. He had very little idea how much the real figure was, but he knew $300,000 was on the low side. It could very well be more than a half million. He couldn't tell if Carlos believed him. Shortly after Carlos finished this line of questioning he had heard Carlos and Miguel argue. Live or die, there was no point in having his family risk more than necessary. Business was business. He also wanted to make sure the ransom was well within the means available to Fran. If the kidnappers got shorted because she was unable to raise the whole amount, there was no telling how their wrath would be manifested. So he hoped Carlos had bought the $300,000 figure - he hoped and prayed.

"Why didn't you tell us about the cell phone?" Carlos asked him, suddenly switching topics without warning.

"You didn't ask. I told Miguel that I did not lie about it. I just forgot I had it. All you had to do was ask and I would've told you.

You know, you should call my wife on that phone - it's probably harder to trace than a pay phone."

"Who told you I was using a pay phone?" Carlos asked sharply. Fischer couldn't see it, but Carlos cast a dark glare at Miguel. Miguel shook his head, indicating he had not said anything.

"No one told me anything. I just assumed."

"You are trying to trick me again. We are too smart for that. Here's what I think of your cell phone."

Fischer heard a loud clatter in the far corner of the room. It was clearly the sound of the cell phone being thrown hard. He heard Carlos's footsteps move toward that corner, then another sharp noise similar to the first. The phone was being smashed again. Those little things were pretty tough, Fischer knew, for he had dropped his on the hard tile of men's rooms or parking lot pavement more than once, with no visible damage. He assumed, though, that even if the phone was still in working condition, Carlos had turned it off. Maybe Carlos would leave it there, broken or not. If so, Fischer felt he still had a chance to get to it and to try to turn it on during some unguarded moment.

"We will have to ask our boss what to do with you," Carlos said ominously.

Chapter 11

Wei-Jun Lee moved his mouse dexterously and rapidly to select the Bulletbird software from the application list, and to load it in the startup routine. Bulletbird was not really one program, but a series of programs, developed by a consortium of scientists, engineers, and investigators. The National Institute of Justice had funded much of it, and the personnel who worked on it cooperatively were from the cellular companies, their major hardware and software suppliers, law enforcement labs such as the FBI and Treasury Departments, and researchers in universities working under grants from the military. Each cellular company used its own proprietary software and hardware, and differing government-assigned radio frequencies. These differences precluded any hope of a single application working for all cell phone companies. Instead, the basic algorithms on which the software was based were modified to suit the electronic data inputs that came from the different systems. That meant that each individual program had to be modified at the source code level for each carrier, and recompiled. Then it had to be tested and tweaked until it really worked in the field. The mathematical formulas used were straightforward enough, but they assumed the surface of the earth to be a perfect sphere and every cell tower and cell phone to be identical in signal strength and sensitivity. In reality topography, buildings, other transmissions, weather, and even the way a caller held the phone affected the signal strength at a given cell site. Some of the carriers were already using the program with success. Broadcoast was not among them. Lee knew that the program had never been put to the test of real-world crime in this region, at least for Broadcoast. He would have been the person trying it. He was determined to make it work now, though, if he could. He typed in the necessary command for the system to shut down and reload.

His monitor, as if incredulous at his temerity, popped up a window asking if he was sure he wanted to cut off all calls in progress and shut down. He clicked yes without hesitation. Then again, another window appeared: was he really, REALLY sure? Yes. The screen went blank for a moment, then the reboot sequence began flashing across the screen. A technician on call came running into Lee's office almost gasping. When he saw Lee was watching the reboot sequence, he realized Lee must already know about it. Lee told him not to worry, there would be a few irate customers, but they'd get over it. People were used to losing cellular calls in midstream. They would not know the whole system went down for a few seconds. He didn't tell the technician that he was the cause of the reload, or why. What was the point? If he told, then there would just be more people to second-guess him. He hoped the FBI agent on the other end was telling the truth, but he didn't really have any doubts that the caller had been who he said he was. Lee knew the company security man had contacts with law enforcement and was scrupulously paranoid about access and legal process. The security man had told him the request was from his regular FBI liaison. What would be the point of someone faking this, anyway? If this was really a kidnapping, it would be in the papers eventually, whether the victim lived or died. He would then know whether the FBI was telling him the truth. Sometimes you just had to trust people. If he could save a man's life, it was his duty to try. He sent the technician away, leaving him unsuspecting this was more than some inexplicable glitch.

The system went back into full normal operation. Lee then selected and ran the Bulletbird program, and watched it build a query window. He filled in the MIN field and tabbed to the ESN field. He typed that in as well, and clicked the Verify on System button. Immediately an error statement popped up. The ESN and MIN did not match. After proofreading both numbers he realized he had made an error in entering the ESN. A well-designed program would not need both, since it could look up one from the other using the account data base, he thought at first; then he realized any typing error like the one he had just made would go undetected as long as the typo produced a valid number. No doubt the designers wanted both numbers as a double-check to make sure the correct number was being queried - civil rights coded into a triangulation application. He corrected the number and clicked the same button. The bi-colored disk on the application window spun merrily, indicating it was looking up the requested information. After several seconds, the first display window showed the message: NO CALL IN PROGRESS. So among the active calls, the target phone was not in use. This was not surprising, since everybody had just been dumped from the system a few seconds earlier. It would take a minute or two for those who had been talking to redial and reconnect. However, the little disk continued spinning, indicating it was still looking.

Bulletbird wasn't just looking for a call in progress. It tried to determine if the phone was detectable anywhere on the network. The normal cell phone network kept this information current on every single account 24 hours a day so that the switch could route any call that might be destined to any number at any time. So there was a constant series of silent transmissions going on between a cell phone and the nearby cell sites, the transmission towers scattered throughout metropolitan areas and busy highway corridors. As the phone moved around, the software decided which cell site had the strongest signal from that phone, and routed the call there. Bulletbird just wanted to piggyback on that information to identify in humanly recognizable terms which cell site that was, and then - this was the key - to use the weaker signals to determine a likely exact location for the instrument itself through the same geometric principles used by surveyors. If the signal and its strength were measurable on two cell sites, there would be two possible locations for the phone, one on either side of the straight line connecting the two sites. If they could pick up the signal on three sites, then theoretically the location could be determined exactly, through trigonometric algorithms coded in the program. This required special software, however, since the cellular companies' own software was specifically designed to disregard the weaker signals and always routed everything only through the strongest site.

The program window had three small dots in a vertical row to indicate how many cell sites detected the signal from the designated account. Lee watched with growing excitement as the first dot changed from tiny and gray to large and black. One site was detecting the phone. Then a second changed in the same fashion. The little disk kept spinning. Suddenly, all the dots returned to gray and the display window read simply MIN NOT ACTIVE. Quickly he brought up another application. This one was a standard company utility to determine if an instrument was active, but it did not tell where it was. It, too, showed that Mobile Identification Number was not in use. The phone had been turn off at the very moment they were trying to locate it.

He gave the bad news to Tobin, who was waiting patiently on the phone.

"Can you tell where the two sites were that picked up the signal?" he asked Lee.

"No," Lee replied. "I only queried whether the number was on the system. I didn't get a chance to activate the triangulate function."

"But if it detected the signal, it should have been able to tell what sites it was coming from."

"I'm sure it had that data at the time, but I did not query it in time. The information wasn't preserved or written to a file. Once the signal disappears, the data evaporates. Each cell site interrogates every phone it detects every two seconds. If it goes for three consecutive interrogations without a reply, it considers the phone undetected, and overwrites any record. In other words, there's no MIN information stored for longer than six seconds after a phone is turned off. Unless the location was captured by the billing data base or Bulletbird, it's gone."

"You can't even estimate?" Tobin asked anxiously.

"I'd guess it's probably in the Western Region. The training material on Bulletbird says that it doesn't query sites outside the region, what you would call the local roaming area, until all sites within the local area have been queried. I could tell from the display that it hadn't finished querying the local region. So that phone is somewhere on the west coast right now."

"Keep Bulletbird up, will you?" Tobin asked him. "That phone could be turned on again at any time, and we need to know that when it happens. And get us the location."

"I will, officer."

FBI Agents didn't like to be called 'officer' since they were agents, not police officers. Defense lawyers often used that form of address when agents were testifying, to try to minimize their training and education in front of the jury. Tobin knew Lee meant nothing by it. "Thank you," he said simply.

Tobin called Jemperson back and relayed the bad news.

"Shit! Knowles'll kill us. The phone was turned off the instant Bulletbird was trying to locate it? If we'd just moved faster by a few minutes - seconds, even. Stroaker told you this was probably a false alarm, didn't he?"

"Yeah, but that's no excuse. You treat every case as if it's life and death, because you never know which one will turn out to be." Even as Tobin said it, he knew it wasn't true. It was impossible to treat everything exactly the same. You had to prioritize, to pick the most important, or at least the most urgent, task and do that first. Something always fell behind. But he was right about one thing: he would have no excuse. FBI Headquarters - the Bureau, as agents called it - would not be forgiving. Bulletbird should have been implemented earlier, they would say.

Jemperson drew the figurative short straw and was elected to call Knowles. After telling the story, Jemperson apologized. "Sorry, man. We moved as fast as we could, but we just didn't quite make it. Even if we had done it, there's no guarantee it would have located the thing. We'll have the GTE pay phone number by the morning, at least."

"Yeah. Thanks, anyway." Knowles sighed. He couldn't help feeling both resentment and frustration that he had not been taken seriously the day before, but he also knew that he could have been wrong. At least he had been vindicated in his judgment, and from now on this case would get treated right. He hung up with Jemperson and turned to Rothman.

"Let's get back to the office. There's lots to do."

Rothman was able to raise the SJRA on the radio. He had the clerk relay a message to Kim that they were coming back in. He also learned that Olson, who had been out, had been informed of the recent developments and was on his way back to the RA. They all arrived at about the same time. As Knowles and Rothman came in the front door, the clerk at reception told them Olson was looking for them. They headed to his office where they found him on the phone.

As he talked, Olson motioned at them to come in. He was obviously talking to the Z-man and bringing him into the loop. This would take division-wide coordination, and Z-man was the Violent Crime Program Coordinator. Z-man agreed to be the one to take the news to Stroaker, since they were both in San Francisco at the moment. That reason was good enough, but an equal motivation for the Z-man was to get "face time" with the SAC on a big case. It would make him look like he was in charge, a leader, even though he hadn't really done anything. Z-man had ambitions of higher office; Olson didn't. Olson was content to let the Z-man handle the boss.

"Cliff, it looks like you were right after all," Olson gushed, as though Knowles had just won the lottery or something equally unlikely. "I was on the fence there, but you had it pegged. Still, we don't know if the wife is involved somehow. Or the husband could have staged the whole thing and hired someone to make the calls. Anyway, we have to treat this as the real thing all the way. I'll call Mo to arrange for SOG support. Z-man is going to arrange for the cash from the Federal Reserve Bank. Can Mrs. Fischer cover the $650,000?"

"I believe so. I haven't really talked to her about it. That's one of the things I was planning to get to last night when Stroaker pulled me off to go look for the corpse at the house. Maybe Rice covered that in his interview."

"Oh, yeah. Well, I haven't seen Rice's 302 yet." This comment by Olson hardly surprised Knowles, who knew Rice's reputation for timely reporting was not the best, and Olson's attentiveness to his inbox wasn't much better. Knowles didn't know whether the 302 had not been typed yet, or whether Olson just hadn't read it. He hoped it was the latter, because now he wanted to see it, too. He needed to know the details of that interview if he was going to work the case. Olson continued, "Tim, you'll coordinate the flight schedule. Work with Mo on that. Get a separate channel from Communications just for this case, and let me know what it is. I want to monitor all surveillances. Cliff, you contact the family and find out if they can cover the ransom, and if so, how fast they can get the money together."

"Okay."

Knowles had not handled a ransom case as the case agent, although he had worked them on a street surveillance team. He wasn't sure how the currency was handled. He knew that the Federal Reserve Bank had a vault of bills set aside just for such cases. The serial numbers were already recorded, the bills photographed and packaged, in all different denominations. However, Olson explained that these bills would be released only if the victim transferred an equal amount of cash to the bank. The bank had no authority to expend public funds to ransom private individuals. If Fran Fischer could get the money together and wire it to the bank, they would release the necessary cash in the right denominations. Someone from the Z-man's squad would pick it up and transport it to the SJRA for special preparation before delivery.

Olson's phone rang, but he ignored it. Kim picked up the line and quickly yelled into Olson's office "Ben, it's the SAC to talk to you."

Olson picked up the line and waved Rothman and Knowles out. They had enough to keep them busy for now.

Knowles called the Fischer house, using the fax line. Louellen Murphy answered. He asked about the money, and was assured that

Mrs. Fischer could get the cash ready to be wired by the next morning. That meant the bank would release the currency that same day, and it would arrive at the RA Thursday afternoon, probably. He wasn't sure how much time it would take to doctor the package for delivery, but he assumed it was an involved process. Next he began drafting an immediate teletype for the neighboring divisions: Portland, Sacramento, Los Angeles, and for good measure, Las Vegas, San Diego, and the Legal Attaché in Mexico. Those latter three offices were not contiguous, but the ransom calls indicated they could be involved. Someone had to bring them up to speed in case a payoff demand gave instructions to travel to those locations, or if they got information the hostage was being kept there. Sending out leads and update communications was a chore normally reserved for the case agent. But Knowles knew the case agent was in Disneyland. Doubtless the case would be reassigned to him by the end of the day.

Rothman pulled out his flight schedule for the month. The number of aircraft was limited, and the pilots as well. During a hostage situation there would always be at least one aircraft, either a fixed-wing or a helicopter, available to take off at a moment's notice, and if an actual surveillance was planned, at least two. That was on top of the normal surveillances scheduled, and any special transport needs, like the SWAT team or executive staff. There would be very little other flying done until this was resolved; for sure all training flights would be canceled. Fortunately, he did not have the overall responsibility for finding the pilots and craft to complete the job. That was the job of one of Mo's reliefs, the Flight Operations Coordinator or FOC. Rothman knew that Olson was contacting Mo Morales to arrange for physical surveillance support, but that would primarily be the ground teams. Mo was neither a rocket scientist nor a pilot, and knew almost nothing about flying. Rothman called the FOC directly and explained what was going on. He was met with a barrage of invective directed at no one in particular. The coordinator would have to reschedule pilots, maintenance, vendors, and everybody else involved with the aircraft, but he knew he would have no choice for a hostage case. At least none of the pilots would be able to claim they had conflicts, since the SAC himself would make everybody cancel everything for this. He confirmed with Rothman that he would find the aircraft and the bodies to put in the pilots' seats. Of course he wanted to know when the payoff was, and when Rothman couldn't tell him, another blue streak filled Rothman's earpiece. Oh well, venting was good for the spirit, Rothman thought.

Both agents continued making calls and dictating communications. Now that time was of the essence, Knowles began dictating into his handheld Dictaphone rather than typing. Kim typed at least twice as fast as he did, so he could save time by dictating. She could also get Olson to sign off on those things that needed it without Knowles having to chase him down. Kim was extremely loyal to Olson, and, in turn, Olson always did whatever Kim asked him to. Knowles began calling other people he knew would be affected, including other part-time pilots in the RA, agents on SWAT teams, and the office support supervisor.

Knowles went back into Olson's office and waited for him to get off the phone. "Should I call the U.S. Attorney's office?" he asked.

"Good idea. I forgot about that. No, I'll do it." Olson called the direct number of Len Schuler, the Branch Chief of the San Jose U.S. Attorney's office. He got voice mail, which was normal, since Schuler was virtually always on the phone when he was in the office at all. Olson left a message that it was an urgent matter and asked him to call back.

"Stroaker will be handling this himself. I just talked to him," Olson informed Knowles. "The Z-man will be down in the RA later today. Stroaker will be here tomorrow for the next ransom call. We're going to use the conference room for our command post. You can help organize that."

"Okay, I'll get with Belinda," Knowles replied. Belinda was the Support Supervisor for the RA, the civil service equivalent of an office manager. "Shall I do a memo so the Rotor can reassign the case?" "Rotor" was an obsolete term for a squad's File Clerk, dating back to the days when rotary files were the only permitted form of storage for pending case files. Though now considered politically incorrect, the term was still universally used.

Olson shuffled uneasily in his seat. "No, that's not necessary."

Knowles was momentarily confused, then he began to redden. "Why not? You aren't going to leave it assigned to Nick are you? He's in Disneyland. What's the deal?"

"I'm sorry. I wanted to reassign it, but Stroaker told me not to. I guess he's pissed at you."

"Pissed at ME? Why? I'm the only one who's given him good advice so far. He's pissed at me for that?"

"Well, he says you should have explained better why you thought the case was for real. You made him look bad because you weren't clear enough, ... uh, forceful enough, like Lark. He thinks you're partly to blame for him saying it looked like a false alarm. At least that's the way he put it. And he says you should have asked if the victim had a cell phone. We could have started Bulletbird sooner if you had."

"Bullshit, Ben. I explained it just fine. As for the cell phone, no one thought to ask because no one from the family or company mentioned it. It wasn't just me; I didn't even get a chance to finish the interview because he yanked me off it to do that wild goose chase at the house. Stroaker just went off on a tangent. He's a complete idiot and always has been. If he feels compelled to blame someone else for that, why doesn't he blame Lark, or even you, for saying the case was bogus? Or Rice. Rice didn't ask about the cell phone either."

"Yeah, he probably should," Olson said, shrugging his shoulders. Some supervisors would take offense at such a reference to their own bad judgment, but Olson and Knowles were good enough friends to be able to speak frankly. Most supervisors would not share with an agent something negative the SAC said about them, for fear that the agent would confront the SAC and bring the wrath of the boss back on himself. But Olson knew Knowles wouldn't betray his frank revelations. He motioned for Knowles to close the door, which Knowles did. "But you know what they say. Hindsight is 20-20. We made our best guess and you made yours. You aren't going to make yourself any more popular if you say 'I told you so' to the boss."

Knowles knew he was right about this, but that just rankled all the more. Not only was he being blamed for what was clearly the SAC's own mistake, but if he tried to get any recourse, he would just get in even greater trouble. The big boss wanted someone to blame, and he was it. Deal with it. "So who's going to do the case agent work? You making Lark come back from Disneyland?" Agents had to file itineraries whenever they traveled, and they were subject to recall for emergencies, although it was extremely rare to make an agent come back from a family trip.

"No, you will. I'm designating you acting case agent. Stroaker said you were the smartest guy on the squad, maybe the division, so I know he won't have any trouble with that."

Acting case agent? There was no such thing, Knowles knew. The only effect would be to make him do all the work, but get no credit for either the effort expended or the statistical accomplishments that the case might produce. Convictions, recovery of ransom money, all of that is claimed by the agent assigned the case. On paper Nick Lark would get credit for rescuing Fischer, if that was the eventual outcome, notwithstanding the fact he hadn't even been aware the case was going on. Even the hours Knowles spent would not show up anywhere. His other cases would languish for however long this took, and that would hurt his stats, but he would get nothing from this case to compensate.

"Look at it this way," Olson said, reading Knowles's emotions correctly. "It doesn't matter who the case agent is. Stroaker's going to take personal charge of this case and call all the shots. If something goes wrong, he'll take the full responsibility, and he'll take full credit if it goes well regardless of who's case agent. You know that. At least you'll be there to give him good advice again. He'll need it."

Knowles took some solace in these words, because they largely followed his own thinking, if not his emotions. The important thing was getting the victim back alive and catching the culprits, not who got credit or blame. He would be in a position to make a difference, and that mattered. He had fought his way out of FCI just to do this kind of work, and now was his chance.

By mid-afternoon the audio tape of the ransom call had been transported and transcribed, Kim doing her usual great work at making out the sometimes garbled speech. Z-man had arrived and set up camp in the conference room. Belinda had taped sheets of butcher paper on the walls to use to make charts or lists, and the phone jacks in that room all had telephones connected. The shades were drawn, and notepads and other necessary supplies were set out in orderly stacks. A sign was taped on the door warning employees that the room was being used for an emergency, and any reservations they had were canceled. This caused no small outcry, since it was the only conference room in the office for over 50 agents. It was always a challenge to get a reservation to use it, so agents hated to lose the slots they had patiently waited weeks for.

Knowles entered the conference room to check out its progress. He had an extra copy of the call transcript which he tossed on the table for the Z-man to read. Z-man was finishing up a call to the SAC. When he hung up he said to Knowles, "Well, tomorrow we get our Peter Stroaker in the RA." He pumped his right hand up and down in the classic jerk-off motion and pronounced Stroaker "stroker." Zwolinksi was notorious for feigning disdain for the brass while doing all in his power to join their ranks. Knowles ignored him. Belinda walked in at that moment with more office supplies. She either didn't notice the obscene gesture, or pretended not to. Z-man laughed nervously when he realized a woman might have seen him; sexual harassment complaints could wreck a career.

"Has Stroaker ever worked a ransom kidnap case?" Knowles asked.

"It doesn't matter whether you've worked a particular kind of case..." Z-man began to answer. Knowles, without really listening to the rest of the explanation, took that to be a negative answer, not only for Stroaker, but for Z-man as well. Great, the boss and his number one man have no experience in this kind of case, and they'll be calling the shots.

Z-man then picked up the audiotape transcript, while Knowles reread his own copy. "This part about the Jaguar - is that a convertible?"

"Dunno. She was driving a full-size Cadillac when I met her."

"We have to have a big car. We need an agent hidden in the car with the girl for her protection. Convertibles are out. We have to give Louellen instructions on what to tell the caller - to make an excuse to use the Caddy."

Knowles was mildly impressed once again. Z-man had been talking to someone who knew something about ransom drops. If the Z-man could stop being so offensive, he could be good management material.

"I've notified the Bureau we have a tape recording," Z-man told Knowles. "They're going to get their linguistics expert to listen to the tape. Can you ship a copy to them overnight?"

Knowles looked at his watch. He didn't have a spare copy, so that would mean duplicating the tape from the original, and then shipping it FedEx overnight. They didn't have time to make the last commercial pickup. He called Rothman's extension. "Can you find a pilot to fly a tape back to the Bu tonight?"

Rothman thought about it briefly and replied, "Probably. I know a United pilot over at San Jose airport who flies night runs to the east coast and back. He's a real Feebee wannabe. He's always asking about our cases when they show up in the paper. If he's flying tonight, he'll do it. He can drop it at the airport police on the other end, and someone from the Bu can pick it up in the morning on the way to work. If we can get it to the airport by 8:00 PM we should make it."

"Tim, can you get the original tape from Kim - she just transcribed it - make a copy, label it, and drive it out to your buddy?"

"You   got   it."

Day 3
Thursday

Chapter 12

"We have before us an immense challenge," Pete Stroaker began. "A man's life may hang in the balance. Each of you will give 110%, and more, I know. I am sure you are up to the task, for this is the finest group of investigators which I have ever had the privilege to work with. I know I don't get to the San Jose Resident Agency very often, but I am acutely aware of what a critical role this RA plays in the FBI, and as iron-clad guardians of Silicone Valley."

Cliff Knowles looked around the conference room. Stroaker, Z-man, Olson, Rothman, Tobin, Morales, Rice, Mike Bean, Hank LaPointe, and Terry Izawa all seemed to be having as much trouble looking inspired as he did. Stroaker often spoke almost entirely in clichés and always mispronounced Silicon Valley. To keep from overt yawning Knowles concentrated on trying to figure out what the role of each person was. Tobin was the Tech Squad supervisor. Olson, Rothman, Rice, and Knowles were the SJRA violent crime squad contingent. Morales, the SOG squad for surveillance. Z-man, the Violent Crime and Major Offenders coordinator. Bean was the chief radio technician; LaPointe was the SWAT team leader. But the rest were there for reasons not yet known to Knowles. Izawa was a senior agent on Z-man's squad in San Francisco. He had some direct hands-on role, Cliff assumed.

"... thorough in your interviews, accurate in your observations, and precise in your reporting. Time is of the essence and waits for no man... or woman. Radio transmissions should be kept to a minimum, but be fulsome in your descriptions."

Knowles whispered to Rothman, "Iron-clad guardians? Silicone Valley? He doesn't even know the difference between silicone and silicon? The only Silicone Valley around here is Carol Doda's cleavage. He wants fulsome descriptions? Do you think he knows fulsome means 'nauseating?' His syntax is fulsome enough."

"Shh, he'll hear. Who's out at the house?" Rothman whispered back.

"Louellen Murphy, Luciana, and Ron Jemperson. Louellen and Lucy are staying there for the duration. Mrs. Fischer and Pam, the daughter, are there; Mrs. Carmody comes and goes. The hired help has been given two weeks off."

Stroaker's voice picked up volume. "The case has been designated a major case by the Bureau. It's titled Fischnap. Ben, why don't you give a short update to the group, for the benefit of the newcomers."

"Sure, Pete." Olson gave a concise and articulate summary of what had taken place. When he came to the second ransom call, Stroaker interrupted him.

"Don, can you play the tape, please. There's a transcript in your packet."

Everybody flipped through the briefing materials until they found the transcript. Stroaker cleared his throat meaningfully to quiet down the increasing murmur and rustle of pages and had Z-man restart the tape. The assemblage listened intently through the entire recording. When it was done, Stroaker resumed.

"Don has been in touch with HQ on this. They got the tape this morning, and they're shipping it to their linguistics expert, some professor in Pennsylvania. They already played him the tape over the phone, I understand. Don, have you heard anything yet on it?"

"The professor gave only a tentative opinion. He thinks it's a male in his twenties, not a native English speaker, but educated in the United States for a period of years. He believes the accent is Arabic."

"Arabic? You got to be kidding." It was Morales speaking. "I'm no Ph.D., but I know a Mexican accent when I hear one. I grew up in El Paso."

Olson spoke up next. "It sounds Spanish to me, too. The caller said in the first call they were taking Fischer to Mexico. How sure is this expert?"

"Not very. He only heard a copy of the original recording played over a telephone once. He should have the tape in his hands within an hour or two. I expect we'll have a more thorough analysis later today. He is good, though. We use him all the time for terrorist threats. He can usually pinpoint not only the language, Arabic, but which Arabic-speaking country."

"Well, let's move on," Stroaker said. "Ben?"

"As you no doubt noticed, the caller said he would call again today. He may leave payoff instructions as early as this afternoon. We aren't ready yet. We don't even have a ransom package, real or dummy. Everyone needs to get their assignment and get moving. Flip back to page one. You'll see a contact list with everyone's regular direct line, pager, and for most of you, cell phone number. You will also see from the list what your assignment is."

Knowles and Rothman started looking over the list. Rothman was the squad flight coordinator as expected, and investigative support. Knowles saw his name listed as case agent, even though he knew Lark was still officially assigned the case.

The Z-man spoke up. "We've been in touch with the Federal Reserve Bank about the money. They're preparing it all in hundreds and photographing the bills. There will be several techniques used to aid us on tracking the money. Tobin will brief you more on that later. Terry will be the ride-along. If the daughter has to do the drop, he'll be her bodyguard."

Everyone looked approvingly at Terry Izawa. At five foot seven he was compact enough to fit in the rear footwell of a car, but at 175 lbs, 3% body fat, wielding biceps the size of footballs, he was not small in any other sense. He was experienced in the role from a prior hostage case several years earlier, and he taught both firearms and self-defense. No one in the room would contest the choice.

Bean was next. He went into detail on the channel assignments. SOG, the three surveillance specialist teams, would stay on their regular tactical channel, Red 3, which SWAT would share. The Buradios in the average agent's car did not have the Red channels. The regular agent teams, known as street teams, would be on a dedicated channel just for this case: Blue 7. During the payoff there would be an aircraft carrying a repeater over the drop car at all times, so that Izawa and the follow car could always communicate. Agents should use the normal Blue channels for everything not directly connected to Fischnap. Cell phones were being issued to key personnel. Bean handed out several cell phones, assignees already identified with Post-it notes stuck to the phones. Make sure to get these back, he cautioned, as they were going on each agent's official property list. He knew from experience the phones would disappear from inventory if agents were not held accountable. Because the street agents don't have the SOG channels on their car radios, he noted, they wouldn't be able to talk directly to the SOG cars. All communications had to go through Radio Control for relay. Radio discipline was key during large-scale surveillances, Bean declared authoritatively. Without it, everyone talked over everyone else, or a mike stuck open, and no one could communicate at all. Though the Red/Blue split meant SOG and SWAT would have to switch from their channel to talk to the rest of the agents, it was necessary, he assured them.

Tobin's pager went off at that moment. He returned the page from a phone in the corner of the command post. He mumbled a brief affirmative, then wrote down something on a piece of paper. The call lasted no more than a minute. He took the note to Stroaker as Bean summed up radio procedures.

"We have the trace on the call from yesterday," Stroaker said. "It was made from a GTE pay phone at a place called The Big Brown Farmhouse in Aromas. A restaurant, I suppose."

Knowles and Rothman shot a glance at each other. The Big Brown Farmhouse was an antique shop just off Highway 101 between Gilroy and Salinas. The place was huge, almost like a big box discount store. Actually, Knowles figured, it probably wasn't antiques they sold, considering the size of the place; more likely it was furniture and artwork carefully represented as "antique style" or "colonial style." Gilroy, better known as the Garlic Capital of the World, was also the local furniture manufacturing area. Both agents had driven by the place many times, but they had never had occasion to stop. It probably had a snack bar, rest rooms, and a bank of phones.

"Cliff, you're in charge of setting out leads, and setting up the regular street teams. I want a team waiting at all major choke points in the area when the call comes in tonight. Ralph, we need to have the next trace in real time, not the next day. I want to catch this guy with the receiver in hand."

"I've got Pac Bell and GTE both on alert," Tobin replied. "We should be able to trace if he stays on longer than a minute or so ... unless he calls from out of the region, or uses a cell phone."

Stroaker turned back to Knowles. "As soon as this meeting is over, I want you to set a lead for agents to get out to that restaurant and find out if anybody saw anything yesterday."

Right, thought Knowles. Everybody else at the phones the previous day would be tourists or local farm labor using the rest rooms. The chances of anyone having noticed anything useful was virtually nil. It was unlikely the agents would even find anyone there who had been there the previous day. But it had to be done, he knew. If they were lucky there would be a security camera covering the area.

"Then, set up street teams. The next call could be from anywhere. Have someone at the Brown Derby, although he probably won't be dumb enough to use it again."

Or dumb enough to mistake an Aromas antique shop for a Hollywood restaurant, Knowles thought. "Right, Pete. How many people am I authorized for this, and how do I know who I can have? Will the supervisors provide me a list of names, or do I get to pick? It's going to take close to a hundred people to cover the southern half of the division."

"Take as many as you need. I told Brad you'd be assigning teams." Brad Williams was the Associate SAC, next in authority in the division after the SAC. Large, black, and dependable, Williams was a regular poster child for affirmative action. "Brad'll run the division while I do this case full-time."

Several eyebrows lifted at this last remark. Everyone had expected the SAC to take charge, give out assignments, and then let the professionals do their jobs. Most SAC's didn't try to micromanage big cases because they simply didn't know much about investigations. It was nearly impossible to get to the level of SAC without serving at least two years in six or eight geographic locations, often many more, and in all types of administrative or liaison assignments. This tortuous path upward usually entailed lots of politics and very little investigation. Most field squads were really run by Relief Supervisors or Stationary Supervisors, the lucky few field agents who were anointed by the SAC to take some of the supervisory slots - people like Ben Olson who actually knew how to investigate a case. The inevitable result was that SAC's seldom had more than a few years of investigative experience early in their career - usually in the relatively unimportant case work typically given to new agents. It was this fact, known to all in the FBI except to those SAC's whose egos precluded them from accepting their own incompetence, that led to the raised eyebrows. The normal practice was to allow an old-time squad supervisor to run the case, with the SAC watching closely from the front office, not calling the shots in the command post.

"Pete, do you think that's wise to let Brad run the whole division? He's only been here two months." It was Olson's tactful way of saying get the hell out of my hair, you empty suit, and go back to San Francisco to give press conferences or something.

"I have every confidence in Brad. He always gives 110%, and more. He's one of the finest administrators to which it has ever been my privilege to serve with. Besides, I get to have some fun, too. You guys always get to run these things while I'm stuck making speeches to little old ladies."

If it had been possible to have a synchronized blanching competition, the agents in that room would have won the Olympic gold medal hands down. The SAC was running the case because he wanted to have fun? There was a man's life at stake, and he thought this case was his personal toy? The familiar aroma of nervous sweat filled the air, but no one said anything for a moment.

"The SAC is required to take personal charge of a hostage case, as you all know." It was the Z-man, reciting the investigative manual, the MIOG. "Brad is a bit green to run the division, but it's just a risk we have to take. Pete can keep watch on him from down here." Z-man was smooth. He knew why the agents were going pale; but he also knew the SAC was interpreting it to mean they were worried about the division in the hands of a newbie ASAC. He was able to capitalize on both impressions to give the agents a graceful way out, and play to the SAC's vanity. Stroaker ate it up. Z-man was destined to be an SAC himself, no question.

"Hank," Stroaker resumed, "I want you to put all SWAT on standby until further notice. We're going to use the ninja suits." The SWAT gear included an all-black outfit specially designed for the FBI, a Velcro and Kevlar contraption with wide, reinforced belt loops for gunbelts and holsters, extra pouches for ammunition magazines and various other gizmos. The black suits were intended for night-time stealth. It was probable that the payoff would be at night, but you never knew.

"Right. I'll notify all three teams to cancel all leave." LaPointe was hastily making notes. Since the first ransom call had come from the South Bay, Team 2, comprised of South Bay personnel primarily, would be considered the lead team. They knew the territory best. LaPointe was already way ahead of Stroaker. "Cliff, I'll give you a current list of SWAT personnel so you don't assign them to the street teams." Knowles had thought of that himself, and intended to ask for it after the meeting, but it was typical of LaPointe to pick up on the need without prompting. SWAT members, like Legal Advisors and part-time pilots, were drawn from all the squads. There was no easy way of knowing who was SWAT without a list.

LaPointe might have been lifted from the pages of a Tom Clancy novel. Raised in the northern peninsula of Michigan, and a descendant of a French Canadian and a Minnesotan, he had a slight regional accent that blended French, Minnesotan, and flat Midwestern American English. Women went gaga over the accent - or perhaps it was the rock-hard physique and dimpled cheeks, improved somehow by a noticeable scar running along the chin line. He looked as dashing as a movie pirate and could back up the image with physical skills and brains. He had been chosen to be the SWAT Coordinator for a reason - many of them, in fact.

Stroaker continued his instructions, "Mo, you have to put a plane in the air for the call tonight. We may end up with a car chase. Ben, what time do you think the next call will be coming in?"

"Hard to say. The first two calls came in around late morning to midday. But the caller also knows that Pam needs time to make arrangements regarding the money. He offered to give her a week. He'll probably figure she'll need most of the day, so my guess is he'll wait until late afternoon or early evening. That's just a guess, though. He may not even call today at all."

Knowles agreed with Olson's analysis. He noticed several nods of agreement around the table. The SAC saw them too and seemed reassured, adding, "That makes sense. Now what about this $650,000? That still seems like an odd figure to me. Has anybody got any ideas about why that number?"

Z-man responded first, "I talked to the VCMO unit back at the Bu. There's a long-time analyst there who's studied every kidnapping we ever had. He said it was unusual but not unheard of. The normal is a round number like a million, but when there is an odd number like this, it's usually because there's a specific need the hostage taker has to fill - a debt to be paid or something they want to buy that costs just that much. Maybe a house or a business. Maybe he thinks Fischer cost him that much in a business deal and this is his way of getting repaid."

"That's good," Stroaker said. "Cliff, contact the family to see if that number rings a bell with them, or there's anybody connected with them, a relative, neighbor, or household help that may have talked about something like that. Maybe someone fired at the company."

Knowles made a note. It was a lead worth pursuing. "Sure. By the way, while I'm contacting them, what do you think about contacting neighbors directly to find out if any of them has seen anything suspicious lately - cars cruising by, prowlers, that kind of thing. Someone may be able to give us a description."

Stroaker knotted his forehead rather impressively. He seemed nonplussed to be asked about a technique he hadn't considered. "Well, that raises a risk of tipping our hand to the kidnappers if one of the neighbors is involved." He looked first to Olson, then to Z-man for support.

Olson immediately replied, "I think Cliff is right on that. There's a good chance of getting some useful information, and the added risk is small. Kidnappers always expect that the victim's family is going to contact law enforcement - that's why they always threaten them and tell them not to. But the reality is that even if the bad guys find out we're investigating, that's what they expect anyway, so they won't do anything different. It's not a busy street, so anyone not a regular might have drawn some notice."

Knowles added, "And the interview at the cleaners proves that Fischer made it to Mountain View before being grabbed. If there was a spy at or near the house, they would've done the snatch there, on familiar ground. Besides, have you seen that neighborhood? Multimillionaires live there. The neighbors don't need to kidnap a friend for what to them is chump change. That raises another issue, too. Shouldn't we notify Mountain View P.D.? It's obvious now the abduction took place at the workplace, not the home."

Rothman kicked Knowles under the table as if to say you've gone and put your foot in it again.

Stroaker's expression grew dark. "Local police have been notified. I called the Chief at Los Altos P.D. myself, and she told us to run with the case. I don't see any reason to contradict her. As for the neighbors, the caller had a Spanish accent just like the Fischer gardener and housekeeper. There are plenty of Spanish speakers who work as domestic help around there, and who don't have money. I don't think we should risk it." Pause. "And I'm calling the shots."

Stroaker seemed miffed at being told what to do by a street agent, and especially upset at being called out on the local police notification in public. By now everyone in the room knew the kidnap must have happened in Mountain View, even if it was just outside the door of the dry cleaners. Stroaker just didn't want a new face, someone from the Mountain View Police Department, to join in the investigation and start second-guessing him. This was a clear violation of direct instructions in the MIOG, and the Z-man, who had been quoting it liberally up to now, was quite content to remain silent on this one. Stroaker's final sentence seemed to give him a measure of satisfaction - like the big kid on the playground who wrenches the ball from his playmates to let them know who really owns it. He shot down a good lead just to prove that he was boss.

But Knowles was too stubborn to let go entirely. "Well, sure, I see that point of view. But the language expert said it was probably an Arabic speaker. I don't think we should focus on the Spanish accent."

Rothman rolled his eyes, wanting to tell his friend to let it go. A couple of the supervisors shuffled uneasily. You just don't argue with the SAC. He'll win every time and you'll pay the price later.

Stroaker didn't have to respond, but he couldn't resist. "We don't need some pointy-headed professor in Pennsylvania telling us that a Chicano is an Arab terrorist. He's used to consulting on that Arab stuff and hears it in everything. He might know an Iraqi accent from a Pakistani one, but he obviously doesn't know a Mexican when he hears one."

Zwolinski winced, not because of the put-down of his trusted expert, but because Stroaker apparently thought Pakistan was an Arabic-speaking country.

"Anyway, let's move on," Stroaker resumed. "Don, you'll be liaison with the Bureau, and I want you to do all the teletypes."

Knowles heaved a silent sigh of relief. That was a case agent chore he wouldn't have to do. Stroaker probably trusted the Z-man to put the right spin on things - saying that local police had been notified, for example, without specifying which department.

"Okay, you got your assignments. Get your cell phone assigned, if you still need one, and give all your corrections on phone numbers to Kim so she can update the list if necessary. Cliff, get someone out to the Brown Derby."

"Roger," was all Knowles could force out. He literally and figuratively bit his lip, and headed out the door.

Chapter 13

Louellen Murphy knocked softly on Mrs. Fischer's door. She was greeted warmly and invited in. The room was actually a suite of rooms: huge bedroom, bathroom with walk-in cedar dressing room, and off the bedroom a sitting room which served as Fran Fischer's den or office. There was a computer, desk, telephone, and a custom-built bookshelf of stained maple. Louellen realized the suite of rooms was easily twice the size of her own entire apartment in Berkeley, and much more expensively decorated.

She asked Fran Fischer about the progress on getting the money.

"I talked to our broker just about thirty minutes ago. He had to liquidate some bonds, but says the account should be credited by the end of the day. How are you doing with the bank?"

"The Federal Reserve is ready to release the money as soon as you wire the funds. Here are the wiring instructions you'll need to give your broker. You don't have to say it's the Federal Reserve Bank. That might raise eyebrows. You just give him the numbers, including this telephone number, and his bursar will know how to do it. This money will look normal, but it's all marked. We don't intend to let the kidnappers keep it, of course, but if it gets away from us, it can be traced and retrieved almost anywhere."

"I don't care about the money," Mrs. Fischer said flatly, and truthfully. "I just want my husband back safe."

"Of course, that's what we all want. But if the money and kidnapper get out of our hands somehow, the money is one of the best ways to find your husband."

"Oh, thank you for all you are doing, Louellen. I know it must be hard for you, giving up your own family life and coming down here. It must seem like being in prison for days." Her eyes got moist for a moment, then she smiled at Louellen.

"No, it's not hard at all. It's what I've trained for, and what the FBI does best. Everyone on this case is dedicated to the same thing - getting your husband back. There's not an agent, not a clerk or secretary, who would hesitate to put their personal life on hold for a week or a month to accomplish this. We came into this job to help people in need, and now is our chance to make good on our part of the bargain. Just think of it as your tax dollars at work."

Fran Fischer heaved a giant sigh, and leaned over to give Louellen a hug. "Oh, thank you for everything. You and Lucy have been so nice and so patient with us, too."

"Okay, now I need for you to give these instructions to your broker, and tell him to let you know the minute the funds have been wired. And remember, it's entirely your decision whether or not to pay the ransom. We cannot order you, or even advise you, regarding your own financial risks. I know I've told you we can trace it, but you need to understand we can't promise that. There's always some risk."

"Don't worry. I have no hesitation whatsoever on that score. They can keep the money for all I care. You'll have your ransom money."

"Thank you, Fran. You've been terrific. You call me now, if you have any questions, or just need a shoulder to lean on." Louellen left the wiring instructions on the desk and left.

Knowles made up a quick list of agent names from the SJRA squad rosters. Olson had handed him the names the other San Jose supervisors had provided to be lead agents, mostly first-office agents - green, but eager. In Bureau lingo "lead agent" referred to any agent covering a lead, not to someone leading an investigation. He sent two he trusted from his own squad, Gina Torres and Matt Nguyen, to The Big Brown Farmhouse to do interviews, and one more, the RA fingerprint instructor, to lift prints from the phone - not that he expected anything from that either. The ransom caller had no doubt worn gloves, and the phone had probably been used at least twenty or thirty times since then.

The next item on the agenda was naming street teams. The plan was pretty standard - have agents positioned evenly around the region so that when the next call was traced, there would be a team somewhere close by. The agents were given discretion to cover their own designated area however they saw fit. There would be teams of four to six agents assigned an area, and one of them would be the team leader. If the call traced back to a phone, perhaps at an airport or at a hotel, the word would go to the closest team to converge on the area and try to locate or identify the caller. Instructions as to whether or not to arrest or stop someone would come from the command post. Even if you missed the caller, the sooner you got to the phone the better; there could be fingerprints or witnesses who saw someone using the phone minutes earlier.

Knowles asked Rothman to help him. Knowles had been in the division for twelve years in San Francisco and three RA's, and therefore knew a great many agents in the division. But he had been in the South Bay for the last eight of those years, so there were a lot of agents that had come into the division during those eight years and were assigned elsewhere whom Knowles did not know well. Rothman, as a pilot, frequently flew surveillances jointly with of agents from other squads as ground teams. Even though there was an SOG squad that did nothing but surveillance, it could not cover every surveillance itself. Most agents spent quite a bit of time doing their own squad surveillances, sometimes with air support from the SOG. Because of this Rothman knew who was good on the street, and who made good team leaders, capable of clear thinking, clear radio instructions, and good navigating. Surveillance was a specialized skill and could be improved with experience and training. Even so, like many other skills, some people just had a knack for it, while others would get lost in a phone booth.

The two of them went over the entire division roster and began selecting names. People who were on SWAT, SOG, or out on maternity leave were eliminated immediately. So were the agents they knew were total bozos. Knowles took out a map and selected areas that needed coverage, then made a list of how many agents would be needed. From experience he knew that the freeways were key. He gave Rothman some names of people he knew he wanted. The list finally grew to 119 names. Each name was assigned to a team, each team had a leader, and each team was assigned an area to cover. They had to let these people know they were working a late shift soon, or they would be gone, make other plans, or simply not get the message in time. And there would be plenty of conflicts that resulted in the agents not being available. Rothman and Knowles simply didn't have any way of knowing who was on sick leave, back at the FBI Academy on training, under subpoena for trial, or otherwise just not available. All they could do was make the list and put out the word that these agents were to form up in teams at 2:00 P.M., or as soon thereafter as they could, hit the streets in the area designated, and wait for instructions on Blue 7. Then there would be a humongous outcry from agents and supervisors complaining about it. They would be tied up with all kinds of other things. The supervisor would want to choose who goes - maybe even dump the laziest or most unreliable agents on the "special" - and so on. Knowles had to count on Stroaker using his weight to shut up the dissenters.

When the list was done, he took it to Olson, who made a few changes, usually for a good reason Knowles hadn't known about. Knowles then took it to Stroaker, who was tied up on the phone with FBIHQ. From the conversation Knowles realized Stroaker was talking to an Assistant Director. When Knowles approached Stroaker, Knowles heard him say, "Hold on, the case agent just walked in." So they were talking about this case, and the SAC was acknowledging, unofficially at least, that Knowles was the man on the street. Knowles showed him the list, and started to explain the idea of choosing the best people for team leaders, and putting people in geographic areas they were familiar with. Stroaker stopped him, and simply said "Cliff, I trust you. If these are the right people for the right places, that's good enough for me. Let the agents and the supervisors know, and if you get any crap from anybody tell them this is under my orders. I'll back you, but you shouldn't have any trouble. Every supervisor and ASAC knows what's going on."

Knowles thanked him and went back to his own office. He then typed up a one-page cover memo with short, crisp instructions, and asked Belinda to have a clerk start faxing the name lists to each supervisor to notify the agents. The faxing started at 11:13 AM. By 11:18 Knowles's phone was ringing off the hook. Just as predicted, there were countless problems and conflicts. Agents who transferred out of the division a week ago, agents who were in grand jury testifying, agents who had really lame excuses, and supervisors who gave no excuses, but just declared that agent couldn't do it and they were naming someone else. Sometimes Knowles pushed back; other times he accepted the change without comment. Sometimes he had a reasoned discussion with the supervisor, explaining his concerns that the assignment not get pushed off on some junior agent or one of the flakes. Most of the supervisors who called him, though, were surprisingly cooperative and deferential. Knowles was the most surprised, since he was outranked by all of them, but he was also well-known and well-respected. He had often appeared for Olson at Supcon - Supervisors Conference - the weekly meeting with the SAC where each squad got the word from on high and shared their latest news with the others, so other supervisors had interacted with him as an equal on many occasions. One supervisor even offered to cover the assignment himself. Knowles told him it wasn't necessary, but the supervisor was serious, and in fact, put himself on the list. The bottom line was that when it came right down to it, every employee in the division knew what was at stake, and they would do what they could to see that the victim got back safe.

Then came the call from Brad Williams, the ASAC Stroaker had put in charge of day-to-day operations of the rest of the division. "Cliff, what're you doing to me? I've gotten at least six calls from squad supervisors saying their squads are being ripped apart with three hours notice. Agents have interviews scheduled, some are dressed for court, or their cars are in the shop for repair, all kinds of things. This isn't the only case in the division."

Knowles was a bit unsettled. He had never had a personal conversation with Williams, due to the separation by geography and rank and the fact that Williams was new. The word was that Williams was a regular guy with street smarts, but he had a tendency to get cross-ways with the brass. He also had some kind of personal family situation that was taking him back and forth from his previous assignment to San Francisco, so he was not in town much and had not yet familiarized himself with the personnel or geography of the division.

Knowles did his best to explain what he was trying to do, and that he had been acting on orders from Stroaker. Williams knew that this part was for real. "Cliff, I know that's the plan, but you have over a hundred agents here. When you throw in everybody on leave, training, or tied up on somethin' or other, we have almost no one left to respond to a bank robbery or walk-in complainant."

Knowles knew this was a bit disingenuous. It wouldn't matter much if agents didn't respond to a bank robbery, since the local police patrol units were always first on the scene anyway. FBI agents worked cooperatively - usually - with the locals on those and could piggyback off their investigation. Walk-in complainants, unless they were disruptive or looked dangerous, were generally handled by clerical personnel. But Williams had a point. It became extremely difficult for a squad to carry out any normal functions when its staffing level dropped below a certain level. There would be some cases delayed and some presidential appointees who had to wait a few days longer for their background investigation to be completed. "Brad, I know this is hard on the division. And you haven't heard the worst of it yet. Tonight is just the first call of what will probably be several. We're going to have to keep doing this until the caller is caught or the payoff is made. Expect at least three more days."

"Jesus," Williams exhaled into the receiver. There was a long silence. "Okay, Cliff Notes, I'll tell the supes to lay off you. We all gotta do what the SAC says."

"Thanks, Brad. You must have been talking to Z-man. He's the only one who calls me that."

"Not talking to him, listening to him - whether I want to or not. He says you're ... some kind of studious intellectual." He gave a short chuckle.

"I doubt that's the exact language he used, but I'll take that as a compliment. Thanks for your backup on this."

"Okay, you got it, but you have to promise me one thing in exchange."

"What's that?"

"Work with the supervisors. They aren't trying to dump weak links on you. I'll see to that. We're all on the same side here."

"I will, Brad. I can't very well pull rank. I don't have any." Knowles said, drawing another chuckle from Williams.

"Well, save this Fischer guy and maybe we can change that. And good work on calling this as legit. I hear you were the only one," Williams replied.

"Thanks. Now I gotta run." Well how about that, an ASAC who was reasonable and who cared about competent agents getting promoted! Knowles was both pleased at getting out of a tough conversation, and even more pleased that there was someone solid in the front office for the long run.

There was very little overt rank differential in the FBI. Every employee fell into one of four basic categories: support, agent, supervisor, and upper management. But anyone on the inside knew that there were vast, if sometimes subtle, differences within those categories. Pay was determined by one's spot on the Government Service, or GS, scale. Support consisted of everyone who wasn't an agent. Even a Ph.D. lab supervisor with 25 years experience and a GS-14 pay level was looked at as a "clerk", and was sometimes viewed as being of lower rank than a GS-10 new agent right out of Quantico. Agents were, in that sense, like officers in the military, only without the saluting. But the 25-, even 45-year support veteran wielded considerable power in many cases, and a wise agent would learn quickly not to cross the Office Services Manager or the SAC's secretary. Within the agent ranks, all supervisors and management were included. They carried guns and had to qualify like the regular "street" or "brick" agents. Investigation, except for lab work, was done almost exclusively by street agents. An ASAC might be four or five grades above a senior agent on the GS scale, but might only make 15% more pay, and actually be worse off financially because of all the moving. In other words, pay meant little.

GS levels notwithstanding, among agents, as among the animals on Animal Farm, some were more equal than others. Agents could be Relief Supervisors or Principal Relief Supervisors, who had supervisory authority in the absence of the squad supervisor - or for that matter in the presence of the supervisor as long as the supervisor granted it. Some agents were named reliefs just so that someone in a remote RA had the authority to sign out a communication if necessary, but they exercised no other authority. Other reliefs virtually ran their squads, if the supervisor was weak, absent, or always traveling trying to line up another slot. For this they received no extra pay. Some were named as Acting Supervisor when there was no supervisor at all, such as occurred after a retirement, transfer, or death. Other agents did not carry the title of Supervisor or Relief Supervisor at all, but had authority in some specialized area, like Principal Firearms Instructor, SWAT Coordinator, or Media Representative. On the firearms range the PFI could order the SAC to stop what he was doing, curse him out, or whatever was necessary to prevent a dangerous situation. A training agent, who could be any agent not on probation, held considerable power over his or her trainees, including the power to declare them not fit to get off probation. Legal Advisors and Equal Employment Opportunity (EEO) investigators also held certain tools of power. Knowles was both. It was possible he could be in a position to declare that an agent, even an SAC, violated a law or discriminated against someone. That could be a career killer. For someone at the brick agent level he was what Nick Lark would call a "high-risk piss-off."

Still, Knowles was a bit awestruck that he had negotiated with an Associate SAC and won. Brad Williams was three levels higher than he was on the chain of command - Supervisor, ASAC, Associate SAC. Knowles had been treated like an equal, and the merits of the case had been given consideration. This colloquy gave him a small sense of well-being, a sense that things might just turn out okay after all. He knew that this wouldn't have happened if Stroaker wasn't the force behind it, but there was also a sense that Williams had learned from Z-man, Stroaker, or Olson that the case was in good hands, that a good team was running it. Stroaker was going to micromanage the case, and would take credit for anything good that came out of it, but at least Stroaker and Z-man seemed to respect Knowles enough to listen to him and maybe even tout him to the rest of the front office.

The phone started ringing again, and Knowles had another full hour of dealing with irate or imploring supervisors and agents. Finally, he had taken as much as he could stomach, and simply stood up and walked out of his office, phone still ringing. He caught Torres and Nguyen coming back in just as he was walking out. He motioned for them to join him, and asked if they'd eaten lunch yet. Neither had, so he led them outside to the rear parking lot. "Let's grab lunch and you can tell me what you found there. Mexican okay?"

"Sure," they replied in unison. As First Office Agents, FOA's, they weren't going to argue with the case agent on a major case; if he'd wanted to eat whale blubber, they'd have gone along. Knowles drove them to a small place just off Hamilton Avenue frequented by many agents in the RA. The two FOA's informed him that they hadn't found anyone or anything of use at The Big Brown Farmhouse. The phone bank had included three GTE phones as well as several Pac Bell and AT&T. The little paper labels on the phones showing the assigned numbers had been destroyed by vandals. This made it hard to identify which phone was the one GTE had identified as the one used by the caller. The Evidence Response Team agent had called GTE and couldn't get a straight answer. No one at the substation knew which phone it was, or if they did, they weren't sure how to tell the agents how to identify it.

"Why didn't you call the number and see which one rang?" Knowles asked.

"We tried that, but just got that recording that the phone didn't accept incoming calls," Nguyen replied. "You know, some phone companies do that to keep the drug dealers from doing business on their phone banks. DEA started that policy and got the carriers to do it in some locations. I guess this was a problem area." Knowles hadn't heard, but nodded anyway.

Nguyen continued his account of how the agents had threatened to just cut the receivers from all three phones and take them all into the office for lifting latent prints. That had prompted a shift to a supervisor, who then gave them the dial code which is used to find out a telephone number of a questioned phone line. Every telephone company has such a number for the workers to dial to make sure they have connected things correctly. The ERT agent had dialed that number on each of the phones, listened to the disembodied voice read back the number they had dialed from, and found the one used by the caller.

There was no security camera on the phone bank. If the caller had come into the store, he would be on tape inside, but there was no way to know if he had. That videotape had been taken as evidence anyway. There was also an exterior camera that might have video of the caller's car pulling in or out of the driveway. The agents had reviewed a little bit of the tape at the store, but the quality was terrible; the tape had probably been reused hundreds of times, and the camera was both out of focus and situated too high. All it contained were grainy shots of tops of cars – no license plates, bumper stickers, or body scratches. It was black and white, so there was no color, either. You could tell a pickup from a sedan, but unless the caller had driven a convertible or a truly unique vehicle, the tape wouldn't help much. On top of that, there was a significant delay between frames - several seconds - which meant the car might not even be on the tape at all, and the multiplexer clock was off, so the time shown on the tape was misleading. Security cameras could be very useful tools, but they had to be correctly placed, focused, operated, and maintained. And the tapes had to be stored, rotated, and replaced. At least they got tape; that alone was a lucky break, Knowles knew, no matter how bad the tape was. Well, another lead to be assigned - have the humps look through hours of videotape.

The interviews had gone even worse. The employees never watched the phone banks in the breezeway, and none of the tourists who were there today had been there the previous day. They all wanted to know what the investigation was all about, and the agents gave them a cover story about a fugitive. Observation showed that the phones were used a great deal by tourists or the general public stopping just for the phones. They counted an average of seven callers per hour using, or at least touching, each of the phones. There could be more than a hundred fingerprints put on that receiver after the ransom caller touched it. The whole trip turned out to be a total waste, Nguyen concluded.

They piled back into Knowles's Bucar to return to the RA. Knowles couldn't turn out of the driveway to the right, the way they would normally go to return to the RA, because of a delivery truck double parked, so he turned left to go around the block. As they moved past the nondescript office building behind the restaurant, Torres called out, "Hey, isn't that Q-ball's car?" She pointed to the parking lot under the office building. Quincy Allen's Bucar was a bright purple Oldsmobile. No one on the criminal squads would drive it because it was too obvious on a surveillance or while meeting an informant, but it didn't matter for applicant work, so Allen had gladly accepted the new wheels.

"I think you're right," Knowles answered. "No civilian would have taste that bad. That looks like him in the driver's seat, too, but he isn't moving. What's he doing there?" He pulled over to the curb and idled across the street. "Gina, go on over there and see if he's okay."

Torres crossed the street hurriedly. She prowled around the car in two full circles, the second time pressing her face up to the driver's side windows, shielding the glass with her hands to block the glare. Then she came trotting back across the street. "He's asleep. Snoring, too. He didn't even notice I was right up against his window."

"This is too good to pass up," Knowles said. "You want to have a little fun?" he asked conspiratorially. The other two agents grinned and nodded, a bit nervously. Knowles sent Torres down to the gas station on the corner, on foot, to use the pay phone there. At Cliff's direction, she called the local police non-emergency line, and reported a dead body in a purple car. She gave the address, then she hung up and returned to the car to watch the fun. Knowles pulled down the street a bit more so as to be less obvious. Within five minutes a marked unit came rolling around the corner from Hamilton Avenue. It squeezed past the double-parked truck and pulled into the parking lot. The officers opened their doors carefully, and crouched as they exited the squad car. The driver of the illegally parked truck came scurrying out of the office building, where he had been delivering bottled water, the big ones used in office water coolers, and loaded the empties on his truck. One cop yelled at him to get out of there or he'd get a ticket. The driver saw the two officers with hands on gun butts, and, deciding discretion was the better part of valor, took off as fast as the lumbering truck could move. The officers approached the Oldsmobile from the rear, moving cautiously from side to side, in case someone was springing a trap on them. As the one on the left side of the car got to the driver's door, he stopped and put his ear to the window. Then he stood up straight, disgust showing on his face. He was obviously telling his partner this guy was just taking an after-lunch nap. The other officer was talking into his lapel mike to run the car license plate. That was standard procedure, to check for wants and warrants. They discussed what to do for a minute or so, then the officer obviously received a response on his radio. They seemed to puzzle over it another minute or so. Knowles was laughing out loud by this point, and the other two agents were snickering. They knew the registration on the FBI car would look normal to an untrained eye, but would not look right to a police officer. The FBI used fake registration addresses. The two officers posted themselves to either side of the Olds once again, and one officer tapped loudly on the driver's window with his nightstick. Allen started, and sat bolt upright. He raised his hands when he saw the officers, although they had not commanded him to do so. They made him get out of the car, and the agents could see Q-ball fumbling with his credentials, dropping them on the ground once. At that point, Knowles started up his car, made a U-turn, and cruised by. The officers, facing away from the street, didn't notice them, but Allen saw Torres and Nguyen roll down their windows and wave that cute little fingertip-only wave as they drove off laughing. He knew he'd been had.

When they arrived back to the office, Knowles checked in at the command post. Stroaker was engrossed in paperwork. The SWAT teams were beginning to assemble in their staging areas. Everyone was on standby for the call to come in.

"The money is on its way down. The wire transfer's been completed." The Z-man said this nonchalantly, like it was routine business for him.

"Great," said Knowles. "No calls, nothing happen at the house?"

"No."

"Hello, Cliff," a female voice said from behind him. Knowles turned around to see Antoinette Bertinetti, the SAC's secretary. She was known as Toni to her friends, but better known among the mere mortals of the office as "AB." She bore a cup of coffee in one hand and a newspaper in the other. She placed both before Stroaker, leaning over to give him a decent view of her very considerable cleavage. Stroaker looked up, eyes hesitating en route to their eventual destination of eye contact, and beamed boyishly at her.

"Hi, Toni," Knowles replied. "Are you going to be with us for the duration?"

"I go wherever Mr. Stroaker needs me." She formed a mechanical smile.

"Great to have you here."

Bertinetti was feared even more than she was ogled. At 46 years of age, she was unusually young for an SAC's secretary. That post was normally filled by one of the most senior secretarial staff who had worked up from squad secretary. In most divisions the SAC's secretary was an ancient biddy who still refused to refer to anyone as "The Director" except J. Edgar Hoover. Several years earlier, though, the previous occupant of that position, a pleasant if plodding widow, had retired - been driven out, actually, by the tyrant who had been SAC at the time. He had been so demanding, so cruel in his criticisms, and so impossible to work for, that she had taken her pension from 44 years of service and retired to Oahu without looking back. That SAC had once taken a framed photo of the woman's son from her desk and thrown it in the trash can, simply because it had been on top of a memo he had been picking up. The secretary had been using the photo as a temporary paperweight because the air conditioning had been out of kilter, and blowing papers off her desk. The SAC couldn't be bothered to move it to another spot on the desk as he picked up the memo; he had just batted it into the trash when it got in his way. That had been the final straw. She had submitted her retirement papers the same day.

No one but Bertinetti had applied for the spot, so bad was the SAC's reputation. Only in her late 30's at the time, she had been junior to at least a half dozen other secretaries, but as is often the case in the FBI, even at high supervisory levels, the job went to the only person who had applied. Her typing and shorthand skills were very good, and she didn't complain about the ungodly hours that were expected of her. She worked very hard at keeping her incredible figure, and the SAC had seemed not to mind having her around. He had stayed a tyrant, but had softened his brutality a bit. He had soon left to become an Assistant Director, and Bertinetti had stayed. Stroaker was now the third SAC she had served. During the interim she had learned how to use, or abuse, her position. She dressed in tight sweaters or blouses with low necklines, and applied makeup with the skill of a television performer. There were rumors she had once had a face lift, but there was no question she was a fine physical specimen of womanhood. There had never been any direct evidence of hanky-panky with her bosses, and she was reportedly happily married to a general contractor named Lou. It was a known fact, though, that the contractor did plenty of remodel work on the homes of SAC's, and some in the office who knew construction said Lou was expensive and not particularly good. Knowles had once seen the Stroakers and Bertinettis dining together at a Palo Alto restaurant, and assumed his house was one in that category.

Knowles went to his office, grabbing his mail from the mail room on his way. At his desk Knowles looked through the day's bureaucratic detritus. Donate to the Combined Federal Campaign. The next firearms qualification was coming up in three weeks. A reply from New York on a lead Knowles had sent out five months earlier - faster than usual for New York. A flyer inviting all to come wish an agent well at his transfer celebration luncheon next week. Kim had put an updated telephone contact list in his slot. He ripped off the old one and stapled this one to the briefing packet. Then he checked his e-mail. There was nothing there that couldn't be deleted or left for later. Then came voice mail. There were eight messages waiting, mostly from agents complaining. Knowles could hardly blame them, since some of them had arrived at 6:30 a.m. expecting a normal day, and might now work until well past midnight. But he was experiencing the same schedule, and there was nothing he could do about it. If the agents could just arrange for the kidnapper to call at predictable and convenient times so they could all go home it would be most appreciated.

Rothman came charging into the office and scooted into his chair. "Cliff. Did you see who Stroaker brought down with him from the City? AB. The Awful Brafull herself You should see the blouse she's wearing. The top button looks like it needs serious reinforcements."

"She's married. Take a cold shower or something. If you're that horny you shouldn't have gotten divorced."

"Hey, my sex life has never been better. But this is different, this is AB. She's... she's... inhumanly convex if you get my drift."

"What about Fischer's secretary, excuse me, *administrative assistant*, Carlotta? You guys looked like you were ready to get up close and personal."

"We're going out for dinner on Saturday if this thing is over by then. That doesn't mean I can't enjoy other scenery."

Knowles rolled his eyes and shook his head like a parent chastising a teenager. They worked through their calls and paperwork, checking in at the command post periodically. An agent showed up about 3:00, told Knowles he had the language report, and headed to the CP to find Zwolinski. Knowles went to the command post to hear his briefing.

Stroaker came right to the point. "So, Don, do you have an analysis of the first tape?"

"I do. The professor has issued a written report, which I just got, hot off the fax machine. Here it is." He handed Stroaker the only copy.

Stroaker read it for a few minutes, flipping through the three pages rapidly. "Well, he's sticking by his Arabic analysis. 'The intonations may be indicative of Northern Mexican Spanish, but the consonantals demonstrate an unmistakable similarity to Arabic...' more mumbo jumbo, hmm here we go '....the speaker, in my opinion, is probably a native Arabic speaker attempting to imitate a Mexican accent. He has lived in the United States for at least three years, probably much longer, and is educated at a level equivalent to two years of college work at least.' This guy for real? Can he really tell an Arabic speaker trying to sound like a Mexican? I have a hard time buying that."

Zwolinski smiled slightly. He was not the type to contradict the boss. "It's hard to say. Does it make any difference? Will you do anything you wouldn't otherwise do if you know for sure whether he's Arab or Mexican?"

Stroaker said nothing. There was no need for him to commit himself, at least not to Zwolinski or anyone else in the Division. He would probably have to answer that question for the Bureau, though. They had gone to the trouble of having the tape analyzed, after all, and now would expect him to start some leads to follow up on the new information. He handed the report over to Z-man and looked at him expectantly. Z-man grunted and said to the SAC, "Let Cliff handle it. He's in charge of leads."

Stroaker handed the report to Knowles, who adjourned to his office. Knowles read through it several times with care. Finally he asked Rothman's opinion. He knew Tim well and trusted his views. Rothman said that he tended to trust the expert, but could not guarantee the analysis. After a prolonged debate, they agreed that leads would be set out to three or four agents in the division who worked Arab terrorism matters to check with their sources about any unusual activity, such as a small group that has disappeared or gone on vacation together recently, or talked about getting a lot of money together for something. Also, they were to ask if any of their compatriots liked to impersonate Mexicans or Latinos for any reason, or had talked of doing so. No mention was to be made to the informants of the kidnapping itself.

Knowles walked back to the command post and began to fill in the Suspect #1 sheet. Three of the butcher block pieces taped on the walls had been reserved for information on suspects as they became identified. Only the first sheet had any information filled in. The only entries so far were 'Male', 'English' by Language(s) and in the Comments section, 'foreign accent.' He filled in the Complexion line with 'dark' and the line for Hair, 'probably black'. Stroaker watched him do so, and nodded approvingly. Knowles's changes applied equally to Arabs and Mexicans, and so were acceptable. Knowles then turned to the Race section and added the words 'possibly Arab or Hispanic.' It was a bit vague, but you might as well give the street teams every bit of information you had. There is no harm in hedging your bets, either. He knew that every bit of information that matched a suspect encountered on the street would be one more fact that could be cited as legal justification for a stop or arrest.

When Knowles was done writing, the SAC's secretary walked over. "I hear you're doing some remodeling," she commented off-handedly.

"Oh, well, we're getting bids. We may not do it. Just, you know, seeing how much it would cost us to redo the kitchen." Where does this witch get her intelligence, he thought. NSA should hire her.

"You may not know it, but my husband Lou is a contractor. He specializes in kitchen remodels, in fact." She stretched luxuriously.

"Oh yeah?" Of course he knew it - everybody knew it - only it was bathrooms he specialized in the last time one of the SJRA agents was remodeling. "I don't know, Toni. Is that such a good idea to do business with friends? What if something went wrong and there was a dispute? I would hate for anything to mar our friendship."

"Cliff, what could go wrong? Lou's the best builder there is. Just ask Mr. Stroaker. Lou did his redwood deck. By the way, I just saw your commendation letter come through for that chip theft case last January. Good job. Work like that could get you a QSI next time around. If I weren't down here I'd be filing that right now. Yuck! There'll be a ton of filing to do when I get back."

Knowles got the point. AB controlled the personnel files. If she lost or misfiled a commendation letter, or just dropped a critical remark on the SAC when it came time to award QSI's, an agent could lose out on a raise. A QSI was a Quality Step Increase, a merit raise that accelerated the agent's seniority. It affected both pay and pension. There were always more agents nominated than awards to give out, and the SAC always made the final cut. He certainly looked in the personnel file to see how many commendations and statistical accomplishments an agent had during the rating period.

"Well, maybe I should get a quote from him, then. Do you have his card?" Of course she did. She handed one to him. Knowles noticed that there was an e-mail address listed, 'FBIBuilder@aol.com'. Using the FBI initials in advertising materials without approval from FBI headquarters was illegal, at least if it implied an endorsement by the FBI of the product or service. This was skirting the law.

"Great, Cliff. I'd love for Lou to be able to help you out. He hasn't worked in Los Altos before. That's a pretty high-rent district for an agent. But I know it's beautiful there. A Los Altos home should have a first-class kitchen."

He smiled at her wanly. He had no intention of hiring good old Lou, but he had to play the game to stay on her good side. He could always say later that he couldn't get the loan. "So you're married to a contractor? I would have guessed you'd be the type to marry an agent."

"Why? Just because you guys carry guns? You think us females can't protect ourselves? I can handle anybody." She spoke with a light-hearted tone, but it was obvious she believed what she said. "And I don't need a gun. I'd never let myself get kidnapped like this Fischer guy. If somebody tried it, I'd just let him have it with a ball-peen hammer." She made a convincing striking motion in the direction of Cliff's crotch to emphasize her point.

"Yeah? Would that be in the ball or in the peen?"

Bertinetti's eyes went wide for a moment. "Why, Cliff Knowles, I'm shocked to hear such language ... and from you of all people." The smile she unsuccessfully attempted to conceal belied her protestations. "I'm going to go work out on my lunch hour," she continued after a pause. "Is there a 24-hour Fitness around here? I have a membership that allows me to use any of them. Do you belong? If not, you could come as my guest. I'd be glad to sponsor you for a session. I just hope you don't mind my ratty old gym outfit."

Knowles had heard of her "ratty old gym outfit." It was a glistening Spandex marvel that had drawn more business to the health club chain than all the supermodels in the newspaper ads. Knowles knew at least four agents who had joined Toni's gym and timed their workouts just to watch her routine. This was her way of rewarding Cliff for caving on the remodel - he was accorded a prime ogling time and location.

"No, thanks, I don't have time today. I think one of the women on the drug squad uses that gym, though. Check with them."

"Okay, thanks, Cliff." She smiled warmly and walked past him out the door, brushing her breast firmly against his arm as she did so. The booby prize. Knowles had heard rumors about this occasional benefaction of hers, but had never seen it happen, much less been the recipient.

Knowles, Rothman, and Olson went to dinner in Olson's car. They headed for an all-you-can-eat place nearby and found a table. Knowles recounted the episode with AB, to the great amusement of the other two.

"I'd be peering in the window of the gym right now instead of wasting my time with you two," Rothman allowed. "If only you'd told me about this sooner."

"You aren't man enough for that kind of a woman," Olson responded. "She'd drain every ounce of your precious bodily fluids like a spider eats a fly. There'd be nothing left of you but a withered shell."

Rothman sank into a momentary reverie. "Maybe so," he said wistfully, "but what a way to die."

"Seriously," Olson continued, "stay out of her way while she's down here. She's dangerous."

Knowles recognized a certain gravity in Olson's expression that went beyond the normal supervisory words of wisdom level. "I have the feeling you aren't telling us everything. What should we know, Ben?"

Olson shifted uneasily in his seat. "Okay, this didn't come from me, understand?"

A hush descended over both agents, and they immediately nodded gravely.

"You know Roger Ardsley?"

Rothman shook his head no, but Knowles nodded affirmatively. "Sure, the Mormon guy with eight kids. He quit to go back to Utah and be an accountant because he couldn't afford to live out here. He worked FCI up in the city. We did some surveillances together on an espionage case."

"He didn't quit voluntarily," Olson said ominously. "That was the public story, but the reality was he was forced out. He had such a big family he couldn't rent or buy anywhere near the city. He was living in some run-down farmhouse north of Santa Rosa. He had about a two-hour commute each way, but he stuck it out for over four years, and was finally about to get transferred to Santa Rosa RA. Stroaker had already told him he was going to get the slot when Butch Feeney retired. He was happy as a clam. No way he was going to quit." Olson took a bite of his food and chewed deliberately.

"So come on, what happened?" Rothman pressed.

Olson lowered his voice even more. "Well, it seems he had a run-in with AB. He'd been recommended by his supervisor for FSI, the Foreign Service Institute run by the State Department, and had the seniority for it. He was supposed to be the candidate for San Francisco that year, and we only get a slot about every three years. But AB didn't get the communication back to HQ in time with our nominee, and San Francisco forfeited the slot. Not only did he miss the school, which is a prestigious one, but his brother was getting married in Maryland that same weekend the school started, and he could have flown at government expense. He ended up not being able to attend the wedding because he just couldn't afford to fly out there."

"I can't believe he'd quit over that," Knowles opined.

"He didn't. What happened is he went into the front office and read AB the riot act when he found out how she'd screwed up. She offered a perfunctory apology, but it wasn't enough for him. He called her an incompetent bitch in front of the ASACs' secretaries and stormed out. That was his mistake. Some time in the next week or so an anonymous caller told the OIG that there was an FBI agent committing time card fraud."

"The Office of the Inspector General at Main Justice?" Rothman asked.

"Yep. Half those guys are FBI rejects. They're always itching to catch one of us at something. They resent the fact that our own Inspection Division does internal investigations of misconduct."

"I know a guy at the OIG," Knowles broke in. "He's not a bad guy. He's a former Buagent, in fact. He left the Bureau because he got fed up with some of the internal politics."

Olson looked at him askance. "Don't let any brass hear you say that. Main Justice is the sworn enemy of the FBI in their minds. Anyway, whoever dropped the dime on Ardsley apparently gave them a perfect description of him and listed the license number and parking place of his car in the basement of the federal building. The OIG isn't authorized to investigate us, but they called out to someone in the U.S. Attorney's Office to check it out before referring it to our people. Their local goon had no trouble documenting Ardsley's time in and out for a week. Building security cameras would confirm it, anyway. When it was referred to us they already knew they had him cold, because he was leaving early by about an hour every day. The U.S. Attorney came to Stroaker and told him he was considering filing criminal charges for Fraud Against the Government. Justice wasn't about to let the Bureau sweep this under the rug."

"Wait a minute. I worked with Ardsley. I don't believe he would defraud the government. He used to work straight through lunch. He couldn't afford to eat in restaurants like the rest of us, so his wife would pack him a baloney sandwich. He'd sit at his desk and eat it while he read, or he'd eat in the car during a surveillance. He was a hard worker."

"I'm not questioning that, but you know the government. You're charged with 45 minutes of personal time for lunch whether you take it or not. You can't work through lunch and take the time off at the end of the day. But that wasn't his excuse anyway. When we did the investigation, he admitted leaving early, but said he dictated his work into his Dictaphone during his commute home. He'd put on his timecard the time that he finished his dictation. He was working every minute he put on his timecard in addition to whatever he donated by working through his lunch. You know FCI; there's a ton of paperwork, more than enough dictation to account for the hour he left early. He offered to take a polygraph to substantiate it."

"Hey, that's credible," Knowles huffed. "He's not the only agent who's dictated during his commute. I've ..."

"Don't finish that sentence, Cliff," Olson cut him off. "He worked FCI, remember?"

Rothman looked quizzically at Olson, but Knowles got the point immediately. Foreign counterintelligence work was classified. If

Ardsley's story was true, of which Knowles had no doubt, that meant the information on the dictation tape was classified even though it wasn't yet on paper or marked as classified. Knowles knew that Ardsley was too conscientious to dictate anything really sensitive in an outside environment like his car, where the tape could get compromised. But he knew also that FCI supervisors overclassified everything. You couldn't say the sky was blue without them slapping a CONFIDENTIAL stamp on it. Technically, if the documents Ardsley was dictating got marked as classified after being typed, he was violating national security laws by "removing" the information from the office while dictating in his car.

Olson resumed, "At first it looked like Ardsley was going to come out okay. But right after the investigation that Chinese physicist case at Los Alamos broke into the headlines. Here we were prosecuting a scientist for removing classified information from one part of a classified facility to another, and one of our own agents was taking classified information home - or at least it could be made to look that way."

"Bullshit!" Knowles exploded. "That scientist lied to get his hands on information, top-secret nuclear weapons information, that he had no right to in the first place. And he lied to investigators about it after the fact. I doubt Ardsley even had access to top secret stuff, and he told the truth when asked. This was information in his head already. We all take home the information in our brains that we learn from our work. I'm sure if he dictated in the car, it was about as sensitive as the daily astrology column in the paper. Trying to equate what he did with the Chinese case is ridiculous."

"Keep your voice down!" Olson ordered. "You may be right, but Ardsley was screwed in any event. The Inspectors figured out that they were stuck with a story that was worse than the original allegation, even though everybody knew he was innocent of any intentional wrongdoing. Fortunately, because the U.S. Attorney had told the SAC they were contemplating criminal charges, Ardsley had been interviewed after receiving the administrative warnings, not the Miranda warnings. He was required by law to answer without an attorney so they could take disciplinary action quickly, but that meant it couldn't be used against him criminally. Since they couldn't prove any other way than his own statement that he'd 'removed' the information, he was safe from prosecution on the classified information matter. The fraud charge required criminal intent, and the

SAC told the U.S. Attorney that the agent had proven he was doing work in his car, so he was safe from that as well. But he couldn't get out from under the classified information problem; he'd still violated security rules and was subject to discipline. The SAC told him that if he stayed in the Bureau the least punishment he could expect was demotion two steps and loss of the transfer to Santa Rosa, and there was a good chance he'd get fired. Ardsley couldn't risk it, so he pulled the plug himself. And here's the real kick in the balls. AB came to his going away luncheon and left him a card on the table that said simply 'Bon Voyage.' It was her unmistakable handwriting, but you know how she initials everything 'AB'? - on the card she initialed it 'IB'."

"'Incompetent Bitch'," breathed Rothman. "Her way of telling him she had done it to him as payback. Did anyone ever prove who the source for the OIG was?"

"No. It was an anonymous call. There was nothing in writing, and apparently it wasn't recorded. The OIG refused to say whether it was a man's or a woman's voice, claiming confidential informant privilege."

They ate in sober silence for several minutes contemplating the deviousness of it all. Eventually the mood lightened. Rothman mentioned that Stroaker was going to have his own helicopter for the payoff. It would be using the Valley Medical Center helipad for its local takeoff point. VMC was almost right across the street from the FBI office.

"You're kidding!" Knowles responded. "What's he going to do with a helicopter? Chase the kidnapper personally?"

"To fly him to the on-site command post wherever it ends up moving to, near the drop site somewhere."

"Christ, how can he tie up the helipad? What if there's a Medevac coming in?"

"No problem," Rothman answered. "The hospital doesn't use it."

"Huh?" Olson countered. "I know I've heard helicopters come in there a few times."

"They have another one on the roof. That's the one they use. The one we'll be using is in the back about 30 yards from the emergency entrance."

This time it was Knowles who had to ask, "So why do they have two? Some boondoggle to rip off the taxpayers?"

"They built the first one at ground level, and used it for awhile. Then the ambulance drivers went on strike - they're Teamsters, you know - and got a clause in the contract that said only their union members could transport patients from any emergency vehicle on the hospital grounds into the hospital building. The management didn't realize that this was a trick clause, so they agreed to it. They thought it just meant the ambulance drivers would wheel the patients the last few yards from the ambulance to the door - no big deal, they were doing that anyway. Then after it was signed, the union demanded to have union drivers on call for every emergency flight in. The helicopter was an emergency vehicle on the grounds, and the clause applied. They took it to arbitration and won. Since the hospital couldn't predict when Medevac flights would come in, the hospital had to pay two paramedics to be on duty 24 hours a day just to roll the gurney 30 yards from the helipad to the emergency entrance a couple of dozen times a year. They didn't even drive an ambulance. Of course, the ER staff could have done it for no extra pay. It was costing over $200,000 a year for this."

"So they built another helipad on the roof so that it was no longer 'on the grounds'?" Knowles finished the story for him.

"You guessed it. The new helipad cost about $150,000, but it was still cheaper than using the old one and paying the wages. Medevac patients now get wheeled through the roof access door, which wasn't designed for it, and wrestled down the service stairwell to the closest elevator. It's more dangerous and less comfortable. And, of course, the paramedics aren't even getting the pay now. It's just $150,000 out of the taxpayers' pockets because of the union."

Knowles smiled. The irony of this remark struck him, because Rothman was the biggest advocate of the FBI Agents Association, and always harping on him to join. Federal law enforcement officers were forbidden by law from belonging to a union, so they called it an association. It acted like a union in every important way except striking and collective bargaining. They went to bat with their lawyers for every drunkard or lazy bum of an agent who was disciplined or fired. Knowles called it the FBI Crybabies Association whenever he wanted to get a rise out of Rothman. "Yeah, those unions are scum all right. Public safety should come before any individual employee's pocketbook. What was the name of that union again, the Ambulance Drivers' Association?"

The gibe was not lost on Rothman. He quickly took umbrage and stuttered a protest. "That's not the same thing at all. These guys were putting their own pocketbooks before people's health. We just stand up for agents who are getting screwed."

"Oh, right. I didn't mean anything by it."

Olson smiled as he watched the needling. This kind of camaraderie was what he liked about the FBI. Everybody was under tremendous pressure, and they needed to lighten up a little. They finished their meal and headed back to the RA. En route Olson pulled through the VMC parking lot to take a look at the helipad. Rothman pointed out all the features of the pad, the special lighting, the severe trimming of the nearby trees, the safest route in to avoid wires, the most dangerous features of the terrain. There were scores of considerations that a trained pilot had to think of that the rest of the world never even noticed.

When they got back in the RA, Tobin was in the command post with a large duffel bag. No one else was there. Tobin groused, "Where the hell is everybody? I thought we had a kidnapping in progress. This place is empty. I can't just leave $650,000 lying around, and I've got to take a leak."

Stroaker, Morales, and the Z-man had apparently gone out to eat. They were likely to come back well-lubricated. AB was at her workout, but Kim and Belinda were around. They were just as trustworthy as any agent, but they weren't armed, and the MIOG was clear that ransom money was to be in the control of an armed agent at all times except when it was locked in an approved evidence safe. Tobin could have found an FOA to watch over it while he ran to the bathroom, but he didn't want to trust it to anybody he didn't know was assigned to the case.

"We'll watch it," Olson said. "Go take your leak."

Tobin hurried out, obviously in distress. The three of them peeked gingerly into the duffel. All they could see were swaths of plastic. They decided not to poke through it, since they didn't know how much doctoring had already been done to it. Several agents saw them fiddling with the bag and came in to see it. This was more money than most of them were ever likely to see in one place. They all commented about what they could do if they had that much money. The buzz level rose in the room to the point where regular business became impossible. Then Tobin returned and snapped at the agents to keep their paws off. They reluctantly broke up the group and moseyed on back to their desks, still talking about how they could finally buy a house in Silicon Valley with that kind of dough.

"So how does the loot get tracked?" Olson asked Tobin.

"It's got eight features we can use. First, the serial numbers are all recorded and entered into the Federal Reserve computer system. Large bills are frequently scanned by banks, and they have machines that read the serial numbers and can check them against a data base. Every one of these is in that data base. Two, they're all photographed on both sides. That way, any bills that have distinct markings, torn corners, and so on, can be easily compared and identified. Three, we put exploding dye canisters in the bundles, like they do for bank bait packs. Only these aren't set to go off when they leave the vicinity of the bank. They go off when the pack is opened. Four, we have a radio transmitter which puts out a beacon that can be tracked on Bureau channels. I can't put that in until the last minute because it's very small and needs a fresh battery when the payoff run starts. Five, an infrared heat source, a whole string in fact. They look black to the eye, but put out enough heat to be identifiable through night vision goggles. We call 'em sparklers. These are scattered all over the exterior of the package; they won't work from the inside. We have to wait for the caller to tell us what kind of package he want it in before we can attach these. Six, is this baby. Don't open it." He pulled out a solid-looking metal jar with the yellow and black danger sign used for radioactivity. "This is an isotope that decays rapidly, so it's harmless to humans unless you swallowed a whole bunch of it or something. You can follow the traces through the air with a Geiger counter if you lose the trail. It's slow, but it works - they say. Seven, is an audible alarm. When this pack of bills is opened, a screamer goes off, kind of like one of those air horns they use at games only smaller. And eight, this is supposed to be the killer. This is new." He showed the agents a small plastic vial with a clear liquid in it, less than a teaspoon. "This is a pheromone. It's for some kind of butterfly that I can't pronounce, but it's supposed to be mating this time of year in California. This is another last minute thing. Just a drop here and there. It's super powerful, according to the lab guy. This was flown out just for this case. It's been tested at Quantico, but never on a real case. They have two other pheromones they've synthesized, but the fauna is different here, they say, so they can't use those. At least it's spring; that's supposed to help. Let's just hope it doesn't stink to high heaven. It only works if the wind is below five miles an hour, though, because the butterflies won't take off in a wind any stronger than that. They can't fly upwind."

The crew inspected all the gadgets. It was obvious that they would need some time to apply all the tracking technology once the drop instructions were given. They all hoped the caller would give them the time.

Street teams had reassembled and taken positions by mid afternoon. The lead agents were still reviewing the security tapes from the antique store parking lot. Izawa and the radio techs were working on the car that would be used for the drop. Now there was not much else to do but wait.

Chapter 14

The phone rang at 7:33 PM. Pam Fischer answered it. Luciana Malarna deftly picked up the extension to listen in on the call, and took notes as the call progressed. Louellen Murphy sat next to Pam to keep her on track and remind her of anything she forgot. Ron Jemperson used the other phone line to notify Pac Bell to start the trace.

Luciana took notes furiously. She paused and picked up the cell phone and called the command post with the preprogrammed autodial button. "We're live," she whispered, shielding the other receiver from her voice. "They're tracing. The caller is playing a tape from the victim. He says the *Chronicle* headline is about an Abortion Law... sophisticated equipment...caller on again, same voice as yesterday.... make sure not to get followed. Hold on." A long pause ensued. "Pam says the money will be ready by eight tonight. Now the caller says how can the money be ready. Eighty thousand in checking...fifty thousand in savings. He's questioning her on where she got the money. She says from her father's stockbroker." Malarna would listen for a few seconds, jot notes, then whisper the gist of it to the command post. "Pam says her mother isn't doing well. He says listen...go buy white T-shirt, jacket, and backpack. Money will go in the white backpack. She's trying to get him to accept a courier. He refuses - says it has to be her. Use the Jaguar. She says it won't start - can she use the Cadillac? He says how about the VW. She says her boyfriend has it. He says listen, do as I say. She's crying. He'll call tomorrow after six. Have white outfit ready. She agrees. He says they'll release the father in Mexico once the money is safely in their control. Where she asks. The city. What city, San Francisco? Yes. He'll call tomorrow." She stopped talking.

The group that was gathered around the speaker phone in the command post let out a collective sigh of relief when the call ended. They had been given a payoff day and a time, and they had at least a day to do what they had to do. In his softest voice Stroaker asked Malarna if the ransom call was over. She confirmed that it was. He then raised his voice and almost bellowed in Tobin's direction, "So where did the trace come back to? That call was over five minutes long. We should have it by now."

Tobin was on the line with the Pac Bell security man on the other phone in the corner - the same one he had used for the previous call. He was starting to raise his voice, too. The others in the room looked over to him, listening to his end of the conversation. Stroaker got up from his chair and walked over to that phone. He pushed the Hands Free button to put the conversation on the speaker for everyone to hear.

TOBIN: We need that number now, not this lame excuse....

PAC BELL: It was the M29 net, I'm telling you, from the Watsonville feed.

TOBIN: What's the M29 net?

PAC BELL: The old-style manually-switched net used for some of the older pay phones. It didn't come from a regular line.

TOBIN: Yeah, of course he used a pay phone. What'd you expect? What's the number and where is it?

PAC BELL: That's what I'm trying to tell you. We can't trace on the M29 net. It's not on a regular switch. We'd have to put a tech at every substation with an M29 junction router to read the line numbers manually.

TOBIN: You're shitting me! I told you we had to trace this to rescue a hostage, and you say you didn't put the manpower out to trace it?

PAC BELL: You never told me it was going to be an M29.

TOBIN: I've never heard of M29. I just told you we had to trace it no matter what or where. You might've just gotten this guy killed.

PAC BELL: The call is somewhere in the billing system if it's a pay phone. It came in from the Watsonville feed, so it's south of here anyway. You'll get it in the morning when the transactions are posted to the main data base.

TOBIN: That's not good enough. Tomorrow is the drop instructions call. We have to know exactly where that call is coming from in real time no matter what, you hear me?

PAC BELL: Well, if he's using an M29 pay phone, I'd have to put a tech at every substation like I said. Who's going to pay for that? That's over $10,000 a night in overtime. I don't have that kind of money in my budget. I want you to commit in writing to pay for it.

TOBIN: You cheap bastards! You're going to let this guy get killed because you're too cheap to man the goddam posts? GTE has an operator and a tech standing by their Bay Area switch right now for as long as it takes. The employees volunteered to do it for no pay when they found out it was a kidnapping. They say they can identify the pay phone within thirty seconds if it's one of theirs.

PAC BELL -- Well, we don't work that way. We're a business. You want our services you pay for 'em. We aren't a charity. What can I do? GTE only has one main Bay Area switch - we've got dozens of substations. I can't be everywhere, or I'd do it myself.

TOBIN -- Listen to me. If you're a business, then you tell your "business" manager that he has a "business" decision to make. Tomorrow night, if we can't trace that call because he's too cheap to pay for the manpower, that hostage could be killed. That hostage is worth about $15 million a year. I will personally testify at the civil trial when they sue Pac Bell for that much, plus punitive damages, and I'll tell them you said it was a business decision to take that risk rather than pay some blue collar guy overtime. That should go over real well with the jury.

PAC BELL (long sigh). Okay, you've made your point. I'll see what I can do. But there's no way I can get you that number tonight. It's in never-never land until it's posted to the main data base. I'll get it to you in the morning.

Stroaker shook his head slowly back and forth. His fists unclenched. From across the room Knowles could have counted Stroaker's pulse from the tiny throbs visible along his temple. Stroaker was still powerfully built, and Knowles could see why he had been a formidable football player. Mr. Pac Bell Security was better off not being in the room just then.

"Okay, I guess that's it for tonight," Stroaker said, refraining from any mention of Pac Bell. "I want everybody fresh tomorrow. It looks like that's going to be game day. I want everybody to be able to give 110%. Call off the street teams and everybody else. Tell them to rest up. We'll meet here at 1:00 PM for a briefing. I want all the team leaders, SWAT, SOG, everybody who's critical, to be here. That still gives them time to get back to their area and stage or prep."

Knowles began radioing or phoning each street surveillance team to relay the instructions. They were happy to get cut loose early. Most of them asked where the call had come in from. They were just told it was near Watsonville, and not to worry about it - it was covered. There was no point in telling them the Pac Bell story. They were frustrated enough already from just waiting around in their cars.

At the Fischer house, Louellen Murphy was pepping up Pam, telling her what a terrific job she had done. This was not just puffery; Murphy knew that the call had been a big success. Pam had convinced the caller that she had to drive the Cadillac, or it looked like it, at least. That was quick thinking about the boyfriend having her car; no one had anticipated that the caller would know what kind of car Pam drove. They had also succeeded in getting the caller to specify a time when the call would come in, and how he wanted the money packaged. They could begin to prepare now. The hostage was safe, based on the recording. The caller was suspicious about the money, about who was handling it and telling her it would be ready. He could have smelled a rat, but Pam had acted so sincere that he seemed to have bought it. The location information was confusing - how could the hostage be released in San Francisco an hour later if he were being held in Mexico? The caller was lying about something, but what? The intention to release him when it's over? Mexico? Murphy knew it was a dangerous situation.

"Come on, girl, we have to get you some white clothes. The stores are still open. Finding that white backpack might be difficult, though." Pam dried her eyes and grabbed her purse. They left by way of the backyard, out what had come to be known as "the FBI entrance" through the gate to the side street, and hopped in Murphy's car. They drove straight to Stanford Shopping Center.

Day 4
Friday

Chapter 15

Even though he had gotten to bed early the previous night, Knowles slept a bit later than usual. He knew it would be a long night, and he had seen in previous all-nighters how some really bad decisions had been made by agents who were simply too slow-witted to function right. As he drove in he could heard radio traffic that told him things were already in an elevated activity status. There were no overt references to any kidnap situation, but an alert listener could have figured out something big was up. There were just too many people talking to too many other people.

When he got to the RA, it was almost 8:00. Stroaker and AB were already there, as was the Z-man, Morales, and Mike Bean, the radio tech. It seemed that there had been a problem with one of the repeaters - the one on Mount Umunhum - and Bean had had to drive up the mountain road to replace a circuit board at 5:30 in the morning. After checking in, Cliff headed to his desk and went through the regular mail and message ritual.

Kim came into his office about 9:00 with the typed transcript of the previous night's call. Knowles began to read:

FISCHER -- Hello?

MALE -- Is this Pam?

FISCHER -- Yes. Who is this?

MALE -- This is the same person who spoke to you yesterday. Now listen. I got a tape for you, and new tape that proves your dad is still alive.

FISCHER -- Okay.

MALE -- I want you to get a piece of paper and a pen, and get back ASAP, because you're gonna have to record some stuff.

FISCHER -- Okay, I'm ready.

MALE -- Okay. Listen very carefully. Uh, one second...

FISCHER -- I don't hear anything.

MALE -- Yeah, hold on.

FISCHER -- Hello? Is anybody there.

MALE -- Hold on, I said. Okay, here.

RECORDING

Pam, to show you that this tape is being made today, which is Thursday, uh, the headline in the morning *Chronicle* says that "San Francisco Judge Strikes Down Abortion Consent Law." I'm very sorry that you're in this position. But you have to realize that my life is in your hands and I ask you not to gamble with it, or with your own. These people are very serious and they have sophisticated equipment. I know they're asking you to withdraw money. Please follow their directions. Don't contact the authorities. They really don't want us to jeopardize our lives or the lives of anyone that we love. Again, I'm very sorry. I love you very much.

MALE -- Hear that?

FISCHER -- Yes, I did. Is my dad, .. he's okay?

MALE -- Your dad is alive and is all right -

FISCHER -- Can I talk -

MALE -- and is being treated well. Now you listen to me very carefully. When you draw that money from the bank or from anywhere -

FISCHER -- The money is all set.

MALE -- Listen. When you get the money, make sure you're not being followed by anybody. Anybody follows you, that means you're in trouble, your dad is in trouble. Make sure the bank is not getting suspicious.

FISCHER -- Okay.

MALE -- The money is ready already?

FISCHER -- Yes, it's ready. Well, it will be ready by eight o'clock this evening. They're trying to get it all together. The banks, I mean. I won't be able to get it until then.

MALE -- How is that possible? Your dad had eighty thousand dollars in his checking, fifty thousand in his savings, and plus ...

FISCHER -- It takes awhile to get it, and I had to get one-hundred dollar bills.

MALE -- Okay, so the money is ready by - by eight o'clock?

FISCHER -- Yeah, they told me it would be ready.

MALE -- Who? Who told you?

FISCHER -- The people who my mom talked to - the stockbrokers, uh, the bank.

MALE -- Tell me everything your dad has and where you got it. We know everything about your dad and what he has.

FISCHER -- I got, or my mom got it really, but I picked it up, the money from my dad's stockbroker. The bank had some, but not enough, so we had to get it from the stockbroker, Michael somebody. My mom knows.

MALE -- Good. Six-hundred and fifty thousand dollars all in one hundred dollar bills?

FISCHER -- Yes.

MALE -- Good. Now you listen to me. Uh.. We know everything....

FISCHER -- It's, ... you're killing us with this situation. Do you realize what you're doing to us?

MALE -- I realize this, but you listen to me.

FISCHER -- My mom is having a really hard time, you could take both my parents from me..

MALE -- Listen. I'm sorry about your mom, but you listen to me. Tomorrow you will go, or today you will go and buy white pants, white T-shirt, and a white jacket, and a big backpack, like the kids use for school.

FISCHER -- What kind, like a..

MALE -- It doesn't matter as long as the money fits in it. You are to put all the money in that backpack, okay?

FISCHER -- Do I have to, I mean, my mom was asking do I have to do this? We could get a courier or somebody from the company. I don't know if I can do this.

MALE -- Don't! Now look, do you want to see your dad again? You have to make the drop, and using your mom's Jaguar. Make sure the car -

FISCHER -- It's, I have to tell you, I'm trying to tell you, the car won't start. I don't know what's wrong with it. Can I use the Cadillac?

MALE -- How about your beetle? I know you have a VW beetle. Nobody else can make that drop. I'm telling you we don't want to have to hurt nobody, but if we have to we will. I know what you look like. We have your picture. Nobody but you.

FISCHER -- I don't have my car. My boyfriend has my car.

MALE -- Don't give me shit! Okay? (unintelligible) Okay, use the Cadillac.

FISCHER -- Okay.

MALE -- Now cut the bullshit. I'll call you tomorrow. Make sure you have the money.

FISCHER -- What time are you going to call? I don't know how long I can take this.

MALE -- Pam? Look, you listen to me. You do exactly like I say, and I don't want to hear no crying. Okay?

FISCHER -- Okay.

MALE -- Have your white clothes ready tomorrow and I'll call you after six o'clock.

FISCHER -- Okay. Tell my dad we love him, and -

MALE -- Okay, enough. Just make sure the money is there if you want to see your dad.

FISCHER -- Are you going to release my dad right after I give you the money?

MALE -- We'll release him in one hour after (inaudible). See, your dad's in Mexico.

FISCHER -- But you're going to release him right after I give you the money?

MALE -- Exactly, yeah

FISCHER -- Where are you going to bring him to?

MALE -- No. It'll be in the city.

FISCHER -- The city? San Francisco?

MALE -- Yes.

FISCHER -- Is he alive?

MALE -- He's alive. What do you mean, is he alive? Didn't you hear him? The *Chronicle*, he read the headline. Don't bullshit me. Are you trying -

FISCHER -- Okay, okay

MALE -- Okay, now I'm telling you, don't gamble with your dad's life.

FISCHER -- Okay.

MALE -- I'll call you tomorrow. Be home after six.

FISCHER -- Okay. bye.

END OF CONVERSATION

Knowles strode quickly back toward the command post. There was a lot of material here to digest. Three or four heads were better than one on these things. He knew Kim had a stack of transcripts in her hand when she gave him his, so that meant the rest of them had copies.

But Just before he got there, Nguyen stopped him. "Cliff, I think we may have something from the videotapes. It's not real clear, but it's something." Knowles followed Nguyen back to the tech room at the other end of the office. There was a video player, multiplexer and tiny black-and-white monitor set up there. The lead agents had been taking turns going through the tapes from The Big Brown Farmhouse. Nguyen rewound the first tape to a specified point he obviously knew by the counter number. "The time shown on the tape is wrong, but we've done the math three times. We timed how much the clock is off when we were there. This has to be the correct time - the time of the phone call, I mean. The first car to pull out of that lot is this one here." He pointed to a dark shape half cut off by the edge of the frame. "This is it pulling south onto 101. It leaves within one minute of the end of the call, if we've calculated right. There are no more cars leaving the lot for the next four minutes. I don't think I'd hang around four minutes if I'd just placed a ransom call."

"Okay, agreed. But you can't see a license plate, color, or make of the car. What good is this?"

"Yeah, but look. Let me go back. I showed you the frame of it leaving. If you back up the right amount of time, the length of the call, and start looking backward, you can see that same car pull in." He rewound the tape some more. First he showed Knowles the frame immediately preceding the one of the car pulling onto U.S. 101. It showed that the car was parked in an area off to the right of the camera view, because it was moving from the far right into the field of vision. The angle was too straight down to identify the car, but at least it showed where the car had been parked. Then Nguyen put it back to a point several minutes earlier. "This is about three minutes before the beginning of the call. Here is the same shape moving into that same parking area. You can't see it park - it's off-screen, so you can't be 100% sure, but we think it's the same car. There are no other vehicles that match the one leaving which came in during the ten minutes before the call." He sped through three minutes of tape and stopped. "See that's the moment the call started."

Knowles scowled. It was really hard to tell whether they had it right, even if their time calculations were correct. "Boy, I just can't be sure." He replayed the sequence himself several times. There were a few other vehicles pulling into the lot during the ten- minute span, but they didn't match the dark sedan that had pulled out right after the call. There were two SUV's, a pickup, and a Mazda Miata. He looked at Nguyen's notes from the clock test at the site, and agreed that they had worked out the time sequence correctly. That dark sedan was the only vehicle that had entered shortly before the call and left just after. "Okay, I'm with you. But it still doesn't do much for us. It's just a dark sedan. The angle is too high to see the plates or even be sure of the make."

"We're pretty sure it's a Ford Taurus. Look at this." Nguyen wound the tape back one more time. "See this shape on the passenger window as it pulls in? I'm pretty sure that's one of those stickers that warn you it has an alarm. I think that's a rental car. I used to work part-time at an Avis lot when I was in college. All the rentals had those stickers on both sides, because that was company policy. But a Taurus is not a particularly expensive car, and I don't think many regular buyers would put an alarm system in and apply the stickers, so I think it's a rental. Anyway, it came from the south, and went back south. At least you can figure the direction. The color is dark, too, which might help. It could be dark blue, gray, maybe black."

"Hmm, you've got a better eye than I have, if you're right. It could be a Taurus, all right, but from almost straight down, they all look almost identical. Ford Escorts and *Mercury* Sables are virtual clones of the Taurus. They all have the same shape these days, the basic sedans, anyway. As for the bright spot, that could be a reflection off the glass, so far as I can tell."

"I think it's a little octagon, Cliff - the shape of a stop sign. That's the shape they use for those stickers."

"Well, I'll go with the car being the right car - a dark sedan. But going for Taurus and a rental car, that's more than I can accept based on this. It's too grainy and out of focus. I'll tell Stroaker your theory, though. Good work on going through the tapes. I know how tedious it is. How many cameras were there?"

"Two inside, two outside. This is the only one that picked anything up, but we had to watch all four."

"Good work." Knowles gave the young agent a pat on the shoulder as he left. To some it might have seemed to be a bit hokey, but it had the desired effect. The accolade from Cliff Knowles meant something to a probationary agent like Nguyen. It didn't take long for even the new agents to figure out who the real heavyweights were.

Knowles finished his trek to the command post. Stroaker, Z-man, Tobin, and Morales were all there discussing the meaning of several items in the transcript. Zwolinski spoke first. "Cliff, where you been? We were looking for you. Have you seen the transcript of yesterday's call?"

"Yeah, I saw it. I was just in looking at the videotape from the security camera at the antique store."

Stroaker looked up. "Antique store?"

"You know, The Big Brown Farmhouse, where the first call - first recorded call - came from."

"Oh, sure," Stroaker said as if he had known that, which clearly he hadn't. Apparently no one had bothered to tell him it wasn't a restaurant.

"Anyway, Nguyen and some of the other FOA's have identified the car on the tape. You can't get a plate or anything, but it's a dark sedan. And it came from south of that spot, and returned south."

"No plate and no make? Color or distinguishing marks?" Stroaker asked.

"No, except a bright spot on the front passenger window. Could be a reflection, but Nguyen thinks it could be a warning sticker like rental companies put on when there's an alarm in the car. He thinks it's a Taurus, but I don't think you can really tell from the tape."

"Not much use. I'll take a look later at the tape. What do you think of the transcript?"

Knowles knew that the SAC was genuinely interested in his analytical abilities. He had an urge to pontificate a bit, but didn't want to overdo it. "Well, for starters, I think this guy is a real amateur, in way over his head. He's lying through his teeth and not good at it. He's incredulous at Pam being able to get the money, and keeps asking her where she got it from, then says he knows everything about the father's money. In the previous call he referred to Pam's brother being in Illinois; I found out he's at Notre Dame, which is in Indiana. He couldn't even get the tape player to work. Pam almost thought he'd hung up. He says Fischer's being held in Mexico, then says he'll be released in San Francisco within an hour of getting the payoff. How is that going to happen - transporter beam? There's no way they took him to Mexico. He's somewhere in the Bay Area, or at least close. They had him read a *Chronicle*. That's not available in Mexico,

I suspect, and would be hard to find even in L.A. The guy is local. He referred to San Francisco as The City. People from outside the Bay Area don't, and that was spontaneous, too. He's been living around here."

Z-man jumped into the mix, "Yeah, I was saying the same thing. They have him here in the area. Just because the call came from the south, that doesn't mean that's where they're holding him. If he's going to be released in San Francisco, he could be north of here, but he's nearby."

"I agree," Stroaker replied. "We have to be prepared for anywhere in the division. I guess the girl got her white outfit last night, but we're having a helluva time finding a white backpack. If we can't find one, we'll have to make one out of canvas or something." Stroaker paused.

Knowles resumed, "Pam did a fantastic job of stalling him. That was a good ploy at the end about 'is my father alive,' but it made him suspicious. It's a shame about the trace. Has it come in yet?"

Tobin heard, and pointed to the corner phone, indicating that when Pac Bell had the number, they would call direct on that line.

"The drop is going to be after nine o'clock," the Z-man volunteered. "That's why the white outfit. He said he'd call at six, but it'll be a late drop. He wants to be able to see her well in the dark and be sure that's her, not some agent decoy."

"Pam'll have to drive the drop car herself," Stroaker said authoritatively. "If we try to put an undercover in, they'll be able to spot it. We're going to have to go with Pam."

Knowles agreed with this decision, although reluctantly. There was always a danger to have a civilian, especially a distraught family member, in the immediate vicinity when the action starts. But there had never been a case of a second family member being kidnapped or shot during the payoff, so far as he knew, at least not in the U.S. So it should be safe. If they put an agent in as a stand-in, the kidnapper might spot her and not make the pickup.

"Izawa can handle the bodyguard duty," Z-man resumed. He was always quick to tout his own squad members. "She'll be safe as long as she doesn't go far from the car. But we can't let her get out of the car and approach anybody. That'll risk a second hostage. If the final instructions involve carrying the money in somewhere, Terry'll have to do it."

"Absolutely. 'First, do no harm...'." Stroaker was always spouting what he considered to be his medical expertise from being married to an RN. "We may not be able to rescue the victim, but at least we don't have to lose another one."

Morales had been silent up to now, but shook his head at this one, and looked sideways at the SAC. That comment was a less-than-resounding endorsement of the FBI's abilities. "We'll get him, boss," he said. "My guys'll be in the tail car, and we'll make a perimeter of the drop zone. And we'll have air cover. They won't get through. If somebody picks up the money, we'll get him."

"I know, Mo. I have every confidence in you. But we don't know what this is all about. This guy Fischer could still be playing us. Maybe there is something fishy going on with the finances, and he's using this as a way to clean out his cash and run off. We just can't let this go on, and let the daughter get drawn into it."

Knowles couldn't believe it. Stroaker still wasn't convinced this was a real kidnapping, and he didn't sound very confident. Why couldn't he just go back to the front office? He was going to be nothing but trouble.

"While I have you and Mo here," Stroaker went on, "here's the surveillance plan. You'll have your street teams distributed throughout the division. Mo will have the SOG concentrating on the key places - they'll tail the Cadillac to the drop point, and deploy personnel around the money when it gets dropped. They will also surround the drop point before she gets there, with any luck, and be in position at the moment the drop is made to cover the perimeter, as Mo just said. They'll film the whole thing if possible. SWAT will be deployed there also, and will be the ones to move in close. If we have SOG in position, we'll surveil to see where the pickup man goes. If not, SWAT will just arrest as soon as the pickup is made. The street teams will leapfrog toward the direction of the drop. So if the drop is in San Francisco, for example, the street team in San Jose will move to San Mateo, past the Palo Altos team which will remain stationary, and the Palo Alto team then moves to the southern border of The City. The teams will be designated as odd or even, so all the odd-numbered teams move at the same time, then the even-numbered teams."

This leapfrog plan was a recipe for disaster. It was much too complex. But even worse was the idea of letting the pickup man go and then trying to follow him. Whenever that was tried, the guy was able to shake the tail. Surveillance is a lot harder than it looks in the movies, and is nearly impossible if you are following someone who suspects you are there and is trying to shake you while you are trying to be discreet. Standard procedure is to grab the person who picks up the cash - simple and effective.

"Pete," Knowles said tentatively, trying not to imply direct criticism of the SAC, "have you run the plan by HQ? I'd be interested to know their experience."

The Z-man stepped in, "They recommend arresting the pickup. And we'll do that if we don't have him locked up tight. We just want to see if there is a hand-off to a second person, jumping into a vehicle, and so forth. We want to get everybody. It could even be a courier sent to pick up the money, with the bad guys watching. We don't want to arrest some innocent dupe and blow the whole thing."

"If you're right about the pickup being late at night," Knowles said, "and I think you are, then they won't use an innocent pickup person. It's hard to get any kind of messenger or courier service after 9:00 PM on a Friday night. And if you don't arrest, we all know how easy it is to lose someone who is trying to shake you."

"Not in my division," Stroaker corrected him. "We have the finest people here. Mo has guaranteed me the pickup will *not* slip through the perimeter. We're going to have snipers in place, too, with night-vision scopes. If he tries to flee, they'll be able to see him. If we have to arrest, and he tries to shoot it out, we'll take him out."

The corner phone rang. Tobin picked it up, and wrote down a few lines. "Here's the traced number from yesterday. It's a pay phone in Aptos. I've got the street address." He flipped open the reverse directory for Santa Cruz County, kept on a shelf in the command post with all the other county cross directories. They're kept for just this type of situation. "It's a Chevron Station."

Knowles took the address and telephone number and headed out the door. As he left, he remarked, "That makes the last two calls south of here, and the video from the antique store shows the car going south. The victim is down in that direction - Monterey County or Santa Cruz County, probably."

"Could be, but the caller used a *San Francisco Chronicle* headline, not a *Mercury News* or Monterey paper, and said the release of the victim would be in The City. It could be anywhere." The Z-man was obviously hoping the drop would be in San Francisco, since his VCMO agents were the ones most likely to be called on to make the arrest if SWAT or SOG couldn't get to the pickup first.

Knowles took the lead to Nguyen and Torres. Since they seemed to enjoy this kind of lead, and had done a good job the last time, he'd give them another chance. When he found Gina Torres in her cubicle, she was stomping around fuming. Torres was not the kind of person to hide her feelings. Her mood tended to vary from perky to persnickety. Those inclined toward ethnic stereotypes might have said she had a fiery Latin temper, but they would have been wrong. Temper, yes, but despite her dark coloring and Latino father, her mother's side was Finnish, a nation known more for reserve and stoicism than excitability. When she wasn't bouncing around trying to cheer everybody else up, she was complaining about something or other. "What's the matter now?" he asked.

"I can't believe it. I was supposed to get off probation today. I've been on for six months like all the FOA's, but an hour ago, Tom Morris from SF called and said I was going to be kept on another six months because my training book isn't done. I never did a white collar interview. I thought the one with you on the chip fencing case counted for white collar, but he said it didn't because the case was carried by a VCMO squad."

Knowles was surprised. This was a pretty strict interpretation of the requirements. "That doesn't make sense. The case was being charged as both Wire Fraud, which is white collar, and Interstate Transportation of Stolen Property, which is VCMO. Just because it was being worked off the VCMO squad doesn't make it a violent crime. It was really a white collar kind of interview."

"I know. I checked with my training agent, and she said they've never been that strict before. That means I can't get my first raise on time. She says that if you're on probation at the time of the first step increase, which I will be, you're not eligible for it. I can hardly afford to live here with three roommates as it is. I really need that within-grade."

That's what tipped Knowles off. They wouldn't hold up pay increases for anything so minor. And he had never heard of such a rule about probation causing it anyway, only letters of censure. "Hmm, Tom Morris called you, did he?"

"Yeah, he's the First Office Agent training coordinator for the division."

"So I heard. He did applicant work for almost 15 years before they moved him over to FOA Coordinator. He's an old buddy of Q-ball, Gina. They've worked appys together for years." Then he stood up straight and shouted, "Q-ball, where are you hiding? Come out now, the game's up. You got her thinking this was real."

A bald pate slowly emerged over the top of the partition two cubicles over. He had been keeping low in the white collar squad secretary's cube. He was smirking gleefully as his full face appeared. He waved at Torres with a dead-on imitation of the dainty wave she had given him when the cops rousted him from his nap. He put his hands together and pretended to rest his head on them, like a child going to sleep, and then sank down again out of sight. Torres's face turned beet red as she realized she'd been punked, but there was nothing she could do. Payback time. Q-ball strolled out and said to Knowles, "I know that was your car, Cliff. I bet you're the one who called the cops on me. I got her, but I still owe you."

"Who me? Innocent I am, and that's my story. Anyway, please don't drive any of my FOA's to suicide until after this case, okay? I need them to do the grunt work. Then I'd have to ask for someone more senior. Someone who knows the territory - you, for example."

"Hey, I've got my assignment for tonight. I'm on one of the street teams down in Gilroy, as you well know. You don't need me to shag leads now. And I still owe you one."

Knowles just smiled and turned to Torres. "Gina, you and Nguyen need to run to Aptos and check out this phone. This is the second call - the one from yesterday. Same drill. Interview everybody, check for cameras, clues, whatever you see. Use your judgment. Take someone from ERT to do the prints and photograph the scene. Take Q-ball." Allen was also on the Evidence Response Team and knew how to lift prints.

Allen poked his head out again. "C'mon, Cliff. Can't you take a joke?"

"I'm not being a poor sport. This is for real. I need to have the prints lifted, and you're ERT."

"Okay. You need it, you got it," he grumbled. He grabbed his kit and slipped on a jacket to cover his gun. "Let's go." He and Torres took off in search of Nguyen.

Chapter 16

Carl Fischer heard the two men talking in another room. He moved his cuffed hands up to his mask and lifted the bottom edge enough to peek out. No one in the room. He couldn't see the cell phone anywhere, but it could be up on top of the table, and still functional. His muscles and joints were stiff from lying down for three days with few chances to stand and move. It hurt just to sit up on the mattress. He noticed his briefcase was in the corner by the door. They had moved it for some reason.

The muted conversation in the other room seemed casual; he couldn't make out any words. They must be speaking Spanish, he reasoned. Then he heard the sound of the screen door opening and closing. He slipped the mask back on. If Carlos was leaving, then Miguel might come back into the room. He waited several minutes, but heard nothing. Miguel was still not in the room. Then he heard the familiar sound of weights, probably dumbbells from the sound of the thumps, hitting the floor. Miguel had been looser with his guard duty in the last few hours, and obviously preferred working out. He'd probably be busy for a half hour or so.

Fischer peeked out again. If he was able to get free from the chains, how would he get out of the room? He craned his neck around the edge of the closet door to see the side of the room the closet was on. No door to the outside, just to the hall. But there were windows on two sides, and this was a first-floor room. If he could get out the window, he might be able to escape.

He slid the mask up to his forehead and lifted the lower ends of the adhesive tape covering the cotton balls. He left the top ends stuck on in case he had to replace everything in a hurry. Now he could see. He scooted up with bent knees so he could reach his ankles with his cuffed hands. He started working on the loosest wrap of chain, trying to slide it down over the heel. His abdominal muscles started to cramp, and he had to lie back and straighten out to make the pain stop. He repeated this process several times, each time being stopped by abdominal or leg cramps. Finally, with a mighty surge of effort, he slipped one loop over his heel. He thought that would loosen the whole arrangement, but he wasn't so lucky. That loop caught just below the heel on another loop around the other foot, and he started cramping again. He lay flat on his back and began kicking his feet in a rapid flutter kick. He tried to be vigorous, but silent. Once, the chains rattled more loudly than he had intended, and he panicked for a moment, thinking Miguel must have heard. He lay still for several minutes, but then he heard the distant sound of the weights hitting the floor again. After ten minutes of straining, he managed to get one foot free. Then came the other.

He stood up, and immediately his head swam. He had the presence of mind to drop to his knees and put his head down on the mattress so as not to pass out. If he were to fall to the floor from fainting, Miguel would certainly have heard. Slowly, he got up on hands and knees, then up on his knees. When his heartbeat went from pounding furiously to merely rapid, he slowly stood again. He was a little dizzy once more, so he just stood still for thirty seconds.

Finally he felt strong enough to venture out of the closet. He walked to the nearest window. It was covered over with butcher paper, the corners fastened with ordinary brown masking tape. He peeled back one strip of tape and lifted the corner. The glass was filthy, and it was hard to tell exactly what he was seeing. It was a yard, covered with dirt and weeds, and he could see a wooden fence about ten yards from the window. But he couldn't tell whether he was looking at a side yard or a back yard. There was an old tire and some scrap lumber. He peeled the paper back a bit more to try to figure out how to open the window. It was an aluminum casement frame, the kind that is hinged on one side, and operates with a small crank. He peeled off the other bottom tape strip so the entire bottom was now loose. As he got a better view of the second corner, he realized that the crank had been removed. There was just the ribbed metal nut protruding. The window was locked with a handle lever on the unhinged side that worked a small curved piece in and out of a slot in the metal trim around the pane. He lifted the handle, moving the tang out of the slot and freeing the pane to move. If only he had the crank, he could open it. He tried pushing on the window, and felt it give a little. The window opened slightly. He could tell, though, that without the crank turning the operator, the gear would strip, and it would probably be a difficult, noisy endeavor.

He decided to check the other window. He closed the handle again, but with the window slightly open, the tang didn't engage the slot. It looked locked, but wasn't. He couldn't close the window without a crank; he just had to hope no one would notice. He pulled the paper down again and stuck the tape back on the wall as best he could. He moved to the other window and quickly determined that it was no better than the first. He was sweating profusely by this time. He listened for the weights and panicked momentarily when he couldn't hear the familiar clunk. Then he heard them clinking, but not hitting the floor. Miguel was doing something that kept them suspended, like curls. Fischer regained his composure.

Despairing of getting out either window, he moved toward the door to see if he could slip out without Miguel seeing him. As he approached the doorway, he was able to see the side of his briefcase that had been turned away from the closet. There was a small brass plaque on the large side, near the handle, on which were inscribed his initials: CMF. The briefcase had been a gift from his children several years back. Directly below the initials he saw something that made his blood run cold. In large, crude letters someone had carved into the fine leather the words 'IS DEAD'. He literally staggered at the sight, and was unable to continue for a full minute.

No sooner had he recovered his breath than he heard the two dumbbells hit the floor, and footsteps approached the hallway. He slipped silently to the closet and leapt onto the mattress, just getting his feet out of sight as Miguel entered the room. If Miguel checked the chains, it would be obvious that he had managed to get out of them. He rolled over with his back to the room, fearing his facial expression, his unmistakable fear and sense of guilt, would betray him. Miguel seemed oblivious and simply parked himself in the chair again.

Carl Fischer lay there, able to think of nothing else but that one foreboding sentence: CMF IS DEAD.

Chapter 17

Olson entered the command post. "I've been at the off site where they're working on the cars. The Jag is a no go. There's no rear seat. Terry would have to sit in the passenger seat. The Cadillac has to be the one. We can't have her go in alone. We need Terry not only for protection but for communication. She can't be driving and using an unfamiliar radio, too. Let's hope the caller doesn't insist on the Jag or the Beetle. If he does, she'll just have to say okay but take the Caddy."

"That's what we were planning," Stroaker agreed.

Olson continued, "We've been scouring the division for a white backpack. There's no such animal. Backpacks get filthy in normal use, so they don't make 'em in white. We've come up with some white canvas sailcloth; if we have to use it we can, but it'll be hard to find someone who can turn it into a backpack." He dropped a blue backpack and a small white bookbag on the table. "This is the best we could do."

Kim came in to give Olson his copy of the transcript. He had been out of the RA when she had typed it. He thanked her, and she turned to go, when Bertinetti addressed her, "Kim, Mr. Stroaker would like some more coffee." She proffered the cup to Kim.

"The break room is just down the hall, first left, then left again." Kim was smiling, and her tone was cordial, but forced.

"I know where it is. He likes it with cream." She pushed the cup another inch forward.

Olson had been engrossed in reading the transcript, and only now noticed trouble brewing. Kim was a good secretary, but she had always made very clear that she was strictly business. She didn't do coffee, even for her own boss. He jumped up. "Here, let me get it. I was going to get some myself anyway."

Kim realized she was causing her boss to lose face in front of the SAC, but she was too angry to think straight. She spluttered for a moment, then snatched the cup from AB's hand. "Why can't you get it, AB? Too busy painting your nails?"

"Oh shit," Olson muttered under his breath toward Z-man, who sat riveted, taking it all in. Everyone called Bertinetti AB behind her back, but no one used that form of address to her face. They always called her Toni. The Awful Brafull moniker, used by many of the male agents, had not made it to Kim's ears. She had heard the "AB" nickname, but thought it just referred to the initials Bertinetti used on routing slips, for her name: Antoinette Bertinetti. This, of course, was part of the joke.

"I'm taking minutes of this meeting," Bertinetti said coolly, holding up her steno pad demonstratively. She hadn't made a mark on it in the last fifteen minutes, but Kim didn't know that. "If you knew shorthand you could be a good secretary yourself. But you can't take shorthand, you can't fetch coffee. Just what do you do for your boss, anyway?" She eyed Kim's skirt line suggestively.

Kim was four inches taller than AB, and had long, gorgeous legs. Young, single, and still available, she wore short skirts that showed them to good advantage. Olson was known for his womanizing, but never with the office help. He was more than twice Kim's age anyway, and knew better. Now he knew this had to be stopped. "Kim, give me that. I said I was going there anyway." He grabbed her arm and hustled her out the door, scolding her half-heartedly under his breath.

Z-man turned to Stroaker and said, "Cat fight! All right!"

Stroaker tried to suppress a grin, not entirely successfully. When Olson returned with the coffee Stroaker continued, "Okay, so where were we? No backpack? Just sew on some white things. The kidnapper doesn't care if it's original equipment, he just wants to be able to see it in the dark."

Z-man replied, "Well, I don't know if I like that idea. If it looks too, uh, altered, then the pickup man might get suspicious and think it's rigged."

"It is rigged." Stroaker said, not getting the point.

"Uh, right. But we don't want him to know that. He's going to wonder what's sewn in between the white panels, and so forth. I'm just saying it might spook him."

"Ah, he's got to figure it's rigged anyway. I'd rather he get close enough to get a good look at it, and get spooked, than not be able to find it in the dark because he can't see it."

The argument became more heated. They decided to ask Tobin his opinion. Tobin picked up the duffel that had been used to carry the ransom money into the RA. It was large and black. Then he picked up the two Olson had brought in. He compared the sizes of all three packs.

"I've got news for you. Both of these Olson bought are too small," Tobin finally declared. He began pulling bundles of cash from the black one and shoved them into the blue one. There was still a quarter of the money left over. "You're going to have to find another one, or alter this black one."

Mike Bean chose this moment to enter the command post. He was obviously in an agitated state. Knowles entered just as Bean began talking. "I can't get a Bureau radio installed in the Cadillac. It has a different electrical system than anything we use in our Bucars. I'm sure we could get some wiring specs for it and get a Bureau radio in eventually, but not today. We're going to have to go with a handheld."

This was bad news. Handheld radios didn't have much range. "Have you tested a handheld in the vicinity of the house?" Stroaker asked.

"Yeah, and it sucks. It won't reach the nearest repeater, which is on Umunhum."

"Umunhum? What kind of a name is that?" Stroaker asked, almost indignantly.

"It means hummingbird in the Ohlone Indian language," Knowles answered casually. It was something he'd picked up in an article in the newspaper some time back, but everybody in the room looked at him as though he were a freak. It was obvious from Stroaker's expression that the question had been rhetorical.

"Whatever. Okay, so that just means the plane will have to stay directly over the Caddy until the drop is made. It'll work fine." Stroaker seemed unconcerned as he said it.

"That's fine if the plane doesn't lose contact," Bean responded. "But if he gets separated by more than few miles, Izawa will have no way of communicating unless there's an SOG vehicle within twenty yards of the car. It'd be awfully obvious to go into the drop with a tail car bumper-locking the drop car."

Olson was more concerned than Stroaker. "That could be a problem. Maybe we'll be lucky and the drop will be in good repeater range; they usually are in a metro area. But without radio contact, there could be all sorts of problems." Olson knew that communications were always the sticking point in these operations. Something always seemed to break down, and now it was happening again. "We need to make sure the SOG and SWAT have cell phones. Terry, too."

"Cell phones aren't all that reliable in this area, either," Bean pointed out. "You know how spotty they can be around here. We got mountains, tunnels ... this isn't the Midwest."

"I'm going to talk to Mo about this. He's got to keep the plane right over the drop car. That's the only way we can be sure we can talk to them." Olson left the command post to go to Radio, the alcove on the other side of the RA that served as a radio room.

"Have you heard?" Knowles inquired of the assemblage once there was a break in the conversation. "Rothman just heard it on the news as he was driving back to the RA. The oil executive in New Jersey was found dead. Apparently he tried to escape and the kidnappers killed him, then continued to demand ransom for over a week."

"Jesus, that's going to be rough on the Fischers when they hear that," the Z-man replied.

Stroaker looked alarmed. "My god, that's all we need. I don't suppose there's any way to keep that from them?"

"Not unless you can stop them all from watching TV or listening to the radio, or talking to close friends who do," Knowles answered.

"Well," Z-man pointed out, "at least we can emphasize that we don't have the same situation here. The tapes of the father reading the newspaper are proof he is still alive. With any luck, there'll be another recording played tonight."

"Let's hope so," Knowles said. "We can't afford to have Pam panic tonight. This can be used at the briefing today to emphasize the seriousness of the situation."

Stroaker formed a suitably grim expression and assumed his pontificating tone. "We must redouble our efforts, and never lose sight of the goal. Our first priority must be to secure the release of the victim. Cliff, are the street teams ready?"

"They know their surveillance territories well now, and they know tonight is the payoff. They should have been able to get plenty of sleep, so they should be okay. The team leaders will be at today's briefing. You can emphasize to them whatever you think is essential. As long as we're asking about preparation, are we going to get a real-time trace tonight?"

"I think so," Tobin answered, "but I can't be sure what Pac Bell is going to do. We have GTE on standby all night - no charge, no protest. It just depends on where the call comes in from. Any luck with the pay phone in Aptos?"

"Don't know yet. I have a couple of FOA's over there now doing a neighborhood, and an ERT agent to do the prints. We should know by the one o'clock briefing. Did we ever get a location for the first call, the one we didn't record? The billing record should show the call, shouldn't it, by reverse search on the dialed number?"

"Only if it's a toll call. I never thought to ask. I'll check." Tobin hit the autodial button on the corner phone. He obviously had programmed Pac Bell Security into this instrument just to save time and errors in dialing; every second counted in an emergency. He spoke briefly with someone on the other end. "They'll check for me. It shouldn't take long, if it's billed through Pac Bell."

"I also had Rothman talk to Carmody and Louellen talk to the family members. No one can figure out the significance of the $650,000 figure. There haven't been any family health emergencies, foreclosures, deaths, or anything else like that with the domestic help, family members, neighbors, Claritiva employees, or anyone else close to them ... at least, not that they know of. Carmody is having Human Resources check to see if there are any special hardship cases he hasn't heard about, but he's pretty sure he would already know of anybody in this category."

Knowles looked over at the suspect board on the wall. So far, they didn't have much to go on. Usually at this point, several people should have been designated suspects, and information gathered about them and posted. Typical suspects would be estranged family members, recently fired domestic help or company employees, people close to the family with mental disorders, and so forth.

There was still nothing in the section on suspect vehicles. He wrote in felt pen "Dark Sedan. Possible white sticker on right front passenger window." As he was writing, Tobin called to him, "We have a hit on the first call - the unrecorded one. It's from outside the supermarket at the Seventrees Center, wherever that is."

Knowles knew the shopping center. There was a bank there that had been robbed more than any other bank in the valley. That shopping center was on the east side of town in an area bordering a poor district and a middle class one. San Jose did not have slums in the same massive, oppressive sense that slums existed in Chicago, New York and other big cities. But some areas were worse than others and the Seventrees Center was close to such a neighborhood. The shopping center was on the east side of Highway 101 near the southern end of town, just where the eastern foothills began. The center was relatively old by local standards, perhaps 25 or 30 years. Originally the area was a mix of moderately-priced housing developments and agricultural land, mostly fruit and nut orchards and dairy grazing. But as the suburban sprawl had pushed growth eastward and southward from city center, these developments became absorbed into the larger carpet of housing covering the valley floor. Economically depressed areas scattered themselves throughout the district, mostly tenanted now by Southeast Asian immigrants. Some of the housing developments, especially up into the hills a few miles, were still quite nice, and quite expensive. Seventrees was the only sizable retail shopping center in that entire section of town, and it did a booming business among all economic strata. For this reason, it seemed to be the logical target or meeting point for robbers, drug dealers, and other assorted low life who had no other handy locale to victimize. It had very easy freeway access, as well, which made it attractive to bank robbers - and ransom callers.

Knowles wrote down the number of the phone. He knew there was no chance anyone was going to remember the caller from Tuesday. The shopping center was enormous, and had a polyglot population of shoppers and staff. Hispanics, Arabs, Filipinos, Indians - all would blend in. Still, there might be a security videotape of the phone area. He could hope. He went back into the cubicle area in search of a lead agent, and found someone assigned to the special who could run the lead down for him. Then he returned to the command post.

"The important thing here," he declared to Stroaker and Olson, "is the location. That makes all three calls south of here. This first one in south San Jose, the next one on 101 near Aromas, and the third one over by the coast in Aptos. We should concentrate surveillance resources on the southern sector. I think we ought to put more teams in that area, and fewer up north. And we should contact the local officials in the southern counties. FBI LA, too, for that matter."

"Hold on, now," the Z-man protested. "We still have the reported drop off in San Francisco, we have the use of the *Chronicle* headline in the recorded message. I think we could find the action up in The City tonight." He still wanted his squad to be the ones in for the kill. He was SAC material; he had to be a glory hound if he wanted to climb the next rung.

Olson countered with support for Knowles. His squad would get the action if the case went southward. A vigorous debate ensued, with Stroaker turning his head back and forth between the two supervisors as if he were watching Wimbledon from a sideline seat. Finally, he announced that everything would stay the way it was, spread evenly throughout the division. He gave no further reason, and probably had none, other than a desire for the argument to stop. Both supervisors were articulate and had some good reasoning on their side, so he just canceled them out and treated the situation as though no new information had come in.

Bertinetti interrupted the conversation by handing the telephone to Stroaker, indicating that it was Bureau headquarters to talk to him. "Stroaker here," he said, grasping the receiver.

The others in the room could only hear Stroaker's end of the conversation. It became apparent that he was talking to the Deputy Assistant Director of the Criminal Division. Now referred to by the Bureau acronym DAD, this position traditionally was called "Number 1 man." On paper a DAD ranked equal to an SAC, but in reality, nobody but the Director or Deputy Director, ranked equal to or higher than an SAC of a major division. SAC's were like potentates in the field - almost absolute rulers in local administrative and investigative matters. Agents knew that their boss was the SAC, and they would follow his or her direction, as long as it was legal. FBIHQ could direct an SAC all they want, but unless the SAC chose to follow that direction, it didn't happen. Many felt that the best position in the FBI was that of SAC of a major division because of its power and independence. Many Assistant Directors "stepped down" to take SAC slots in the field - if they were lucky enough to get them. In contrast to Washington, D.C., the cost of living in the field was usually low, the autonomy high, the public scrutiny a lot less, and, for the most part, the FBI was respected, even idolized, there. The field was also where the real action was. Cases weren't solved at the Bureau.

Stroaker was explaining that indeed, the DAD had heard it right, he was planning to surround the drop site and have the SWAT and SOG follow the pickup person to see where he went. Stroaker's voice elevated only slightly, but his face assumed an expression of exasperation. He listened impatiently to the DAD, and then repeated that it was his plan, and he felt it was the best thing to ensure the safety of the victim. He reassured the DAD that if it looked like they would have any difficulty following the pickup person, they would move in and arrest. This apparently did not mollify the DAD, as his elevated voice could now be heard from the earpiece of the phone by others in the room. He was almost screaming that that plan just wouldn't work. The personnel could overhear a few choice words like "lamebrain idea" and "goddam nuts." Stroaker responded with a patronizing speech on how he was the man on the spot, he was the one with a life in his hands, and how the DAD would someday understand if he ever got to be in his position. This last comment was a jab at the DAD for not ever having been an SAC even of a small division - he had gone from ASAC to DAD. It was also disingenuous, because the DAD, while ASAC in Detroit, had run a kidnapping case in which the victim was rescued and the ransom money recovered. He had more real street experience than Stroaker at this kind of case.

Olson, Tobin, and Knowles exchanged nervous glances. This was getting to the crux of the investigative strategy, and they knew they could be in trouble if this was not resolved. The fact was they knew the DAD was right and the SAC wrong in this argument, but they had to follow the SAC. If he persisted in this course, then they would be in a no-win situation. If the payoff was made, and the pickup person ended up losing the surveillance because they followed the SAC's direction, there would almost certainly be a nasty post-incident review of the whole thing and everybody involved would be picked apart mercilessly, especially if the victim was killed or the kidnappers weren't apprehended. If the SAC and FBIHQ agreed on a course of action and things went awry, well, they played the odds right, and you couldn't win 'em all. But despite the possibility of criticism, demotion, or other possible personal penalties, the main thing on their minds was rescuing Fischer. They all waited breathlessly for a sign the SAC was weakening in his position.

It never came. Finally, Stroaker told the DAD that he understood his view and would reconsider the whole situation, but couldn't promise anything. Then he turned the phone over to Z-man to discuss further details of how to apprehend if that was the choice. This was an insult to the DAD, since Z-man was only a squad supervisor, and it implied that the man running the operation, the SAC, didn't need to concern himself with this detail since it probably wouldn't happen. When the conversation ended, Stroaker turned to Z-man and asked, "So, do you think the Niners are going to trade for some help in the defensive secondary?"

This was a sign that the SAC's brain had absorbed all the strategy and argument it could handle. He was going to decompress with football talk. Knowles left the room in disgust.

Chapter 18

Carl Fischer heard Miguel get up and go to the bathroom. After he flushed, the toilet ran again. This irritant only got worse with each passing day. Why couldn't these bozos just jiggle the handle? Fischer had developed a habit of asking to go to the bathroom a few minutes after they had, whether he really needed to or not, just so he could stop the infernal noise. This time, however, he heard Miguel's footsteps moving away, toward the screen door. Then the slam of the door told him Miguel had stepped outside. That meant both men were out of the house - or apartment or whatever it was. Fischer still wasn't sure exactly what kind of place he was in.

Fischer had resolved to try to escape if he got the chance. The words scratched into the leather on his briefcase meant only one thing to him - they planned to kill him when this was over. He might not get another chance. The payoff was supposed to be today or tonight. He waited two or three minutes to hear if Miguel would come right back in. Then he made his move.

His feet were still loose from the chains. He stood up, slowly this time to allow his blood pressure to equalize. His hands were still cuffed in front of him, but he had no trouble removing the mask. Then he tiptoed to the bedroom door. He could hear no sound - other than the toilet running. He poked his head around the doorway into the hall. Still nothing. He remembered the path by which he had been led to this room, which would be to the right. He figured that route would lead him out to the screen door Miguel had just slammed. That would not be wise. Better to look for an alternate exit. He turned left and found himself in the kitchen. It was charitably described as shabby. There was an ancient gas stove, free-standing about eight inches from the wall, gas line plumbing clearly visible. The counter top was a sickly green Formica, cigarette butt shapes burned into the edges, corners peeling, and pieces missing here and there. A plain but sturdy-looking wooden table stood in the middle of the kitchen. The plywood cabinets were inelegant and in disrepair. One cabinet door would not close, and Fischer could see unopened soup cans on the lower shelf. There was a heavily mottled sink, with dirty pans still sitting there from the previous evening's meal - hot dogs and beans. In the back of the small room was an incongruously new-looking refrigerator. Next to that was a door to the back yard.

Fischer hurried to the door. He opened it, and was immediately confronted with a screen door. Was this the same screen door he had been hearing slam, he wondered? Could Miguel be in the back yard? Or was this simply another screen door, similar to the one through which they had entered? He saw no car or garage outside, so he was sure this was not his entry route. This must be a different screen door from the one he had used before. But was it the one he heard slam just a few minutes ago? He couldn't be sure. Gingerly, he stepped outside.

No Miguel. He let the screen door close ever so carefully. It made no noise. Examining the yard, he could see he was still far from being out of trouble. The fence was constructed of vertical redwood boards. The horizontal members, presumably two-by-fours, were out of sight on the other side of the fence. On this side were smooth boards side by side, with no spaces between. The top of the fence was a good seven feet above ground level. With his hands cuffed, his bad leg, and no horizontal members to grab or stand on, there was no way he could get over the fence. From what he could see, there wasn't anything on the other side, anyway. All that was visible were fruit trees; prune, he guessed. He thought it was an orchard on the other side, but it may have just been a back yard with a lot of fruit trees. Because of the high fence and the trees, he could see no other structure in any direction. He wasn't sure whether there were other houses next door, or if they were out in an isolated farming area. He looked around quickly for something he could use to climb on, but the garbage cans and old tires looked too unstable and it would be noisy and time-consuming to pile them up.

He decided to go around the side of the house to the front. He could see a gate on the left, which looked like it would be too noisy to open. Stealthily, he crept around the right side. The right side led around to a driveway - or at least a pair of ruts in the dirt that suggested wheeled vehicles of some sort had traversed the route regularly over the years. From the driveway he could see a detached carport in the front of the house. It was possible to enter the carport from the road in front, and drive all the way through to the back yard, as the carport was not enclosed on either end. At the moment there was no car in it. Fischer continued to walk as quietly as possible toward the front of the property. When he got to the carport, he walked straight through, taking care not to trip over any of the old tools, Mason jars, and general debris lining the corners. As he reached the far end of the carport, he could see the street layout for the first time.

The road was more of an alley than a street. It had once been paved, but had needed a repaving for at least a decade. It was mostly dirt and gravel now, punctuated with large potholes. There were houses both directions, but spaced farther apart than in more urban areas. The buildings did not seem to be of any consistent design, but all seemed to be old, small, and cheaply made. The alley had the look of an old farm road. Directly across the street from him, Fischer saw a dilapidated backhoe on a large trailer, parked at an angle in the yard of an even more dilapidated house. An enormous pepper tree filled that yard, dripping wispy foliage and knobbly peppercorns down over the top of the backhoe. A sign on the trailer said "Alvarez Backhoe" and provided a telephone number. Because of a large hedge on the front yard property line where he was standing, Fischer could not see to his right. To the left he could see more houses, pickup trucks and signs of habitation. He saw no Miguel, or for that matter, people of any kind. Due to a slight curve and all the trees he could not see the left end of the block, but he could see on the opposite side of the street a yellow caution sign reading "No Outlet." From this he concluded that it was a dead end to the left, and there was probably an intersection close by on the right. He had to make a decision, and he did not have much time for analysis. Miguel might have re-entered the house while he was coming around through the carport. Miguel could come out looking for him any instant.

Fischer walked quickly to the street and turned to the right, moving around the hedge. There was no sidewalk, only a worn strip which bore signs of use for that purpose. To his right was a row of old houses with untended yards, and to his left was a row of assorted vehicles, mostly pickup trucks and a couple of ridiculously large-finned American sedans of yesteryear. At the end of the block was a U-Haul truck. One of the pickups bore an almost-obliterated advertisement for a gardener named Ortiz. Fischer did not have time to reflect on the irony of a gardener living in the adjacent house, with a weed-covered yard that bore more resemblance to a junkyard than to a residence. There was no address or city listed, but there was another telephone number. Fischer looked at the telephone number, but there was no area code. He looked back across the street at the backhoe. No area code there, either. He didn't even know what area code he was in, much less what town. He had no idea how to give directions to someone, even if he were to reach a telephone. He tried to memorize the telephone number on the truck, but after walking a few more yards, realized he had already forgotten it.

He decided not to worry about memorizing anything, just to get out of the area. He still saw no signs of anyone being home. This was late morning on a weekday in May. Apparently the adults were all working, and any kids would be in school. He had no idea if the neighbors would assist, even if he could find one. This appeared to be a Mexican neighborhood, and they might not even understand him. He spoke no Spanish. Perhaps they would return him to Miguel, or be illegal immigrants who would be afraid to call the police. He decided to walk on the street, so that the row of cars and trucks would help obscure him from the houses on both sides, at least until he got to the corner. He stepped between the front of an old pickup and the back of the U-Haul. As he stepped past the U-Haul into the street he came face to face with a short, heavily-muscled man with curly black hair. Fischer had not seen the face before, but he recognized the shoes. It was Miguel. Only something was wrong; Miguel didn't look Mexican.

Miguel pulled out a large knife with frightening rapidity. "So you have come for some fresh air, I see. We will go back now. Turn around." He spit the words out venomously and pressed the knife up against Fischer's throat.

Fischer turned around obediently and began to walk back to the house. He was in no position to fight, and he knew it. "What are you going to do now?" he asked. There was no point in trying to make excuses to Miguel. He had tried to escape and had been caught. There would be repercussions.

"Now, I cut off your balls." He gave a quick jab of the knife to Fischer's left buttock. It was just enough to prick slightly, but not break the skin. Fischer moved faster.

They walked in the front door, and Fischer got a good look at the portion of the house he had not seen. As he entered he noticed the number on the front of the house next to the front door - "15." He assumed it was the street address, although he still did not know the street name. Then a thought occurred to him. He had now seen Miguel's face. He could identify him. Did this mean Miguel would have to eliminate him as a witness? Was there even any point in trying to pick up any more evidence to tell the police? The picture of that briefcase inscription resurrected itself before him: CMF IS DEAD.

Miguel shoved him forcefully into the closet with the mattress and ordered him down on his knees. Fischer complied. "So you think you can escape, huh? That is not possible. My organization controls this whole area. If you are seen outside again, they will kill you. I trusted you, but you turn out to be a cheater and a liar. Now you learn the penalty for trying to escape. Are you Jewish?"

"No, I'm a Catholic." The answer came reflexively, but as soon as he said it, Fischer's heart sank again. Miguel did not look Mexican because he wasn't. He was an Arab. And apparently not one who cared much for Jews - or rich, American industrialists whose government supported Israel. Would Miguel think he was lying about being Catholic to cover up being a Jew? He tried to think whether he had anything on him that would prove it. No crucifix, no Saint Christopher medal, no bible. His wedding ring was a plain gold band. He could recite a rosary or some other Catholic prayer, but Miguel didn't look like he would know a paternoster from patent leather.

Miguel unbuckled Fischer's belt, fed one end through the handcuffs then around his waist to the small of his back. He closed the buckle there, over the shirt, but outside the belt loops. Fischer knew his hands were now trapped. With time and privacy, he could pull the buckle around to the front again, and unbuckle it to free his hands from his waist; but with Miguel watching him, he could do nothing. His hands were trapped. But why hadn't Miguel used the belt loops? That would be more secure. He had his answer all too soon. Miguel unsnapped Fischer's waistband, so the pants fell to his knees. Then he yanked down hard on Fischer's shorts, pulling them to mid-thigh.

Fischer mumbled a prayer. He prepared himself mentally as best he could to be castrated without anaesthesia.

One o'clock came and went. Knowles looked at his watch. Stroaker was already 15 minutes late, and the natives were getting restless. There were over fifty people here for the briefing. They had staged in an empty office next to the FBI space in the commercial office building that housed the San Jose RA. There was no furniture, so people were sitting on the floor, or standing. Some were still milling around the adjoining office space of the RA, using the phones, computers, or copier. Stroaker was nowhere to be seen, which meant he was probably in the corner office - Olson's. Belinda had already distributed to the personnel a briefing packet which Olson had dictated and Kim had typed. Some were studying it, but most had already scanned it and learned what they could. It was primarily reference material: telephone numbers, radio channels, addresses of the calls, dates, descriptions of Fischer, of the Cadillac, of the suspect and his car. Patience was wearing thin. Some people had brought fast-food lunches with them into the space, and now they had burger wrappers and ice-filled paper cups to dispose of, with no wastebaskets. Knowles asked Belinda to find some wastebaskets from the RA space. She did so promptly, once she realized the mess could alienate the property manager. She had imposed upon him to open the space to them for a "special training scenario."

Knowles decided it was time to get the show on the road, before more people started to leave to make phone calls or go out for a smoke. He stood up in the middle of the room and called out an instruction to sit down and be quiet so the briefing could start. He was used to calling a group to order from his years as legal instructor; he deepened his voice a bit and said it like he meant it. The noise level abated, and he began.

"Tonight you have the chance to save a life or cost someone his life. It is that simple. Carl Fischer was taken hostage on Tuesday morning from the parking lot of his workplace in Mountain View. He's the President and Chief Operating Officer of Claritiva Software. His net worth is in the hundreds of millions of dollars. He is reportedly a brilliant engineer, a popular boss, and a loving family man. There are only a handful of family members and coworkers who know of his kidnapping, but they are all hoping that tonight the FBI proves what it can do.

"There have been three ransom calls. The first, on Tuesday, was not recorded because no one knew until then he had been kidnapped. The remaining two have been recorded and analyzed. All three calls were made from pay phones in public areas near freeways. The first from Seventrees Center, a large shopping center just off 101 in south San Jose. The second from a tourist trap just off 101 near the Santa Clara County southern border. The third from Aptos, just off Highway 1. That's just south of Santa Cruz for those of you who don't know the South Bay well.

"The last two calls were taken by Pam Fischer, the victim's daughter. Ben, can you play the tape of the last call?" Olson started the tape player. Everyone who had not already heard it strained to catch each word. When it was over Knowles resumed, "As you can hear, Pam did a fantastic job. She followed our instructions perfectly, and when necessary, improvised. She's proven herself adept at stalling the caller. We should be able to trace tonight's call in real time. Most of you here will be doing surveillance, either on a street team or with the SOG squad. It's critical that you stay in communication without tying up the radio channel, and you respond quickly and efficiently when you are given a lead. We want to catch the caller at the phone booth, if possible, or if not, at the drop site. Our linguistic expert, a professor in Pennsylvania, believes the caller is an Arabic-speaking male in his twenties or thirties who has been educated in the United States for several years at least."

A hand shot up from one of the SWAT members. "That sounds like a Spanish accent to me," he said. His comment was met with a murmur of assent from several others.

"To be honest, it does to me too," Knowles replied, "but I am repeating what the expert says. He thinks it is an Arabic speaker trying to imitate a Mexican accent. You should consider the possibility that either Hispanics or Arabs, or both, are involved." Knowles pointed to the suspect sheet which had been moved from the Command Post to the briefing room. At least one of the people involved is likely to be a young, dark, adult male. We also have some vehicle information, although it is sketchy. As you can see from the sheet, the caller was caught on a security camera in a dark sedan. It's not much, but it's what we have. There are no eyewitnesses to the abduction or to any of the ransom calls."

Another hand went up. "Cliff, who is the Mountain View P.D. liaison officer? I don't see a name on the sheet."

Knowles had not expected the question, but smoothly responded, "The SAC is handling local liaison personally. If you need to pass a request to County Communications for local officers or the highway patrol, go through the command post. The CP will handle all contact."

Stroaker walked in at a leisurely pace, almost dawdling. He was chatting with the Z-man until he realized suddenly that the briefing was already in progress. He shot a glare at Knowles, who said, "Here's the SAC now to give you the briefing." Knowles stepped back into the crowd next to Rothman.

"I can't tell you all what a privilege it is to lead you tonight," he began. "This is the finest group of investigators it has ever been my privilege to work with. Tonight is the championship game, and we want that trophy!" He shot his fist up in the air. "This is not a night for 90% or 95% effort. Tonight is the time for 110% effort, and I know I will get it from every one of you." He looked about grandly.

Knowles could see several pairs of eyes glaze over. The sports trophy metaphor, heard too many times already, was more of a lead balloon than a gold cup. Stroaker was the only person in the room who was there for the glory of winning. This was beginning to sound like all his other speeches.

"Now you all have the descriptive information on the missing man and the caller. You are looking for a young Hispanic male or an older, tall, stout white male with a white handlebar mustache." He flipped to the sheet with Fischer's photo and pointed it out to the audience. Several flipped to the page and studied the photo. Knowles noticed that he did not refer to Fischer as the victim, but as the missing man. There were several sideways glances towards Knowles from other agents who had noticed this and some other minor discrepancies between Knowles's version and Stroaker's, such as the omission of the possibility of Arabic ethnicity. "I would like you all to hear the caller's voice. Ben, can you play the tape?"

Olson replied, "I did already while you were out. They've all heard it."

"Oh." This stopped Stroaker in his tracks. He had not planned to go on just yet. Clearly he was irritated that his material was being usurped. "All right then, let's talk about your role. You will be taking your positions throughout the Bay Area. We don't know where the payoff drop will be. It could be near you. We will have the drop car, driven by Pam Fischer - you heard her voice on the tape - and a tail car go to the site. Terry Izawa will be riding as protection for Pam. The drop car will be a brand-new Cadillac, license and description on your briefing sheet."

"Now as for the surveillance plan, the SOG will be the tail car, and after running as cover car for Pam, will separate from her once the drop is made and she's away safely. Other SOG units will surround the general drop area before she ever gets there to form an outside perimeter. SWAT will be in place to surround the scene. When the pickup is made they will communicate what is happening and follow my instructions. Observe, follow, arrest, as is appropriate.

No one is to fire a weapon or attempt an arrest or stop unless instructed to do so. Unless, of course, you are attacked with deadly force. You may defend yourself, as always. We will have snipers prepared to shoot if that becomes necessary. We have to assume the subjects will be armed and dangerous. There could be others involved we do not know about. Don't assume that anyone may be safely ignored just because they are not a Mexican male. What I want from you when we give the signal, is for every other team to move toward the designated drop area, filling the spot of the second team ahead of you, which will have moved. Once that set is in place, I want the other teams to leapfrog in the same manner. When you get to the location of the team you replace, stop and wait there."

Knowles saw agents start to scratch their heads and whisper to each other. Finally one of the brasher agents broke into the presentation. "Pete, I don't quite follow that. How are we supposed to know whether we are the team that is supposed to move first, or wait, and how do we know which team we are replacing and where they are?"

The complexity of Stroaker's automotive choreography was sinking in rapidly with the agents. Stroaker seemed to have given little thought to the actual logistics of executing his plan. The street agents knew they needed a clear instruction and didn't have it. "Hmm, that's a good question," Stroaker replied. It was actually three good questions. "The odd-numbered teams will move first. Just go to wherever the next odd-numbered team is in the direction of wherever the drop is. Then when all the odd-numbered teams are in place, the even-numbered teams will do the same thing."

This was just getting worse and worse. The teams had been numbered for ease of reference when giving radio instructions, but they had not been allocated territories in a line in strict numerical order. They were scattered in two dimensions, with odd-numbered teams sometimes adjacent to each other in some directions.

Another hand shot up. "How will we know when all the odd teams are in place? Do we have to wait for the very last car of the very last team before we move? What if all the teams on our side of the bay are already in place - do we have to wait for someone to move from Eureka to Mendocino? Why don't you just give the word to everybody to move toward the drop area as soon as you learn of what it is?"

Stroaker was now getting visibly annoyed. "We don't have time for all these questions. I've set forth the strategy. Cliff here will give you the details. I assume you've worked out a plan, haven't you, Cliff?"

All eyes turned to Knowles. Great, he thought. Now everyone will blame me for this lame-ass leapfrogging fiasco. "I'll clarify it after the briefing. Every team leader - leaders only, please - meet with me for a quick post brief." He'd figure out how to deal with it in the meantime.

Stroaker resumed, "Now remember to use the radio, Red 3 for SWAT and SOG, Blue 7 for everybody else, only when absolutely necessary. We have over a hundred units out on this. If you need to talk among your own team members, go to an alternate tactical channel. Your sheet shows you which one you're supposed to use for your area. The main channel should be used only for instructions and information from the CP to you, and for direct responses to questions we give you. Do not acknowledge instructions unless you are specifically asked to do so. If we ask for your team to verify it is in place, only the team leader should respond when you are all ready. Now you'll get a briefing on the money."

Tobin stood up and explained that the money was marked and recorded. He explained some of the techniques, but not all. There was no point in publicizing the ones the general group did not need to know about. The radio signal, for example, was on a channel not accessible to the agents' car or handheld radios. So that was not mentioned; only SOG or SWAT could follow that signal and they would get their won briefings. Similarly for the infrared signals. He mentioned the exploding dye pack and the pheromones, since the street agents might see overt signs of these during a surveillance or car stop. Someone asked him what the package would look like. He told them it would be in a backpack that was white or partially white, but he could not show it to them now. He did not bother to explain their attempts to buy or design a white one.

Stroaker took center stage once again and launched into another pep talk. Rothman shot a glance at Knowles and whispered to him, "I'll take 'Size of the fight in the dog'."

Knowles replied, "Okay, I'll take 'Reach down deep inside'." They waited to see which cliche would be the first to appear. Knowles won. "Okay, I owe you a beer," Rothman said. "and I need to talk to you when this briefing is over."

When it ended, Knowles realized that Stroaker had intentionally left the agents unaware of his actual plan to follow, rather than arrest, the pickup person. He had left it for them to observe, report, and then follow instructions. That sounded normal enough, but they would all be expecting to receive the instruction to move in and arrest once the pickup was made.

"Cliff," Rothman said. "We have a potential problem. The weather report forecasts heavy fog tonight for much of the area. All the coast, and some of the inland areas. This last ransom call was from Aptos. If the drop is anywhere near the coast, there'll be no air cover for surveillance. We should be able to stay airborne at altitude, above the fog, so you'll have an airborne repeater, but they won't be able to see anything on the ground or stay together with a surveillance."

"How far inland will it come in?"

"Hard to predict, but probably over the lowest hills. All SF and the Northern Peninsula, Oakland, Berkeley, of course. The Monterey peninsula and coast for sure, maybe even the Salinas area."

"Okay, keep me posted. Be sure to tell Stroaker, too. He was planning to use that helicopter, you told me."

"His chopper pilot is reading the same weather reports I am."

"Okay, Tim, thanks. I'll let Olson know."

Knowles had to deal with the team leaders next, on the issue of the leapfrogging physical surveillance, or fisur as it was abbreviated in Bureau lingo. He waited for the SAC and Morales to leave, and then commandeered a distant corner of the empty lease space they were using for a briefing room. He looked around. There were about 20 agents, all relatively senior and savvy - hand-picked by Knowles and Rothman to be team leaders. Knowles decided to take the plunge, although he knew he was taking a chance.

"Okay, here's the deal," he began. "This leapfrog fisur just won't work. If anybody dimes me out to the SAC I'm dead meat, but I'm going to trust you. Just forget that plan, and go where I send you. I'll get to Radio, or call them, and send individual instructions by team number. If I can't do it, I'll try to get Ben Olson to take over. Most of you won't move, but I may tell you to cover a larger area while I pull another team out to support the drop area. If you don't hear your team number specifically assigned to do something else, just continue to stand by in your area until you get the 10-22." 10-22 was the standard police code for Discontinue. "Our radios are scrambled, so use the code sheet in your packet to keep communications secure."

Most of the team leaders nodded and smiled conspiratorially. A couple gave the thumbs up. One of them said hesitantly, "Cliff, what if the SAC gives us a specific order? I mean, we ..." then he saw a couple of the more senior agents glowering at him or shaking their heads. The agent cleared his throat and resumed, "Well, ... I guess we can assume that things change during an operation and we should just follow the instructions we're given." He looked and saw the senior agents nod and smile.

"That's right. I'll take the responsibility. Whatever orders I give you tonight, I'm the case agent, and I've been delegated the responsibility by the SAC to implement the ground surveillance from the regular agent street teams. You heard the SAC in the briefing. Now remember, the SOG will take the close-in roles, such as the tail car and the perimeter on the drop zone, but I've done these cases before. They always end up needing regular street teams to run down leads or join the chase. If we pick up a tag from a suspect vehicle, we'll run it and have you check out the address. Things like that. Even long after the drop, there could be things for you to check out, so don't tune out just because you end up a hundred miles from where the action appears to be. It's going to be a long night for all of us. We don't know yet when the call will come, but the consensus guess is that the drop won't be until after 9:00 at the earliest. When you get on post, find a place that'll be available all night to get coffee and take a leak. That's it. Good luck."

Knowles sought out Ben Olson, eventually finding him by Radio. Olson was checking to see what the communications were like from Radio to various points in the Bay Area. Mike Bean was with him. Olson did not seem sanguine about what he was finding. Even with the repeaters tuned and the best channels selected, the coverage was just as spotty as always throughout the South Bay.

"Ben, sorry to bring you more bad news," Knowles broke in, "but it looks like air cover is going to be spotty as well. Heavy fog predicted for the coastal regions, maybe even inland."

"Jesus - bad radio, no air support, and the backpack still isn't ready," Olson fumed. "This is all screwed up. And we've got the SAC..." His voice trailed off as he glanced down at Bean and the radio operator. He wiggled a finger at Knowles in a "follow me" gesture, and stepped into the supply room adjacent to Radio. Knowles followed. "The boss is micromanaging this thing to death. He's going to kill us with this follow-the-crook business. He wants to have the SWAT in their Ninja gear for dramatic effect, so the bad guys will just lay down their arms. He's scared to death of a shootout because of all the bad press that's happened at Ruby Ridge and Waco. He wants to be the 'humane FBI' instead of 'inhuman FBI.' And this leapfrogging business is absolute crap. He read some paper by some theoretician in the Law Enforcement Bulletin." The Law Enforcement Bulletin, or LEB, as it is better known, is a glossy magazine published by the FBI Training Academy. It contains articles by FBI instructors and a politically correct diversity slate of police officials from around the country - the world, even. Most of the articles offer badly written, oversimplified explanations of the law, forensic techniques, or how to address law enforcement issues. Its primary purpose, like so many other academic journals, is to provide a place for its contributors to get published so they can avoid the second option in the "publish or perish" dichotomy facing all academics. The FBI Academy was a prime example of yet another canard - "those who can, do; those who can't, teach." Neither the authors nor the usual reading audience had any substantial knowledge of the subject matter discussed in the magazine. Olson continued, "He has no idea how impossible it would be to coordinate in this area. We know how bad the radio reception is in the Bay Area. After the first 'leap,' half the division will be unable to find out whether everybody else is in place because they won't be able to hear from half of them. And..."

Knowles interrupted him, "Don't worry, Ben. I've taken care of it."

Olson looked at him askance. "Why...what did you tell the team leaders in your post-brief?"

"That I'm the person designated by the SAC to implement ground surveillance by the street agents. To follow my instructions." He kept a straight face as a lopsided smile crept over Olson's visage.

"So... that sounds right," Olson replied. "I guess I don't need to know the details." Olson was preserving his deniability in case the SAC found out about the countermanding of his leapfrog orders. Knowles knew that Olson wouldn't have cared, but why get one more person in a jam? Olson appreciated being given the out. "On a similar topic..." Olson said, with a meaningful jump of his eyebrows, "does this fog mean the SAC's helicopter won't be able to take off tonight?"

"I think it can take off, since the fog never comes inland this far. It just can't land, or descend below the top of the fog bank. Rothman says the chopper could come down on wires, steeples, anything, if it tried to come down in the fog."

"Okay, keep me informed. There's nothing we can do about the weather."

Carl Fischer had been blindfolded once again. He was now trembling and shivering with fear. The wait seemed interminable. He could hear Miguel moving around him cautiously to look at him from the front. "You're circumcised," Miguel declared accusingly. "You're Jewish, aren't you, you lying bastard! You're a lying Zionist pig!"

"No, no, I'm not," Fischer replied, but the words were barely intelligible, his throat was so dry. "Everybody's circumcised in this country. I'm Catholic, really I am. You can check any way you want. You said you know everything about me. You should know that. I go to mass at Saint Simon's on Grant Road, just off Foothill. The priest is Father Muldoon. We gave them $100,000 last year for repairs to the children's pre-school wing. Call them - it has my name and my wife's on a plaque."

"I don't believe you. You lied about your daughter's car."

Fischer was suddenly overwhelmed with a vague but very real sense of shame. He knew he was fighting for his life. Much as he wanted to excoriate the Arab terrorists, he saw no point in false heroism before an armed Muslim fanatic. Such a declaration could only serve to increase Miguel's desire to kill him. At that moment, though, Carl Fischer knew something had changed. He had always thought of himself as neutral about the conflict in the Middle East. He had always thought there were good people - and fault - on both sides of the Israeli-Palestinian conflict. But now he understood his sympathies would be irrevocably with the Israelis. He replied simply, "It's true. I'm Catholic. Check it any way you want." In any event his Christian faith was real and he wasn't ashamed of it.

Miguel seemed to think about this for awhile. "Don't move, or I'll cut off your balls," he said. Fischer could hear him walk across the room. Fischer couldn't have moved if he'd wanted to; he was so paralyzed with fear. He heard some slight shuffling in the vicinity of the card table. After an eternity passed, Miguel spoke. "Your health insurance card says here, 'REL: RC.' What is that?"

Salvation! His insurance card - why hadn't he thought of that? "That stands for 'Religion - Roman Catholic' - you know, so they would know how to treat me or give me last rites if I was in the hospital in an emergency or something."

This seemed to convince Miguel. "Okay, you can pull up your pants now. I will take your word for it about the Catholic. But if you try to escape again I will kill you, I swear I will. And then I will blow up your house."

"No, no, I won't try again. I'm, I'm … sorry. I'll be good."

"And I will have to report this to the leader of the cell. He is in Santa Barbara. He will decide what to do about it. You should not have tried to escape."

It took at least ten minutes for Fischer's shuddering to subside. Even after he recovered, there were several more episodes of uncontrolled shaking as he fixated on how close he had come to being maimed by a muscle-bound religious zealot. He had always thought of himself as righteous, even pious, for having watched *Sophie's Choice* and *Schindler's List*. His adult discussion group at church had even discussed these films, and many of the men had solemnly declared how they too would have sacrificed their lives to fight against such evil if they had lived in that generation. What sanctimony! He had been silenced by nothing more than the sight of a knife. His keen intellect told him that he had done nothing wrong, that this was just a form of survivor's guilt. He was only doing what was necessary to survive and fight another day. But his own moral compass was telling him he had come up very short. A deep, black self-loathing enveloped him.

When Carlos returned, Fischer estimated that it must be early afternoon. He was hungry, and Carlos had brought another fast-food meal. He could smell it. Fischer was getting rather sick of McDonald's by now, but he had not been fed much during the entire ordeal, and it had been at least six or seven hours since the meager breakfast of cereal and milk. He could hear Miguel rush out to meet Carlos as he entered the house. They talked *sotto voce* for about five minutes, and Fischer strained to make out what they were saying. He realized this was foolish, since they must be talking Arabic. He could comprehend a few words of Spanish from having lived in California, where it is almost a second official language, but not a whit of Arabic. Still, he knew his fate could be decided during this conversation, and he tried mightily to pick up some idea of tone or emotion.

Carlos entered the room, and the aroma of the food grew stronger, causing the digestive juices to flow in Fischer's gut. His stomach began to rumble. "So, you think you can escape from us?" Carlos asked rhetorically. "That was very stupid. We will have to see what to do about you. We will have to receive orders from our superior. He is in Santa Barbara, so it will be some time before we can talk to him. You have no idea how powerful we are. I'll show you something." He uncuffed Fischer and led him still blindfolded into the next room. Carlos placed Fischer's hands on a smooth round surface near the floor. Whatever it was rolled slightly at his touch, and Fischer judged it to be heavy, cylindrical, and metallic. "It's a torpedo," Carlos stated proudly. "We're going to sink one of your navy ships."

"That's very impressive," Fischer said with as much sincerity as he could muster. He didn't know whether to believe Carlos, or how this thing connected with his abduction. If they already had a torpedo, they didn't need his money to finance a terrorist operation. His stomach continued to make noise.

This gave Carlos an idea. "So you are hungry, no?" He waved the bag under Fischer's nose.

"Yes, I'm hungry."

"Well, I have your fish sandwich here - like you asked for. Doesn't it smell good?" He made another pass with the bag.

As if on cue, Fischer's midsection emitted a Guinness Book of Records-sized gurgle. Carlos and Miguel both laughed. Even Fischer thought it was funny; he was relieved to have the tension broken. "Yes, it smells good. I can't deny it. My stomach tells you the truth." Then inspiration came to him. "See, it's fish! I asked for fish because it's Friday. Miguel didn't believe me, but I ordered fish because Catholics eat fish on Fridays."

"Yes, you are Catholic. I know that already," Carlos said, uninterested. But Miguel muttered something in Arabic that gave Fischer the impression he was only now coming around to believe him. "Well, Catholics are supposed to suffer on Fridays aren't they? Isn't that why you give up meat for fish? Hah! Some sacrifice! That is like giving up a Mercedes for a BMW. I will teach you to suffer for disobeying me. If you touch that food, Miguel here will hurt you in ways you cannot imagine." He gave a gleeful chortle.

Fischer could hear the rustle of the bag being opened, and some of its contents being placed on the floor very close to him. The food smells were obviously intended to torment him as a lesson. Negative reinforcement, they called it in psych class in college. But, strangely, a great wave of relief washed over him. He knew that this was a test of his faith. He was saved from death or dismemberment by the fact he had declared his religion openly - on his insurance card, in the food that he ordered. His adherence to ritual had indeed been his salvation. God was testing him, and he had passed. He was saved because he was a devout man, a godly man. The self-loathing dissipated in an instant, and he relished the chance to suffer in penance. Carlos had intended to be sarcastic, but Fischer knew that he was being asked by God to endure this deprivation to determine whether he was worthy of redemption. He was determined to prove that he was. He tried to genuflect, but couldn't with his hands belted to his waist. He lay down murmuring a quiet prayer.

Chapter 19

Hank LaPointe gathered the SWAT team members at the assembly point behind the main gym at Moffett Field. There were three teams. Each team had a leader, but LaPointe was the overall commander. He ran them through a few calisthenics to get them pumped up and to shake out the jitters, but he didn't want to get them overly tired. They would need endurance and sharpness tonight. Most of them had gone to bed late and slept in until close to noon in preparation for a possible all-nighter tonight.

The main blimp hangar loomed over them like a man-made Matterhorn. Its immensity was difficult to fathom until one had walked through it. That hangar was the largest undivided, enclosed space in the world - in short, the world's biggest 'room.' So big, in fact, it had its own atmosphere. It had been known to rain indoors. Built between World Wars I and II, it was intended to be the cornerstone for west coast operations of the expected dirigible fleet, but, after the Hindenburg disaster, had been put to other uses. Now it protected elements of NASA's fleet of experimental aircraft. NASA Ames Research Center was situated just to the north of Moffett Field. On the south end was Onizuka Air Force Facility, named for one of the astronauts who had perished in the Challenger disaster. The facility, however, predated that disaster by decades, and had been known both before and since by the more popular name "The Blue Cube," for its color and general shape. The newspapers liked to append the modifier 'super secret' before the name. Onizuka was the west coast satellite tracking station for the Air Force, following and directing everything from Vandenberg satellites to Space Shuttle launches. LaPointe, however, was oblivious to the high-tech wizardry today. His only concern was getting his troops ready. He started the whole group on a slow jog around the golf course. Their usual warm-up was five miles with gear on; today he would cut that to three, and keep the pace slow. He did not want to wear them out. He had ordered light clothing and no weapons for this warm-up, as he wanted to stay low-key with the other users of the base. They finished the run easily and needed to blow off more steam. He gave them a few more push-ups, and then they settled into a classroom for a separate SWAT briefing. LaPointe told them what Stroaker had not at the general briefing - that the primary plan was to follow the pickup person, not arrest. Several of the members put up a howl of protest.

"Follow?" one of the team leaders said. "At night with our gear on when we don't know where we're going or what mode of transportation he'll use? The kidnapper could have a motorcycle, an ATV, a mountain bike - anything. We have to nab him when he grabs the loot."

"Don't worry, the SAC assured me that if it looked at all like we could lose the subject, we'll get authorization to arrest immediately."

"That's going to be too late," Gerry McMurtry complained. McMurtry was one of the oldest SWAT members, and he had put on a few pounds in the last few years. He was powerful enough to get the duty of holding the steel and Plexiglas shield used for advancing, but he couldn't keep up with the younger, fleeter members in a footrace. "You don't know you're losing him until you've lost him. If you're close enough to move in and arrest, that means you weren't about to lose him. We'll never get the order to arrest when it's still possible to execute it."

LaPointe was unyielding. "An order is an order. We don't want a shoot-out if we can avoid it, especially if the victim's daughter is nearby. We wear the black ninjas, and the SAC thinks the guy'll surrender when we confront. But that happens only after an order to arrest. The black ninjas will be good camo in most rural environments. If he has the ransom dropped in downtown San Francisco, we'll be rather obvious. SOG will take any discreet surveillance on roads or streets."

The SWAT was the most militaristic of the field elements of the FBI. LaPointe had made it clear this was an order, so an order it was. SWAT played with guns rather seriously, and there was simply no room for dissension or "creativity." Everybody did things exactly as planned and as ordered. Surprises were deadly. Predictability was survival. They routinely practiced arrest commands, handcuffing, takedowns, and weapons deployment. These were all things they had done hundreds of times, but then that was the point. Training was meant to make such activities so routine they were performed correctly automatically every time.

Then came the vehicles. Each team was to be deployed as a unit, so they all traveled together in a large, nondescript van. Each of the three teams in a separate van, each team in a different part of the

Bay Area. The team drivers checked over the vehicles, making sure they were gassed up fully, all systems performing as planned. An inspection of the exterior confirmed there was nothing to indicate a federal or law enforcement affiliation. The vans were moderately colorful, rather than government gray, but not so colorful they would stand out and be noticed on a surveillance. The license plates appeared to be ordinary civilian plates.

Torres and Nguyen called in from Aptos. Nothing of significance had been found at the phone booth from the last call. No one had seen anything, and there was no security camera. The gas station was just off the Seacliff Beach exit from Highway 1. Quick freeway access was clearly an important consideration for this caller. The exit was a mile or two from the beach. Seacliff Beach was a state park, and access was controlled and fee-based. If someone had used that beach, the ranger would have a record of the user's license plate. The park was used primarily by vacationers in trailers who wanted an overnight spot. But the same freeway exit was used for access to the much larger Rio Del Mar beaches, which were free, uncontrolled access, and used by local families and body surfers. Knowles figured there was no chance the caller would have descended the cliffs to the beaches anyway. The previous video had proven he liked to hop back onto the freeway as soon as he finished his call. Knowles told them to come on back to San Jose.

Knowles then checked with Rothman. The weather was still looking like fog. Aptos was certainly going to be fogged in by dinnertime. Knowles knew that ransom callers tended to make their calls closer and closer to the eventual drop point as time goes by. In other words, Aptos was more likely to be close to the drop point than San Jose or Aromas where the first calls originated. That was bad news, since that meant the fog was likely to be a problem.

Rothman also had been in charge of other leads - the credit cards of the victim. He had just received a report from the security manager of one of the banks. A withdrawal had been made from an Automatic Teller Machine using Fischer's bank card on the day he had been kidnapped. Seven hundred dollars had been withdrawn, apparently right about the time the first ransom call had been placed to Mrs. Fischer. There had been no activity on the card since that call. The caller was at least smart enough to figure the cards were not safe to use once it was known they were in the hands of the kidnappers.

"Tim, that ATM is not far from here. That's right between Mountain View and the Seventrees Center. The kidnappers must have driven right down 101 and holed up for awhile in South San Jose somewhere. Call the manager back and have him pull the videotape from the ATM, not only for that use of the card, but for several minutes on either side. Have him check the records to get the account information for the customers using that ATM within that time frame. If we can identify who used the same ATM during that same period and show them the videotape, they may remember seeing the person who used it right before or after them."

"Right," Rothman replied. "Cliff, do you want to run out there ourselves if the other customers are local? This could be a big break."

"Yeah, I think we can. I don't have anything else urgent until the ransom call comes in. The street teams are all on their way to their staging areas." Knowles looked at his watch. It was 3:45.

Rothman called the security manager back. He agreed to isolate the video segment from the ATM that included the period from ten minutes before the transaction with Fischer's card. He assured Rothman that he could also get the transaction information and identifying information on the other users of the ATM around that time - if there were any - but only if they used that bank's ATM card. If they got cash using a card from one of the other affiliated issuers, for example, then he could get the transaction information, including the card number and issuing bank. The FBI would have to contact the card issuer to find out who the cardholder was. He said he could have the information available by the time they got out there.

Knowles checked in with Olson, who was back in the command post by this time, and let him know what he and Rothman were working on. He said he'd pass it on to Stroaker. The two agents then left the RA. As their elevator descended, it stopped at the second floor. A young man, with a long brown ponytail, entered the elevator in a motorized wheelchair, with considerable difficulty. Rothman and Knowles were accustomed to this, since the second floor was the location of a center for traumatic brain injuries. The young man looked at them and asked, "Hey, you guys G-men? What's going on? I see your people all over the place with guns strapped on their thighs."

The man's speech was a bit slurred, so it was difficult to make out what he was saying, but he spoke fluently. Rothman deciphered the question before Knowles did. "Training exercise. We do this every year. This year it's here in San Jose."

"Bullshit. You're bullshittin' me. I been coming here for seven years and I never seen anything like this before. I heard some talkin' in the bathroom. 'S no training exercise. They were talking about live ammo and hoping they didn't have to kill anybody tonight. What's going on? You got a top ten fugitive?" The man's eyes glistened with excitement.

Knowles was taken aback. If this guy was brain-damaged, the damage was restricted to the motor functions only. His perception and cognitive functioning were just fine. Knowles knew better than to enter into a debate or extend the cover story. "You seem like a sharp fella. We're just out doing the people's business. Wish us well."

"Yeah, okay. You can't talk about it. I know. Drive careful - that's what I didn't," he said cheerily as the agents got off at the first floor. He waved goodbye to them, as he continued to the basement for the wheelchair entrance to the garage.

"That's the problem with these RA's out in public office buildings," Knowles commented. "It's hard to be discreet. At least in a federal building you can be pretty anonymous. They give you a separate elevator and everything."

Rothman laughed. "Well, I'm sure we could arrange for you to be transferred back to San Francisco, if that's what you like."

"No, thanks. It was just an observation." They both knew how lucky they were to be in a resident agency, out of the view of the bosses. The cost of living was incredibly high in Silicon Valley, but it was a major metropolitan area, which translated into complex – and interesting – case work. San Jose, the eleventh largest city in the United States by population, was the only one in the top 20 that wasn't an FBI Field Office. Working in the San Jose RA was a mixed blessing. If you could afford to live there, it was as good an assignment as existed in the FBI. Big if.

Rothman drove, since he had talked to the bank security manager and knew where they were meeting him. When they arrived at the bank, the manager walked up to them before they even reached the front door. "You guys from the FBI?" he asked. It wasn't hard to guess when two guys in suits and ties get out of a battered Taurus.

"Yep. I'm Tim Rothman, this is Cliff Knowles. I'm the one who talked to you on the phone."

"Nice to meet you. I've got everything all ready for you inside. Follow me."

Proper practice dictated that they show their credentials, and check his identification, but the reality was that law enforcement and corporate security managers could easily tell who was who. There was a little ritual they always went through. The manager started it this time, "So you know George Davajarian?"

"Oh, sure," Knowles replied. "He retired about five years ago. He used to work bank robberies out in the East Bay. I hear he sold his house and moved to Reno. His son played football for one of the Pac Ten teams. I wonder if he ever made pros."

"No, the son became an actuary for some insurance company. He never got drafted into the NFL. George is playing golf up in Reno, all right. No state income tax on the federal pension there. We go fishing together once a year in Baja. I used to be on the force in Walnut Creek myself until I ruptured a disk in a training exercise."

"Yeah?" Knowles replied. "You must know a guy named Oliveros. I forget his first name - great big guy with a crazy laugh. He and I had a case on a fugitive once."

"Ollie? Yeah, that's him. He's crazy for sure. He can outdrink anybody I know. But he's good on that fugitive stuff - he recruits all his snitches in the bars. He knows everybody in those places."

The vetting over, they could rest easy that they were among friends. They didn't need no stinkin' badges, as the saying went. The manager sat them down in a chintzy break room in the back of the bank. Banks were all notoriously cheap about security. The video player was right next to the employee microwave. He turned on the player. The video recorder at this ATM ran continuously, even when no one was at the machine. Unlike a home VCR, it recorded only one frame every twenty seconds during general use. This sped up to every five seconds when someone began a transaction. Motion was thus very jerky. After three or four minutes of nothing, they saw a fat white woman stand in front of the camera and withdraw cash. She had to try her PIN three times. The fisheye lens must have added an extra 50 lbs to her avoirdupois. The manager pointed to a name and address on a printout he had placed on the table. It was obviously the identifiers for the woman in the video.

"You understand, I didn't give you that information. I would need a subpoena for that. But there's no law that says I can't print it out for my own use. If you happen to see it, well, I can't help that."

Knowles hated when they did that. Some people were too lazy to go through the legal process. They expected the FBI to cover for them by lying so they didn't lose their jobs. There were other ways to get the information besides a subpoena. The manager could have called the woman and explained that the FBI wanted to talk to her because she might have witnessed something they were investigating. Most people cooperated and allowed their name and number to be given out. Knowles made a note of the name, address, and phone number on his legal pad. He hadn't asked for the name or address, and he hadn't promised to keep the manager's secret. He'd cross that bridge when and if he ever came to it. He knew the chances were slim that he would need to.

The video continued playing. The woman could be seen walking away. At least two full minutes passed; then a man approached. He was wearing a sports coat, collared shirt, and no tie. The video was black and white, so no color could be determined. The fisheye lens put everything in sharp focus, but it distorted the shapes. It was hard to tell how heavy-set this male was, but he was clearly not as heavy as the woman had been. It was also impossible to tell what he looked like because he wore a motorcycle helmet with the tinted full-face visor pulled down all the way. He also wore gloves, although the day must have been over 80 degrees. He inserted the card and punched in the PIN expertly. He had obviously planned this very carefully and was trying to minimize the time he was in front of the ATM. He had probably waited until no one was around the machine before venturing into the open. The manager said, "That's him." The man was gone in a little over a minute with $700 of Fischer's money. There were no logos or names on his clothing. The helmet was dark, with a thin white stripe around the border of the visor, presumably some sort of plastic piping. They replayed the sequence several times, but that was all they could get – a male of average build wearing a sports coat and motorcycle helmet. There would be no fingerprints on the ATM, and, Knowles now knew, there wouldn't be any of this man's prints on the phone receivers they had dusted. Finally, they let the video resume playing. About thirty seconds after helmet man departed, a small, elderly Asian male approached the machine and withdrew money. Knowles looked down at the printout. There was a transaction number and notation, but no name and address.

"That guy used another bank's ATM card. National California Bank. They don't have a branch around here but they're part of the network that can use our machines. There was no one after him on the tape for the next ten minutes."

"National California. That's Mike Boggus's bank, isn't it?" Rothman asked. Boggus was a fellow Bureau agent and part-time pilot from Los Angeles division who had retired about a year earlier to take a bank security job and double dip - pension plus paycheck. Rothman knew him from flight training, but Knowles was not familiar with the name.

"I think so," the security manager replied. "I don't know him, but his name is on our association list. We all talk to each other about the robbers and fraud schemes. There's no competition between us like there is with the business units. We're all basically cops. We have regular meetings and all, but he's down in L.A. And I'm up here. I think that's the name on the list, though." He pulled a directory out of his briefcase and started to flip through it. "Yeah, that's the name - or at least one name. He's only regional manager, not director, so he's got someone over him. Here's the number."

Rothman asked to use the phone, and was directed to a wall phone next to the garbage can. He called the number from the directory. The line was busy. He cursed under his breath. "Busy. Cliff, the fat lady won't be able help us - she left before the subject got there. But the old Asian guy was right after him. He might remember our guy, tell us what kind of car, better physical description, whatever."

"I agree. We need the ID on that guy. We have to check out the woman, though, too. She could have walked away, but come back, or seen the subject waiting for her to leave. Let's do them both. Write down the number, and call your buddy later. Let's go try to find the woman." They made sure they had the account number of the Asian man, thanked the manager, and left with a printout of the ATM photo of the helmet man.

The woman lived in Fremont, which was about a half hour away in late afternoon traffic. Knowles called her on his newly assigned cell phone. She wasn't there, but her husband answered the phone. When Knowles introduced himself, the man was happy to tell him how to find the woman. She worked in a department store about three blocks from the bank, in the linens department. Knowles thanked him profusely and sincerely. That saved them an hour of rush hour driving. They got to the department store in record time. They had no difficulty locating the woman, who was as pleased as her husband to help the FBI. She didn't even ask what this was about. That was rare. However, when Knowles showed her the video printout she said had not seen the man. She remembered going to the bank on Tuesday, but just couldn't remember if anyone was around her at the ATM. Dead end.

That left the Asian man. Rothman called the number again for Mike Boggus. It rang this time. "Mike Boggus speaking."

"Hey, Mike. It's Tim Rothman, from flight school."

"Tim, how ya' doin' man? A voice from the past."

"Great. Hey, Mike, I'd love to catch up on old times, but I'm working a breaking case - a seven matter." Every FBI investigation fell into one or more classifications. The file number began with the classification number and a hyphen. All kidnap cases began with "7-." "We need your help."

"What can I do?" Boggus said it matter-of-factly, as though it was a given that he would do whatever he could.

"The bad guys used the victim's ATM card to withdraw money. One of your account holders was right after him at the ATM. We need to identify him to interview him."

"Do you have a subpoena?"

"No time - the payoff is tonight. The grand jury only sits on Tuesdays. As you know, we only have admin subpoena power for drug cases, not VCMO."

"The victim is still being held hostage? This is life-or-death, then?"

"Yeah."

"Okay, give me what you got. You should get me an emergency letter, followed by a court order. There's a procedure under the RFPA; your Legal Advisors know how to do it. You know I don't care if I get fired from this shitty job for helping you. I've about had it with tellers who don't know how to push the red button when they get robbed, and executives who treat us security like the janitorial crew. To save a man's life, I'd do it in a heartbeat, but I don't want to see you have the evidence suppressed if the witness turns out to be valuable."

Rothman relayed the gist of the last comment to Knowles. Rothman knew the RFPA referred to the Right to Financial Privacy Act, but didn't really knows the details of the law. After a moment of discussion he said to Boggus, "Mike, I'm working with one of our Legal Advisors; he's the case agent, in fact. Let me put him on."

"Mike, this is Cliff Knowles. Thanks for helping us out. We'll get you a letter to cover you, if you need it, but we don't need a subpoena or court order to make this legal. Name, address, and account number of a person involved in a financial transaction isn't restricted by the RFPA from law enforcement disclosure, as long as we get you a formal written request."

"Yeah? Our Chief Counsel says we can't give anything out without a court order or subpoena."

"Your Chief Counsel is an idiot, like most bank lawyers. There's a specific statute. The account holder isn't even remotely a suspect, and won't object anyway. The only person whose 'privacy' could be 'violated' is the account holder, not the defendant's. The witness's testimony won't be suppressed. From the ATM picture, it looks like an elderly Japanese man. I studied Japanese in college. They don't believe in privacy. They don't even have a word for it. Their translation is a word that really means loneliness. It's something they find oppressive, not something they'd sue to protect. In any event, it won't hurt the case."

"Well, you're the lawyer. I'll take your word for it. Give me what you got."

Knowles pulled out the printout and read the transaction numbers to Boggus, including exact date and time. He waited while Boggus started looking things up on a computer. He could hear the clicking of the keys in the background. It took a minute or two, and it was obvious that Boggus was not particularly proficient with a keyboard. Soon, he came back on the line. "Ready to copy?"

"Go ahead."

"Ichiro Tsuruda, 4949 Golden Coast Drive, Santa Monica, telephone (310) 555-5324"

"Super. Thanks, Mike. I'll fax you an emergency letter as soon as I get back to the RA."

"No problem. Good luck."

"Thanks again. Gotta run."

"Bye." They hung up.

Knowles showed Rothman the information. "Could be worse. Santa Monica isn't far from Westwood. LA is already on standby for this case, so we shouldn't have any trouble getting an agent to run down I-10 to cover this if we can't do it by phone."

They tore back to the RA, with Rothman's driving reflexes tested to the limit. They weren't authorized to use red light and siren, but they weren't concerned about getting a ticket. Knowles tried to get through on his cell phone to the telephone number Boggus had provided, but there was no answer. When they got to the RA he tried one more time, without success. Then he dialed the LA office of the FBI and got their main switchboard. He asked for the VCMO squad.

"Which one?" the switchboard operator asked.

He'd forgotten how big FBILA was. They had multiple VCMO squads. "Whichever one handles kidnappings. It's a seven case, and it's urgent." Operators usually refer to a chart that has the violations organized by classification. She transferred him to an extension.

He was put through to the squad secretary first, and explained that he needed a lead agent to run out immediately to Santa Monica to try to locate a witness on the breaking kidnap case.

"I thought that the guy was found dead. What's the rush?" the secretary answered, showing only moderate interest.

"That's the one in New Jersey. I'm calling from San Francisco. We have a payoff tonight with a live hostage still out there. This is immediate!" Knowles almost yelled.

"Okay, well everybody's out on bank robberies right now. I don't have anyone to send."

"Where's your Supervisor or Relief on duty?"

"The Supervisor's here. She's in a meeting with the ASAC, though. I can't interrupt that."

"You're going to have to. This is really life-or-death. I thought your whole squad would be on stand-by for this case. The SAC here said he talked to the ADIC there." ADIC was the acronym for an Assistant Director in Charge. Only New York and Los Angeles were big enough to warrant that position.

"Yeah, I think I heard something," the secretary said, barely stifling a yawn. "I thought that was up in Santa Barbara RA, though. A surveillance or something."

At least she knew he was not making it up. There would be agents on standby in Santa Barbara, the northernmost L.A. Division RA, to support the surveillance in case it headed south. But there should be agents on standby throughout the division for things like this - leads. "Look, I really need this. Please go get your supervisor. Tell everybody I absolutely insisted - I'll back you up. They won't blame you, I promise."

"Okay, if you say so." Knowles was put on hold for what seemed like an age. He gritted his teeth as he waited, because he could see the little red message light on his phone indicating he had messages, but he didn't dare put this call on hold to listen to them. Wasted time always gnawed at him. He looked over at Rothman, who was getting another weather report. Finally the squad supervisor came on the phone with a curt "Yes?".

"This is Cliff Knowles, the case agent on the seven case that's breaking in San Francisco tonight. You should have gotten a teletype last night about the payoff tonight."

"Sure, the Fischer case," the supervisor seemed to know all about it. Thank god the Z-man was sending out nightly teletypes to other divisions as planned.

"That's it. I need a lead covered in Santa Monica. A Japanese man used the ATM right after one of the kidnappers in our case used the victim's card. He might have seen the subject or his vehicle. I've got the address and telephone, but we haven't been able to get through on the phone. No answer. I need someone to run out and try to find out where the guy is. Apparently he lives down there, but was up in the Bay Area on Tuesday."

"I've got two agents working a late shift to cover this case for you. They're scheduled for a four-to-midnight, so they should be here by now. They'll work as late as you need. Give me the name, address, and telephone number of the witness." She was clear and efficient and did not need a recap. She showed no signs of pique at having been yanked out of a meeting with her ASAC. If only some of this conscientiousness could rub off on the squad secretary.

Knowles gave her the information. She told him she would track down the standby agents and have them cover it immediately. They would call him back with the results. She took his direct dial number in the RA and pager number, and they ended the conversation.

Rothman filled him in on the weather. No change. Fog predicted in coastal areas, clear above. Then Knowles started on his phone messages. The lead agent who had gone out to Seventrees had done massive interviews in the area, but found no one who remembered anything unusual at the pay phone on Tuesday. There were no security cameras covering the area of the phone. The phone was in near-constant use, so they didn't see any point in trying to dust it for prints; scores of people had used it after the ransom call.

Louellen Murphy had checked in from the house. Her message said Pam was holding up, but under a great deal of stress. They still hadn't found a white backpack. There were several others, none very important. A lot of people were just checking in to say they were ready. Some of the team leaders for the street teams needed clarification on what territory they were supposed to be covering.

Knowles didn't bother to return any of the calls immediately. Instead, he rolled his chair over to the computer he shared with Rothman and located a previous RFPA request letter he had drafted for another agent. He plugged in the name and address of the National California Bank, and the transaction numbers he had given Boggus. It took him ten minutes to print out a finished letter. He went to Kim's desk to pull it off the printer. This had to be signed by the SAC, so he took it to the command post. Stroaker was there talking to Len Schuler, the Branch Chief of the United States Attorney's Office in San Jose.

"Hi, Len," Knowles said casually as he entered. He and Len got along well, perhaps because both were attorneys and both had graduated from the same university. Len always provided good service on FBI cases, unlike some of the prosecutors in the U.S. Attorney's Office. Len had his briefcase all spread out and a cup of coffee on the table. It was obvious he was here for the duration of the night's events. It was normal to have an Assistant United States Attorney, or AUSA, stand by on big events like this. It was unusual, and therefore a sign of importance, to have the Branch Chief do it himself.

"Well, Cliff, as I live and breathe. Are you working this case, too?" Schuler asked.

Knowles looked at Stroaker as he replied, "Yep. I'm the case agent." This was a silent challenge to Stroaker. In effect he dared the SAC to tell the prosecutor that the 'real' case agent was in Disneyland. It still stuck in his craw that he had not been assigned the case officially. Schuler raised his bushy eyebrows quizzically, but remained silent as he shifted his gaze toward Stroaker. It became obvious to Knowles that Stroaker had been briefing Schuler as though he, Stroaker, had been running the whole thing almost single-handedly. "I hate to break in like this, but I need a signature from Mr. Stroaker. It's a request letter under the RFPA for financial records." He explained the situation, without mentioning that Boggus had already provided the information.

"Certainly, I'll sign it, Cliff," said Stroaker, scribbling his name at the bottom and handing it back. "I'm here to support the agents out on the street chasing down all the leads, no matter how small. They're the ones who do the real work, you know, Len." This was so blatantly intended to show both magnanimity and overall command of the war that Schuler gagged audibly. He covered it with a cough, as though his coffee had gone down the wrong pipe. Stroaker continued, "Now, you'll have to follow this with a search warrant, won't you, in two days? We always do everything strictly legally in my shop."

This was a show put on for Schuler's sake. Knowles was not surprised Stroaker got it wrong, since he never came to mandatory annual Legal Instruction. The requirement to follow a request letter with a court order or search warrant applied to intercepts, not the RFPA. Schuler, on the other hand, took for granted that all agents knew the law on all such things, since that was his own stock in trade. He seemed a bit appalled that the SAC thought a search warrant was required, and shifted uneasily, but, not wanting to embarrass Stroaker, said nothing.

Stroaker picked up on Schuler's body language, but misinterpreted it. "Is there something wrong, Len? If there is anything in the least illegal about this, then I won't sign." He reached to take the letter back from Knowles. Knowles turned so his back was partially toward Stroaker, making it appear that he was just trying to get face-to-face with Schuler. He made a huge grimace at Schuler, who got the message unmistakably.

Before Knowles said anything, Schuler declared confidently, "No, no. Nothing illegal at all. I was just thinking of ... manpower issues. By all means, sign it. If you need to talk to this witness, do what you have to do to save the victim. I'll take care of everything in court."

Knowles began to catch the command post personnel up on what he had learned from the phone messages, but Stroaker brushed him off disdainfully, making clear they already knew all that. He implied that if Cliff hadn't been off chasing down street agent leads, he would be up-to-date on the big picture like the executive team. This was, once again, an obvious ploy to impress another agency head.

Knowles took the signed letter and faxed it to Boggus. Then he dictated an FD-302 for Boggus's interview. Since the woman at the department store did not provide any relevant information, he did not do a 302 for her. No one had to know about the other bank manager providing her information without an order, although he could have done a letter for that bank just as easily.

Knowles then checked with Tobin to see if there had been any further activity with the cell phone. There was none. Strike-outs on the investigations at Seventrees and Aptos, the cell phone, and the fat lady. The FCI and terrorism squads had reported that there was nothing of interest from the Arab informants, and similar leads to the agents who worked Mexican gangs had come up dry. Their only active lead was the Japanese man in Santa Monica. If that didn't pan out, it would all be up to the surveillance team at the drop tonight. He wished he could talk to the neighbors of the Fischers, since it seemed pretty obvious now that they weren't being watched by anyone nearby. The caller had lied or bluffed about a number of things, such as knowing all about the finances, and the victim being in Mexico. So far as he was concerned, there was no danger the neighbors were involved, but the SAC had made that call, and he was not going to buck that. There was a difference between doing something without asking permission and doing something after permission had been denied.

As he walked back to the mail room to see what paper had shown up in his box, he walked past the entrance to the break room. The fragrance of pizza wafted his way, and his Pavlovian response kicked in. He was famished. It was now after five o'clock, and he had skipped lunch. Some kind souls had chipped in for the pizza, and left a few pieces on the soggy cardboard box. He grabbed two pieces, now cold, and a small slab of birthday cake left from the previous day. He couldn't even read whose birthday it had been, but it was food. He picked a spare coffee mug from the cabinet and filled it with tap water to wash down the cardiologist's nightmare. Rickie would kill him if she could see what he was calling a meal.

As he choked down a large glob of frosting, his pager went off. His hands were slathered in pizza grease and frosting, so he looked for something to use to wipe his hands. There was nothing. The paper towel dispenser was empty - as usual. There were no rags or wipes of any kind. His beeper continued to cry for attention. He would get grease all over his suit pants if he grabbed it now. He walked back into the mail room and fished a memo out of the trash can. The slick printer paper did not make the best napkin, but he got most of the goop from his hands. He walked back into the break room and ran his hands under the tap, rubbing them vigorously. With his hands still wet and a bit greasy, he pulled his pager from his belt and pushed the button. The beeping stopped. He read the number in the display window - a Los Angeles area code. One of the lead agents must have something. They had probably called him at his regular desk extension, and, when he didn't answer, called the pager. He rushed back to his office and dialed the number.

"O'Neill," was the terse answer in a decidedly sexy female voice.

"Hi, this is Cliff Knowles. Did you page me?"

"That was quick. I'm working this lead to locate the Japanese guy on the Fischer case."

"Yeah, great. Do you have something?" His tone told her he was eager for even the smallest scrap that could be of any use.

"I think so. There was no one at the house, so I started knocking on doors. A neighbor says the Tsurudas both work, but when I mentioned the name Ichiro, they seemed puzzled, since that wasn't the homeowner's name. Then I said it was an elderly man, and they said that must be guy's father who came out to live with the son about a year ago. They hardly ever see him out. He doesn't drive, and doesn't speak much English. They gave me the son's work telephone number."

Knowles looked at his watch. Five-fifteen on a Friday meant the son was probably stuck in a long L.A. commute right about now, and would be unreachable anytime soon. He crossed his fingers, hoping that O'Neill had had the brains to call the guy herself, rather than just getting a number for Knowles to follow up on.

"So I called it," O'Neill continued. "He was just getting ready to leave. He said his father is up in the Bay Area visiting the other son's family - this guy's brother. He gave me the name, address, telephone number, and work number for his brother." She read him off the details. "He said his father won't answer the phone there, because it's not his, and because he doesn't speak English well, but he'll pick up if he hears a voice he knows in Japanese on the message machine. I told him to try to reach his father or brother and have them contact you. I gave them your direct dial number. I hope that's all right."

"Absolutely. God, this is great. Thanks, uh, O'Neill .. sorry I didn't get your first name."

"Christine. No problem. Do you want me to follow through here or do anything else?"

"Not right now. We'll need a 302 eventually, but not tonight. You sound like you're at a pay phone."

"I am."

"Give me your pager so I can reach you if I need any other leads covered down there."

She recited it to him. "Hey," she added, "do you know Hank, the SWAT guy?"

"Yeah, he's working the SWAT lead on the operation tonight."

"Yeah? Well, he'll nail the bastard if anybody can. Hank's good at nailing people." She laughed with a throaty chuckle. "Tell him Crazy Christine from L.A. says hi."

Good at nailing people? Knowles decided this fell into the category of more than he needed to know right now. "Sure will. Thanks again, Christine. I'll call you if I need you."

Knowles saw the red message light on his phone glowing. He was hoping that one of the Tsurudas had called him, but the only message was from O'Neill - her original attempt to reach him before she had paged him. She had considerately left the whole message including all contact information on his voice mail, so he had it for easy reference if he needed it. We need more agents like Christine O'Neill, he thought.

He told Rothman what he had on the Tsurudas, and they split up the telephone numbers to call. The San Jose brother had left work for the day, and no one answered at the home. "We're going to have to run out to the house," Knowles said. "The father might be there, but he doesn't answer the phone, they said. We need to show him the picture anyway."

One more time they told Olson and Stroaker where they were going and why, and headed out. The condo complex where the man was visiting was only two blocks from the bank where the ATM was. Clearly, the old man had gone to that bank because he didn't drive. If only they had known how close he was when they were out there before, they could have saved a lot of time. Fortunately, there were two of them in the car, so they could use the car pool lane. They would have had no compunction in using it, even as solo drivers, but the Highway Patrol would have kept pulling them over, since they didn't have marked cars. The commute in Silicon Valley was brutal heading south on a Friday night, but with the car pool lane boost, they made it in under half an hour.

Arriving at the Tsuruda residence, they noticed a small stone lantern by the front door. Some Japanese calligraphy hung on a vertical cloth banner from the eaves. Rothman knocked on the door. After a short wait, they heard tiny footsteps approaching. The door opened, and they recognized the man before them as the same person in the ATM photo, a wizened, minuscule patrician in an elegant print robe. Knowles pulled out his credentials. He opened them carefully so that the badge as well as the photo ID was visible. He figured the man probably couldn't read the words, but would know what a badge was. He said slowly, "We're with the FBI," and pointed to his credentials.

The man's eyes lit up, and he responded quickly, "Ah, efu bi ai! Hai, hai." He formed a pistol shape with his thumb and forefinger and pointed the finger barrel at Knowles's chest. "Ka pao, ka pao!" he said, imitating a gun's recoil with two kicks of his hand, then giggled. He took a close look at the proffered credentials and began laughing uproariously. He kept laughing until tears literally streamed down his cheeks. This exercise in hilarity caused one gold incisor to be prominently displayed. Then, smiling brightly, he bowed deeply, stepped back and said, "Dozo."

Rothman shot Knowles a look that was usually reserved for cases of trouble. Knowles returned it with a nod, but shrugged and stepped in, nodding to Rothman to follow. They had no choice but to try. As he stepped inside Knowles took a quick look at his own credentials. Taped neatly over his photo was a photo of the Jack-in-the-Box clown. That's what had set off the gut-busting laughter. Knowles knew instantly that Q-ball had gotten him back. Discreetly, he peeled off the clown photo and returned the creds to his jacket pocket. Inside the door was a genkan, a small, tiled area for street shoes. Knowles told Rothman to take his shoes off and leave them here. They proceeded into the living room in their socks, and sat on the sofa as indicated by the man's gestures.

So far, Knowles had not heard any English from him, so he strained to recall his basic Japanese from his college course twenty years earlier. "Eigo ga dekimasu-ka?" he asked. 'Do you speak English?'

"Sukoshi. Ritteru bitto."

Knowles had to translate the 'ritteru bitto' as 'little bit' for Rothman. The accent was so strong that Rothman hadn't even recognized it was English. Knowles withdrew the photo from the ATM, and showed Tsuruda. The old man took it and studied it at length.

"Fuishai rensu," he announced.

Knowles had to mull that over, then responded, "Ahh, yes, it's a fish-eye lens. Do you remember that man? Kono hito ga oboemasu-ka?"

Tsuruda looked again, and seemed unsure. "Where this? Kore doko?"

"ATM," Knowles replied. When this met with blankness, he added, "Ginkoo."

"Ginkoo? Banku? Hai. Hai, oboemasu. San .." he paused and held up three fingers, "torii day ago. I go to banku." He nodded confidently.

"Yes, yes, on Tuesday," Knowles responded, urgency in his voice.

"I rimemba. He come befo I come."

They were making progress, but it was slow going. "Yes, he used the machine, the ATM, before you. Can you describe him?"

"I rimemba," Tsuruda said again, smiling.

They were so close it was tantalizing, but several more tries at questions resulted only in assurances that he remembered. Knowles did not remember enough Japanese to use words like 'describe' and could not understand the responses he got except for the 'I rememba.' He tried a different tack. "His car. Kuruma ga oboemasu-ka?"

"Kuruma? Hai, oboemasu." He remembered the car.

"Nanno kuruma?" What kind of car?

"Amerikano kuruma." American car.

"Dochira no..." which.... Knowles couldn't think of how to say 'make' or 'manufacturer.' "For example, Ford, Chevrolet, Chrysler.."

"Wakaranai." I don't understand. Knowles was not sure if he meant he didn't understand the question or didn't know the answer. The response could mean either. This was so frustrating, Knowles wanted to pick him up and just shake the answers out of him. From somewhere in the back of the condo the rhythmic hum of an electric motor sounded. The clunk, clunk that accompanied it signaled an automatic garage door, rolling up panel by panel. "My son. He herupu. He speak English good." He pronounced the last words, "Supikku Igirisu guddo."

The younger Tsuruda entered the condo from somewhere in the rear and came walking into the room cursing in Japanese. He threw his briefcase on the counter separating the kitchen from the living room. Tough day at the office for the salaryman, Knowles surmised. Then the younger man spied the agents and his features took on a mask of serenity. He bowed slightly and without only a slight accent said, "Hello. I am Martin Tsuruda." He put out his hand.

Knowles returned the bow, and shook the hand. "I'm Special Agent Cliff Knowles of the FBI, and this is Special Agent Timothy Rothman. We're speaking to your father about a case we are investigating. He's being very helpful, but we have some language difficulty. Would you be willing to translate for us." Knowles displayed the credentials once more, this time without the clown face.

Martin shook Rothman's hand. "I'm pleased to meet you. I will help you however I can."

Knowles explained that Martin's father had been to the bank on Tuesday and had seen the man in the photo, which he displayed. The son seemed slightly relieved to know his father was not directly involved, but was just a witness. He exchanged rapid-fire Japanese with his father for a moment.

"He says he went to the bank on Tuesday and remembers this man in front of him at the money machine - the ATM."

Knowles did not see any point in telling him that they had already gotten that far. "We would like to find out if he can provide any further identifying information on this man. Can he describe him, for example?" More rapid Japanese.

"He says he was tall. He remembered him because he thought it was funny he was wearing a motorcycle helmet when he was driving a car."

How tall is tall? Ichiro Tsuruda could not be more than five foot one. Someone five four might seem tall to him. This was a common problem with the way witnesses gave descriptions, and the agents were used to narrowing it down. "How tall, Mr. Tsuruda," Rothman asked. "As tall as your son?" Martin was about five seven. He translated.

"More tall my son. Maybe. Litteru bitto." Tsuruda senior was trying to show off his English still, but this was still unclear. The son was a little bit taller or the subject? Martin clarified it by standing up and holding his hand over the top of his head about three inches. Then Ichiro said something else in Japanese.

"He says he could not tell how tall because of the helmet, but taller than I am, he thinks," Martin translated.

"What about the car? Can he describe it? Make? Color?"

After more consultation, "He says it was American. He does not know the American makes, only Japanese cars. He doesn't drive and does not pay much attention to cars. He says he is sure it was not a Japanese car. It was a four-door, dark car. Maybe black, but he's not sure."

"Did he notice anything distinctive about it," Rothman asked, "license plate, bumper stickers, broken or damaged parts?"

"No, he doesn't remember anything like that," came the eventual response.

"How about the clothing? What was the color of the clothes?"

"Dark sports coat, white shirt. He says white shirt, but the Japanese word really means dress shirt. Could be any color. No tie."

"Was there anyone else in the car?"

"Not that he remembers. He's pretty sure the man was alone."

Further questioning brought little more information. This was turning out to be less useful than they had hoped. Finally, Knowles looked at his watch and decided they had better be getting back to the RA. The payoff instructions could be coming soon. They thanked the Tsurudas and prepared to leave. As they put on their shoes, Martin said he would walk them out. All four men walked out to the curb, and the agents got in the Bucar. Knowles rolled down his window to thank them again. Ichiro Tsuruda said something to his son, and started laughing again.

"Hold on," Martin said. "He says the man's car was a lot like this one. Only darker, and newer."

"A Ford Taurus? Is he sure?"

"No, he says he can't be sure it's the same manufacturer. All the American ones look alike to him. He's laughing because he thought it was so funny this guy wore this sporty motorcycle helmet and yet was wearing dressy clothes and driving a boring, average-looking car. It wasn't even a convertible."

Knowles nodded, animated. This was at least a little better. They could eliminate Japanese cars, and this added to the probability it was a Taurus like Nguyen had thought. Progress. He jotted some notes, thanked them again, and rolled up the window. As they pulled away from the curb they made a U-turn. Knowles looked over and saw Martin Tsuruda running across the street toward them. He told Rothman to stop. Martin ran up to the driver's side window.

"This might be important. He said he realized why the man had on the helmet when he drove out."

"Uh, yeah?" Rothman said, not yet seeing the significance, since he knew the reason was to disguise his face for the ATM camera.

"Yes. He drove over to the stores across the street from the bank. There's a motorcycle shop there. My father assumes the man had a motorcycle there for repair, or was buying one there. He probably just kept the helmet on after he dropped it off or was going back to pick it up and drive it away."

"He saw where the man drove to?" Rothman asked, incredulous. It's always that question you don't ask. He kicked himself mentally for not thinking of it during the interview. He just assumed the subject had driven away, and a person on foot wouldn't be able to follow and see where he went.

"He says he saw him drive across and into that shopping center over there. There is a Suzuki cycles place there. He knows that because it is Japanese - he can see the sign from the bank. There's a Japanese restaurant in there, too. My father has been in there."

The agents thanked Martin yet again, even more profusely, and took off. The Bureau radio ground out a staticky message which Knowles recognized as his call sign. He picked up the mike. "Go ahead."

"Number One is asking where you are. It's after six, and the training scenario will be starting soon. Your friend called again." That was code for the night's operation could be starting any time; get your ass in here. "Your friend" was the ransom caller. Number One referred to the SAC.

"Did my friend give the mailing address?" That was code for drop instructions.

"Negative." So the instructions were yet to come. They had to wait for another call.

"OK, tell Number One I'm on my way. We got some good material for the exercise here - tell him that."

"Roger."

Knowles told Rothman to make a pass through the shopping center where the motorcycle shop was. It turned out to be a dingy strip mall with a number of seedy businesses. The motorcycle shop,

Sy's Cycles, was a repair shop that had a few bikes for sale on consignment in the window. Asian Adult Entertainment stood next to that, with a cheap sign advertising "XXX videos" in the window. Ume Restaurant, apparently the one referred to by Martin, was little more than a bar with a Japanese name and decor, but they probably served some yakitori or sushi from the bar. Next to that was Deep Thought Diving, then Stan-Mike Furnace and Air. Knowles told Rothman to show the photo - Rothman had a bad photocopy he could display - to the restaurant, the diving place, and furnace repair, and Cliff would take the motorcycle shop and the porno place. They were running late and had to get this done fast.

Knowles surveyed Sy's from the parking lot and noticed that it had a small Suzuki Parts and Accessories sign in the front window. It was not a new cycle dealer. This sign could not be seen from the bank, contrary to what Tsuruda the younger had said. Nor could it be seen from the area in front of the restaurant/bar, because that stretch of shops was recessed, while only the cycle shop and porno place protruded out closer to the street in a shallow L configuration. One could see the sign only from directly in front of the cycle shop - or the Asian porno place - and Ichiro Tsuruda did not look like a motorcycle aficionado. Perhaps the elder Tsuruda was not quite so genteel as he had appeared. When Knowles entered, the sales clerk, a tattooed biker straight from a television type-casting session, looked at him with a jovial grin, revealing very bad teeth. Knowles showed his badge, and the grin disappeared. He showed the biker the photo of the helmeted man in the sports coat, but all he could get from the clerk from then on was a grunted "no" and a shake of the head, massive arms crossed defiantly over the chest. This guy wouldn't identify his worst enemy to the FBI, Knowles thought. He clearly was not an Efrem Zimbalist, Jr. Fan Club member. There was no one else there, and Knowles gave up. There was no point in wasting more time there.

He went next door to the video store, where the man at the register glanced at him suspiciously as he e-entered. The suit probably set him off, Knowles thought. He took a quick look around, and saw the videos on shelves with crude, hand-written signs indicating language or nationality: "Chinese", "Viet Nam," "Japanese," "Thai." Some of the signs had characters in the native language. There were a few customers browsing, and they looked at him even more suspiciously than had the man up front. There was a large table near the register that bore a sign in felt pen "New Release." On it were a dozen or so VHS tapes with hand-made labels showing major studio first-run movie titles. These were obviously pirated copies. Something to report to the white collar squad, Knowles figured, but now wasn't the time. He showed the clerk his credentials, then the ATM photo. The clerk put on a show of studying the photo, squinted, and said no, he'd never seen him before. Out of curiosity, Knowles asked about Ichiro Tsuruda. The name meant nothing to the clerk, and Knowles did not have the ATM photo of Tsuruda, only helmet man. He described Tsuruda as very short and thin, white-haired, with one gold tooth in front - Japanese. At this description, the clerk's face lit up with recognition so obvious that he might as well have drawn the cartoon light bulb over his head. However, he did not respond directly to the question, instead asking what this was about.

Rothman walked in at that point and said, "Nothing down there. Any luck here?"

"Naw, nothing. Let's go." Knowles decided it wasn't worth pursuing the angle on Tsuruda. Fortunately the older man had not personally told the agents he had seen the Suzuki sign from the bank; that had come from the son. If Ichiro had said it himself, it would have had to go in the FD-302, and that would have damaged the credibility of the old man if it ever became necessary to use him as a witness. He had obviously not wanted to tell his son that he saw the Suzuki sign during his frequent forays to the video store.

They hopped back into the car and took off for the RA. Knowles checked on the radio once more, and the drop instructions call still hadn't come in. They weren't late for the action. Even so, Rothman drove like a fighter pilot getting back.

Chapter 20

Carl Fischer heard the screen door, followed by the sound of footsteps. These footsteps, however, sounded different from the others - louder than Carlos's or Miguel's. The sounds increased in volume until they were obviously in the same room. Fischer turned around to face whoever had entered. He could still see a little, from under the mask. The shoes he saw were work boots, new-looking. Carlos's shoes had always been dress shoes or sneakers, and Miguel always wore athletic shoes.

"Mr. Fischer, we seem to have a problem with you," the voice began. "I am Ruben, the leader of this organization. I will decide your fate." The voice was deeper, more authoritative, than the others. But Fischer wondered why they bothered to continue using Spanish names. He had seen Miguel, and gone through the religious inquisition. It was obvious they must be all Arabs. Carlos and Miguel spoke a foreign language together; though they were careful not to speak it where he could hear them, and it was unlikely one was Arab and one Mexican. "Did you try to escape today?"

"Yes, I did." Lying would have served no purpose.

"I have not decided yet how to punish you. Will you try again?"

"No, no, I swear I won't."

"What did you see when you had your blindfold off? Do not lie to me. Your punishment will be worse if you do."

"I saw the kitchen and the back yard. I saw the carport, but no car. I saw Miguel briefly, but only for a moment. I don't think I could identify him." Fischer did not know for sure whether or not he could identify Miguel, he had been so panicky and the encounter so brief, but he wasn't about to say he could.

"Describe him to me."

"Short, maybe five feet ten, black curly hair, beard and mustache, dark complected - like Mediterranean." Fischer knew Miguel was no more than five six or seven, and was Middle Eastern Muslim - Arab, or possibly Turk or Persian - but he was intentionally being vague in the hope that his poor description would be deemed so bad that they would consider him not much of a risk as an eyewitness. If his description was too accurate, he would be setting himself up for elimination. "The mustache was sparse right in the middle, under the nose, and formed little sharp peaks on the cheeks in the growth pattern." He hoped that this level of detail would convince them that he was being truthful and guileless in his disclosure. He focused on the facial hair, because he knew that they would not be worried about that - Miguel could easily shave and no longer fit the description.

"What is this place?"

"It's a house. I didn't get the street name. I don't even know the town we're in. I was almost blinded by the brightness of the sun, I've been blindfolded so long." This was truthful as far as it went, but he did not mention that he saw the number on the house or name of the Alvarez Backhoe business across the street. He could give investigators enough information so they could find this place, but he hoped Ruben would not ask those specific questions, as he could not be sure how good he would be at lying.

"All right. I will let you live - for now. If you try to escape again, I will not make the same decision next time. You will make another recording for Carlos." With that pronouncement, he turned on his heel and left.

The screen door and accompanying footsteps heralded Carlos's return. "You heard what Ruben said?" he asked.

"Yes, I heard. I understood. I won't try to escape again, and I'll cooperate with you in making another tape. Whatever you say."

By the time Knowles and Rothman got back to the RA, Kim already had the transcript typed.

FISCHER -- Hello?
MALE -- Pam?
FISCHER -- Yes.
MALE -- Is the money ready?
FISCHER -- Yes, it's ready.
MALE -- Okay, which car will you be driving?
FISCHER -- The Cadillac.
MALE -- The Cadillac. Okay, that's good. Did you get the white pants, white shirt, and white jacket?
FISCHER -- Yeah, but I'm still working on the book bag.
MALE -- Good. Put all the money in the backpack.
FISCHER -- Okay. Is my dad okay? Can I have...
MALE -- Another tape? Yes, you're gonna listen. Get the San Jose *Mercury News* and keep it with you.

FISCHER -- Uh, the evening edition, or do they have two editions? I'm not sure.

MALE -- Get the morning edition.

FISCHER -- Okay.

MALE -- We will contact you at ten o'clock tonight with specific instructions.

FISCHER -- Can't we do it earlier? My mom is a nervous wreck.

MALE -- Listen to me. You...

FISCHER -- No, you listen to me. My mom is almost in the hospital. We just want to get this over.

MALE -- I can't listen to you. This is non-negotiable. I will call you at ten o'clock tonight. I'll let you hear a tape.

FISCHER -- Can I hear it now?

MALE -- We don't have it yet. It has to come from Tijuana. Understand?

FISCHER -- Oh, okay.

MALE -- We'll contact you tonight. Don't do anything stupid. If you're being followed, the mission will be canceled. No games. If your car...

FISCHER -- No, no I won't. It's just me here.

MALE -- Okay, listen to me.

FISCHER -- I'm trying to hold down the fort by myself. This is hard without anyone to help me. My mother is almost in the hospital.

MALE -- Look, just listen to what I'm saying. This will all be over tonight if you do exactly as I say. Make sure...

FISCHER -- Well, how do I know you're not going to kidnap me? Or hurt me?

MALE -- We don't want nothing to do with you. Why would I do that? All I want is the money.

FISCHER -- When I drop the money, am I going to see my dad?

MALE -- Our organization will release your dad in a few hours.

FISCHER -- You, you, no, ... before you told me one hour.

MALE -- Well, yes, one hour. Maybe two at the most. He'll be dropped in The City.

FISCHER -- Where in San Francisco? Do you have any idea? How is he going to get in touch with me?

MALE -- Right after you make the drop, you will go directly home and wait for his phone call.

FISCHER -- Okay.

MALE -- Okay, now listen. In about ten seconds I'm going to have to hang up.

FISCHER -- Okay.

MALE -- If you're being followed, or there's any kind of transmitter this whole thing will be canceled.

FISCHER -- Do you think I'm stupid? I understand about being followed.

MALE -- Good. Good. Now be home by ten o'clock and I'll call with further instructions.

END OF CONVERSATION

"Did we get a trace location?" Knowles asked as he hurried into the command post.

Stroaker cast a disapproving glance at him. "So there you are. Yes, we got a trace." He looked down at his notes. "It's at the Prime Outlet Center in Gilroy."

Gilroy was about twenty miles south of San Jose. The factory outlet center had over 150 stores, Knowles knew, and was really three huge shopping centers juxtaposed. It would be impossible to locate the specific phone and witnesses in a timely manner. "Has anybody been dispatched there?" he asked.

"Yeah, I sent the street team in Gilroy. Q-ball is the team leader," Olson replied. Stroaker gave another withering glance at Knowles, as if to say, see, we had to cover for you since you weren't here to do your job.

"Okay, great. I'll get on the radio and see how they're doing. I got some lead information on the car." Knowles synopsized the investigation with Tsuruda.

"Hmm, well, it sounds to me like all we got was a confirmation that we're looking for a dark sedan, make still unknown, and a male, average height and build," Stroaker reviewed with his own spin on it. "It doesn't sound like much of an improvement." He was still trying to minimize the importance of what Knowles was doing when he should have been up in the command post.

"Well," Knowles countered, "that's pretty much right, but now we know he probably visited a motorcycle shop, and had a helmet. He may try to make an escape tonight by bike or ATV."

Stroaker turned to Morales and inquired, "Mo, do you have cycle and ATV capability?"

"We already have motorcycles out on the street, Boss," Morales replied, "and they have all-terrain tires. Our people are trained in motorcycle pursuit."

Stroaker beamed at him approvingly and replied to Knowles, "Well, we had that covered already. We have the best SOG in the western U.S., maybe in the whole FBI. But it's good that we have this bit of information to pass on to the street teams. Mo, you let the SOG units know about the motorcycle angle, and Cliff, you inform the street teams."

"Sure, Boss," Morales said, hustling out to Radio to do as he was bidden.

"What about the call?" Knowles asked. "What do you think of it?" The question was directed to all the command post personnel. Knowles was a bit late to this party, and knew that they must have already discussed it. He looked around expectantly first at Stroaker, then Z-man, Schuler, and Olson.

"This guy's full of bullshit," the Z-man proclaimed. "He's no pro. He can't get his story straight on when he's going to release the victim, one hour or two, and he can't get a tape from Tijuana tonight, especially if the victim is close enough to be released in San Francisco. He's hiding somewhere locally."

"And we're sure now he's Spanish speaking," Stroaker said. "The way he said 'Tijuana' is the correct Spanish pronunciation. We heard the tape. Most Americans say 'Tia Wanna' or something like that. You can drop the Arabic part from the description." He pointed his finger at the suspect board. Knowles nodded, but did not move to make any change. The briefing had already been given, and the street teams had heard it. The board made no difference at this point. "Fischer is out getting a *Mercury News*. It's hard to find at this time of night. There aren't many vending boxes on the sidewalks in Los Altos and the ones that are there are empty by now."

"Well, you shouldn't let her buy one there, anyway," Knowles offered. "They get the Peninsula Edition, whereas whatever is going to be on the next tape will probably be from the Metro edition or Monterey Bay edition. All the calls have been South Bay. If he reads something from the Metro edition, covering San Jose, that isn't in the Peninsula edition, Pam may freak out. He may even give instructions by referring to particular articles, ads, or page numbers that are in the edition he has, not realizing hers is different. She needs to ask specifically which edition, the area, I mean, not the morning or evening, if the instructions are like that. What if he says go to the bus stop across from the shoe store in the ad on page 14? We need to make sure that same ad is on the same page on what we're looking at."

Stroaker looked over at Olson, whose head started bobbing in assent. Stroaker, in his office, got all four major Bay Area newspapers, The San Jose *Mercury News, San Francisco Chronicle,* San Francisco Examiner, and Oakland Tribune, as well as clipped articles from other, more local, papers. It was his duty to stay current on news coverage of the FBI and their cases. He did his newspaper reading in San Francisco, and tended to rely most heavily on the *Chronicle* and Examiner, so apparently never noticed that the *Mercury* came in several localized editions. He only saw one. No one else had thought of this, and Knowles could see the exasperation in his face when the SAC scowled at Olson and Z-man for having missed it.

"Good catch," Schuler piped up cheerily. "You should get a copy of each edition and run it over to the house." He could see that Knowles was the brains behind the operation, and needed reinforcements.

"I'll see if I can round up the Monterey Bay edition here in the RA. Several employees live over near Santa Cruz and might have brought one with them. If not, I'll have one of the Santa Cruz County street team members drive one over. Our local RA copy will be for San Jose Metro. Did Pam ever get a Peninsula edition?"

"Yeah, eventually she found one," Olson answered.

"Okay, good then. We're covered. Do you want me to call Louellen and give her the instructions about clarifying the correct geographical edition with the next call?"

"No, I'll take care of it," Stroaker said, picking up the phone to call her. "Just check to see what the story is with the backpack. We need that now."

"But it doesn't have to be white," Knowles said. "We can use the original black duffel it was brought down in. That was clarified in the last call. We all had it wrong."

Stroaker hung up the phone. "How do you mean? I remember Luciana saying specifically that he instructed her to get a white backpack."

"She did say that. But she said it wrong while she was trying to relay the call. Look back at the original transcript, and again at this last one. He says white pants, white shirt, and white jacket, but he does NOT say white backpack. I finally noticed it when reading this latest transcript. I don't think he cares about the color of the backpack at all."

A flurry of pages ruffling filled the room as five or six people flipped through their copies of the transcripts. Stroaker read over the transcripts with a concentration so intense he looked to be on the brink of brain overload again. Finally he looked up and shook his head disgustedly and called over to Tobin to get the black duffel bag prepped. Tobin began to wire the sparklers onto the outside of the bag.

"Cliff, I want you in the CP when the next call comes in," Stroaker said. "If you have more leads to run down, give them to the other agents."

Knowles left to get back to his office to check his phone messages and e-mail. He now knew that he would have a few more hours before the drop. He stopped at Radio on the way and notified the street teams of the expected time of the drop call, the motorcycle angle, and the possibility of directions being given by reference to the *Mercury News*. He also let them know the last call was traced to Gilroy.

Knowles was becoming concerned with how he was being perceived by the SAC. The command to be in the CP during the drop could be taken as a vote of confidence, or as a sign the SAC wanted to keep his eye on him. It was the right place for him, in any event. He could not tell whether Stroaker resented being shown up for not having noticed either the newspaper or the backpack problems, or whether he appreciated that he had someone he could rely on for the details. Maybe a little bit of both.

Knowles checked in with Kim to see if there was anything else going on, then reviewed his phone and e-mail messages. He returned calls to several team leaders who had questions, then called Radio to see if Quincy Allen's team had made any progress at the outlet mall. The Radio clerk said Allen would be calling him in a few minutes. He then checked with Rothman, who confirmed that the weather forecast was unchanged and told him that the SAC's helicopter was ready and waiting at the hospital helipad.

His phone rang. "Cliff Knowles," he answered.

"Cliff, it's Quincy. I'm at the outlet mall."

"Any luck yet?"

"We've located the phone he used. It's a single pay phone on a masonry pillar outside the stores, close to a parking area. There's a video camera on the general area. It isn't focused specifically on the phone. It's a wide-angle coverage shot. I'm in the mall security office now. They've pulled the tape, and we're reviewing it. We haven't gotten to the spot on the tape that has the ransom call, but based on what we have seen of others using that phone, it'll be impossible to make any identification. It's a really small image, the view is of the back of the head, and even that is partially blocked by the next pillar down. There's no shop facing the phone where someone might have noticed who used the phone. We're still interviewing, but we don't expect to find anyone. From what you said at the briefing, we assume this guy wore gloves, but we've removed the receiver for later dusting at the office, just in case. There probably weren't many people who used it after the call. It's in a low traffic area."

"Okay. If you can recognize the caller on the tape from his clothing, not his face, I mean, but you can pick him out of the crowd there, see if you can spot him on other camera views coming from or returning to his vehicle. It could be a motorcycle, which means it might be up close to the main part of the mall where the video might capture it. We'd like to know if he is using a cycle tonight. But don't get too bogged down there. The payoff is going to be in a few hours, and your team is likely to be close to the action. You have four people. The closest teams to you north and south are Salinas and the Coyote area. You need to spread out and cover Hecker Pass Road and Pacheco Pass, too. That's a lot of real estate for four people."

"We'll take care of it. I still owe you one, by the way."

"Yeah, right. I know that was you with the clown picture. I got thoroughly embarrassed on an interview today. Truce, okay? This is just not the time. The SAC is giving me more grief accidentally than you ever could on purpose anyway."

"Okay. I admit nothing, but we're even."

"Bring me a good picture of that caller, and I'll paste the clown photo back on myself."

"We'll try. Talk to you later."

The time was creeping up on eight, so Knowles checked with the command post to see if it was okay to take a meal break. The pizza and cake from lunch wouldn't hold up alone through the night. Olson said they were going out in shifts since no action was expected for a couple of hours, and gave Knowles permission to grab a bite. He suggested Knowles be back by nine to see the final packaging of the money. Knowles rounded up Rothman, Nguyen, and Torres and went over to the Greek restaurant across the street from the RA so they'd be close. They found a booth in the corner where they could talk without being overheard.

Nguyen and Torres had been assigned to stay on lead duty in the RA, rather than be on a street team. There were always things that needed to be done - checking records, making phone calls, running stuff to someone somewhere - or just to serve as a reserve. They had never been on a big operation like this, so they had a lot of questions. Knowles went over the plan with them again. The call would come in at around ten, they assumed, and instructions for the money drop would be made. Pam Fischer would take the ransom money in the Cadillac. Terry Izawa would be with her, hidden in the back, communicating with a handheld radio on the SOG channel, Red 3, to units nearby. The SOG aircraft would fly as close to overhead as possible, providing visual coverage of the car and serving as a radio repeater. One SOG vehicle, a souped up tow truck with a hidden compartment, used for special cases such as this, would be the tail car to provide added protection. If the Cadillac was stopped or isolated in some way, the truck could zoom in and protect Pam. There would be additional fisur units consisting of the street teams assigned to the Los Altos area. They were staffed by agents from the Palo Alto RA, the closest RA to the Fischer home. Their job was to stay close enough to respond quickly to a radio call for assistance, but far enough away from the Cadillac so that anyone looking for a tail would not spot them - definitely not within line of sight of the Cadillac. When Pam got to wherever the caller instructed her to go, she would not take the ransom to a person, for safety reasons; she would leave it where instructed and go. If the caller's instructions were to leave the car to meet someone, Izawa would be the one to do it. The air cover would then peel off from her and follow the ground surveillance around the money. The SWAT, in their black ninjas, would presumably get to the spot first and form the close observation team. There would be snipers in place with night vision scopes. SWAT would also have night vision equipment, if needed. The SOG would form the distant perimeter to prevent anyone from escaping.

When the money was picked up, the pickup person would be followed. Usually, but not always, the kidnapper drove off in a car. That would be the critical time. The ransom would be treated with all the methods mentioned in the briefing, so the surveillance teams should be able to follow where it went, but it was always dicey. In past cases the pickup always had a plan to shake any surveillance, and they occasionally succeeded - swapping cars, speeding at 100 mile per hour or more, going into parking garages or other places where they couldn't be seen by airplanes, having the loot thrown over a bridge or using some other way of separating the money from the people following it, having a paid messenger who knew nothing about the customer who ordered the delivery pick it up, and so on. Knowles had never heard of a case where the kidnappers had not expected the drop to be covered by law enforcement, and so there was always a plan to evade capture. Sometimes the plan had worked for awhile, but almost never long enough for the kidnappers to enjoy the spoils of the crime.

Rothman listed the many factors that affected the air coverage. Fuel was a big one. The plane always took off as late as possible, so as to maximize the amount of time it could spend in the air, but if the surveillance lasted more than a few hours, it might have to leave the area. For tonight's operation, they had a second fixed wing aircraft assigned to relieve the first one. Planes, unlike cars, can't park in one spot and wait. Once airborne they have to keep moving at over 100 miles per hour, so they were constantly flying in circles when waiting for something to happen. That meant they had a good chance of being headed the wrong way when the critical moment arrived. It was difficult to identify the target car, especially at night. It worked best if an SOG vehicle, with special markings visible from the sky, could get right next to, or right behind, the target so the pilot could lock onto the one he was supposed to follow. That was easier said than done. While all this was going on, the pilot had to fly the plane, a non-trivial task. Since the pilot had to focus on the target on the ground, there had to be an observer in the plane to watch for other air traffic, help with the radio if necessary, take notes, and look things up in the reference materials. Tonight there was the added problem of fog; it was expected to be dense enough at ground level to kill visibility, but not too thick - it would be clear above a few hundred feet in altitude. If the payoff was anywhere near the coast, the plane just wouldn't be a factor in the visual surveillance, but it would still be able to serve as a radio repeater up above the fog.

Nguyen asked about the chances of a gunfight. Knowles told him that was mostly television and movie fiction. It could happen, but it was rare. Kidnappers knew they couldn't win a gun battle with law enforcement. Their plan was always to get the ransom money away without being observed or caught. If they got into a situation where it was obvious the game was up, they invariably surrendered - unless they were suicidal or fanatics of some sort. One might try to claim he was an innocent who just happened to come by. One case he remembered was a guy dressed as a bum who had left instructions to leave the money, packaged in a garbage bag, in a public trash can in a park. He had waited patiently more than two hours, trying to determine if the police nabbed the people who threw things in the trash or rummaged through it for cans. When he saw they didn't, he ambled up and started rummaging, then slipped the loot into his own can bag. He was arrested as he left the park. What he didn't know was that we had figured out what he must be doing - watching from somewhere - after a half hour or so, and sent in an undercover dressed as a homeless bag lady. She went through the garbage and left with some cans, and no one touched her. That lulled him into a false sense of security and he broke cover.

The waitress brought their dinners, all of which consisted of some concoction wrapped in grape leaves. The orders had all been different, but they smelled and looked the same upon arrival. They all had feta cheese crumbled over the side salad. Knowles had taken no more two bites when his cell phone rang. Since this phone was issued by Communications especially for this case, the only people who had the number were people he could not ignore. He decided to take the call at the table. There were no secrets from the other agents, and they were in a remote corner of the restaurant where no one would overhear him.

"Yeah, Knowles," he mumbled through his mouthful.

"The shit hit the fan," the Z-man said. "The girl just heard from her mother, who heard about it on the TV upstairs - about the oil executive in New Jersey getting offed. She's freaking out."

"That's all we need. Is Louellen on top of it?"

"Trying to be, but the Fischer girl is saying her dad is going to be killed. She wants to just pay the ransom and not be followed."

"No, we can't allow that. The best chance for her father is for us to grab the kidnapper and make him lead us to him."

"Shit, I know, but convincing her is another matter." Behind the Z-man's voice Knowles could hear bedlam in the command post.

"Do you need me to do something?" Knowles asked.

"I don't know yet, but you should probably get back over here. The SAC's calling Carmody personally to try to get him to help calm the daughter down. I think Louellen is the best person to deal with her. That's what's she's trained in. I don't think Pam's going to pay much attention to Carmody."

"Okay, I'm on my way." Knowles briefed the other agents on what had just happened, telling them they could stay and finish eating unless called. Then, knowing this might be his last chance to refuel before the fireworks started, he picked up his plate and shoveled his entire meal into his mouth. He opened his wallet and threw a $20 bill on the table, then scurried out, still chewing. The other agents would have to do the arithmetic later.

Knowles dodged dangerously through heavy traffic across Bascom Avenue to the RA and ran up the stairs. When he got to the command post, chaos still reigned. Len Schuler saw him come in and grabbed him by the elbow. "Pam's threatening to withdraw consent to monitor the phone again unless we promise to let her go with no tail car. She's afraid that they'll kill him if she's tailed. We need to go for an emergency court order to monitor the phone based on probable cause rather than consent. Can you do an affidavit?"

"Len," Knowles answered, "there's no way we can get an affidavit and order drafted, and to a judge in time. And if Pam withdraws her consent, the order probably isn't going to change anything. She can refuse to do what we say, she can yank the second phone off the wall, or unplug the phone patch. There's a million ways she can sabotage us, order or no order. Someone's got to convince her to cooperate. Lie to her if necessary."

Schuler gasped audibly at the word 'lie'. "But that wouldn't be valid legal consent if she gave it under false promises. That could taint the admissibility..."

Knowles cut in, "C'mon Len, get real. The defendant won't have standing to raise that if he even finds out it ever happened. Think about it. The victim is still alive in this case. No kidnapper's going to kill a victim because they detect surveillance. They expect it - always. It's much more likely that if we don't follow her, and she makes the payoff by herself, that they'll keep the father and try to do it again, since they know it works. Or just kill him so he can't identify them.

That's the real danger. If we capture the pickup guy and get him to take us to the victim, Pam isn't going to complain that she gave her consent under false pretenses. Besides, we still have the mother's consent, and it's her phone line."

"Yeah, but you know the law says it has to be a party to the conversation. Besides, this could get tried in a California court, if it doesn't turn out to be a true interstate case, and California law is stricter than federal. I'm not sure your standing argument would hold up there. The California Penal Code statute is very strict. The defendant might be able exclude the evidence because we violated Pam Fischer's rights."

Knowles mulled that over; he hadn't considered the California law angle; it was a valid concern. But the bottom line was the same. "Len, give up on the court order. There's no time. Let's see what Louellen can do."

Knowles elbowed his way over to where the SAC was talking to Tobin. It became clear from what Tobin was saying that if the equipment was physically removed from the house they could not intercept the call from another location. It would take too long to get another line run to some monitoring site. It had to be done in the Fischer house if it was to be done at all. Knowles decided against letting the street teams know what was going on. It would just cause confusion and a million radio inquiries he didn't want to answer.

After twenty minutes or so of recriminations and hand-wringing, the SAC's phone rang. It was Louellen Murphy. "She's on board, Pete," Louellen said. "It took awhile, but we got her calmed down. She realizes that her best course is to rely on us. There's no problem with the consent."

"Great work, Louellen. I had utmost confidence in you the whole time." He gave a thumbs up sign and a big wink to the collected agents who were trying to eavesdrop. Smiles broke out all over, and the strident arguing mutated into nervous laughter and a few "I told you so's".

Tobin whispered something to the SAC, who nodded assent. Tobin went back to the evidence room, and the evidence technician, unflatteringly referred to in Bureau lingo as the "Bulky Evidence Clerk," opened up the main safe. She withdrew the ransom money in its plastic packaging, and gave it to Tobin. He placed the money into the duffel and carried it back to the command post. The room had emptied out a bit, since several agents, who had put off eating dinner because of the non-consent crisis, had decided to grab a bite while they still had a chance. Rothman, Nguyen, and Torres, however, had rejoined the assemblage.

Tobin counted out the money bundles, forty in all. He pulled out the metal jar with the yellow-and-black radioactivity symbol on it and opened it. He sprinkled some of the gray powder liberally around the bundles. He then removed an electronic device from his briefcase and examined one of its dials. He moved a switch and lifted something that resembled a microphone from its clamped position on the side of the device. He adjusted yet another knob, labeled "gain" and a crackling noise sounded from a small speaker on the device. He moved the detector wand to a position almost touching the powdered cash bundles. The crackling roared to a crescendo.

Stroaker asked, somewhat nervously, "So what is that, a Geiger counter?"

"Yup," Tobin responded, "but don't worry, this stuff has a half life of only 20 hours. Half the radiation will dissipate in less than a day."

"So we have to wait a couple of days for it to be all gone," Stroaker said, alarmed. "It still sounds hazardous."

Knowles remarked off-handedly, "Actually, if it has a half-life of 20 hours, it won't all be gone in two days. It'll be more like three-quarters gone. It may still be detectable several days after the payoff." Stroaker seemed to take great umbrage at this, and said rather sarcastically, "Cliff, this time ...." Then he stopped. He sensed he was getting on shaky ground and decided not to push his luck.

"Actually, boss," it was the Z-man. He had been about to explain that Knowles was right, intending to stop the SAC while there was still a face-saving way out. As a chemistry major he understood radioactive decay well enough himself, but when he saw that Stroaker had silenced himself he took a different tack. He continued, "...I'm not sure those lab guys know how any of these things behave in the real world. They're so immersed in theory, they couldn't investigate a real case if their damned lives depended on it. We won't know how long this'll last until we try it."

Stroaker's expression brightened immediately, and he seemed to sense somehow, without understanding why, that he had been let off the hook. "Ain't that the truth," he agreed. "That's why we put on all these different techniques. You just never know which ones will really work. Goddam lab geeks."

Tobin continued to prep the package meticulously. The one thing that had to wait until the call came was the pheromone. Unlike the radioactive powder, it was not possible to get more if needed for the next day. He closed the duffel and handed the vial and eyedropper to the agent who would courier it to the Fischer house. They couldn't wait any longer. The package had to be ready to go within minutes once the call came. "You'd better get over there," he said.

The courier was the same agent who had driven the money down from the Federal Reserve Bank in San Francisco. He grasped the duffel and said, "All right. Oh, I almost forgot, here's a picture of the butterfly that's supposed to be attracted by this chemical. Look for these." He tossed a color photograph on the table and headed out the door.

After he left, Stroaker turned to the Z-man and said, "He should have given us that photo before. We could have made color copies and included them in the briefing material." He studied the photo a bit. "This is more colorful than I had expected from the written description. Toni, get these duplicated - in color. Make twenty, no fifty, copies." He handed the photo to his secretary, who murmured a yessir and left the room.

As soon as she was out of Stroaker's sight she stopped one of the clerks on duty and ordered him to make the copies immediately. When the clerk protested that the RA had no color copier, she angrily demanded he take the photo to a 24-hour copy shop or whatever he had to do, but if he valued his job, he'd better be back in the command post in an hour with fifty color copies. He fled in fear, photo in hand. Bertinetti sauntered over to the ladies room for a touch-up.

The Z-man tried to convince Stroaker that the agent, one of his squad members, had not done anything wrong - that it didn't matter whether the photo had been copied and distributed. Olson and Knowles watched the whole discussion with a detached bemusement. For once they were not the ones on the hot seat; it was Stroaker's toady, the Z-man. Nguyen and Torres, naive in Bureau politics, recoiled at the scene, and sneaked out quietly. Until then they had nursed an impression of a controlled precision, a smooth operational plan forming and being executed from above. Instead they had witnessed an SAC who was too dumb to know what a half-life was, who was obsessed with petty details, and who was engendering rivalries in the command post.

Rothman was sitting with Stroaker's pilot to go over flight conditions. Tobin was on the phone with Jemperson, then with the Pac Bell security man. Izawa reported in that he was suited up and ready to go. Soon thereafter, Izawa reported in from the Fischer residence that the money had arrived. Morales said the plane was in the air and headed for the residence; the tail car - truck, actually - was waiting on the route outside the home. There was nothing to do now but wait for the call.

Chapter 21

It came at 10:08 p.m.

FISCHER -- Hello?

MALE -- Are you ready?

FISCHER -- Yes.

MALE -- Listen, I've got a tape from your dad. Listen very carefully to what he says.

RECORDING

Hi, Pam. Hi, Fran. This is Carl. I'm well. I love you very much. I'm sorry that we're in this situation. To prove that I'm still alive and well, the headline in the San Jose *Mercury* for the day is "Voters Lost in Barrage of Candidate Attack Ads." Pam, I remember often saying that if I was stuck on a desert island, you're the one I would depend on to pull me through. I trust you with my life. I ask you to pay close attention to the directions you've been given and not to gamble with your life, or mine. Make sure that no one accompanies you in the car. Make sure there are no electronic devices on you or in the money or on the car. These people have ways of determining whether those devices are present. I'm sure that if you follow all of their directions, we'll be seeing one another in the morning. I'm looking forward to seeing you, and I love you very much.

FISCHER -- Oh, you sucker. You promised me that...

MALE -- Hear that?

FISCHER -- You promised me he'd be released within the hour. Not in the morning.

MALE -- Yes, he will be released within a couple of hours, but he has to be flown in from Tijuana. Now you listen to me very carefully.

FISCHER -- Oh god, let's just get this...

MALE -- Listen to me goddammit! I'm gonna say this only once. I'm gonna hang up if you don't listen to me. Do you have a paper and pen ready?

FISCHER -- Yes, I do.

MALE -- Okay. From your house you get on 280 south.

FISCHER -- 280 south. Okay.

MALE -- South to 101 south.

FISCHER -- To 101 south.

MALE -- All the way until you hit 156 west.

FISCHER -- 156 west.

MALE -- It'll say "Monterey Peninsula."

FISCHER -- Okay.

MALE -- You go all the way on 156 west to Highway 1 south.

FISCHER -- Highway 1 south.

MALE -- Keep going straight on 1 south until you get to Reservation Road. You exit on that and make a right.

FISCHER -- Okay, a right on Reservation Road.

MALE -- Okay, and then an immediate right on Dunes Drive. D-U-N-E-S.

FISCHER -- Dunes? All right.

MALE -- That's a right on Reservation Road then another immediate right on Dunes Drive. Do you have that?

FISCHER -- Yes, okay. I got it.

MALE -- You go all the way to the end of the street, you drop the money, and keep on going.

FISCHER -- Where do I drop it? How can I keep on going if the road ends?

MALE -- At the end of the road, just drop it. Make a U-turn and keep on going.

FISCHER -- Is there, like a place to put it, or just in the street?

MALE -- The street will end. Just drop it at the very end of the street, and turn back. There is one more thing. If there is anyone with you, they'll be shot.

FISCHER -- I understand.

MALE -- (inaudible)(electronic beeping noise)

FISCHER -- Hello? Are you there?

MALE -- Yes, now listen. Right now it's 10:10.

FISCHER -- Yeah.

MALE -- By midnight, or before, you're going to be there.

FISCHER -- How long does it take to get there? I have no idea.

MALE -- From your house you can do it in one hour and a half, driving at 65. Don't drive any faster than 65.

FISCHER -- Okay, okay.

MALE -- You don't want to get pulled over.

FISCHER -- I won't drive too fast.

MALE -- Okay.

FISCHER -- How do I know you aren't going to kill my dad as soon as I give you the money?

MALE -- Because your dad has not seen our faces. He doesn't know who we are. We are just unknown Mexicans to him. All right? Get going.
END OF CONVERSATION

Luciana Malarna relayed the substance of the call to the command post as it took place, just as she had in the previous calls. As soon as she hung up, the original tape was removed from the recorder and the write protect tabs on the cassette were punched out. She marked the tape with proper evidence labels and placed it in her pocket. She was the first to leave the house.

"South." That one word instruction was spoken with Stroaker's "command voice." He looked directly at Mo Morales as he said it. Morales hesitated a minute with a questioning look on his face. "South, Mo, send them all south. You heard her - the drop is in Monterey." Morales looked around at the other inhabitants of the command post, but they were all involved in their own responsibilities. He rushed out.

"Who's the SRA of Monterey RA?" Stroaker asked.

"Nick Lark," someone replied.

"Oh, yes. Some genius sent him to Disneyland," Stroaker said, his voice dripping with sarcasm as he made eye contact with Ben Olson. Olson put on a suitably sheepish face, even though he knew he could have pointed out that he had cleared the decision with Stroaker before approving the annual leave. "Don, get a hold of whoever is next in seniority there and have them establish a forward command post with the Monterey PD."

"Uh, boss," Olson said, "I don't think Reservation Road's in Monterey. "Cliff?"

"No, it's probably Marina. I'd have to look at a map. It's north of Fort Ord." Knowles had attended the Defense Language Institute, known as DLI, in Monterey back in his early career. It had been his ticket out of New York. He knew the Monterey Peninsula pretty well.

"Well, wherever the hell it is, contact the locals - or use the military if it's close enough - and set up a forward command post there. We'll fly down and run the drop from there. Cliff, let the street teams know to start the leapfrog down toward Monterey."

"Okay, Pete," Knowles said, glad to have an excuse to get out from under the bedlam for a minute. There was a cacophony of voices from every corner of the room - Tobin talking to someone, either

Jemperson or the Pac Bell security man, Olson talking to Belinda, the chopper pilot trying to talk to Stroaker without success, Harry Rice on the phone to the Fischer house, Z-man on the phone to the senior agent in Monterey. Mike Bean was radioing to a technician in a radio truck to get up to a high point around Marina to establish a mobile repeater running off the truck's engine power.

Knowles got to Radio, and as he did so, Morales had just finished transmitting instructions to the SO. Mo had his own transmitter/receiver unit set up right next to the regular RA radio so he could give instructions to the SOG without interrupting the regular radio traffic. Knowles took the radio mike from the clerk and gave instructions to the street teams. He wanted them to know it was his voice, so they would follow the instructions without being worried about who was giving them. He told the units around the southern end of the division territory to converge in the general vicinity of Monterey/Marina. He assigned several units specific intersections - freeway interchanges - and spread the more northern units farther south to cover the territory that was being vacated by the southern units. He needed them more densely packed around the drop area to jump into a surveillance when the action came that far. He did not give them a specific location for the drop, because he knew agents too well. There could be some hot dog who would show up at the drop site to try to get the glory or the action.

Rothman came running up to him. "Cliff, has anyone contacted the Coast Guard? That drop area is right off the beach. They could have an escape boat ready."

"That's right. No, no one notified them yet. It's technically Z-man's job to do liaison and notification, but if you have a contact, do it. It can't hurt if they get notified twice."

"Yeah, we coordinate with their sea rescue people and flight coordinators all the time when we have to overfly the water. I have the number for their 24-hour controller."

"Tell them the whole story - don't try to be cozy. Let them know the victim's life is at risk. They can get a surface ship out there off the coast, but I guess no helicopter, huh?"

"Not a chance. The fog is socked in there. Visibility less than 40 feet."

"Does Stroaker know about the fog?" Knowles asked.

"I haven't told him myself, but I know his chopper pilot is very aware of it. He's been trying to get Stroaker to listen for the last five minutes."

"Okay." Knowles got back on the radio and asked one of the team members from the Monterey team to call him on his cell phone. Then he headed back to the command post.

"This is going to be fun! This is the most action I've had since Quantico," Stroaker declared enthusiastically. He was standing now, and pacing around with no apparent destination in mind.

"I've just talked to the chief down at Marina," Z-man announced over the din. "We've got our forward CP. The PD is right up the hill from the drop site."

"Great, great work, Don. Show me on the map," Stroaker replied. They walked to the wall map and began to examine the Marina area.

Marina is a small, tough burg separated from the posh Monterey vacation spots to the south by Fort Ord. Fort Ord was a major west coast army installation prior to the base closings and downsizing during the Clinton administration. The military was still using a great deal of it, but a huge chunk of it had been donated to the State of California for use as a new campus in their California State University system. The campus was formally named the California State University at Monterey Bay, or CSUMB, but colloquially was referred to as UFO - the University of Fort Ord. Most of the army operations had been moved to other bases, but the sizable military presence there still fed the economy of Marina. It was, in essence, an army town, with bars and prostitutes mingled with trailer parks and low end retirement home clusters. The beaches there were beautiful, no less so than in Monterey or Carmel, but they were surrounded by barbed wire fences to the south and artichoke fields to the north. Marina just didn't have the cachet of the other local towns, and as a result, the police there dealt more with pimps and welfare fraud and bookmakers than with the ritzier white collar crime on the other side of the base. That made them competent to deal with violent crimes; they saw more of it than the larger Monterey Police Department did. They also had good liaison with the FBI because of the base. The FBI has jurisdiction over Crimes on a Government Reservation - known as CGR in bureau parlance - if it involves a civilian. That required a regular interaction between FBI agents and the detectives in the communities adjacent to the base.

Z-man pointed out to Stroaker where the police department was, to the east of Highway 1 in the commercial area next to the base. The drop area was about two miles away, on the beach side of Highway 1, on a short street populated by motels catering to the tourist trade. One could walk to the beach from the end of the street where the drop was to be made. Stroaker was nodding sagely as he drank in the topography.

At the Fischer house, Jemperson deftly placed fresh batteries in the electronic tracking devices - the sparklers, radio beacon, and screamers. Then he sprinkled the pheromone on the plastic bundles and the outside of the duffel bag. Pam Fischer watched anxiously as this preparation took its course. She urged him to hurry up, saying that she needed to get going to meet the caller's deadline.

Terry Izawa, meanwhile, checked his weapons for perhaps the fiftieth time. The ammunition magazines were full and secure, the first round chambered in his Smith & Wesson 10-millimeter pistol and ready to fire. He had two backup guns, a Sig Sauer P228 9-millimeter semiautomatic and a five-shot snub-nosed .357 revolver, secreted in places he didn't want to talk about. Then, suddenly, he had to relieve himself. Accomplishing this was no small feat for someone layered in Kevlar and weighed down with lethal hardware. He disappeared into the nearest bathroom, knowing this would be his last chance for several hours. He rued that last cup of coffee he had drunk for the caffeine. He didn't need the stimulation, he was so hyper already.

Louellen Murphy held the Cadillac keys herself so that Pam could not change her mind suddenly and take off without Izawa in the car. Fran Fischer and the Carmodys emerged from upstairs and hovered, murmuring meaningless assurances to Pam. Fran Fischer's eyes were rimmed red and bleary from the crying. She held Mitzi Carmody's hand in a near death-grip.

After what seemed an eternity, Izawa emerged from the bathroom and checked his weapons for the fifty-first time. He announced he was ready to go. Pam Fischer slipped on the white jacket and Izawa carried the backpack out to the garage. Izawa climbed into the rear footwell and assumed the semi-fetal position he had practiced for several days. Pam activated the automatic garage door opener and backed out into the night.

"She was nervous after that last call about having us follow her, but the talk of getting shot convinced her to have Terry with her," Louellen Murphy told Stroaker on the phone as soon as she had driven away. "I think she'll be okay. She was getting real nervous about the time limit, though." She looked at her watch. It had been twenty-two minutes since the caller hung up. Pam still had time to make it by midnight, especially in a Cadillac. "You warned the Highway Patrol not to pull her over? You gave them a description of the car?"

"Don says he talked to the CHP just minutes ago. They already knew about the kidnapping at the commander level, but they have now put out to their units not to make any stops of traffic heading toward the Monterey area without checking with us. We don't want our street teams or SOG units stopped either."

"You'll keep us informed of developments here?" she asked.

"Of course. Olson and Z-man will stay here in the CP, and I'll be going to the forward CP in Marina with Mo and the team. We'll be controlling SOG and SWAT from there. How's the family doing?"

"Hanging in there," Murphy replied.

"Great, great, Louellen. Thanks - you're doing a great job. Now just relax and enjoy it." He hung up.

Murphy made a sour face at the final remark, and hung up. Relax and enjoy it? Didn't he know the association that phrase had with rape? How could anybody enjoy this? His tone had been so casual and the comment so insensitive she was glad the family members hadn't heard it.

"We have a trace," Tobin stated aloud. The remark was directed to the room in general; he was not looking at anybody, but copying information on a piece of paper. As soon as he hung up he wrote the number on the butcher paper sheet that was used as the phone call log. The address was a number which meant nothing to anyone in the room, but below it Tobin wrote "McDonald's, Reservation Road, Marina." Knowles crowded behind Olson and Stroaker to look on the large wall map. The call had been placed from a fast food about half way between the drop site and the police station where the forward command post was being set up. It was less than ten minutes driving time from the phone to the drop site. Everyone realized the caller by now had no doubt already driven to, or been dropped off at, the site and set up wherever he was going to set up.

"Cliff, Toni, Mo, I want you guys to come with me to the forward CP," Stroaker announced. We need to get going. Buzz, are you ready?" Buzz was the helicopter pilot.

Knowles looked at his watch. It was now 10:40. If they were going to drive, they should have left at least fifteen minutes ago. It took time to set up a CP and establish radio communications. They were going to be driving up to the police station about the same time Pam Fischer was going to be dropping the money.

"I've been ready, Boss," Buzz said. "But the fog is even thicker now than when I last told you."

"Okay, well just put it down as close as you can, and we'll have a street team drive us over. Mo, where's the Cadillac now?"

Morales looked at Stroaker blankly. "I don't know. You had me pull off my units."

"What? I didn't have you pull off your units," the SAC said, flabbergasted.

"Sure you did, Boss. You said to send everything south to Monterey, so I did."

"I didn't mean the tail car. I just meant to implement the plan we already had - send the south teams to form the perimeter around the drop site. You at least left the plane to follow from the air, didn't you?" Stroaker's neck veins were popping out. Knowles could see the throbbing bulges well enough to count the SAC's pulse from across the room.

"I thought everything meant everything. I sent them all to Monterey just like you said." Morales was cowering now, head down, and his suffering was almost palpable to everybody.

"You...." Stroaker obviously wanted to curse a blue streak, but he had the sense not to humiliate Morales and cause greater confusion and recriminations, so he stopped himself. "Who's following the Cadillac?" He looked at everybody in the room. Every person there made eye contact with every other employee, but no one said a word. They all realized that Pam Fischer and Terry Izawa were out there speeding to the payoff site all by themselves. "Jesus Christ. Okay, Cliff, get the closest street team to find them and follow them in. Have them radio the location if they spot the car. Make sure you have the teams on 101 south and 156 on alert to report the car when they see it. We're going to have to wait here until we get a positive response."

It was hard to imagine a worse beginning. They lost the victim's car even before she left the garage, and all because of a single ambiguous instruction and a supervisor who was too insecure to clarify it. Knowles was almost sick to his stomach. He ran to Radio and raised the two teams closest to the Fischer residence to follow the Cadillac. All instructions were in code so eavesdroppers could not follow what was going on. The teams reported back that they had seen the car go by a few minutes earlier, 15 minutes or so after the SOG pickup, and would try to catch it. He phoned that back to the command post. Stroaker told him that would have to do, and to get back to the command post.

"Ben," Stroaker said to Olson as Knowles entered the room. "you're to take over ground operations if I lose communication. The plan is as we discussed. Follow the ransom pickup to a car or structure to identify others. I plan to be giving the orders from the forward CP, but we're running late now, so I want a chain of command in place in case of problems. Don will handle liaison with the Bureau and the forward CP. You've got agents to help you here..." he waved his hand vaguely in the direction of Torres, Nguyen, and two or three other agents who were standing by, "... so I'm taking Cliff and Rothman and Mo. Toni will be with me to help set up the CP. I'm sending Rice down by car to follow up whatever we need and an extra car could come in handy. We can't fit everybody in the helicopter. Don, don't tell the Bureau we lost the drop car, just say it's on the way and we've got it covered."

"Right." The Z-man wasn't about to tell FBI headquarters that the operation was already screwed up if he didn't have to. He did not even have to dial the number; he had an open line, on hold at that moment, direct from the RA to FBIHQ, a line he was required to keep open throughout the entire operation. The Deputy Assistant Director was on the other end; he would follow events until it was over. Z-man punched the button for that line and began to relay Stroaker's message in a voice resonating with confidence. Knowles had to admit the Z-man had balls. Or maybe he was just a good liar. He'd done deep undercover work earlier in his career. You had to be a good liar to succeed at undercover.

Stroaker strode from the room, motioning for the entourage to follow. They hurried to match his pace as he headed down the stairs and out across the street. Morales carried a mobile radio, the largest Knowles had ever seen, with a headset attached. He was able to keep contact with the SOG personnel apparently, even when airborne. Knowles had no way to contact the street teams. He had to hope Olson and the radio clerk would keep them in the loop as needed. He would resume directing them when he got to the forward CP.

"Come in, Dog 1, come in," Terry Izawa repeated into the handheld radio for the third time. Dog 1 was the code name for the SOG tail car - the specially outfitted tow truck. The transmission was on the SOG radio channel. There was no response.

"Shit, where are those guys?" he yelled to Pam Fischer. "They're supposed to be within radio range. We tested this just half an hour before the call. Can you see them in the rear-view mirror?"

"No, at least I don't think so," she replied. "I see some headlights now and then, but I don't think it's the tow truck, just cars that I pass. Is something wrong?"

"No, no. Don't worry. It's just these crappy radios they give us. I'm sure we're just in a dead spot. Are you staying within the speed limit?"

"Yes, sure," Fischer answered. But Izawa noticed just a hint of hesitancy in her voice. He was an experienced interrogator and sensed she was not being truthful. He sat up so he could see over the back seat. As he did so, he heard and felt the car slow considerably. He caught sight of the speedometer needle falling toward the 70 on the dial. He realized she must have been doing at least 85, maybe more. She was slowing because she could hear him getting up to do some literal back seat driving.

"Jesus, Pam," slow down. "They may have hung back out of visual range to stay discreet, and expected you'd stay at 65 like we planned. They may be out of radio range and not know it, thinking you're just ahead out of sight. We need them for backup. You don't want to get there alone, do you?"

"Oh God," she said. "The man said I had to be there in an hour and a half. You took so darn long getting ready. We should have left immediately. I'm just trying to keep them from killing my dad."

"Take it easy. We have enough time. If you keep going this speed we'll get there by 11:30. The kidnapper gave us until midnight. You aren't trying to lose the tail car are you?"

"No, I swear, I'm not. I told you guys I'd cooperate. That stuff about shooting scared me. I want you guys there. I'm going to make the fastest U turn you ever saw and get the heck out of there."

Izawa then noticed a road sign. It read "California 85." She had taken a different route. Highway 85 was recently opened to speed access between the northwest corner of Silicon Valley, the Mountain View area, to the southern end. It was more or less the hypotenuse to the approximate right angle triangle it formed with highways 280 and 101. The kidnapper had timed the route using the two major freeways, 280 and 101, and the instructions were based on those. The route she was taking not only cut 15 minutes off the directed route, but was one the surveillance teams would not expect. If they had lost visual contact with her car, they would not be looking for her on this freeway. He considered at the same time that even if she had lost the tail car fairly quickly, the plane should still be able to follow and hear his transmissions. Why weren't they answering up when they heard him unable to raise Dog 1?

"Pelican, Pelican, do you read?" he barked into the radio.

No response. They were on their way to the drop site by themselves without a tail. If she lost control and ran off the road at 100 miles an hour no one would even know where to look.

"Tim," Knowles whispered to Rothman, "What the hell are we doing? I thought the whole Monterey peninsula was socked in. Where are we going to land?"

"Beats me. There's no place to land anywhere within thirty miles - maybe fifty miles - of Monterey. This makes no sense. We should be piling in cars, not a helicopter."

Stroaker led them to the helipad behind the hospital. Buzz's copilot had already warmed up the Huey. It was idling, waiting for the passengers. They clambered in en masse, and within two minutes, they were airborne. Stroaker sat squeezed between and slightly behind the pilot and co-pilot, as close as he could get to up front without interfering with the stick. To his right was Morales with the mobile radio headset, his head almost hanging on Stroaker's right shoulder, giving the SAC a running account of what he was hearing from the agents on the ground. To Stroaker's left, behind the pilot, sat Toni Bertinetti, squeezed exceedingly tightly against the SAC's left arm. She had her notepad out to take down any instructions, but Stroaker was engaged in a continuous dialogue with Morales. The pilot was on a different radio channel, communicating with civilian air authorities about his position. The FBI had permission to fly in places and in a manner the general public could not, but they had to follow strict rules nonetheless, and the pilot had to make sure they were not interfering with other aircraft. Knowles was directly behind Bertinetti, and Rothman was directly behind Morales. There were also two SWAT agents designated as Stroaker's own personal bodyguards when they went into action, and a senior clerk who could help with record searches and general CP operations when they got set up.

No one who has not ridden on a military helicopter can appreciate how difficult it is to communicate with each other inside the cabin for those without headsets. The Huey is huge for a rotor craft, and the power of the engines is not muffled from the passengers. It is intended to transport military personnel, not paying customers. The noise is quite literally deafening to anyone who has to endure it repeatedly without ear protection. The pilot and co-pilot have industrial-quality earphones and radio mikes that bend almost to touch the lips. The ordinary mortals in the rear can do nothing but shout at the top of their lungs into the ear of the person next to them. There is no hope of hearing anyone farther away. The craft is also unheated. Soldiers are not mollycoddled, and neither are FBI agents.

The inside temperature was below sixty degrees, and falling. Knowles had not planned on riding in the helicopter, and he sat there in his business suit, looking very out of place. He kept a heavy coat and change of clothes in his car, something he always did when on surveillance or other big operation, but that would do him little good up in the Huey. Rothman, ever the pilot, had switched his suit coat for a heavy fleece-lined flight jacket before boarding. Rothman glanced at Knowles and pointed to Bertinetti, who was still squeezed tightly against the SAC's left arm. She had on a light jacket, but it was unzipped about halfway. The sweater she wore underneath was a very lightweight, form-fitting cashmere job that served as a perfect relief map of the contours it covered. Every bump and bulge was evident to the astute observer, and Rothman was as astute as they came. Bertinetti was actually rubbing up and down very slowly on the SAC's arm, his triceps buried deep between her breasts. The bodies were packed so tight that Rothman was the only person in a position to view this spectacle, and he was drinking it all in with a wonder better reserved for a first time view of Yosemite or the Grand Canyon. Stroaker continued to converse with Morales while he pressed his meaty left arm back against his secretary's chest. He apparently had become so accustomed to this treatment, that he could concentrate on the operation while copping his feel with one arm. Knowles hoped so, at least. The chopper made a sudden swerve and everybody braced against something - or someone. Bertinetti fell backward and to the right. Rothman reached out to break her fall, and his hand landed on her rib cage under the right arm. His fingertips made unmistakable contact through the jacket with her right breast as he helped her back to an upright position. She gave him a baleful glare as she straightened, and zipped her jacket all the way to her chin. She moved an inch or so farther away from the SAC, who seemed not to have missed her ministrations.

"You're only a GS-12, Tim," Knowles shouted to Rothman, his hands cupped around his mouth and Rothman ear's in a sort of transmission tube. "You have to be Senior Executive Service or hire her husband for a remodel to get the booby prize, I guess." Despite Knowles having shouted this from a position directly behind Bertinetti he had no fear of her overhearing. It was barely possible for Rothman to understand him.

"What'd you say?" he replied, screaming back over the rotor noise.

"Nothing. Listen, where's the closest place to the drop this chopper will be able to put down?"

"I'm not sure. Why?"

"It looks like Morales is having trouble with the radio. I think he has the wrong kind of earpiece for this chopper. It doesn't block out the rotor noise."

"Yeah, it's hard to hear," Rothman agreed.

Stroaker was now instructing the pilot. "Buzz, if you can't land at the PD parking lot, just put it down at the airfield at Fort Ord. We can have a ground team run us over to the CP."

"No can do, boss," Buzz replied. "Fort Ord is buttoned up, too. They won't give permission to land."

"What do you mean? We're the FBI. Just do it. Screw 'em - we don't need their permission." Stroaker waved his hand forward in a dismissive motion.

"Yeah, boss we do. I could lose my pilot's license for landing against ground orders, but more importantly, I'm not real interested in killing us all. Visibility is almost zero. I couldn't even find Fort Ord if I wanted to, under that blanket."

"Jesus, then where are we going to land?" Stroaker asked, growing hoarse from the shouting. He was incredulous that he couldn't just fly to wherever he wanted.

"I tried to tell you, it's all closed. The whole area. The closest is probably San Martin, South County airport. That's clear enough to land, although there's a little haze there too."

"I thought you could navigate with GPS or something. It's clear up here. Why don't you just fly directly to the coordinates of the Fort Ord airstrip and then go straight down into the fog."

"The instruments are good, but not that good. You have to be able to see the ground. There could be a live wire or a ground vehicle within a few yards of the landing point, even another aircraft on the landing strip. If I read the GPS wrong, or even right, I could kill us all."

Stroaker did a slow burn. He was keeping his tongue in check surprisingly well considering all the setbacks, but he clearly was not having the fun he had expected. "Okay, go as far south as you can. Let's see where this fog layer begins." He turned back to Rothman. "Tim, you're a pilot and you know this area. Where can we land?" He was bellowing at the top his lungs in order to be heard over the rotor noise.

Rothman answered back, "I'm used to fixed wing strips, not helicopters. There may be some places I don't normally think of. These pilots should know better than I do, since they fly these things." Knowles had not been able to follow the conversation due to the noise, so he nudged Rothman on the shoulder. Rothman turned to him and shouted to him what the SAC had just asked.

"Tim, is there a spot in Gilroy?" Knowles asked, sudden inspiration striking.

"Not a landing strip per se. These things can land in a lot of places, though."

"What about the outlet mall?"

"The parking lots are huge, but they're full of light poles and cars moving around. You'd never be able to control the ground well enough. You'd be better off at some law enforcement site, like a sheriff's office. At least we could communicate - the pilot could, anyway. Hang on." Rothman leaned over to the co-pilot and yelled something in his ear. The co-pilot lifted his left earpiece and made Rothman repeat it. Then he pulled out an aviation map and started pointing at it. They continued shouting back and forth for a minute or so, then the copilot adjusted his mouthpiece and said something to the pilot. The pilot nodded and glanced at the map momentarily.

"Boss," the pilot said to Stroaker, "we might be able to put it down in the CHP substation in Gilroy. They use it for a truck weighing station, but it's probably closed this time of night. I can confirm that with CHP over the radio."

"How far is that from Marina?" Stroaker asked. He had been SAC in the division for years and still didn't know the territory.

"About thirty or forty road miles, maybe. You have to drive through the mountains on 156 to get there. It's not a freeway, just a two-lane country highway. That's the same route Pam Fischer is driving."

"Can we get there before she does?" Stroaker asked.

"Not likely. She got a fifteen- or twenty-minute head start on us," Buzz answered.

"But you can fly in a straight line direct there, and go 125 in this baby. I've had the showcase ride."

"Not here I can't. There's no way to navigate without a radio beacon at the CHP station except to overfly the freeway. I'll have to go straight down 101 to know where I'm going, just like a car. We're only going 100 or so, not much faster than a car, and I can't go any faster safely in these conditions."

"Okay, then, let's try to get down farther. Fly on down to Gilroy and let's see if we can land there."

Morales broke in and started to brief Stroaker on what he was getting over the radio. Eventually the substance of it filtered back to Rothman and Knowles. The street teams still hadn't located the Cadillac. No one had heard from Izawa. Apparently the two people in the drop car were out of both visual and radio contact - in effect, lost. FBIHQ was adamant that the SWAT should try to arrest the pickup person rather than follow, but Z-man was being non-committal. Olson had sent one of the Monterey RA agents to the pay phone at the McDonald's. It turned out to be in the foyer to the rest rooms, and therefore not on the security cameras. There was no video of the vehicle either. No one saw a thing. There had been several customers come and go on motorcycles, and of course many more in sedans, but no one could say whether any of them had used the phone. Yet another dead end.

Gina Torres sat in her car with the engine running and the heater going. A thin layer of haze was creeping over the Santa Cruz

Mountains, fanned by a noticeable onshore breeze. It was getting downright chilly, unusually so for late May in California. She turned on the AM radio to catch the news, but kept the Bureau radio turned up in volume to make sure she would catch any operational transmissions. The teams had been exercising admirable restraint. There was no news of the kidnapping on the AM radio. The radio discipline lecture had been effective, she judged, since there was only the occasional terse, cryptic transmission and response. The street teams were continually repositioning themselves, or seeing something they felt warranted looking at further. One team in Oakland had witnessed a hit-and-run accident, and radioed ahead to another unit who pulled the perpetrator over. It turned out to be a criminal defense lawyer who was stumbling drunk. While standing next to his mangled front fender, still dripping plastic shards from a broken signal light, he denied being involved in any accident. That had been the only real radio traffic she had heard since she had started her car. She was just now arriving at her assigned position, and planned to get comfortable. She could be here a long time - or not.

Torres was exhausted and somewhat disheartened. This case had not gone the way she had expected. Rather than the display of precision and organization she assumed would occur, the whole thing had been something of a cluster-fuck. The neat one-hour wrap-up of TV drama fodder it was not. She had had too little sleep over the last few days and her mood was anything but upbeat. She was single and living with two roommates in a dowdy apartment to make ends meet. Her mind drifted to her personal life. She had been hit on only twice in the year she had been in the San Jose RA, once by a lesbian agent and ex-volleyballer who must have assumed she swung the same way, and once by an overweight garbage disposal installer who was at least ten years older than her and during the install had exhibited the grossest butt-crack she had ever seen. For a moment she reflected on her assets: she was smart, having graduated cum laude from the University of Texas, employed in a good professional position, and had great hair. But was that what men wanted? Somewhat flat-chested and strong-boned, she knew she wasn't competition for the clerical staff in the beauty department. None of the male agents had paid her much attention. She began to wonder if her decision to join the FBI had been a mistake, much as she loved the work.

A crackle on the radio brought back to reality. Ben Olson had dispatched her, Nguyen, and two other agents as soon as Stroaker had left. He had told them to post themselves all along 101 south from San Jose to the 156 exit to try to pick up the Cadillac, in case the regular street teams couldn't. She had drawn the spot just south of the 85-101 interchange. She decided against trying to find a parking spot off a frontage road. It would be too far from the freeway. Instead she had pulled over onto the right shoulder just past an overpass, and then backed up to the overpass abutment. That way, no one could rear-end her car and she couldn't be seen except by someone looking to the side or in the rear-view mirror. She had a good view of the traffic going by. She had just finished adjusting the mirrors when she saw a Cadillac sail past. She had not even been in position long enough to get into a routine. This was only the third or fourth car that had come past since she had backed in. She caught only a partial plate - the three numbers at the end, but they sounded familiar. She looked down at the briefing sheet. The numbers matched the Fischer Cadillac.

"Matt, this Gina," she said over the air, forgetting to use call signs. "I think I just saw Cat southbound at 101 and 85. It was going at least 90. Can you confirm?" Cat was the code word for the Cadillac.

Matt Nguyen had the next post south of her. "I'm still moving," he responded. "I should be in position in about two or three... holy cow, hold on. I think that's Cat." The Cadillac blew by him in the left lane as he held the radio mike in his hand. "Yes, confirm. Cat is southbound on 101 at Bailey Avenue. No Dog in sight."

"Control to unit calling. Confirm your call sign and location." That was the radio clerk at the RA, Nguyen realized, and he gave the required information. "Pursue Cat. Repeat, you are to try to catch up with Cat and get ahead of it if possible. Please confirm."

"Overtake and get ahead. 10-4." Nguyen pushed the accelerator to the floor, but the Bucar he drove was assigned in accord with his seniority, or lack thereof, and he couldn't get the speedometer past 95. He could still see the Caddy's taillights in the distance, but he wasn't catching it. "Control, I'm unable to overtake. This unit just can't go that fast. Copy?"

"10-4. Wait one."

After a minute or so Ben Olson's voice came on the air. "CP to Q, do you copy?" Olson didn't know all the team designations the way Knowles did, but he knew Quincy Allen was the team leader in Gilroy, which was what he wanted right now.

"Q here," Allen replied.

"We need you to execute a slowdown maneuver on 101. We've got to put the brakes on this vehicle. Can you do it?"

"I'll try. I'm not exactly CHP, you know. I've never been trained in that."

"Use all your team units if you have to. You're authorized to go Code 2."

"What's Code 2?" Q-ball didn't do a lot of high-speed pursuit doing applicant work.

"Lights, but no siren."

"10-4."

Allen gave instructions to his team members to follow him onto the on-ramp together, and to take positions blocking each of the four lanes of traffic. It took several attempts for them to get aligned properly, and other traffic cut between them, horns blaring. Once they got in position, though, they slowed to 60, then 50, coordinating by radio. Traffic behind them was accumulating rapidly, and car horns began signaling a building road rage. The FBI cars each had only a single red light - all that was required by California law - but it was inadequate for this situation. The cars behind them could not tell they were law enforcement, since the cars were unmarked and there was no light bar on top. Eventually, Allen's team figured out to turn their red lights facing backward, which silenced the first row of vehicles. The horns farther back eventually went quiet, too, once the drivers realized there was nothing they could do about it, anyway. Allen radioed in that he had slowed traffic to 50, and would hold it there pending further instructions.

"Super, Q," Olson acknowledged.

Within five minutes Pam Fischer came upon slowing traffic. But this wasn't the backup from Allen's maneuver, this was the normal Friday night congestion. A lot of vacationers head south or east from Silicon Valley for the weekend, and this was the main route out. Even at eleven o'clock there was a knot at this point. She was still almost twenty miles from Gilroy. This delay didn't last long, but she was getting more anxious as she looked at the clock on the dash.

"Keep it slow now, Pam. You promised me," Terry Izawa cooed, trying to sound calm. He felt like throttling her and taking over the driving, but reality prevented that. "This traffic is just fine. You have plenty of time." He looked at her closely. Beads of sweat had gathered congenially on her forehead in evenly spaced rows as if about to march in a parade over her brow. Her knuckles were white on the steering wheel. "Just keep it slow and easy. We'll make it and your dad will be fine."

Pam Fischer said nothing, but her eyes were moist. She drummed her thumbs nervously on the wheel. Izawa kept talking, trying to ease the tension, but as soon as traffic broke Pam pushed the speed back up to almost 100.

The slowdown had allowed Nguyen to catch sight of her again, though, and he reported her position to Radio Control. By this time the two Palo Alto RA street teams that had been assigned to try to catch her were following the chase, and had pushed their vehicles to the limit. They were only a mile or two back when they reported their positions. This gave Ben Olson the information he needed to be able to report back to Stroaker that they had the drop car in sight and would be able to follow it in to the payoff location. He did so, using the SOG channel to relay the message through Morales. Morales confirmed that he understood, but it took several tries. Communication with the helicopter was getting worse by the minute.

Olson then got on the radio to the street teams to advise them of the location of Cat. Most of them had been able to follow the progress by listening to the radio traffic, but Olson knew that it was always good to give the street teams a sense of being a part of what was going on, even if they were a hundred miles away. The tension mixed with boredom was a tough combination to live with, and he wanted relieve as much of it as possible. They might be needed at any moment. He called to Z-man in the CP and told him he was going to stay up at Radio. The Z-man was able to follow what had gone on via the speaker that Bean had rigged into the CP, but there was no microphone there. He told Olson he would let the Bureau know they were still on the drop car moving toward the payoff site.

It took another ten minutes for Pam Fischer to reach the back end of the traffic jam caused by the slowdown maneuver. She was now south of Gilroy, and the Q-ball slowdown was backing up traffic for miles. Traffic crawled at less than 50 miles an hour, when 75 was normal for this time and place. She started pounding the wheel in frustration. "Oh God," she said, "what's the matter now?"

"Must be an accident or something. Someone just driving too fast and hitting a tree or something," he hinted, peeking over the rear seat again.

The Palo Alto street teams managed to work their way through the jam by putting on red lights and passing on the shoulder. Eventually they spotted the Cadillac, worked their way back in, and flipped off the emergency lights. As soon as one was in front of her and one behind her, they notified Radio.

"10-4," Radio replied. "Units holding the slowdown maneuver in place may now discontinue. Repeat, 10-22 on the slowdown. Let the traffic go. Dog team with visual on Cat, keep Cat's speed to 65. Box her in if necessary."

All the units acknowledged, and Quincy Allen's team finally pulled over to the right to let the backup go. More than a few drivers gave the one-finger salute to them as they sped past. His team was ordered to get back to Gilroy to cover their original position.

The Huey flew within ten miles of Fort Ord, at an altitude of five thousand feet, before Stroaker was convinced that they would never be able to land anywhere near there. The air was crystal clear at this altitude, but the fog below enveloped the landscape like someone had stuccoed the entire countryside with cotton candy. Even the coastal hills were completely invisible. He realized that he had no idea whether they were over water or land himself, and the white blanket below was unpenetrated by a single light or geographic feature he could recognize. Finally he conceded defeat and directed the pilot back to the CHP substation in Gilroy. They had wasted at least twenty-five minutes trying to get ahead of the chase, and as a result, were going to end up thirty miles behind the action. He ordered the co-pilot to relay through the regular channel to have the two closest street teams meet him at the substation.

Toni Bertinetti was by this time hunched in a ball. She was feeling queasy from the frequent unexpected movements of the helicopter and was trying to stave off airsickness. Rothman recognized the symptoms, but decided not to say or do anything about it. If he embarrassed her in front of her boss by offering a plastic bag she didn't actually need, for example, she would make him pay some day, somehow. Better to let nature take its course; she would ask for help if she needed it. Rothman looked at Knowles, who didn't look much better. The copter ride was no jumbo jet cruise. It was noisy, bouncy, and cold, and there were no seats, just a hard metal floor to sit on. Rothman was used to flying in all conditions, and it didn't bother him. But he had seen some of the highest brass, including an

FBI Director once, decorate their shoes with their lunch while taking helicopter tours in better conditions than this ride. This was going to get real ripe if someone lost it up here. He fished through one of the kits and pulled out a can the male agents used to urinate in when they had to. He handed it to Knowles, who took it gingerly, but didn't bring it anywhere near his face. The smell wouldn't have improved the situation.

The word was passed back that the number one SWAT team was in the vicinity of the drop site and members were now taking positions. The first SOG unit was also close, and they were about to set out the perimeter line. Then the word came that the drop car had been found and was being tailed. The tide seemed to have turned, and Stroaker relaxed noticeably. The Huey moved far enough inland to be past the thickest fog, and some ground lights once again appeared through the haze, although dimly.

"That's the CHP weigh station there," Buzz said to Stroaker, pointing to a dark area just off the freeway. "We should be able to land, but it'll be difficult. Visibility is still marginal." Stroaker nodded.

"Pete, the Cadillac is about ten minutes away from the drop now," Morales reported. "One of my teams is forming a perimeter along Dunes, out of sight from the end where the drop will be. There's a trailer park there and a bunch of motels."

"Buzz, get this bird on the ground," Stroaker ordered. "Things are a'poppin'."

"Roger." The pilot made a sharp swoop downward, banking at least 45 degrees as he did so. A low moan emerged from Bertinetti. Stroaker seemed oblivious to her; his eyes were glistening at the prospect of entering the action. The chopper set down with a thump on the empty expanse of asphalt designed for big rig parking. Occupants of the craft piled out quickly, with Bertinetti surging forward urgently, right behind Stroaker, trying to get out before her stomach rebelled completely. She probably would have made it, had it not been for the fact the substation was surrounded on three sides by garlic fields, lading the atmosphere with an overwhelming pungency. Instead, she splattered the door sill, catching most of the eruption with her hands as she jumped down to the ground. She stood directly in front of the doorway heaving for a minute as the other passengers attempted to crowd past her, trying not to inhale as they realized what they were climbing over. The garlic smell was bad enough without that. The senior clerk finally grabbed Bertinetti's elbow and led her away from the helicopter to finish her business out of the way. Several employees began wiping their shoes on the pavement, trying to rid themselves of the smell. One of the SWAT members was swiping at the back of his pants, as he had made the mistake of sitting on the door sill as he got out. It was evident that several of them had been fighting the same nausea, and the stench was not helping in their containment efforts. So much for the thrill of the chase.

Stroaker, still oblivious to what was going on behind him, marched purposefully to the small brick building that housed the Highway Patrol office. There was a pay phone on the wall nearest the parking lot. He dialed the command post and Olson came on the line. On one side of him stood Mo Morales, trying to follow the SOG transmissions on his headset, relaying snippets of information as he heard them. On the other, Knowles stood with a notepad, ready to take any instructions or write down any items Stroaker received from the command post. This was Bertinetti's job, but she was in no shape for it at that moment.

It became clear that the radio communications between the drop site personnel and the forward command post at Marina PD were less than perfect. Most of the information they were getting was coming from Marina officers who had been assigned to join the outer perimeter in a standby mode. Stroaker learned that in the Marina PD conference room that served as the forward command post, the police channel was playing from one speaker while the mobile radio unit from one of the FBI radio techs was broadcasting the SOG transmissions. The Monterey RA agent who was taking care of liaison with the police chief had his RA handheld unit on the regular street channel, while talking to Olson on the phone and to the chief standing next to him. There were thus three radio channels broadcasting accounts of the same general scene in the same room, while personal conversations were going on. Rice had just arrived and was being brought up to speed at the same time. All this was being relayed to Stroaker through Morales standing on one side, and through the San Jose command post on the phone. It was nearly impossible to make sense of it.

The street teams had dropped back from the Cadillac as it approached the Reservation Road exit, and the SOG tow truck, now rejoined to the surveillance, had eased into the lead position, still well back. Terry Izawa finally had an SOG unit on his channel responding to him; they told him he was about eight minutes from zero hour.

"Pete," Olson said on the phone, "Marina PD has something. A patrol officer saw a heavy-set man with a gray mustache. He thinks it's Fischer. He's moving through the trailer park on Dunes."

"I knew it!" declared Stroaker triumphantly. "This is a set up. He's going to grab the loot and hightail it to the Caribbean. Arrest him. Arrest him now!"

Olson passed the command to Olson to give to Marina PD, while Morales spoke into his mobile unit. Stroaker realized that Morales had misunderstood, and was telling the SOG team to move in and arrest whoever picked up the loot.

"No, not you, Mo. The PD saw Fischer - that's the arrest. Your people should back off the drop." Morales reversed his instructions, but it wasn't clear whether anybody on the SOG team had heard either instruction. Morales tried to get a confirmation response, but no one answered up. The radio reception, and especially the ability to transmit, was horrible in this particular corridor.

Stroaker tried to get Olson to confirm that the arrest was being made, but it was obvious Olson was having problems determining what was going on with the police, and it wasn't clear that the officer would act on orders passed from Stroaker to Olson to the Monterey agent to the Marina PD to the patrol officer. The police chief might have other ideas. Stroaker grabbed the headset from Morales, but shoved it back in disgust almost immediately when he heard nothing but a few semi-intelligible words between bursts of static.

Quincy Allen pulled into the substation lot at that moment in his purple Oldsmobile. He drove to the entourage at the phone and started to get out. Stroaker rushed over to him, waving his hand in a motion for him to get back in the car. Allen did so, rolling down the window.

"The drop is about to go down," he said to Allen. "Get us down to the forward CP in Marina, on the double." Stroaker looked around hurriedly and pointed to Morales and Bertinetti, ordering them into the back seat of the Olds. The front passenger seat was occupied by a pile of briefing materials, Allen's briefcase, a shotgun, a bag with the telephone receiver from the outlet mall, and half a bag of fast food. Stroaker decided to squeeze one more body into that car, and signaled for one of the SWAT bodyguards to jump in front. Then he barked out a curt "Take the next one!" to the remaining personnel as he, Morales, and Bertinetti crammed into the back seat. The doors slammed and the Olds spit dust and gravel as it circled back out to the freeway, fishtailing as it went.

Knowles was secretly relieved not to have to join that crowd, especially with AB smelling the way she did. He was still motion sick himself, and the fishtailing couldn't have improved the situation. He knew one thing in addition that Stroaker probably did not, and that is that the radio reception was almost non-existent in this particular stretch until he got through Highway 156 out to the Monterey Peninsula. Cell phone coverage was bad, too. The SAC would be totally out of contact with the other elements of the FBI within minutes, and stay that way. The agents jokingly called the area Radio Free Europe.

Knowles went back to the pay phone and saw the receiver dangling by the wall. He picked it up. The line to the RA was still open.

"Ben, are you there? It's Cliff."

"Yeah, hi. Is Pete there?" Olson replied.

"No, he's with Q-ball heading south this moment. Has the drop been made?"

"Not yet; another couple of minutes. We have Claude Becker in position with the sniper scope, fitted for night vision. He says he has a perfect view of the end of the street. He's got a cell phone that works like a charm. The night's black and totally socked in with fog. There's a path that leads out onto a stretch of beach that goes for miles. If the subject gets through the perimeter he's a free man."

"Listen, Ben. The SAC is headed into Radio Free Europe now. He'll be totally out of contact for at least fifteen minutes."

"Was that your idea to put down in Gilroy?" Olson asked.

"I had a little help from Rothman."

"I owe you big time. Did you hear that Randy Finkman was arrested by Marina PD?"

"Your kidding," Knowles said. "Is that who Stroaker authorized to be arrested.?"

"Yeah. Mistaken identity. He has a beard and is on the pudgy side, but he can't be more than five-eight and 41 years old. Fischer's six-two, has a mustache not a beard, and is in his sixties. Besides, Randy has that long ponytail - you know those SOG guys. The cop must be blind. I guess it was the adrenaline. Two little kids came out of their trailer just as the cop drew down on Randy. We almost had our first casualties. Hold on. I hear the boss on the air now. I guess he's not quite in the zone yet."

Stroaker was hearing the SOG channel through Morales's headset, and the second sniper was relaying via radio what Claude Becker was telling Olson over the cell phone. Becker could see the Cadillac approach the end of the street now. The driver's window was coming down... a backpack was being dumped on the pavement at the end of the cul-de-sac. The car was turning around and heading back out. Now the tow truck could be seen pulling into one of the motel driveways a block down the street.

"Any sign of a pickup yet?" Stroaker asked.

"10-9, you came in broken," the sniper replied.

"Can you see anybody?"

"Negative. Wait, I see movement. A body was hiding in the dunes. He's moving toward the package. Looks like a male - just an outline."

"Surround and follow. Repeat, surround and follow. Do not arrest. SWAT Copy?" Stroaker bellowed at the top of his lungs.

"Copy, do NOT arrest. Pursue and keep in sight." It was Hank LaPointe.

LaPointe watched the figure through his night vision goggles, as it crouched low and crept out of the dunes area into the street. The figure sprinted to the backpack, grabbed it with one hand as he kept his head up, looking up and down the street. Barely slowing down, he reversed direction and zigzagged back into the sand dunes. LaPointe had been viewing this scene from the embankment next to Highway 1, just off the shoulder, perhaps a hundred yards from the street. Night vision goggles could penetrate the fog better than unaided eyesight, but LaPointe was still at the limit of what he could see. Between him and the drop site the ground made a series of dips and rises. He relayed the order to his team, then began to run at a moderate pace in the direction of the figure. The dips and rises, however, caused him to lose sight of his quarry once or twice. He couldn't run with the goggles on, they were just too obstructive. So he would run in the general direction of where he had last seen the figure, slip on the glasses, and look for the infrared sparklers. Once he got a new bearing, he started off in that direction, giving directions over the radio to the rest of the team. Occasionally the SOG team members on the perimeter, chiefly up on the highway shoulder, would spy some movement and relay its position, but it was impossible for them to tell whether they were seeing the subject or their own SWAT members.

Had it been daytime, the SWAT team might have gotten a better feel for the terrain. The street ran north-south, parallel to the coastline. There was a footpath radiating at a right angle from the end of the cul-de-sac due west toward the beach. It was narrow and the footing was soft sand. It was tiring to walk over, exhausting to try to run through. North and south of this path ran undulating dunes carpeted in spots with iceplant and Bermuda grass. There was an entire mini-ecosystem of plants, bugs, and birds populating this strip, and the state park service had considerately posted educational signs around giving Latin names and habitat details for many of the species. Of course, no one had the time or inclination to read them just then. The 'Stay On Path' and 'Area Closed for Habitat Preservation' signs were completely ignored. Due north of the drop point was a chain link fence, erected to deter entry to the more fragile habitat areas, but it was not difficult to walk down the beach path a few yards and then turn north to access the area. Immediately to the east of the drop area was a small trailer park - the one where Finkman had been arrested, and on the other side of that, farther to the east, Highway 101 ran north-south parallel to Dunes Road. The strip of land between 101 and the ocean was about a half mile wide and continued north more or less unbroken all the way to the Salinas River, about two miles away, and beyond that, to the power plant at Moss Landing another ten or twelve miles farther. To either side of Dunes Road south of the trailer park were several motels, the economy-class versions of a Monterey vacation destination. All of them were sizable and the parking lots were nearly full of vehicles of various sorts. The units on the west side of the road opened directly onto the beach. Reservation Road, at a right angle to Dunes, ran west toward the ocean, then curved into a parking lot tucked behind the first motel There was a public beach marked by a rest room and drinking fountain at the edge of the lot.

LaPointe, despite his conditioning, was becoming winded. Running in sand, loaded down with body armor, weapons, and a radio while trying to call out orders was simply not something anyone could do for long without becoming exhausted. He had seen the subject, Fox - FBI code name for whoever picked up the ransom - head west toward the beach, then cut northward at a forty-five degree angle over the vegetated portion of the dunes. He radioed to the SWAT and SOG to close the area to the north and east - along the highway and across the dunes somewhere to the north. As soon as he had caught his breath he took off again, this time due north on a path he hoped would intercept the figure. After ninety seconds he crested another dune and looked through the night goggles. He saw nothing but black.

Back in San Jose in the command post Don Zwolinski, the Z-man, spoke assuredly to the Deputy Assistant Director. "We have the subject in sight, and are following him at a discreet distance."

The response was immediate. "No, no, you shouldn't try that. I told you our policy is to arrest. This is a very risky action you are taking. You'd better move in now to arrest." The volume and vehemence in his voice did not make it sound like a mere recommendation.

"This is San Francisco you're talking to, not some Podunk division in the Midwest. We have the premier SOG and SWAT teams west of the Mississippi. We have things under control. If he gets out of sight, we'll tighten the loop and move in."

Stroaker ripped off the headset and shoved it back in Morales's lap. All he had heard for the last three minutes had been static. He reached up over the front seat of the purple Olds and grabbed the dashboard microphone. He tried the regular street team channel, "This is number one. I repeat this is number one. Does anybody read? Please respond."

Random bits of crackle spewed from the speaker, but nothing that sounded like a response to his transmission. Allen spoke up, "Pete, this is a bad radio area. You're probably not going to get through to anybody until we get through the pass."

"Christ almighty, what's that stench?" Stroaker bellowed. He looked around accusingly at everyone in the car. Bertinetti was doing a dishrag imitation, draped limply on the armrest. She had not had time to do a proper cleanup job, just a quick wipe of her hands with a tissue, and her aroma betrayed her. The SWAT man in the front seat had been the one to sit on the wet door sill, and his clothes contributed to the smell. He pointed to Bertinetti and did a creditable impersonation of a woman vomiting into her hands. He didn't want to rat her out audibly as he knew of her reputation for retribution. "Toni, are you okay?" Stroaker asked, concern in his voice.

"No. Sick. Can he drive slower?" Laying as it did more or less in a straight line through the hills, the road was not so much curvy as it was challenging. It had steep places, both uphill and downhill, and switched from freeway to uncontrolled access, with side streets and even driveways to commercial zones joining in sporadically. The traffic was heavy enough to require Q-ball to zig and zag around other cars, and hit the brakes suddenly at times. Bertinetti was green, and not with envy.

"Hold it, Q," Stroaker ordered. "We can't just stop, and she's too sick to keep this up. This car... holy shit, it stinks in here." The smell was a combination of the emanations from Bertinetti, the SWAT guy, the bag of half eaten fast food, and the garlic fields that still surrounded them. "Pull over at the next thing that looks open." Within seconds they reached a stretch of lights on the right. There was a gas station, now closed, and a cheap bar, which was open. The bar, charitably described as a dump, looked like it catered to the local Mexican farm labor, with a neon "Tecate" sign glowing in the window. Stroaker ordered Bertinetti and the SWAT agent out of the car, and told them to call back for someone to pick them up. The agent protested, but Stroaker was adamant, so he got out, and watched as the purple Oldsmobile pulled away in the night. Despite his formidable weaponry, he felt anything but comfortable walking into a Mexican bar in his ninja suit and bandolier, a sick woman on his arm. And not just any woman - the fearsome Awful Brafull, who would make him pay dearly if she was treated with disrespect, ridiculed, leered at, anything she didn't like. Bertinetti, for her part, was overjoyed at being on solid ground once again, and would probably have been happy to spend the night in the ladies room.

"From the Barfing Man to the barfing woman. This case has certain symmetry to it, y'know," Rothman said to Knowles, both still at the CHP substation. "Sort of a yin and a yang." He was outwardly casual, displaying the sick humor and forced machismo so ubiquitous in law enforcement in really hairy situations.

Knowles was trying to relay to him pieces of what Olson was telling him over the pay phone, and Rothman would in turn relay those bits to the clerk and SWAT agent who had stayed behind at the weigh station. He shushed Rothman with his hand.

"Who has the eye?" It was Olson's voice, but not spoken into the phone. Knowles recognized it as Olson's radio voice - asking the surveillance agents who could see Fox. For ten interminable seconds there was nothing but silence. "Repeat, who has the eye? Please respond if you know where Fox is." More silence.

A sickening tension grabbed Knowles's gut, and he knew at that moment that the worst had happened. They had lost the pickup man. The ransom was gone and they had nothing.

"CP to number one, come in. Number one come in." Olson called on the SOG channel, from up at Radio. No response. He didn't hesitate a moment longer. This was his chance to rectify the worst of the SAC's decision. "All units, number one is out of radio contact. This is the CP. You are instructed to move in and arrest Fox. Repeat, arrest the subject on sight. Use whatever force is necessary, but remember that we do not have a location for the victim. We want him alive if possible. Copy?"

There were two or three responses of "Copy" but Olson could not tell how many agents had heard the command. Radio reception was spotty there, and some might not have heard. He punched the button for the phone line that Claude Becker had been on. He hoped the line was still open. "Claude, are you there?"

"Still here, but I can't see the subject any more. He took off to the north."

"Arrest the subject. Repeat, arrest Fox. I put it out over the air, but I'm not sure everybody heard it. Please repeat it there on the tactical channel - they should be able to hear you where you are."

"10-4. We'll get this sucker, Ben. Talk to you later." The line went dead, and Olson could hear Becker's voice on the SOG channel repeating the command to arrest, although it was broken and faint.

Chapter 22

"We've decided to move in and arrest," Z-man told the DAD.

"Do you still have him in sight?" came the response.

A pregnant pause - so pregnant it was ready to give birth. Z-man delivered: "Not at this time."

Back came a torrent of malediction so vile the Z-man had to hold the phone at arm's length. Z-man could outcurse a drunken sailor, but this stream of invective had even him grimacing. He turned to Tobin and Schuler and said, "He says we should have arrested him when he told us to the first time." The paraphrasing was unnecessary, as every occupant of the room could get the drift without the commentary.

"No shit," Schuler said calmly. He looked down at his notepad and jotted something.

After many minutes that seemed like hours the second car from Allen's team showed up at the highway patrol station. It was a tight fit, but the remaining helicopter passengers climbed in. Knowles gave the instruction, "Back to the RA."

"I thought we were going to Marina PD," the driver remarked doubtfully. She was a medalist in the California Police Olympics in weightlifting, and she dwarfed both Rothman and Knowles.

"Too late. Head back to the CP in San Jose. It took you long enough to get here," Knowles answered.

"Couldn't help it. Unit 7 was going to pick you guys up, but he got a call on his cell phone to go to some dive in Aromas to pick up AB. Stroaker dumped her off in the middle of nowhere because she was too airsick - carsick, whatever - to keep going. The reserve SWAT guy, Stroaker's goon - Jim somebody, you know who I mean - is with her. He says she's okay now. Once she took off her jacket and jiggled her boobs a bit, every farmhand in the place offered to buy her a drink. At least that's what he *thinks* they said; they don't speak English and he doesn't speak Spanish. The bartender is breaking out the really good stuff, too, and she's already half-sloshed, I hear." She shook her cell phone to indicate the infallible source of all this scoop. "She's on some sort of pedestal there and loving every minute of it. The SWAT guy is pissed as hell, and is feeling like an idiot in his Batman costume, and missing all the action. Anyway, Stroaker left orders to send the next car for them and to get them to the forward CP as soon as AB recovers enough to ride. So you guys got pushed to third place. That's me."

Knowles sat in front, ostensibly so he could use the radio, but also because he was still a bit rocky from the helicopter ride. He grabbed the mike and tried to reach Olson. It took about ten minutes before they got into a spot with good enough reception to get through. The communications clerk acknowledged his call sign. He asked the clerk if there had been any progress in locating Fox. The answer was negative. Knowles told the clerk to advise the street teams that Fox was loose with the package and tell them to stand by for orders. He was glad he was not there to hear the responses that would bring. Then he settled in for the ride. He figured it would take at least forty minutes; his only consolation was that he wouldn't be stuck down at the Marina Police Department with Stroaker.

As soon as Claude Becker got the go-ahead from Olson, he relayed it to the other SWAT team members on his handy-talkie. Every one of them acknowledged. The chase was on, and they knew it. The team was together and communicating clearly since they were all in close proximity. LaPointe heard the transmission and asked for every team member to state his position, in order. They had a set radio order for such situations, to avoid stepping on each other over the air. Once they had rotated through the order, LaPointe was able to determine that they had the south end of the area well blocked. There was a team member at the public beach by the rest room area, who assured him that he could see anyone moving south on the beach or dunes from his vantage point. Becker had been on the knoll to the southwest of the drop point, between the drop and the motel area. He had reported the subject moving northwest, toward the beach and away from the street, just as LaPointe had seen. Another member had run down the sandy path directly to the beach, so the subject would have to creep past these three agents to reverse back to the south; this seemed unlikely, since Fox had last been seen making tracks northwest. The second sniper had been up on the embankment near LaPointe at the beginning. His job, like Becker's, had been to keep the subject in view with the telescopic night vision sight. Once the order came to arrest, he had headed due north on foot along the roadside for about a hundred and fifty yards before cutting westward over the dunes. Because of the solid footing at the top of the embankment, he had made good time in the northward direction, and despite his later start, had gotten farther north than LaPointe had.

The SOG teams were now lining up along the highway to the east, blocking off any escape that direction. There were two teams on site, with a third on the way. Each team consisted of four or five agents, so there were nine agents manning a stretch of highway about 600 yards long. All of them had pulled their blue nylon raid jackets over whatever else they wore, so the huge white letters 'FBI' were visible in the headlights of cars traveling past. At a suitable break in traffic they pulled two SOG vehicles out onto the highway and set the emergency lights - both hazard blinkers and red lights - to stop traffic in the southbound lanes. They began to search every car at this makeshift roadblock, ordering every driver to open his trunk. They carried shoulder weapons and didn't get any back talk.

The Monterey RA street team consisted of only three agents, since Nick Lark, the fourth agent in the RA, was on vacation. One agent was up at the Marina PD command post, but the other two, at Olson's direction, were beginning to conduct interviews in the trailer park, which was the closest occupied location to the drop point. It seemed half the park had seen the arrest by the police officer of that nasty-looking criminal with the ponytail. They all had a theory about whether he was a drug dealer, child molester, or terrorist. The agents nodded knowingly at these descriptions, but declined to advise the witnesses that it had been their own SOG agent who had been arrested. Nobody had seen anything or anybody else unusual or suspicious. They relayed their information by radio to the Monterey RA secretary, who had dutifully stayed late to cover the drop, although no one had thought to order her to. The Blue channel normally used by these agents was crystal clear in this area, since it was specifically designated for this region, and the local repeater was set for this channel. It would have been ideal for the entire operation, except, ironically, it was impossible to get everybody to switch to that channel due to the bad radio reception on the dedicated operation channel. SOG and SWAT were on Red 3, and the street teams were on Blue 7; there was no way all of them could hear a transmission telling them to switch. In fact, not all of them even had the right crystal in their Buradio for this channel. Radios were customized for the area the assigned driver covered. So such an instruction would serve only to divide the groups, not unify them. Nevertheless, for these agents, the communication was not difficult; they continued to interview and report back to the CP via the squad secretary, who relayed by phone, without causing any clutter over the air.

With SWAT to the south, SOG to the east, and the ocean to the west, the only direction LaPointe was really worried about was due north. He had radioed to have that closed off, but he did not know if anyone was in position yet to the north. A transmission came over his handy-talkie, "This is Four. I've spotted something significant, I think. There is an underwater tow lying flat on the beach. Fox may have made an ocean escape."

"Roger. Team 1, to repeat, Four has spotted an underwater tow on the beach. That's one of those motorized underwater scooters like Jacques Cousteau used." LaPointe, as a former Navy Seal, knew what it was, but he wasn't sure every team member was familiar with the term. "Does anyone know if the Coast Guard is on alert?" LaPointe asked.

"Four again. There are some running lights of a vessel 80 yards offshore, but I can't tell if it's Coast Guard. If not, it's a pretty sizable pleasure or fishing boat. The fog is too thick to see markings. Whoever they are, they're shining a searchlight this way. It could be a signal to Fox."

LaPointe asked Becker to call the command post via cell phone to find out. Becker did so and reported that the Z-man was checking. LaPointe continued his northward pursuit, without even knowing if he was going in the right direction. Then his flashlight picked up something in the sand. There was a trail of footprints. He stopped to examine them closely. The indentations had sharp rims. He suspected they were fresh, but he was not a trained tracker. He swung the light over a broader expanse to see if there were other, similar tracks. There were none. There were a few indentations here and there, but nothing that looked like human footprints. All the smaller undulations were smooth and wind-eroded. The tracks must be fresh. He got on the radio and checked everyone's position once more. One agent, the second sniper, was north of him, but off to the east near the highway moving toward him. None of the agents could have made these tracks. They had to be Fox. He told the team to ignore the ocean route, and follow him. He was tracking Fox northward.

Knowles and his fellow passengers continued to monitor the situation over Blue 7, but it was surprisingly quiet. All the action was with SWAT and SOG on Red 3, which they couldn't access from their radio. Knowles fumed at not being able to hear what was going on, but he remembered having been involved in another kidnap payoff years earlier when everyone was on a division-wide channel, and a single remote street team car unknowingly got its mike stuck open. The result was that the entire channel was blocked for half an hour with their personal chatter. Not only had they seriously interfered with the surveillance, but they had said a number of things over the air that weren't intended for public consumption. The last words they broadcast division-wide as they noticed their error were, "Oh shit." The occupants had been unable to receive the repeated warnings from the CP to fix their mike because, of course, it had been stuck in broadcast mode. Knowles knew it was necessary to limit the tactical channel to the small number of front line people who really needed it, but it did not reduce his frustration.

Every once in awhile one of the street teams would call in, asking for an update. Radio would respond with a bland, uninformative statement such as "Situation remains unchanged. Continue to stand by."

Stroaker marched into the small conference room at the Marina Police Department, accompanied by the police chief, who had come out to meet him in the lobby. Calling it bedlam would have been an understatement. All three radio channels were still blaring, and two uniformed officers were crowded in the room arguing with Harry Rice. Stroaker asked for an update from Z-man. Stroaker had learned via radio only a few minutes earlier, when he came through the mountain pass onto the Monterey side, that the SWAT and SOG teams had lost the subject and Olson had ordered pursuit and arrest of Fox.

When the status report was finished, Stroaker murmured, "All right. Well, Ben did the right thing in implementing my plan, but he waited too long. I specifically said that if it looked like they were going to lose the subject, they should move in and arrest. They shouldn't have waited until they had already lost him."

The police chief cheerfully volunteered, "Oh, I think he ordered the teams to move in and arrest just as soon as he could. You had just ordered them to follow, and then your radio cut out." He smiled benignly, like the guileless child who presents his mother with a beautiful mud pie, unaware of the significance of the trail of splotches on the new carpet behind him.

Stroaker glowered at him blackly and replied, "The information I had was that they still had the subject well in control. If *Supervisor* Olson knew something different, he should have said something earlier. At least my men didn't mistake one of your officers for the victim." He emphasized the word supervisor as if that would signify to the chief that it was a mere inferior manager who had taken matters into his hands; the unspoken assumption was that as a fellow top commander, the chief would understand and concur that the subordinate must have been at fault if he was that low in the command structure. This attempt to win the chief as an ally was undercut by his gratuitous shot at the Marina P.D. for its arrest of Agent Finkman.

The Chief, unfazed, replied, "Oh that. Well, it was dark and we didn't have a photo of the Fischer fellow, just a description. Your agent met the description, so we stopped him based on your order. We didn't really arrest him, you know, just an F.I. We let him go as soon as he identified himself." F.I. was cop talk for Field Interrogation.

Stroaker decided to get back on track. "It sounds like Fox has gone north, but he probably has a vehicle stashed to the south, somewhere around Dunes Road. He had to have driven in there from the McDonald's. Maybe at the hotels or at the public beach lot. Mo, have every available body form a tight perimeter along the south edge of the area between the drop and the motels to prevent him from doubling back. He might even have a room rented at one of those."

Morales put out the orders over the SOG channels, and the police chief told his dispatcher to assign some officers to check every vehicle trying to leave the area. Dunes fed onto Reservation Road, and there was no other route away from the beach area. There was a natural choke point right at Reservation and Dunes. One of the Monterey RA agents was assigned to assist them.

"Chief," Stroaker continued, "what's to the north of this area besides the river? Anything?"

"There's a sand plant facility right on the beach. Building materials company. They scoop tons of sand with these huge machines and process it into cement. They have a private road that leads down to their plant, coming off of Lapis. Beyond that there are artichoke fields running almost up to the beach. Castroville is the Artichoke Capital of the World, you know." Castroville was the next town north of Marina, situated at the intersection of highways 1 and 156. Stroaker had seen the welcome signs on the way in on route 156, advertising this claim to fame right next to the Kiwanis and Elks Lodge crests. From Gilroy the Garlic Capital to Castroville the Artichoke Capital, he was pretty much maxed out on any interest in vegetable capitals. "After that," the chief continued, "the marshy area of the river. It would be very tough to slog through that, but he could swim upriver and climb out anywhere. There are lots of places - boat docks, fishing landings, bridge abutments, you name it."

"We've got to get someone to cut off the north end, too. Mo, do we have anyone there?"

"Boss," Morales replied, "I've got one car - two guys - at the Del Monte Road exit. They've been instructed to block off the north end, but that's a half a mile of fields and dunes to the water, blacked out by fog, not even starlight getting through, and they don't have night vision equipment. They've spaced themselves as best they can, but that's a loose net at best."

"What about the ocean? Could he take a boat?" Stroaker asked the chief.

"We have a regular channel open with the Coast Guard. They have a cutter just off the beach. That was good thinking of you guys to alert them before the drop. They say no small craft have left the beach area, although they occasionally see people on the beach with lights. Probably your SWAT team. The tide and breakers are too strong for anyone to swim out from there right now, so they don't think anybody came their way."

"It looks like it rests on the shoulders of the SWAT team," Stroaker stated flatly.

Becker caught up with LaPointe. The tracks were still clear, and still headed north. They kept up a slow run, but had to stop periodically to make sure the trail was still there. They crested a dune and saw a huge industrial complex ahead, enormous conveyor belts leading from the ground to a silo-like structure several stories tall at one end of the building. Lights were still on within. The tracks led directly toward the entrance to the plant. They picked up the pace and ran almost full bore to the doorway which opened into a small paved parking area.

"Careful. He could be inside with a hostage or hiding," LaPointe cautioned under his breath. They listened at the closed door for a few seconds, but heard nothing besides the low humming of machinery. Becker tested the doorknob gingerly.

"It's unlocked," he whispered.

"Let's do it. On three," LaPointe directed. He counted to three, and simultaneously the agents entered the plant in a low crouch. They found themselves in a short hallway. Mounted on the wall to the right was a time clock, replete with employee cards neatly arrayed in slots to one side. On the left was a featureless wall, separating them from some interior space; they couldn't tell whether it was office or industrial in use. They continued forward until they encountered a small break room on the right furnished with what could have been war surplus tables and chairs - which war was harder to say. The smell of burnt coffee permeated the atmosphere of the room. As they exited the end of the hallway, they came into a large factory floor area. There was a high counter to the left, and a raised platform behind it elevating two desks. There was a lamp turned on at one of these desks, but no one sitting there. Then a clatter resounded from their right. They stepped forward to peer around a file cabinet and spotted a large man wearing a flannel shirt and a yellow hard hat stenciled with the logo of the company. He was rummaging through a box of metal parts.

"FBI," LaPointe called out to the man. "We need to talk to you." They both had their handguns drawn, but depressed toward the floor. The man turned around, startled, and stared.

"No shit? He was telling the truth then, I guess. You looking for that guy?" the workman answered.

"Who? Did you see someone come in here?" LaPointe asked.

"Yeah, not two minutes ago. He offered me $500 cash to drive him out of here. He said the cops were after him."

"Where is he now?"

"I dunno. He left. I told him no."

"Did you call 9-1-1?" Becker asked.

"No," the man answered blankly, as if to say, why would anybody do that. Becker wanted to grab the guy by the throat and shake him.

"Did he go back out this hallway?" LaPointe asked.

"No, out the other door," the man said, pointing to a metal roll-up door that opened onto the beach.

LaPointe turned to Becker. "Claude, get a description from this guy and whatever else he has. I'm going to continue the pursuit." The SWAT leader took off at a run out the roll-up door.

Becker resumed the questioning, "Can you describe him?"

"Uh, not really. I mean he was smaller than you. What's this all about, anyway?" the man replied. He surveyed Becker's black ninja suit and blurted out, "Are you really FBI or are you with the U.N. forces?"

"He's a kidnapper. We're trying to save a man's life," Becker informed him, lifting his pocket patch to show his FBI seal.

"I don't know. You going to burn this place down like you did Waco?" The man's belligerence was unconcealed.

"The Branch Davidians burned down their own compound at Waco. We never fired a shot; all we did was rescue people. Look, we're trying to save a life here. Please, what was the man wearing?"

"Sweatshirt, pants, dark," the workman said grudgingly, after a short pause. "No hat. I didn't notice his shoes."

"Backpack?"

"No. No backpack."

"Did he show you any cash or just say he'd pay you?" Becker tried to show enthusiasm, to give the man a sense he was being a help, although in reality he felt like punching the guy's lights out.

"He had it in his hand. He shoved in back into the pocket of his sweatshirt when I turned it down. You know, those kind in the front where you can put both hands through."

"What race was he?"

"White. Young."

"Not Hispanic?" Becker asked.

"Coulda been. Dark hair. Not black or Oriental, though. He didn't look like the wetbacks who work in the fields around here, but maybe higher class Mexican. No accent as I noticed."

This one's a real model of open-mindedness, Becker thought. "Mustache or beard?"

"I don't remember. He was only here a few seconds. I didn't pay much attention."

Great, a man comes in saying he's fleeing the police and you don't call 9-1-1 or get a description, Becker felt like saying, but bit his tongue. "Were there any words or pictures on the sweatshirt? A school team logo or something like that?"

"I don't think so."

"Would you recognize him again?"

"Probably. I'm not sure."

"How tall was he?"

"Like I said, smaller than you," the man said almost accusingly, as though Becker had not been listening. Becker was six foot three and 220 lbs. Being smaller than he was didn't narrow down the field very much. The workman was perhaps an inch taller than Becker, and heavier, although it was all in his gut and neck. Becker figured the man must think everybody below 250 lbs was a shrimp, not worth trying to tell apart. The man let the glare sink in for a few seconds, then reluctantly continued, "less than six feet, kind of thin, I think. Hard to tell; the sweat shirt was bulky."

"Is there anything else you can think of to help identify him," Becker asked, again putting on the smile in a faint hope of encouraging him to produce something useful.

"Nope." The man stood there, acting exasperated the FBI had wasted so much of his valuable time already. Becker took his name and phone number, thanked him, and took off after LaPointe.

LaPointe had continued northward toward the Salinas River, which was another mile and a half away. The sandy strip of rolling dunes and fine, sloping beach narrowed considerably after a quarter mile. On the flats to the east of the dunes were artichoke fields, plowed neatly. A barbed wire fence surrounded the fields. Along the southern edge of the field ran a dirt road connecting the beach area with the public streets to the east. The western end of this road broadened into a crude dirt parking area where there stood a metal gate through the barbed wire. At that point was posted a wooden sign identifying this as the Access Path to Salinas River Recreation Area. LaPointe crested the dunes at this point and spotted the fence. Charging out through the narrow pedestrian opening next to the gate he heard a shout, "FBI! Hands up!"

He dropped his weapon, an MP-5 rifle, instantly, and put his hands in the air. Now was not the time to fool around. "It's me, LaPointe," he called out in reply, although he could not see whoever had called out to him.

"Hank?" the voice called.

"Yeah, it's me. Who's that?"

"Tom Horvath." Horvath was on the SOG squad. "Sorry. The fog's so thick here, all I could see was a moving figure."

LaPointe picked up his rifle. "No problem. Has anybody else come this way?"

"Not that I saw. You're the first thing I've seen move since I got out here. To be honest, though, if you hadn't been running like a bat out of hell I probably wouldn't have seen you. I can see along the fields okay - it's flat and open, but toward the beach, someone could probably crawl past, walk even, and I wouldn't see 'em."

"He came this way," LaPointe said. "Get more help and close this area off. He might have doubled back or run out to the ocean. I'm going back." He keyed his radio and transmitted "Claude, anything from the witness?"

"White male, possibly Hispanic, less than six feet, thin build, wearing a dark sweatshirt and pants. Black or dark hair. The sweatshirt has one pocket in front you can put your hands in from both sides. And the back pack is not with him."

"Roger. Team copy?"

The other SWAT team members came on the air in order and acknowledged the description.

Mo Morales heard the transmission and relayed the information to Stroaker. The description was put out over Blue 7 for all street team agents. More street teams were arriving from farther north, so they were dispatched to help seal off the northern edge of the area. Manpower continued to flood in for the next fifteen minutes; all of it was channeled into closing the perimeter.

LaPointe backtracked to the sand company methodically, but he realized that it was impossible to tell whether he was following his own tracks or those of Fox. The stretch of sand right outside the roll-up door was so crisscrossed with tracks, that he concluded it was not even possible to be sure which direction Fox had gone from there. He had assumed the subject had continued north because he was being pursued from the south, but he could have cut down toward the water, doubled back southward, or run up the private road from the cement factory that ran eastward under the freeway. Without the backpack, he would have been able to make better time than LaPointe and the SWAT who were weighed down with weapons, body armor, and communications gear. The man was reportedly young and thin, which suggested speed and agility. With a bitterness he could taste, he finally concluded that the trail was cold. They had lost Fox. He keyed his radio and reported to the command post that there were no tracks to follow, and no reported sightings; Fox was either holed up inside the perimeter or he had escaped.

Knowles, Rothman, and the remainder of the helicopter draftees trudged into the SJRA command post heavily. They had not been able to monitor Red 3 from the car, but the cryptic transmissions which had come out over the Blue channel were enough to let them know what had happened. The subject had been lost and the victim was nowhere to be found. The only bright spot was that the ransom was apparently stashed somewhere in the area of the drop zone, and should be recoverable.

Olson and Z-man looked at Knowles. "Any ideas?" Olson asked.

"How about a flyover with the plane to locate the money with the beacon?" Z-man suggested. "There could be prints on it that would give us leads."

Rothman said, "Won't work. The fog is too thick. The plane can fly over, but won't be able to see where they are to give landmarks to the people below, and the agents on the ground won't be able to see where the plane is. We'll have to wait for the fog to clear. That won't be until late morning tomorrow at the earliest."

"Maybe not," Knowles countered. "How about if the plane flies over, and when the signal is the strongest, the plane tells the ground units. Even if they can't see it, if it flies low enough they should be able to tell whether it's north or south of them. They can call out to each other to see who was the closest to the plane when the word was given."

"Won't work," Rothman said. "The plane will be lucky even to be able to get in the general vicinity of the beach. You can't see a thing up there for miles around. The plane could be flying to the east or west of the beach, or at an angle, and not know it. The ground units won't be able to tell when it's directly overhead, anyway. The fog muffles and changes the sound."

"What else do we have?" Z-man asked plaintively.

"How about the radioisotope?" Olson asked.

"Yeah, we should give them all a try," Knowles agreed. "It won't hurt to try now, but I don't hold out much hope. The wind is blowing off the ocean at twelve knots, I heard. Anything in the air, like the radiation and the pheromone, will have been blown miles away from its point of origin within minutes. If the guy dragged the bag on the ground, it might be possible to track it, but it's not likely. Still, we have to do something."

"Becker said he had a perfect shot of the Fox. He could have taken him out with one round." Olson said it with a shake of the head and an angry scowl.

"And if it had turned out to be a hired messenger service?" Z-man scoffed.

"No point in recriminations," Olson responded. " Let's get Stroaker to order the Geiger counter team in and try the radio beacon with the plane. It's better than nothing."

Everyone around the table nodded wearily and Olson picked up the phone.

"Where's our peter stroker when we really need him," Z-man said, miming his signature jerk off motion. "Shit, he's going to be pissed."

Day 5
Saturday

Chapter 23

"He should have been back by now. It's after one. Something's wrong." Miguel paced frantically up and down on the linoleum. He began muttering something Fischer assumed was Arabic, since he could hear an "Allah" every once in awhile. "If your family did not pay, you will. Pah!"

Fischer ran all the possible outcomes through his engineer's brain. The probability tree was not branching in the directions he had hoped. The numbers were swelling on the side labeled "Death" and shrinking on the side labeled "Rescue." He began to reconsider that slender twig labeled "Escape." It was obviously hopeless while Miguel was in the room, but at least if he got out at night there would be lights on at the neighbor's to identify who was home and who wasn't. Synapses triggered silently as the hunches and fears were converted to likelihoods in his analytical engine.

"Do you think he is coming back?" Miguel asked, suddenly.

This was the first sign Miguel might be influenced. Up to now, everything Fischer had said to him had resulted only in threats, distrust, and accusations. He considered his response carefully. His first decision was whether to interpret Miguel's remark as implying a distrust of Carlos's intention, or as worry that he had been captured. "Has he been honest with you so far?" he said, finally, deciding to plant the seed of doubt if it wasn't already there.

"He is a fellow Mus...a man of his word," Miguel said, biting off the end of the word. Apparently he had been told to keep up the Mexican charade even if Fischer knew better.

"Well, then, you should have nothing to worry about. I'm sure my family has paid the ransom. Carlos is probably just being very careful before returning here. Or maybe there was trouble in finding the right place to put the ransom ... um, money. Where was the payment?" He kicked himself internally for reminding Miguel by use of the word "ransom" that they were criminals at risk for a big jail term. Miguel probably did not think of the money as ransom but as some sort of reward for devotion.

"Monterey. He should be back by now."

Incredible! Miguel had actually given him some information. Still, it would be of little use, since his family and the police would know the payoff location already. At least he knew he wasn't in Southern California or the Central Valley. Miguel had been gone perhaps four or five hours at the most, he estimated. Fischer could not look at his watch, but he knew it hadn't been long after dark when Miguel had driven away. There had to be time for the call to be placed, and for Pam to drive the money from Los Altos. If Carlos was really due back by now, that meant the driving time to Monterey from wherever they were could not be more than one to one-and-a-half hours, five hours minus two, the driving time from Los Altos to Monterey, divided by two. That was assuming everything moved like clockwork.

"I have to go to the bathroom," Fischer said. Miguel unlocked his handcuffs and leg chains, and led him to the toilet.

"Don't try anything. I still have my knife," Miguel said, pushing the flat of the blade against the back of Fischer's neck. Miguel closed the bathroom door halfway.

Fischer moved the blindfold up onto his forehead while he used the commode. This gave him a chance to stretch his muscles, readjust his eyes, and think privately for a few minutes. Perhaps if he were able to get his hands on a knife or club of some sort, he considered. There might be something in the kitchen. The toilet tank lid was heavy enough to do some damage if wielded with surprise and force to the right place. But he didn't see how he could expect to succeed coming out of the bathroom with it in hand. Miguel always listened closely, keeping the door ajar, and would surely hear if he picked up the heavy porcelain piece. Miguel was too young and quick to be caught off guard when he emerged, anyway. That wasn't the answer. After washing up he came out of the bathroom with his blindfold back in place. Miguel led him back to the bedroom closet and reapplied the handcuffs. Then, as Fischer got down on the mattress and extended his feet to be chained once more to the floor bolt, he pointed his toes upward, toward his knees, as much as possible and pushed his heels apart just a tad. He hoped this would prevent the chains from being looped too tightly for him to replicate his previous escape. Miguel seemed not to notice any attempt to resist his efforts, and the snap of the padlock reassured Fischer that Miguel was satisfied with the security of the chains. Fischer relaxed his feet. The tension in the chains eased. The chains still felt tight, but he decided he could get them off over the heels again if he had to.

"Where is he? If he has cheated me, I will kill him. I will kill his whole family." Miguel seemed to want to enlist Fischer in his campaign of Miguel the Poor Victim.

"How long have you known him?" Fischer asked.

"Only one year. But he is devout. We met at the mosque. He would not cheat me."

This was getting good. Both confirmed as Muslim, they attend the same mosque, Carlos has a family in the area. These are things that could help identify them. "If he cheats you, you should not take revenge on his wife or children, only on him. They may be innocent."

"You are right, but they will suffer if I kill him, all the same."

Excellent! So Carlos does have a wife and children; he was able to narrow down the term "family." "And you, what will happen to your wife and children if you take revenge on him? Perhaps one of his relatives will take vengeance on you. They would be left alone."

"Me?" A silence descended. "Quiet. You just worry about your own family. If they let you die, they will be the ones to suffer for their own perfidiousness."

Perfidiousness? Where did he learn that word - and why not use perfidy? This was probably not the time to correct his English. Fischer decided Miguel had finally realized he was blabbing too much. Better not to say any more unless spoken to. He sat silent.

Stroaker made it back to the San Jose command post around 2:30 A.M. No one had gone home. "Ben, good call on sending the SWAT in, but you really shouldn't have waited so long."

Olson knew when to bite his tongue. "Sorry, Boss - radio problems." This had the benefit of being both true and non-accusatory. He simply omitted the part describing the radio problem was the SAC using it to tell the SWAT to follow Fox instead of arrest.

"Yeah, I had my own problems with that. Well, no one could have done any better. We have the best people there are. You win some, you lose some."

Several agents nodded their agreement to this bit of sagacity.

"Pete," Knowles asked, "any progress with the Geiger counter or the radio beacon?"

"No. The wind is blowing too hard for the Geiger counter. It got a good solid reading in the street where the backpack was dropped, but after that nothing. If we get within five feet of it again, though, they say it should detect it."

"How about the beacon?"

"No. The plane flew over and the pilot said he was getting a faint signal. But he couldn't tell where he was, and we couldn't either, because of the fog. Agents a mile apart both thought it was right overhead at the same time. Maybe tomorrow. The screamer didn't go off, either. I guess he hasn't opened that pack." The disgust in Stroaker's voice was manifest.

Olson and Knowles looked over at Rothman and gave him a nod - a silent acknowledgment that he had been right about the radio.

"What about the SOG and SWAT out there? Are they staying all night?" Z-man asked Stroaker.

"I've ordered them to maintain the perimeter with as few agents as they can, and send the rest home. There's going to be a lot of work to be done tomorrow. We need somebody who has been rested. Cliff, you should send the street teams home."

Knowles nodded assent. He had wanted to do it long ago, when it had become obvious that they would have nothing to do. He left the room to go to Radio. When he put out the broadcast, the team leaders all acknowledged the message, none happily. The voices conveyed a mixture of anger, disappointment, sadness, and concern for the victim and his family. Knowles had no doubt they blamed the failure on the Command Post, of which he was the primary spokesman. He was too weary to care. He returned to the Command Post.

"Rice and Mo are still down at the forward CP," Stroaker was telling Z-man, "along with several agents, one from the Monterey R.A., and some from the street teams. We'll leave it like that for now. What did the Bureau say when you told them we lost the subject?"

"They weren't happy. You don't want to know the exact verbiage." Z-man shrugged and gave a dismissive wave to the telephone, as if to pooh-pooh the ignoramus still on hold there. "Do you want to talk to him? They're still on hold."

"I'd better. Gimme that." Stroaker picked up the phone as Z-man punched the blinking line. "Hi, this is Pete Stroaker....So he's gone home? Who is this?.... Uh huh.... Okay, Sam, well, we seem to have hit a snag, but it's only temporary. Our radio problems were the cause. If you guys would give us the funding for decent communications these things wouldn't happen. I'll mention it to Louie when I see him...anyway, we're keeping the area buttoned up, and we'll start again in the morning when it's light.... Yeah....That's right, you tell him that. No point in keeping the line open. We'll call when things start up in the morning. Bye."

Knowles wondered whether the blatant use of the Director's name would really save Stroaker on this one. The DAD had to have been tear-ass, and, unlike everybody in this room, had the ability to put Stroaker on the hot seat. There were fifty or sixty other SACs who were happy to put a bug in "Louie's" ear about the screw up of their colleague cum rival SAC. Egos and ambition dominated at that level and San Francisco was a plum assignment.

"Okay," Stroaker addressed the room, "we're ceasing active investigation for the night. I suggest everybody go home and get some rest. Be back here in the morning, first light. We want you fresh for the real fun."

"Who's staying here in case something breaks?" Z-man asked him.

"I'll be here myself," came the answer.

"I'll stay, too," Z-man said. Stroaker beamed with pleasure.

"Count me in," Olson agreed. His motives were slightly different. He knew the Z-man would not be sufficient influence on the SAC to keep him from screwing something else up. He could also see that this was a test. Stroaker was seeing who was really ready to give 110% and more, what was the size of the fight in the dog, who would reach deep down inside. He looked at Knowles and Rothman and jerked his thumb toward the door. He knew it was actually a good idea to have a level head or two go get rested for the next day.

Knowles stood up. "Well, it looks like you have plenty of help to cover for tonight. I'll see you in the morning." Rothman followed suit. They both lived within short commuting distance, and could get home in time to get maybe three hours sleep. Knowles hoped the brass stretched out on the floor and got some shut-eye there in the RA. He had seen too many big operations where the commanders had stayed up all night and been zombies by midday the next day. The decision-making was always terrible when that happened. In fact, he was convinced that most of the time that happened, the people in charge *intentionally* impaired their own judgment by staying up all night so they would have a ready-made excuse for when they blew it.

It always sounded okay somehow when they said, "well, maybe you're right, but you have to understand, we'd been up for 36 hours straight, and ..." In Stroaker's case, Knowles knew the decision making would be atrocious either way, so maybe it wouldn't matter. He and Rothman walked out.

"Where can he be?" Miguel moaned. "He has cheated me. I will kill him."

Carl Fischer started awake. He had not really been sleeping. He was too wired for that. But he kept nodding off for a few moments, only to be awakened to sheer terror. He could feel his heart thumping in his chest, and panted for a minute or so to clear his head. At least he was still alive. "Miguel, what time is it?"

"4:30. He has cheated us. Either that or he has been caught. They will torture him, but he will not talk. He will not betray us."

Fischer chose not to point out the inconsistency of believing Carlos was capable of running off with the loot and leaving Miguel behind, but was too loyal to break under torture. "My family would not call the police. They are honest people. They said they wouldn't. You're safe from the police. The cops'd be here already if Carlos had been caught. I think you may be right about Carlos, though. I think he may have left you with me so he could absolve, ... so he could leave you holding the bag. If you do anything to harm me, it will be you to take all the blame, not him."

"Aiiee," Miguel cried out, as if in pain. "I will kill him."

"I can help you. I will tell the police that he is the thief, and that you treated me with kindness. You should have killed me, but you didn't because you are a good man."

"Shut up! SHUT UP!" he screamed. "You are lying again. You will do nothing to help me. I put a knife to your throat."

"No, really, I don't even know who you are. I don't know your name or where we are. You could leave me here with some food and water, and just go. I'll be okay."

"No! Shut up, I said. I mean it!," Miguel said. His voice held more menace, if less volume. He picked up the knife and started toward Fischer. Fischer could not see the knife, but he felt the anger and heard the footsteps. He froze and held his breath. The knife point pressed into his neck, right below the chin. A small trickle of blood run down to his collar. "Shut up, I said."

Hank LaPointe and Claude Becker sat shivering. The wind from the ocean had blown steadily all night, and its heavy fog sapped the therms from their bodies as they sat. The Kevlar fabric of their body armor served to trap moisture. This normally made them too hot when exercising, but at night it merely served to hold in the sweat and make their skin feel clammy. It did nothing to ward off the cold. Each had chosen a high point near the north end of the controlled area. The SAC had ordered them out of the area, leaving the perimeter sentries to take over. But LaPointe could not bring himself to abandon the search. His gut told him the Fox was still there somewhere. The subject had been running too fast and furiously to have made it past Horvath and the north line without being seen. He must have stopped and hidden, or found a way under Highway 1 to the east.

"Claude," he whispered into the handy-talkie, "Anything?"

"Nothing. Just the wind and fog. I've been checking with the night vision every few minutes."

"10-4. Same here. We'll stay until it gets light. If nothing turns up by then, we go."

"10-4."

Knowles woke to the kitchen timer, having again slept on the couch to avoid waking Rickie. He could barely force his eyes open. It was already 5:50 and there was just a hint of light in the sky. He needed to get moving. He must have misjudged the time of sunrise when he'd set the timer. Clad only in his underwear, he ran into the kitchen, ripped open a package of sweet rolls, crammed a large bite into his mouth, and started pouring a glass of milk. He finished the roll and the milk in less than one minute, and moved on to his morning ablutions - no shower today, just one quick pass with the washrag and soap. He swished with mouthwash, not taking the time to brush properly, and grabbed his shaver. He tiptoed into the bedroom, crept to the closet, and pulled out a clean shirt and socks. He pulled yesterday's suit on and was in his Bucar in less than ten minutes from the moment the timer had gone off. The sky was definitely starting to lighten now, although the sun was not over the horizon yet.

He buttoned his shirt with one hand as he steered with the other. The news station on the radio was reporting last night's news on the dead oil executive in New Jersey. The Bureau radio was crackling with activity. Agents were already out on the scene in Marina, starting to search. He stepped on the accelerator, and glided into the carpool lane although solo drivers were not allowed there. He arrived at the command post within fifteen minutes. Rothman was already there.

"Olson got a crime scene team out there," Z-man told him as he walked in, still unshaven. It had been difficult for him to organize a team, since half of them had already been assigned to street surveillance teams, and many were neither fresh nor properly equipped. Not all of them were in their own cars, and some had their evidence kits in the office rather than the vehicle in which they were doing street team duty. Still, some had been on notice that they were on call for a morning search if anything turned up. Every one of them had been ready and uncomplaining when they were dragged out of bed.

"They found a gun!" Olson called out to the room. He was on the phone, and copying down something on a yellow legal pad. "Got it. Thanks." He ripped the page from the pad and handed it to Belinda. "Run this in CII and see if its registered in California. If not, give it to the Z-man to have the Bureau run it through the manufacturer." CII, the Criminal Information Index, was the computer database run by the California Department of Justice, used to check out criminal histories, warrants, and gun registrations. It was part of the larger network known as CLETS, the California Law Enforcement Teletype System, which included Department of Motor Vehicle records, the FBI system known as NCIC, and interstate messaging between law enforcement agencies. The gun was a gray Interarms Astra A-60 semiautomatic 9 mm pistol. It had been found loaded, with no indication of recent firing. The serial number had not been filed off or covered in any way. It had been found sitting in a clump of iceplant about fifteen yards from the original escape route, probably tossed there by the Fox. It was in good condition and couldn't have been there long.

The room was electrified at the news. Murmurings and whispers started, but stopped again when Belinda returned in less than three minutes. "It's registered," she said. "Here's the printout." She handed Olson a single sheet of tractor-feed paper that had been ripped off raggedly at the bottom. Stroaker leaned over Olson's shoulder as he read. Then the SAC took the paper and walked slowly to the suspect board. Under Suspect 1 he wrote:

NAME: MAHMOUD AL-ENWIYA
SEX: MALE
AGE/DOB: 7/25/66
ADDRESS: 1487F PLUM ORCHARD LANE, SAN JOSE,
CALIFORNIA 95128
OCC: ENGINEER

He added a few more details, such as driver's license number and telephone number, then looked up.

"Rothman, you take two agents and go over there," he said. "Don't knock on the door or do anything to heat up the place. Be careful. We just want a general idea of what it is - house, apartment, condo, and if there appears to be anything out of place. No interviews; just look and report. Belinda, run this guy in NCIC, CLETS, Bureau indices, everything." He handed the sheet back to the office manager.

Rothman nodded to Knowles, but Stroaker caught the motion and looked over. He hadn't seen Knowles up to that point. "No, Cliff, I want you here. Tim can handle it. Take some FOA's."

Knowles wasn't sure whether he was being punished for going home to sleep, or getting in "late", or just valued too highly by the SAC to be allowed to go out. The phone rang. Everyone else at a phone was already talking on their own calls. Knowles picked up the flashing line and said, "Command Post, Knowles."

"Cliff, this is Chet Murray." Murray was one of the ERT members. "We're going through the motel parking lots. There must be two hundred cars if you count the trailer park and all the motels on Dunes. It's getting light now, but there's condensation all over every car. You can't see inside. I've made a list of dark sedans and where they're parked, along with their license plates. What do you want us to do next?"

"Where are you calling from?" Knowles replied.

"The lobby of one of the motels."

"Can you fax me the list? Does it have makes and models?"

"I think they'll let me fax it from here. The hotel staff is being really helpful. No makes."

"Okay, here's what I want you to do, Chet. Start with the Fords - Tauruses and Escorts. Do *Mercury* Sables, too. If any of them have white or light stickers on the right front passenger windows, do those immediately. Wipe the condensation off the windows and look inside for anything related to the case. Did you go to the briefing yesterday?"

"No, all I know is what I got from Olson the guys in the Marina CP. I have the briefing packet, though."

"Okay," Knowles replied, "that has most of what you need. Look for a motorcycle helmet with a visor covering the face, a sports coat, anything related to that diving tow found on the beach, like a wet suit, anything connected to the locations where the calls were made - those are on your sheet - and any weapons, cassette tapes or tape players. Eliminate anything with a moon roof or roof rack. The photos we have don't show those. I'll have someone run the plates once I get your list. Did you hear about the gun?"

"Gun? No, where?"

"Down there, in the sand somewhere near the path. Just minutes ago. It's registered to a Mahmoud Al-Enwiya of San Jose. It looks like our subjects could be Arabic. Look for anything Arab related."

"You got it. I'll fax you the list, and then start looking. I'll call you if I see anything significant."

Len Schuler entered the room, looking tired and carrying an enormous mug of coffee. The mug had the seal of the United States Attorney's Office on it. He had gone home before Knowles, and returned later. This made Knowles feel better, somehow, not so guilty for having caught a couple hours of sleep. At least he wasn't the last one to the party. Schuler asked Knowles about the progress, and was cautiously pleased to hear they had found the gun. "But still no subject and no victim?" he asked.

"No. And it's getting light. If they don't find Fox in the next couple of hours, we have to assume he got away clean. The ransom is probably still on the beach. If the fog clears, we can run the plane overhead low and see if the beacon is still working. Maybe one of the other techniques will work once the wind dies."

LaPointe and Becker on their separate dune tops did calisthenics - jumping jacks, running in place - anything that kept them from falling asleep, kept them warmed up, and allowed them to stay on their feet. Pushups or sit-ups would have limited their field of vision. They had to stay alert and keep looking in every direction.

"Claude, status?" LaPointe asked into the handy-talkie.

"Same. Nothing." Becker sounded weary.

"The other two teams weren't sent home until 3 A.M. There won't be any SWAT out here to relieve us. ERT's going to organize a grid search soon. Once the line gets to our positions, we'll be cut free. Hold it! I think I see somebody." LaPointe strained to make out the shape in the faint predawn light. The fog was still thick, but the wind had subsided to a moderate breeze. The shape looked like a person walking slowly along the beach southward, right at the surf line. "Claude, move up here to assist me. I see someone walking your way at the water's line. I'm going to approach."

"10-4, I'll back you up."

The two SWAT agents converged on the moving figure. As they approached, they could see it was a male in his twenties, wearing a Hawaiian print shirt and shorts. His feet were bare. He was walking solo with a casual pace, looking out at the water periodically.

"FBI. Stop!" LaPointe commanded. The man stopped immediately. Becker came running up from the front, MP-5 in hand.

The man remained motionless, his hands in his pockets. "What's this about?" he asked.

"Take your hands out of your pockets slowly," LaPointe instructed.

The man complied, removing his empty hands and lifting them into the air at about shoulder height. The agents observed that he had a wedding ring and wristwatch on his left hand. "What's your name?" LaPointe asked.

"David. David Moussafa. Can you tell me what this is about?"

"What are you doing here?"

"Walking on the beach. Is that illegal?" Moussafa asked with a note of resentment in his voice.

"Where did you walk from?" LaPointe continued, ignoring the question.

"From the motel down there," he replied, pointing toward motel row to the south. "I walked down to the water, then up to here, and now I'm going back. I like to take a morning walk on the beach."

"Do you have any identification?"

"No, not on me. I didn't think I'd need it to walk on the beach. Really, now, why the third degree?"

"We're investigating a kidnapping. Do you have a room key?"

The young man patted his pockets. "No, my friends are in the room. They'll let me back in when I knock. I didn't bother to take the key. There weren't enough keys for everybody."

Becker looked the man over with the practiced eye of an experienced investigator. He judged Moussafa to be about five foot eleven, maybe six feet tall. His build looked fairly athletic, but his face was quite thin. A larger man could have judged him as less than six feet and thin. He was definitely Arabic in his features, not Hispanic, though, and he was not dressed the way the sand company worker had described. He also showed no signs of fear or nervousness the way most criminals did when stopped and questioned closely. He acted like a vacationer. But something didn't seem right.

"Why are you dressed like that? Aren't you cold?" Becker interrupted. The temperature had to be around 50 degrees, and there was enough wind and fog to make anyone cold who wasn't bundled up.

"No, I like to dress casual for the beach. If I get chilly, I jog a little bit."

The agents looked at him. There were goosebumps all over his arms. As if on cue, Moussafa began to shiver noticeably. LaPointe, keeping one hand on the butt of his handgun, keyed his handy-talkie with the other. "CP, this is SWAT 1. We have an individual stopped for questioning. He was observed walking on the beach. He gives his name as David Moussafa."

There was too much noise in the San Jose command post, and the signal was too broken, to be heard and understood there, but one of the other SWAT team members on the beach replied. "Hank. They just found a gun in the sand - Arab registrant. Be careful."

LaPointe and Becker simultaneously drew their weapons and stood back a yard to triangulate the suspect. "Put your hands up," LaPointe ordered. Moussafa obeyed. "Now turn so your back is toward me. Okay, stop. Back toward me slowly. Stop. Put your left hand behind you, in the small of your back." As the hand came down, LaPointe cuffed the wrist. "Now the other hand." The other hand followed, and the second wrist was cuffed. LaPointe patted down Moussafa's clothing, what there was of it. He felt no weapons, wallet, or room keys; the pockets were empty. "Come with me. We're going to check out your story." They began the walk back toward the resort complex.

"Give me the name again," Z-man said to the agent in the Marina command post. "Do you have a spelling? Okay, we'll try it phonetic for now. Radio LaPointe and ask for spelling, address, and date of birth." When he finished making notes, he grabbed Stroaker's arm. "Suspect in custody, boss. Arab male, David Moussafa - phonetic spelling. LaPointe and Becker are walking him back to the motel area where he says he is staying in a room with friends."

"Where did they find him?" Stroaker asked.

"Walking on the beach."

"Does the clothing match the suspect?"

"No, but the physical description does, except he's Arab instead of Hispanic."

"Len," Stroaker asked Schuler, "Can we arrest on this?" He explained the facts reported. Knowles bent over to listen.

"That's questionable without more," Schuler replied. "Stop and frisk is okay. They have reasonable suspicion, but no probable cause yet. Better to question him more and resolve it. Did you say they're moving him?"

"Yeah. Back to the resort to see if someone there can verify his story."

"I don't like that," Schuler replied. "The courts usually hold that moving someone from where he was is an arrest, unless it is necessary to move him out of danger, like the middle of the street to the sidewalk. Can't they resolve it without moving him? We could lose any evidence we get from this, including his fingerprints, everything."

Len," Knowles interjected, "They're just walking him to the same place he said he was going anyway. That's less intrusive than the usual court cases you're describing. Besides, the big question here is what was he doing inside the perimeter area? How did he get there without being seen? If none of the other agents saw him enter the area, then I think you have PC to arrest. It strongly suggests he was there all night."

"You have a point there," Schuler replied. "Pete, can you do a quick check with the other agents who would have been stationed along the path he says he took from the motel?"

Stroaker picked up the phone and called Radio. "On Red 3 ask all personnel manning the perimeter around the motel area if they saw a man walking from the motels to the water, then northward into the interior of the perimeter within the last hour."

Z-man handed the name David Moussafa to Belinda and told her to run it in CLETS for a driver's license. He warned her that the last name was only phonetic.

"No problem," she told him. "CLETS needs exact spelling for the first name, but uses Soundex for surnames. There's only one way to spell David, so far as I know. If we're anywhere close on the last name, and the name is in the system, it'll turn up. The only question is whether we'll turn up too many. Can you get an age or an address?"

"We're working on that."

She left to have the name searched.

The Radio clerk called Stroaker back. "Mr. Stroaker, one of the SOG agents reported that she was stationed on the highest dune directly between the resorts and the waterline. She says no one could have walked past her in the last half hour, since it got light. She can't swear that someone couldn't have snuck past in the dark before that, but it would have been difficult. She was scanning regularly with night vision equipment. She says for him to get by undetected in the dark he would have had to have been dressed heavily - his clothing would have had to prevent any body heat loss."

Stroaker relayed this information to Schuler and Knowles. "Z-man, how was the suspect dressed?" Knowles asked.

"Shorts and a Hawaiian shirt. Bare feet."

"Len, that means this guy can't have taken the route he said, unless he left more than half an hour ago dressed like an Eskimo, and shed all his clothing after he crawled past the SOG agent. I doubt anyone could do that, even dressed that way. That line was set pretty tight just to prevent anyone getting past. There were more agents farther up the beach toward the sand factory...The sand factory. Jesus, that's it. We have a witness there. Pete, have Hank take the guy back to the sand factory to see if that's the guy who offered him money. Len, investigative detention cases have always held that it's okay to bring a suspect to an eyewitness for an identification if you can't bring the witness to him."

"I doubt the guy is still there," Olson, who had just joined the brainstorming, remarked. "He was night shift." The entire crew looked at their watches simultaneously. It was 6:56 A.M.

"If he works a midnight to eight we're okay, but if it's an 11:00 to 7:00, they'd better hustle," Schuler remarked. "If this can't be resolved with about 15 minutes of investigation, you'll either have to let him go, or arrest him and risk having all evidence you gain from this, his name, description, fingerprints, all of it, suppressed."

Stroaker picked up the phone to Radio again - the extension was busy. He ran out of the room to the other end of the RA.

Reaching the separate SOG transmitter set up next to the regular radio, he grabbed the mike. "Hank, this is number 1. Come in."

"This is SWAT 1," came the garbled reply, barely intelligible.

"Go back to the sand company with the suspect. Have the witness ID him or eliminate him, if possible."

After thirty seconds a broken transmission came back, "...off at seven o'clock...."

"Hank, it's four... now three minutes to 7:00. Haul ass over there." Stroaker thought he heard a 10-4 in response.

LaPointe told Becker, "Claude, the SAC says to have the witness at the sand company do an ID. He knows you. Can you get back over there before he leaves?"

"I'll try. You walk this guy back to me. I'll see if I can get him to wait."

Becker didn't hesitate. He headed due north at a fast run along the surf line, just a yard or two up from the water's edge, where the sand is relatively firm and faster for running. He could feel the water soak into his boots, and his heels began to form blisters, but he gutted it out. He came running into the parking lot at a full sprint. He heard a car door slam. Looking to his right he saw a pickup truck bearing a bumper sticker "U.S. OUT OF U.N." Probably the right guy, he figured. He ran over to the truck as it began to back out. The driver saw him and stopped. Becker, panting, motioned for him to roll down his window. He did.

"What do you want now?" the workman asked, irritation apparent on his face. Becker recognized him now. He looked different with his hard hat off.

"We have a suspect. We're bringing him to you now. Can you wait five minutes? We'd like you to see if he's the same guy who offered you the money last night."

"I'm off work now. Can't this wait until Monday night?"

"No. The law requires us to get an immediate identification or let him go. It'll only be a few minutes."

"Is there a reward?" the man asked, shifting from reverse into forward, but keeping his foot on the brake so the truck didn't move.

Becker hesitated, still catching his breath. "I thought you didn't want any money. You turned down his $500 last night," he said.

"Yeah, well I figured if we got stopped you goons... uh, cops, would think I was in on whatever it was he did. This is different. There's nothing wrong with getting paid a reward, is there?" He gunned the engine slightly as if to suggest he was about to leave.

"Right, right. Nothing at all. The victim in this case is very rich. I don't know if there is a reward or not, but if you provide information leading to an arrest, I'll make sure the family knows it was you. It has to be the right guy, though. If you identify someone else as the man, you lose any chance of getting a reward." Becker wanted even more than last night to throttle the bastard, but he just gritted his teeth and smiled.

The workman seemed to mull this over, then took his foot off the brake and started to move forward. Becker thought he was leaving. Instead, the man pulled the truck back into its parking spot. "Okay, I'll wait. But make this quick, okay?"

"Sure, as quick as we can." Becker radioed LaPointe that the workman was willing to wait a few minutes, but to hurry up. LaPointe acknowledged.

Within three minutes, LaPointe walked into the lot with Moussafa in tow. The workman stepped from his truck when he saw them approach. Without hesitation he announced loudly, "That's him. He was wearing sweats last night, but it's the same guy." Moussafa's face twisted into an expression of furious indignation.

"No, mister, you are mistaken," he said emphatically. He turned to LaPointe, "I have never seen this man. I just walked down the beach from the motel for a morning walk. I've done nothing."

The workman laughed. "That's the voice, too. You should have paid me the full five grand, you cheapskate. Five hundred is nothing. You deserve to get caught." He turned to Becker. "So now I'm the hero, right? You'll tell the family I helped you catch the right guy?"

Becker and LaPointe exchanged glances; the workman had not mentioned any bargaining for five thousand the previous night. "Sure thing. You're a real hero all right. I'll let 'em know," Becker replied evenly.

The agents reported the identification over the radio. Morales immediately sent the SOG agent covering the entrance to the factory road down to pick them up. It took him less than a minute to get to the lot. LaPointe announced to Moussafa that he was under arrest, pulled out his Miranda warning card, and read him the advisories. They placed Moussafa into the rear seat with Becker; LaPointe rode shotgun. They drove to the forward command post.

Fischer heard the screen door slam. Miguel had gone out without saying anything. It might be for a few seconds, or he may have fled altogether. Anything was possible at this point. He thought about initiating a second escape plan, but decided he'd better wait a few minutes to see what Miguel's intentions were. Within two minutes, the door slammed again.

"It's light out now," Miguel announced. "He cannot be coming back. He has taken all the money or been captured. I will have to decide what to do with you."

"What about Ruben?" Fischer asked, stalling for time. "You can't just make such a big decision. Ruben's the leader. You should contact him in Santa Barbara."

"Ruben! Forget Ruben," Miguel spat out contemptuously. "I am in charge here now. No one else. I decide whether you live or die. Remember that."

"Of course," Fischer replied soothingly. "I just meant it should be a joint decision - what is best for all of you."

"What is best for me, you mean. I have to decide how to save my own skin now."

"I'll tell you the best way. Drive me out to some place far away from here and leave me blindfolded. I'll wait thirty minutes for you to get away before I remove the blindfold and walk out to some place where someone will pick me up. I'll never be able to find this place again, and I don't know who you are. You'll be safe. They won't look for you very long since there was no one hurt. If you kill me, they'll hunt you forever and execute you."

"Drive you out in what? You know he took the car. Pah! You stay here. I am going out again. If you try to escape again, you will make my decision easy." Miguel checked the ankle chains to make sure they were still secure.

Fischer heard footsteps retreating, then the screen door slammed once more.

Toni Bertinetti called to Stroaker, "Mr. Stroaker, Tim Rothman is out at the residence of Al-Enwiya. He wants to talk to you."

The SAC picked up the phone. "Stroaker. What's it look like?"

"Pete," Rothman said on his cell phone, "it looks quiet. Belinda gave me the tags and descriptions of two vehicles registered to this guy. Both cars are here in the complex. One's in a carport, one's parked in the visitor slot. I had Torres walk by and feel the hoods; the engines are cold, and there's no sign of the cars having been moved in the last few hours. This is a condo complex, nice landscaping, generally looks like a decent place. It's only a mile from the RA at most. 1487F is an interior unit. It would be awfully risky to bring a kidnapped person in and out of a place like this. People would see."

"Okay. Can you sit on the place without getting burned?"

"I think so. We can see the two cars from the parking lot of the complex across the street. Neither one would be able to pull out without using the driveway, and we'd be able to follow. But we can't set up to see the front door of the condo itself. It opens under a stairwell facing the pool area. We'd have to set up right at the base of the stairwell."

"No, don't go inside the complex, just watch the cars for now. We have a suspect in custody now, positively identified by the factory worker. He gives his name as David Moussafa. Can you take a look at the mailboxes there and see if there are any Moussafas or anything like that? He's clammed up, so we can't get the exact spelling. Belinda is trying to get something on him from CLETS now."

"Sure. I'll have Gina do it. Women are viewed as less threatening. There's no rental office or property management on premises, so I can't ask there. You might want to find out the complex owner's name and number from the County Tax Assessor's office. It's usually a homeowner's association or property management company who owns the grounds, and the individual owners only own their own condo. We could interview the management or association about the people in 1487F. In fact, that condo may be owned by someone else, and rented out. The Assessor's office can tell you the owner of the individual unit, too."

"Will they be open on Saturday?" Stroaker asked.

"Good point. I don't think so. Let me see what we can do here."

Knowles handed a copy of Chet Murray's fax to Belinda and said, "Can you put a clerk on running these plates? Our subject may have driven one of these to the drop off area."

"We only have two CLETS machines. One is in full use trying to get something on this Al-Enwiya, and the other on Moussafa. I can try to do this as soon as we get a break on either machine." She looked at the list. It had over 200 license plates on it. "Cliff, this is too many. It'll take forever. Can you narrow it down?"

"I've got ERT trying to do that now. Okay, don't start on it just yet. I'll try to whittle it down."

Chapter 24

The doorbell chimed merrily. Luciana Malarna peeked out one window and saw a heavy-set middle aged woman at the door, dressed in jeans and a sweatshirt. She ran upstairs and knocked on Mrs. Fischer's door. "Fran, there's a woman at the door. Possibly a neighbor. Heavy set."

Fran Fischer emerged from her suite looking haggard. She had been awake all night in a state of extreme agitation. "I'll get it," she said. The bell chimed again. She started down the stairs as Jemperson and Murphy moved out of sight of the front hallway. Both kept their gun hands free. Malarna stood just behind the door with her hand on her gun butt as Mrs. Fischer opened the door a few inches. "Oh, hi, Marlene," she said as she recognized the lady on her welcome mat.

"Good morning, Fran," the woman replied. "Are you all right? I was worried about you. I'm sorry if I disturbed you too early, but I know you and Carl are usually up by now. You don't look too good, hon."

"I haven't been feeling well, Marlene. I'm sorry, I'm just not up to chatting right now."

Marlene attempted to peer over Fran Fischer's shoulder, craning her neck left and right. "Fran, what's going on here? I saw cars coming and going in the middle of the night, and someone sneaking in your side gate off the driveway. That's the third time this week their car has woken me up in the middle of the night. I just wanted to make sure you're okay. You and Carl are the kind of neighbors we can't just ignore if you're in trouble. Can I help?"

"Marlene, you're so sweet to worry about us. We'll be okay, really. I'll tell you about it later when I'm feeling better." She raised one hand as if to wave goodbye.

"Does this have anything to do with that car that came by two weeks ago, and the guy snooping in your mailbox?" Marlene asked, undeterred.

At that, Malarna stepped from behind the door. She pulled her credentials from her fanny pack, raised and opened them in a single deft motion and said, "Would you step inside, please?"

The woman's meaty jaw dropped onto her top neck fold and her eyes widened. She mouthed the letters F-B-I, but no sounds accompanied the motion. Malarna grabbed her arm gently and guided her inside. The woman did not resist.

"I'm Special Agent Lucy Malarna of the FBI," she said. "These are agents Louellen Murphy and Ron Jemperson." She gestured toward the other two, who had stepped back into view. "We need your help."

"Omigod, omigod, what's happened?" was all the woman could say.

Louellen Murphy took over. "Marlene, is that your name? Hi, I'm Louellen. Just relax. All we want is a little bit of help." Murphy's manner was so smooth and her smile so engaging that the woman visibly relaxed and returned the smile. She shook Murphy's extended hand.

"Of course, whatever I can do."

"We couldn't help but overhear that you saw a car last week with someone snooping? Can you tell us more about that?" Murphy asked.

"Yes, I did. It was an old beat up Toyota, and two men were in it. I saw them drive by several times slowly. I was in my side yard, gardening. I don't think they noticed me because I was kneeling, over my azaleas. But this street is pretty quiet, and I usually notice the cars that come by, if I'm in the yard. This one didn't look familiar. I figured it was just another gardener or repairman at first, although usually those are pickup trucks." She paused for breath. "What's this about, anyway?" She seemed finally to realize that her question had never been answered, and that she was in a position to get it answered.

"Mr. Fischer has been kidnapped and held for ransom. Any information you have may save his life. Please tell us everything you can remember about this car and the people in it."

"Omigod. Fran, are you okay? Hon, I didn't know. Oh, dear," she rushed upon Fran Fischer like a linebacker charging the quarterback, and grabbed her in a hug that was somewhere between heartwarming and bonecrushing.

"Oh, Marlene, thank you," Mrs. Fischer said, tears welling up again, "please just tell the FBI what you know. That's what you can do." Marlene apparently felt extending the hug another thirty seconds was a higher priority, but eventually she let go.

"Of course, of course. Whatever I can do." She turned back to Murphy. "So I saw this Toyota, and then it drove back the other way.

Well, I figured it was either lost, or just having trouble finding the house. The addresses are hard to see on some of them, you know. I started to get up to walk out and see if I could help. Then I saw the car stop one house down on the other side of the street. I live on the other corner, on the south of this house. They stopped across the street on the north side. So I just watched through a bare spot in the hedge. I need to plant something there that will grow better. There's not enough sun there. Oh right, right, you don't want to hear about my gardening." She apologized, apparently picking up on some body language of impatience coming from Ron Jemperson. "While I was looking, the mail truck came by and started putting the mail in the boxes. It put something in your box, and then came on down to my house. So as soon as the mail truck was out of sight, one of the men, the driver, got out and looked up and down the street quickly, like he wanted to make sure he wasn't being watched. He ran across the street and opened up your mailbox and looked at the mail. It was very quick. Then he ran back and jumped in his car and they left. I could hear him saying something to the other man as he was getting back in, but I was too far away to hear what it was. He was nodding though, and looked like he was happy with whatever he saw."

"Did you call the police, or tell anyone about this?" Murphy asked.

"No, no, I meant to tell Fran, but you know how it is. Well, I told my daughter - she goes to Los Altos High. You can ask her - when she wakes up, I mean. It was all over, and I could see he didn't take anything, so I just let it go. I didn't see them again. I would have given the police the license plate if I had known it was important."

"You got the plate?" Murphy asked, excited.

"Oh, yes, I did. I wrote it down somewhere. Now where is it - I would have to find it. I ran inside and wrote it on one of those Post It things. I think I stuck it to the refrigerator. Unless my husband pulled it off there to make room for another note. He does that sometimes."

"Can you please go over right now and see if you can find it? This is very important. But first, give me a description of the car and the two men."

"Of course. The car was a Toyota 4-door - one of those small ones. Corona, Corolla one of those. It was a reddish-brown, like rust-colored - it fact, it looked so beat up it probably was rusted. The paint was gold or rust-colored though, I don't mean, well, you know what I mean. It had those burned spots on the top and hood like they get when they sit in the sun for years. I didn't see the man in the passenger seat very well, only the driver who went to the mailbox. He was short and stocky. Not heavy-set like me, more like a wrestler. And dark - foreign maybe. He looked like he might be Indian or Pakistani - real dark. Young, maybe 25 or so. That's all I can remember. It was over a week ago."

"That's great. That's very, very helpful," Murphy assured her. "Now please run on over and see if you can find that license plate. Then come back, even if you can't find it. We have some more questions to ask you."

"I'll be right back." She gave Fran Fischer another huge hug and hurried out the door.

Bob and Mitzi Carmody walked down the staircase, Pam right behind them. They had all stayed awake all night awaiting the outcome of the ransom payoff. They had listened in on the conversation at the doorway from the landing, and waited until this break in the interview. Bob Carmody spoke. "Louellen, what is going on? All we get are bland reassurances that everything is all right, but it isn't all right. Carl was supposed to be released by now. We're all sick and tired of waiting, and you're telling us nothing." The others stood resolutely behind him, obviously attempting to impart a sense of solidarity.

"I really don't know. I just know that if he had been released, you would have been told. I do know that the ransom money was picked up, and they followed the suspect, but he disappeared in the fog. We think he left the ransom behind somewhere in the area. A witness saw him trying to escape without it. You were told all this last night. Nothing has changed, but now that it's light out, it will be easier to conduct a detailed search of the area. And this lead from your neighbor Marlene could be crucial. I'm sorry it hasn't been resolved already, but please just let us pursue every lead we can until we find Mr. Fischer. I promise you that we'll tell you everything we can. We can't tell you every detail of the investigation, but if there is major news, you'll be informed."

"Aren't you the ones who said not to talk to the neighbors originally?" Carmody asked, accusingly. "You could have had this lead last week if you had interviewed her."

"That's true," Murphy answered. "Or, one of the neighbors we talked to might have been involved, and decided to kill Mr. Fischer rather than risk a payoff with the FBI in the case. It was Fran who was most concerned about the people near the household finding out about us being called in."

"I think we should have just paid the ransom without calling the FBI," Carmody said, jutting out his jaw a bit.

"You did the right thing in calling us, believe me. This isn't over yet. Please just hang in there. The odds really are on our side." She looked at Pam, who stood a couple of steps up the stairs. She had obviously been crying. "Pam, you should be especially proud of yourself. Not many people could have hung in there the way you did and performed so beautifully on the phone. You came back safe and sound, just like we said. You followed our advice and it worked. Let's be optimistic. I think we'll have good news before the day is over."

The doorbell rang again, Louellen opened the door immediately. Marlene bounced into the room waving a small blue square of paper triumphantly. Murphy took it and walked straight to the phone in the family room. She dialed the San Jose command post.

"Pete, it's Louellen," she said when Stroaker came on the line. "We just caught a break in the case. A neighbor saw some men in a car last week snooping in the mailbox. Young and dark, like Indians. We have a plate number." She read it to him.

"How'd you find this out? I told you not to interview the neighbors - too risky."

"I know, we didn't, but she came over asking about Fran. She'd seen us coming and going late at night, and knew something was up. She asked Fran if it had anything to do with the men in that car she saw, and we asked her to step in."

"Okay, good work. We'll run the plate. It probably ties in. We have a suspect in custody now, found walking on the beach. Arab male. The witness identified him as the one trying to pay him to drive him out last night. Tell the family. We're going to solve this thing."

"Okay, thanks, Pete." She related the new information to the Fischers and Carmodys. There was an audible sigh of relief. Bob Carmody put his arm around Mitzi, and Pam Fischer grabbed her mother's hands and gave them a squeeze.

Chet Murray sounded hoarse as he spoke, "Cliff, it's a zoo down here. Everybody giving orders and nobody following them. Rice and Morales can't decide who's in charge. The ERT keeps getting pulled off this car thing to do something else. Most of us are out on the sand looking for the money and the sweatshirt. Sorry we aren't making progress on the cars as fast a you'd like."

"That's okay, you're doing what you can. Give me what you've got so far."

"Okay, this is only for the TraveLodge. Katie is doing the Best Western now, and there's another one farther back. I've found eighteen Ford sedans, both Tauruses and Escorts. No Sables. Half of them are rental cars, judging from the license plate frames. Three had stickers on the passenger window just like you said - a little stop sign that says "Protected by Sentry Sounder - Warning alarm will sound."

"Colors?" Knowles asked.

"One white Escort, one black Escort, four more dark Escorts, the rest are all Tauruses, dark colors, including red, bronze and gray."

"Give me the plates on all eighteen." Murray did so. Knowles checked off each plate on the faxed list as Murray read them off. "Which three are the ones with the stickers?" Murray read those off, and Knowles made an additional mark on his list for those. "What are the colors on those three?"

"All dark. One dark Escort - navy blue, and the other two are Tauruses, one dark gray, one navy blue."

"Did you look inside those with the stickers like I told you?" Knowles asked, trying to be methodical, but impatient to get to the real meat.

"I tried. It was hard. In addition to the condensation, some of them had those folding sun shields over the dashboard, and one was parked so close to a big SUV that I couldn't get by on the passenger side. But here's what I saw. The Escort has a bunch of kid's stuff in the rear: a car seat, probably toddler size, toys and children's books, a Raffi CD. Looks like a family vacation. One of the two Tauruses, the dark blue one, had two helmets in the rear seat area."

Knowles's heart skipped a beat. "That's it, Chet. We need to find out about that one. Let me get Len to see if we can force entry."

"Hold on, Cliff," Murray replied. "Not so fast. The helmets looked like bicycle helmets, not motorcycle helmets. No visors. You know the type that cover above the ears only with that lightweight foam material. These would not be mistaken for motorcycle helmets. But there was a flyer labeled 'Riding Trails of the Monterey Peninsula.' It showed a picture of mountain bikes and ATV's on the flyer; it could be useful for a motorcyclist or bicyclist. The other

Taurus, the gray one, had some flippers in the front passenger foot well."

Knowles wasn't sure he heard clearly, as Murray's cell phone cut out slightly. "You sound like your battery is getting weak. You're breaking up. That second car sounds promising, too. Could you see anything else to narrow it down?"

"No, both are just parked out here in the cold, covered with condensation. I can run inside to see if these three are listed at the desk on the registration cards. Or I can keep going to look at some of the other cars. I noticed as I was going through that there were several other makes that had those white stickers on them. And the Best Western is bigger than this one. I'll bet Katie will have another half a dozen Fords for you with stickers. This lot is the one closest to the end of the street, though, which is why I started here."

"I know. Hold on, before you go on to the other makes. Take a look again at the flyer and helmets, and at the swim fins, in those two Tauruses to see if you can spot a city name or store name so we can tell if those are associated with any of our locations."

"I tried the first time, but I'll take another look. There isn't much light yet. The fog's still pretty thick, and the stuff in the foot wells is really hard to see. I'll use my flashlight to see if I can get a better view. Hold on, I'm at the gray Taurus now." The signal quality was definitely getting worse. "Cliff, there's part of a logo visible on one of the fins. The other fin is on top of it, upside down, covering most of it. It looks like two words in a fancy script, one over the other. You can only see the first two letters of each word. I'm not sure at all, but it looks like DE- something TH- something. Like 'death throes' or 'deep throat.'" Murray gave a momentary chuckle. "I don't think a swim fin company would use either of those." Then the phone went dead.

Stroaker addressed Ben Olson, Z-man, and Len Schuler: "We need to force the situation at this Plum Orchard location. I just talked to Rice, and they're making no progress with the suspect in custody. He denies being the man they're looking for. He says he was just vacationing with friends. They confronted him with the gun, and he said he didn't know anything about it. He says he doesn't know the name Al-Enwiya. Finally, he just shut up and said he wasn't going to talk any more if they weren't going to believe him. He asked for a lawyer. They can't find anything to tie him to the gun or anything else. No wallet, no car keys, nothing. "

"Have they tested his hands with the Geiger counter?" Olson asked.

"I don't know. I didn't think of that. I'll have them do that." Stroaker responded enthusiastically.

"You can do that, and it'll be good evidence if you get a positive response," Schuler broke in, "but you still can't interview him any more once he asks for a lawyer. If you keep questioning him now, everything from this point on is inadmissible."

"We've already got the identification by the witness, the prints and photos - and his own body. We won't lose those will we?" Z-man asked.

"No," Schuler answered, "those are still good. The arrest was made with PC once the witness identified him. But there's another problem. You'd better find out how long that radioactivity lasts before you try it. If you put the Geiger counter on him and it doesn't register, you will have hurt the case. The defense can use that to show you picked up the wrong man - mistaken identity. It sounds like that factory witness can be impeached as willing to ID anyone for money."

"Well, all the more reason to get someone out to Plum Orchard. We need a SWAT team. Whoever is there could be holding Fischer hostage right there, or in league with them." Stroaker stopped to read the printouts Bertinetti handed him. The first was the registered owner of the vehicle seen by the Fischers' neighbor. The second was a driver's license record for that name. "Here's the owner of that Toyota. Ahmed Shaikh, an apartment in Santa Clara, '89 Toyota. Hold on, here's his horsepower. Five six, 188 pounds, age...21."

"Good," Schuler chirped, "we don't have to worry about trying a juvenile."

"This doesn't sound like Suspect number one," Olson noted.

"Right," Stroaker agreed. "Toni, write this up on the suspect board under number two. Put the full description." Bertinetti dutifully copied the data onto the butcher paper. "We need to get this to the SWAT team for Plum Orchard. Who's going to do the interview once we make entry?"

"Knowles or Rothman," Olson replied, nodding toward Knowles, who was frantically and unsuccessfully dialing some telephone number, unaware of this new information.

"Rothman's right there at the condo," Stroaker said. "Let's keep Cliff here. Don, get Hank and find out where the number two SWAT team is now. Home in bed, probably. We need to get them over to this condo complex."

"Got it, Boss," Z-man said, picking up the phone.

Gina Torres was examining the names on the mailboxes at the condominium complex when she noticed a catering truck pull up to the service entrance of the clubhouse. There was a swimming pool for the residents, and a clubhouse next to it, with a ping pong table, bulletin boards, and some sofas that looked like they'd endured considerable abuse over the years. The driver of the catering truck walked to the rear of the vehicle and withdrew three bakery boxes. She carried these into the clubhouse. Through the sliding glass window Torres could see her arranging pastries on a large tray. The bakery smells wafted over the interior of the complex, and Torres eyed the pastries with more than an investigative interest. Within minutes several residents emerged from their condos and converged on the clubhouse. The caterer continued her routine, apparently making coffee and tea. One or two of the residents left with a couple of doughnuts on a paper plate. Some of the others stayed inside, socializing.

A short, thick-necked woman in her thirties strolled toward the clubhouse from somewhere in the interior. She had thick black hair, cut stylishly just above shoulder length, and strikingly exotic eyes, expertly emphasized with eye-liner. She looked ... Arab, Torres thought. The direction from which she had come was the general area of 1487F, although Torres couldn't see that unit from where she was standing. She had no time to get guidance from Rothman. Subscribing to the notion that it is easier to ask forgiveness than get permission, she decided she had to act before the woman returned to her condo. Torres sauntered casually into the clubhouse and headed for the food counter. The black-haired woman had already piled three doughnuts on a paper plate and was grabbing some napkins. Torres walked up behind her and reached for a pastry.

"This is nice," she said to the woman. "Do they do this every day?"

"No, just Saturday and Sunday. Part of your condo association dues," the woman responded, casually. "Are you new here? The homeowners association gives a booklet."

"Oh yes," Torres replied, "we're just renting from the owners for a little while until we find a permanent place. My boyfriend is an intern over at Valley Med." At the word 'boyfriend' the other woman cast a glance at Torres's ringless finger, a glance Torres interpreted as disapproval. "We're over that way," she continued, pointing the opposite direction from the way she had seen the woman come. "How about you?"

"We're over in 1487. We've been here two years now. This is a nice place. You'll enjoy it here. The doughnuts are nice, and they keep the pool warm. There's a hot tub, too. My two-year-old loves these," she said, holding up the plate. "My husband and I do, too," she added, slightly sheepishly. "We like them fresh and warm. I like to get here when they first arrive." With that she nodded genially and made a motion toward the door. "Nice to meet you. My name is Reena. I'll see you around, I'm sure."

"Reena," Torres said, "that's funny. My name's Gina. Gina and Reena, we rhyme." Torres was getting desperate. How was she going to get this woman to tell her more. Reena smiled wanly and started to back out of the door. "Reena, before you go, maybe you can tell me if you know of anybody who needs child care. I'm thinking of doing some day care in my home to make a few extra dollars. I don't have a job here, and I did that in our last place. It worked out great. I just love kids." She smiled her winningest smile.

Reena's eyes widened. She pushed the door open with her foot and virtually dragged Torres out of the room to the poolside. "And your boyfriend's a doctor you said? Do you take newborns?" she gushed eagerly. Torres could see she was almost drooling, and it didn't seem to be from the smell of the doughnuts. Reena looked down at her own midsection and smiled beatifically, then back at Torres.

"You? Pregnant?" Torres exclaimed with convincing amazement. "I'd never guess. When are you due?"

"Not until November. But I have a two-year-old boy now. The place I use won't take any babies. I'm going to have to find another day care soon. If you'd agree to take my baby, I'd let you start with the two-year old now and pay you for both even though you're doing one. What do you charge?"

Torres had heard that affordable day care was almost impossible to find in Silicon Valley, and had taken a wild shot. It was obvious she had hit the bull's-eye. Reena was evidently ready to pay double whatever the going rate was just to guarantee a spot with a total stranger who may not even be around in November. She had no idea what the going rate for day care was, however, since she had no children and was totally faking it. Her palms began to sweat.

"Hmm," she said, after some thought, "well, I don't know. Your boy is two, is he?"

Reena nodded. "A perfect little angel. So easy to care for."

"Well, I've had some trouble with kids in their terrible twos. Boys especially. I like newborns, though. Of course, I may fill up before November."

"Oh, please, take us now. My boy is no trouble," Reena pleaded, desperate already. "I can't afford to go on maternity leave again. We need both incomes. It's so expensive here. I make more than my husband, but he won't take paternity leave to care for the baby. He's very traditional; he says it's my job."

"What do you do? For a living, I mean?" Torres asked.

"Software developers, both of us. C++ for me, Java and html for him."

Torres did some quick mental math. That meant a household income of at least $150,000 a year, maybe twice that. These didn't sound like kidnappers, especially with a two-year-old in the house. "Well, what if I meet the boy to see how we get along?" she suggested.

"Of course, of course. Come right now, please. You'll like him, I know you will." Reena walked Torres over to the 1487 condo block. It was a two-story building with a total of eight units - four on top and four on the bottom. Torres still wasn't sure if Reena lived in Unit F. Units A through D faced the parking lot, while E through H faced the pool. When the walkway forked, Reena continued straight. They came to Unit F and she opened the door and called out. "Mahmoud, I am bringing a visitor. She runs a day care center."

Torres followed her inside. She heard some shuffling in the bedroom area, and a man emerged in a bathrobe over blue striped pajamas, unshaven. He was fair-skinned, but had thick black hair like his wife. His eyes were a lustrous mahogany brown.

"Hello, I am Mahmoud Al-Enwiya," he said effusively, bowing slightly. "Please pardon my appearance. I did not expect visitors so early." He looked at his wife and said something in Arabic. The tone was pleasant, but from Reena's reaction Torres gathered he wasn't commending her initiative at bringing someone in when he was not presentable.

Reena rebuked him, "Now, Mahmoud. I just met Gina at the clubhouse. She has just moved in. Her husband is a doctor, and she is starting a day care right here at Plum Orchard. She takes *newborns*," she said with heavy emphasis on the last word.

Torres saw that Reena had promoted her to the rank of wife and day care center manager for Mahmoud's sake. She kept her ringless left hand in her jacket pocket and shook Mahmoud's hand with the other. "Hello, Mahmoud, it is nice to meet you."

Mahmoud kept smiling and murmured something in response. He made a graceful motion with his arm to indicate she should be seated.

"Actually, I just came to meet your little boy. Reena said I could see if he would make a suitable, uh, customer for me. Is he here?"

"I think he's still asleep," Reena said, sounding relieved. "In here." She motioned for Torres to follow into the first bedroom.

Torres peeked into the minuscule bedroom, where she saw a thatch of black hair protruding from a rumpled lump of bedclothes. Junior was sleeping soundly. The room was a mess. Several toys on the floor showed signs of recent combat with a larger and more destructive force. There was a scribble of crayon on the wall in one corner. She decided celibacy had its good points and heaved an invisible sigh of relief that the kid was still asleep.

"See, isn't he a sweetie?" Reena cooed.

"Yes, I can see that he is a real doll," Torres replied sweetly. She cast a glance toward the remaining bedroom and bathroom, trying not to look as furtive as she felt. She estimated the whole place at about 1200 square feet: two small bedrooms, one bath, a small laundry/utility, kitchen and living room. This condo would run about $300,000, she knew from her own house hunting. That was about right for two people in their income bracket. They would be able to afford this, and there was certainly no kidnap victim being concealed here. "Well, I have to run. I'll check with my husband about the day care situation. I haven't checked the association rules to see if we're even allowed."

"Oh, don't worry about that," Reena protested. "Businesses aren't allowed but the Association president has a little girl who's four. If you take her girl, she'll let you do it."

"Well, it's been so nice meeting you both. Give me your phone number and I'll let you know. Why don't you put both work numbers and your home number," Torres said. She pulled out the small spiral notebook she always kept handy and jotted down the numbers Reena recited to her. Reena did not seem to think it odd that an unemployed day care operator would keep a notebook and pen at the ready at 8:00 on a Saturday morning at home.

Torres left the apartment at a brisk walk, and immediately spotted Matt Nguyen pacing around the mailbox area. He saw her a moment later and made a frantic gesture she could not quite interpret. She jogged on over to him.

"Where the hell have you been?" Nguyen demanded. "We got worried. You were supposed to be checking the mailboxes. They're sending in the SWAT team."

"No, we gotta stop that. I just came from the condo. There's just a husband and wife there with a two-year-old. No kidnappers there."

"You got *inside?*" he said, incredulous.

"Yeah, it's a long story. I'll tell you later. Let's get that SWAT team canceled first." They ran out to Rothman's car. "Get the SAC and tell him to cancel the SWAT team, Tim. I was inside the place. There's no kidnap victim there, just a husband, wife, and kid. That gun must be stolen, sold, or lost."

Rothman opened his cell phone and called the command post. It took him a couple of minutes to get Stroaker on the line, but when he did the SAC agreed not to bring in SWAT. He instructed Rothman to take Matt Nguyen and do a knock and talk, to find out how Al-Enwiya's gun happened to be lying in the iceplant at Marina State Beach. Torres could stay outside and watch for anyone or anything suspicious. In the meantime, Stroaker said he would send a surveillance team out to the site to watch once they left, in case the suspects threw their belongings in a car and fled afterwards.

Knowles gave up trying to reach Chet Murray after the fourth attempt. He kept getting a message that the subscriber was not available. Chet's cell phone battery must have died, Knowles decided. He picked up the briefing sheet to look for someone else who could get a message to him. Unfortunately, the ERT personnel were not listed on the briefing sheet, and he had no idea who else was in that particular vicinity. What was the other name he had mentioned ... Katie? He didn't know who that was.

"Toni," he called to Bertinetti. "Toni, I need to ask you something."

Bertinetti leaned over his way with mild irritation. "What is it? I'm busy here," she said.

"What's the last name of an agent named Katie who works on ERT with Chet Murray?"

"Katie ... that might be Katie O'Connell. White collar in Concord. Been here almost two years. I think she just got selected for ERT."

Knowles pulled out a copy of the division telephone list. O'Connell...Kathryn P. He dialed the pager number shown, and entered the direct dial extension of his phone in the command post. Within forty-five seconds the phone rang. It was a woman's voice.

"O'Connell."

"Katie, this is Cliff Knowles in the CP. Are you with Chet Murray?"

"Yes, well, no actually. I'm at a different motel, but we're both going through the parking lots. I have a list of Fords here. He said you wanted Fords and..."

"Never mind that for now. I think he's found it, but his cell phone just went dead. I need for you to go over to where he is and let him use your cell phone. Tell him the one with the swim fins is our car. Tell him that logo - it's 'Deep Thought.' Our subject was seen driving into a shopping center in San Jose where that diving store is located. You need to get into that car and see what else you can find."

"Without a warrant?" She asked.

"You have PC to search, and it's an emergency. Do it. I'll authorize it. I'm a Legal Advisor."

"Have you cleared it with the AUSA?" she asked, still not convinced.

Knowles looked for Schuler, but he wasn't in the room. Time for a quick decision, he decided. "Yeah, I checked already. He says we're good. You don't need a warrant."

"Okay, then. I'll go let Chet know. We've got a PD officer around here somewhere. I'll see if he can get us into the car with a shim." She hung up.

Knowles then took the license plate list and headed to the CLETS machines. There was a clerk on each. He went for the one with the juniormost clerk, the one with whom he had a good personal rapport, and rolled her, in her chair, away from the keyboard.

"Hey, Cliff," she complained, "what are you doing? Belinda said I ..."

"This'll only take a second. One plate, that's all." Knowles said, undaunted. He punched the control key labeled "VEH REG" and waited. In two seconds a new screen appeared, full of blank fields. He typed the license plate of the gray Taurus into the first field and hit ENTER. Within ten seconds the screen repainted. The registered owner was Pinnacle Rent-a-Car, South San Francisco. That was all he needed to know, but he hit another key and waited another ten seconds for the information to printout on paper. He ripped the sheet from the roller and headed back toward the command post. The displaced clerk punched him on the arm half playfully, half seriously, as he left. He looked back over his shoulder and thumbed his nose at her. She stuck out her tongue and turned back to her keyboarding.

Knowles walked to the cabinet near main switchboard that had phone books for the entire Bay Area. He dug around until he found the one for northern San Mateo County, and carried it to the command post with him. He looked up Pinnacle Rent-a-Car. There was an 800 number. He called it. He was met with a recorded message that told him his call was very important to them and his call would be handled in the order in which it was received. He tapped his foot nervously, hoping one day he would have an excuse to shoot whoever it was that designed these infuriating phone systems. After seven or eight minutes, his call was answered by a young female voice.

"This is Candice. Thank you for calling Pinnacle. How can I help you?" she asked.

"Candice, this is the FBI calling," Knowles said evenly. He had done this before and knew he could cause the operator to think it was a joke and hang up if he overdid it. "We need some information on a car you rented. This is an emergency. It is not a joke, and I can tell you how to verify I am really with the FBI. Can you get a Security Supervisor on the phone, please?"

"One moment please," Candice replied. Ten seconds later an older woman's voice came on. "Who is calling, please?" she asked.

"This is Special Agent Cliff Knowles with the FBI in San Jose. We have an emergency and need to find out who rented one of your vehicles. Can I get your name and direct telephone number, please, in case we get disconnected."

"This is Lynette. You can dial the same 800 number you just called, and when it asks if you know the specific extension, dial 4657. Can you give me your call back number please?"

"Yes, if you want to verify who I am, you can call 415-553-7400, which is the published main switchboard number for the FBI in San Francisco, and ask them to transfer you to me in the San Jose Command Post, extension 9962. Please look that first number up in the telephone book if you have any doubt about who I am."

"Thank you. What can I do for you?" Her voice was professional and well modulated. She showed no signs of being disorganized or overly excited. She was exactly the kind of person Knowles had hoped for. He was not always so lucky.

"One of your vehicles, a grey Ford Taurus, is directly involved in a crime of violence. We're trying to locate the driver. We consider this a matter of life and death. Can you please look in your records and tell me who rented it, when, and any address or other information that might help us determine where he is now."

She asked him for the license plate, which he gave. He also gave her the vehicle identification number, or VIN, to demonstrate that he had access to law enforcement records, although that information could be obtained by anyone walking up to the car and reading the number off the dashboard VIN plate. She told him she would have to call him back. He made sure he had her direct dial number jotted down correctly, and they hung up.

Len Schuler scooted over next to him. "Cliff," he whispered conspiratorially. "Who's in charge down there with this Moussafa fellow - the interrogation?"

"There's Harry Rice, an agent from Monterey, I'm not sure which since Lark is in Disneyland, and Mo Morales," Knowles answered.

"I know. My question is, who's in charge?"

"Good question. I don't know which one Stroaker put in charge. Knowing him, he didn't put anyone in charge. Clarity is not his forte."

"That's my point. You've got Harry, Curly, and Mo, the FBI's version of the three stooges - no offense - and nobody knows who's in charge. Can't you or Olson take over? Getting that guy to cooperate is the key. We don't know how much longer we have before something very bad happens."

Knowles had thought of the same point already, although he wouldn't have had the guts to call them the three stooges to another government agency employee. But he didn't see how he could change anything. Stroaker wasn't going to let him or Olson drive down there and jump in the questioning at this point. Even if he thought they were better interrogators, they were two hours away, and there was no guarantee they would get any better results. The suspect had already invoked his right to counsel anyway. His phone rang. He held up a finger to Schuler to indicate he should hang on a minute.

"Mr. Knowles, this is Lynette from Pinnacle," the voice began. "I have your information. Are you ready to copy?"

"Yes, go ahead," he replied, clicking his cheap black U.S. government pen to the ready.

"That car was rented last Sunday from our San Jose International Airport office by a Michael Al-Enwiya, 1044 Poppy Crest Way, San Jose." He jotted down the information. She followed with his telephone number, California Driver's License number, credit card number, and intended length of rental - two weeks.

"Any other driver listed?" Knowles asked.

"No."

"Would there be a security videotape of the transaction?"

"Possibly. You'd have to check with the personnel in that office. There should be a photocopy of the driver's license and the credit card. That's standard procedure, and the data base has checked off that it was done." She gave him the telephone number of that site, but could not guarantee anyone would be available early on a Saturday morning to get him the information.

"Thank you, you've been very helpful," he said sincerely, and ended the call. He wished every investigative telephone conversation was so productive. "Len," he said, turning back to Schuler, "this may be our solution. I just got off the phone with Pinnacle Rent-a-Car. They rented a gray Ford Taurus on Sunday to a Michael Al-Enwiya of San Jose, same last name as the registrant on that gun found at the drop site, but a different address. The car matches the description of the car seen on the videotape from the second ransom call location, and the car driven by helmet man using the victim's ATM card. This car is now parked in a parking lot at one of the motels on Dunes Road. We need to search that car now for a clue to the location of the victim, and don't have time to get a search warrant. I think that's plenty of PC. Do we have your OK to go ahead? If I can get something on where that car has been, like a gas station receipt, we may not need for Moussafa to cooperate."

"You got it. As long as the rental company says it was Al-Enwiya, the same last name as the gun registration. That makes probable cause, and emergency obviates the need for a warrant. Can you check with the motel to see if he was registered there? If he wasn't, and just parked in their lot, they can call the local police to tow the car. The driver's reasonable expectation of privacy is much less if he parked illegally and trespassed. Once it's towed, an inventory search is legal, which means we have inevitable discovery now. The public safety exception probably applies in any event."

"And if he's registered there, we have a room to search," Knowles added.

"Right on. Go for it."

Knowles called Katie O'Connell's pager again. Murray called him back. "Cliff, it's Chet. I got a spare battery for my cell. You can call me direct again."

"Okay, will do. Hey, can you do this for me? I just called the car rental company. The person renting it is Michael Al-Enwiya, same last name as the gun registrant, different address. I suspect that's Moussafa's real name. He's probably related to Mahmoud Al-Enwiya and got the gun from him somehow. There's another guy, too, named Shaikh, seen driving a Toyota around the Fischer home right before the kidnapping. Can you check with the motel people to see if there is any guest using the names Moussafa, Shaikh, or Al-Enwiya? If there is, we're going to want to search the room. Let me know, and then get back to search that car." He spelled the last names.

"10-4. I know they already checked with all the motels for a Moussafa, and there is none. I'll check on the other two names - or Katie will. We're still working on getting into the car. Katie called Marina P.D. to get an officer out here with a shim, but I've got a coat hanger in there now, and I think we'll have it open in a second. If not, the cop should be here soon."

"Okay, keep me posted on progress. If you can't get in any other way in the next two minutes, bust the window with a rock or tire iron. Just get in. Anything you get, give it to me immediately."

"Right."

Knowles carefully phrased his comments so that Schuler, who could overhear Cliff's end of the conversation, was not aware that Knowles had already authorized the entry to the car before finding out about the rental to Al-Enwiya, and before getting the prosecutor's approval. At the same time he made sure Murray wasn't aware that Schuler had approved entry only after Murray had started to get in, and had asked for the check with the motel to bolster justification for the entry. Knowles knew the search was legal, since they had the probable cause before making the actual entry and finding anything, but there was no point in giving people something to worry about, and he didn't want them hedging on their testimony if it they got questioned about it. If they were ever asked under oath if they had the determination of the AUSA that there was probable cause, they could truthfully answer yes.

Knowles joined the conversation among Stroaker, Zwolinski, and Olson. He told them about the rental car being found, the name Michael Al-Enwiya from the rental company, and Schuler authorizing search of the vehicle. Stroaker's eyes lit up and he began a slight bouncing in his seat like a three-year-old when his birthday cake is lit. "That's him. I'll bet my Niners season tickets that Moussafa is this Michael Al-Enwiya. Get Rothman this name. Must be a relative of Mahmoud."

"Rothman and Nguyen are already inside talking to Mahmoud now, Pete," Olson advised. Let's see what he brings out of it. If he doesn't mention Michael, we'll have good reason to suspect him of involvement."

"Toni," Stroaker said to Bertinetti, "have someone run this DL number. It should come back to a Michael Al-Enwiya. Verify that, and if so, get DMV to send a photo immediately." Bertinetti took the paper gingerly. She had no idea how to do investigations, and wasn't even sure she understood what she was being asked to do. Stroaker seemed oblivious to her uncertainty, but Knowles could see she was having problems. He walked around the table and volunteered to help her find someone.

He walked her to Moira, the same clerk he had pushed out of the way before, and asked her to run the driver's license number. Moira looked at him with a playful imitation of being cross and said she wasn't sure she couldn't interrupt her current assignment for this. Knowles knew she was kidding, as he saw her log off the job she was doing and hit the DDL key. Bertinetti, however, took her seriously, and screeched, "Listen, you little piece of crap, don't you ever talk to an agent on a major case that way. This is a direct request from the SAC to be done *immediately*. I'll vouch for that myself." She thrust out her massive chest as if her vouchsafing for Knowles settled the matter in eyes of the world. Moira, agape, almost threw the paper she had been handed right back at Knowles, but he had stepped back during Bertinetti's outburst just far enough to be out of her peripheral vision, and made a helpless and apologetic expression, then mouthed the word "bitch" as he rolled his eyes at Bertinetti. The clerk caught enough of Knowles's pantomime to understand he was an innocent party, and began to type the information into the CLETS machine. But Knowles could see she was doing a slow burn. He made a mental note to do something later to make amends. Once they verified that the driver's license number belonged to Michael Al-Enwiya, he told the clerk that they really needed a picture transmitted from the Department of Motor Vehicles here and to the Marina PD. She said warmly, "Since it's you, Cliff, who's asking, I'll be glad to." As she turned to pick up the phone to dial the 24-hour emergency number for DMV she cast a scowl at Bertinetti so cold Knowles shuddered. He didn't want to be around when these two crossed paths again. Maybe Kim and Moira could quietly garrote AB in the stairwell when this was over.

Chapter 25

Miguel walked into the bedroom, his stride now easily recognizable to Fischer from its sound. "Lift up your hands," he ordered. Since Miguel had not rebelted his cuffed hands after the bathroom run, Fischer was able to raise both arms from his lap to approximately chest high. Miguel grabbed his left wrist roughly and Fischer could feel the handcuff being removed. The sensation of relief was exquisite. Then he could feel the padlock on his ankles being unlocked. Was he being released? Taken to be executed? His stomach churned once again.

"Turn over on your stomach, with your hands where your feet were," Miguel ordered. When Fischer had done so, Miguel pulled the single strand of the left cuff back 180 degrees from its locked position to form a McDonald's double arches curved M shape. He fed the point of the single strand through the eye bolt in the floor, then slowly worked the hinge and double strand through until the eye bolt was around the chain between the two cuffs. He grabbed Fischer's hand again and slapped the cuff back around the wrist.

At first Fischer was relieved just to have the change of position. This new arrangement allowed him to move his feet around and lie prone with comfort. Miguel did not even bother to relock his ankle chains. But when Fischer heard Miguel leave the room again the reality of his situation dawned on him. He may be more comfortable for now, but he could no longer escape. He had been able to slip his feet out of the chains locked to the bolt the first time; but now, since he could not break the cuffs or pull up the bolt, he was trapped.

He listened for the screen door to slam, but the familiar sound didn't come. He thought Miguel had walked into the next bedroom, but couldn't be sure. Usually that meant the weights would start clinking, but he did not hear them either. What was the significance of this? He just could not figure it. His best guess was that Miguel was preparing to leave on his own somehow - on foot, call a taxi, he didn't know - and wanted to make sure Fischer was well-secured so as to give him maximum time to make his escape. But if that was the reason, why was there no sound of weights or kitchen equipment being gathered? Was he abandoning it all because it was too heavy to take? Wouldn't that lead to him later through fingerprints or tracing of products? There had been a single thump in the next room, but it hadn't sounded like weights. More like a suitcase hitting the floor, he judged. This gave him some measure of comfort as he decided that must be it. Miguel was preparing to leave.

After another fifteen minutes Fischer heard Miguel go out the screen door and stay outside for about five minutes. Then he returned, and went directly for the other bedroom without looking in on Fischer. Another fifteen minutes passed, and there was another trip out the front. Fischer was puzzled by this pattern. It couldn't take Miguel this long to pack. Mentally and emotionally exhausted from trying to discern meaning in the sounds around him, Carl Fischer turned again to prayer. This brought him an inner peace, however transitory.

Rothman walked into the command post with a distracted look. Stroaker hustled him over to the collected group of Olson, Z-man, Knowles, and Schuler. "Give us a brief," Stroaker commanded.

"I interviewed Mahmoud, telling him we were just interested in locating a gun registered to him, but not telling him why. He said he owned an Astra A-60, but he loaned it to his brother. His brother has an Arabic name, but uses Michael as his legal name in English. Mahmoud and his brother came to the U.S. ten years ago from Iraq. His parents are still there. I got the address for his brother, and telephone number. He said that Michael came to him about two weeks ago and asked if he could borrow the gun for a diving trip. He said he wanted to have one on the boat to shoot sharks."

"Is that the same address?" Z-man asked, pointing to the suspect board, now filled in with Michael Al-Enwiya's data. Rothman looked at it, and confirmed it was the same. "We got that from a rental car company. The car's been located at a motel near the drop site."

"Did you get a photo of Michael from his brother?" Olson asked.

"Yes, a snapshot of Mahmoud, his wife, and Michael and his wife on a picnic last year. It's pretty small, but it's the best he could do."

"Does he know where Michael is now, or who he's with?" Stroaker asked.

"No. Michael said he was going on a diving trip with a friend, but didn't name him. Mahmoud wasn't sure, but thought he said something about the Pismo Beach area, but can't remember if that was something Michael said specifically for this trip, or he just remembers it as a place Michael once talked about going. I asked if there was a way to reach Michael, like a pager or cell phone, but he said no. He called over to Michael's house - they rent here in San Jose - and talked to his wife. He was very cooperative, and did not mention anything to her about the gun, just said he was trying to locate Michael, very casual like. She said Michael was on a diving trip, and hadn't left a number to reach him. He told her he wasn't sure where they were going to stay, and may camp out on the beach. She wasn't happy about it, but wives don't have a lot of say in Iraqi culture, apparently. Michael works as a car salesman in Palo Alto, and doesn't make much money. She's pregnant with their first child, and he's using up his vacation time to go on a diving trip without her. She didn't know the names of any of the people he was going with."

"Did you ask about Shaikh?" Knowles asked.

"I did. I made it sound like he's really the one we're interested in, not Michael. Mahmoud had never heard of him. He could be lying, but he seemed credible to me. Mahmoud didn't ask Michael's wife about Shaikh. Has anybody checked out Shaikh's residence?"

"Yes, I sent a team over there," Stroaker replied. "No activity. Mail piling up in the mailbox. The Toyota parked there, on the street. It looks like it hasn't been moved for a week - spider webs forming."

Olson summarized for the group. "So it looks like this Michael Al-Enwiya and maybe Shaikh went together on this trip. The cover story was to go diving. And there could be more people involved. Michael is probably this Moussafa person, but he's clammed up and is asking for a lawyer. Shaikh and any others are presumably holding Fischer somewhere, expecting Michael to return with the money, and now wondering where he is. The money's still out there somewhere. What's our next step? Any ideas?"

"ERT is searching the car," Knowles offered.

"Getting Moussafa - Michael, that is - to talk is the key," Schuler opined. "He's got to tell us where Fischer is. The hell with his right to counsel. We keep questioning him until we get him to talk. We've got enough to charge him now, even if we lose further evidence."

"But how do we do that," Stroaker almost whined, "we can't just beat it out of him. This isn't NYPD Blue."

"If we confront him with the photo of him and his brother, and let him know his brother told us all about the gun and the diving trip, he may crack," Olson suggested. "I think that's our best shot."

"I'm with you, Ben," Stroaker agreed. "I'm the one with the helicopter. I'll fly it down and do it myself."

Knowles turned to Rothman, and a questioning look passed between them. Rothman nodded a covert affirmative. "Okay, Pete," Knowles said, "but let me make a photocopy first so we have something to work with here - to show to witnesses." Stroaker handed him the photo, and Knowles left the room. Stroaker sent Bertinetti out to find Buzz and have him get ready.

Knowles headed for the copy room, but looked behind him when he got the hallway that led there. Stroaker wasn't looking, so he continued to the back exit of the main FBI space and walked across the hall to the white collar squad. One of the agents there worked computer crimes, and had a sophisticated computer setup. Knowles saw that the agent was not in, unsurprising on a Saturday, and booted up his computer. There was a scanner and cheap inkjet printer attached, and Knowles was familiar with the scanning software. Within two minutes he had scanned the photo, enlarging the area of Michael's face. He selected the print command to produce a high-speed color printout, and while that was printing, took the photo back to the command post. He handed it directly to Stroaker, who put it in his breast pocket.

"Keep working the leads up here," the SAC told the group. "Ben, you're in charge of operations here. I'm going to get this scumbag to tell us where they've got Fischer. I've leave Toni here this time." With that pronouncement he marched out the door.

A few minutes passed and they heard the rotor noise from the helicopter as it lifted from the concrete pad behind the hospital. Olson made eye contact with Knowles and Rothman, then asked, "Is it still socked it with fog down there?" Rothman nodded and smiled. "And this time there's no street team in Gilroy to pick him up?"

"That's right," Knowles confirmed.

Schuler watched the exchange, and broke out in a loud guffaw, until he noticed several of the others in the room watching. "Slow learner, is he?" he asked Knowles rhetorically, under his breath. Olson caught the remark and broke out in a grin, but Schuler was careful to keep it out of earshot of the Z-man.

"Well, I could make a few choice remarks about the U.S. Attorney, if you want to get into that," Knowles replied.

"Now let's not cast aspersions on my boss," Schuler shot back, placing one hand over his chest in mock shock.

Olson broke in, "Really now, we don't have the photo to use to confront Moussafa with. The boss has the only good copy. Cliff, did you make a photocopy? I don't think it was a good enough photo for that to come out."

"I went across the hall to the white collar squad and scanned it," Knowles answered. "I've saved it as a jpeg. It's printing now, enlarged and in color. We can show it here, and we can e-mail the file to the Marina PD if they have an e-mail account. They can confront him without Stroaker's copy. Besides, they'll have a copy of the DMV photos on Al-Enwiya and Shaikh in a few minutes. It doesn't prove the tie to the gun, but it might be enough."

Bertinetti, holding the telephone receiver in her hand, called to Olson, "Ben, this is Rice. He asked to talk to Mr. Stroaker, but since he's gone, he's asked for you."

Olson took the call. Rice told him they received the photos faxed from the Department of Motor Vehicles on both Michael Al-Enwiya and Shaikh. They were able to make a positive ID of Moussafa being Michael. They laid the photos on the table in the interrogation room, without saying a thing, and left. When they came back, he asked to talk to them about cooperation. They were asking for guidance as to whether they could talk to him, since he had previously "invoked," i.e., asked for a lawyer.

"Tell him, hell yes, they can talk to him. Just don't make promises." Schuler told Olson, as he overheard the gist of the conversation from Olson's end. "If he reinitiates the conversation, they can go back into it. Even if the court finds that the laying of the photos on the table was an illegal 'interrogation', which I doubt, we can afford to lose whatever evidence he gives up at this point. Let's just get the victim back. We'll argue the legalities later."

As Olson and Schuler were discussing their options on the phone, Chet Murray called Knowles back. "Cliff, we're into the car. We checked with the motel manager, and there is no Al-Enwiya or Shaikh registered here. The car keys were left on top of the front wheel. We didn't even have to break in. That's an old diver's trick, I understand from the police here. They don't want to have to take the keys into the water where they could get lost, so they hide them on the car. Anyway there isn't much in here except the rental agreement and the swim fins, but there are a few things in the trash bag. One I thought you'd be interested in especially. It's a receipt. I just put it on the fax here in the manager's office. Belinda should be bringing it to you any second."

As he heard Murray say it, Knowles looked up and could see Belinda walking down the hall with a paper in her hand. She caught his eye, and he waved her toward him. She brought him the sheet. "Chet, I have it now. It's really hard to make out. Maybe it's just a bad fax, but ..."

"No, it's just a scrawl. Except for the date at the top, 5/1. The number on the next line looks like a 15 or 13, or possibly 75 or 73. I can't read the writing after that."

"Something like 'NINGINOZZO'," Knowles said, tentatively. "It makes no sense."

"Maybe 'NINGIMOZZO'," Murray replied. "It looks like a sheet from one of those receipt books you buy in the stationery store. Yellow, maybe three by six. The signature at the bottom is just a wiggly line. Looks like it starts with a capital H and ends with something below the line, a 'g' maybe. I dunno, I thought it might be a receipt for some kind of weapon or diving equipment or something."

"Keep looking for something else that might explain it. See if there are any markings on the fins or on that underwater scooter they found. We still don't know if that's connected. The subject didn't even run toward it when he picked up the ransom, from what I hear of it. I don't see a dollar sign on the receipt. Is there a dollar sign in front of the number?"

"No, I don't see one either."

"Okay, Chet, thanks. Keep at it. We'll work on this."

"Cliff, they found the duffel in the dunes. No money inside. The beacon's with the duffel, so you aren't going to find the cash with the radio."

"Shit. Okay, I'll tell the rest." He hung up and dialed the Marina command post. Morales answered. "Mo, we've got something from the search of the car. Chet Murray found a receipt of some kind. If you can get him talking, ask him what it's for. I'm going to fax it down to you. What's the fax number of the Marina PD."

"Hey, if we can get him talking, we'll just ask him where Fischer is. But if you want to fax it, go ahead." He gave Knowles the fax number the command post was using.

"Okay, thanks. Also, can you check to see if anyone at the PD has access to an e-mail account? I can e-mail a photo from his brother, the one he got the gun from. You can show him that and tell him we're planning to arrest the brother. Maybe that'll put pressure on him to come clean. So how does it look for him talking?"

"Still nothing, really. He's admitted he's really Michael Al-Enwiya, but he claims he doesn't know anything about Shaikh or anything else. He's wavering though, hoping we'll strike some kind of deal. He keeps asking what if type questions, like what if he could find out where this kidnapped person is."

"Hypotheticals?" Knowles asked.

"No, no needles on him," replied Morales.

Knowles's mind reeled for a moment at the non sequitur. Then he let it pass; he realized he should have known better than to use a five-syllable word when talking to Slow Mo. "Okay, Mo. I guess you know Stroaker is on his way down there to get this guy to talk."

"Yeah, I heard. I'll ask about the e-mail. I'll call you back." He hung up.

Knowles rejoined Olson and the others. Olson was updating them on the reports from different sources. The surveillance team at Plum Orchard had seen nothing since Rothman's interview. Mahmoud apparently saw no need to go anywhere or do anything in response to the FBI's visit. Similarly, there was a team on Shaikh's Santa Clara apartment, but there was no activity there, either. However, the ERT found the sweatshirt and sweat pants Al-Enwiya was wearing. They were buried in the sand near the sand company. "There's detectable levels of radioactivity on them," Olson was explaining. "And one bundle of loot was in the front pocket of the sweatshirt. Five thousand dollars, just like the witness said. I guess the witness tried to extort the whole bundle from our buddy Michael. He should've paid it; he might've made it. His wallet's there, but all it has is his driver's license, which we already had from CLETS, a photo of his wife, his credit card, and health insurance card. Plus $72 cash."

Has anybody tried to check out that Pismo Beach lead?" Knowles asked.

"No, not yet, but you don't really think they're going to be down there, do you?" Olson asked. "Why give a cover story to your relatives and give the real location?"

"Besides," Rothman added, "the timing won't fit. That's too far for the subject to be driving every time he makes a ransom call."

"Yeah, yeah, I know. I agree with all that, but I still think we ought to let L.A. know."

"You're the lead guy, Mr. Case Agent," Olson offered.

"Maybe I should assign this to Nick Lark to handle. He could stop there on his way back from Disneyland." It still rankled Knowles that he was not officially assigned the case. "Anyway, I just got this from Chet Murray, from the trash in Al-Enwiya's car. It's some kind of receipt, but we can't make heads or tails of it."

The cluster of agents bent over the sheet. "Could this be a rental receipt? A motel or cabin or something?" Schuler suggested.

"That would be ideal," Olson agreed, "and the 5/1 date suggests rent - the beginning of the month, but it doesn't really say anything like that. None of the words you'd expect: 'rental' 'deposit' 'damage' 'nights' and so on. No dollar amount."

"Could that be an address?" Rothman wondered aloud. They all studied the paper some more.

"It seems unlikely. The number is two digits, not four or five like most counties use, and I've never heard of a street 'MINGINOZZO'," Olson answered.

"'MINGINOZZO'?" Z-man said, "that looks like 'HINGIMOZZO' to me, although that's still no street name."

"Look, give me the credit card number and the health insurance card numbers," Rothman told Olson. "Maybe he used one of those to rent a room, buy something, get medical attention, whatever. It's a lead." Rothman had a good liaison list of card issuers, and his work on the ATM card had worked out to get the Japanese witness. "Somebody needs to do something." Olson handed him the information on a slip of paper.

"Sorry, I didn't get you that credit card number earlier, Tim," Knowles said. "I got it from the rent-a-car place, but you were still interviewing the brother.

"No problem. Let's see what it turns up." Rothman left to make the calls from his office where he had his list of contacts.

Knowles said, "Tim has the right idea. It's time to try something. Everybody look at this receipt and try to figure it out. It's recent. I think it might be the name of an Italian Restaurant or Pizza Place. Maybe they had pizza delivered somewhere. 15 or 13 could be the item number from the menu. If we can find it in a phone book, we can ask to see their delivery records."

"I still think it could be an address," Z-man said. "I'll check all the map books for any street that starts Ming, Hing, or Ning."

"Okay," Olson agreed, "but be sure to include Monterey and Santa Cruz Counties."

Z-man headed out to the switchboard area to find someone with a complete set of Bay Area maps. Knowles decided to go back to his office to see if anyone left him useful leads on voice mail or e-mail. On his way out the door he handed Belinda the fax for Morales, then he stopped by the mail room. His slot was getting full, but it looked like general crap - the government equivalent of junk mail. He grabbed the stack, then poured himself a cup of coffee and headed to his office. He dropped the pile of junk mail on his desk, and sat heavily. Rothman was on the phone with the credit card company, on hold. Knowles's phone had a red message light brightly lit.

"They're having a hard time finding someone who can authorize this based only on a phone call on Saturday morning," Rothman said, hold music blaring loud enough from the earpiece for Knowles to hear it from his desk.

Knowles started playing his voice mail messages, on hands-free mode, coffee cup in one hand, while he flipped through the mail with the other. Multi-tasking was an essential at a time like this. He stopped to take notes for several of the voice mail messages. Agents had called him with ideas, questions, general update information all morning, apparently, but most of the information was useless now, overtaken by events. Still, he made a list to follow up on later. He kept flipping through his mail, slurping the coffee. As he picked up the state bar journal, a monthly newspaper for attorneys, he intended to toss it on the pile of stuff to look at later - much later, if ever - but something caught his eye. The headline on the front page story read "Big Brother in Your Rental Car". He began reading. The article was about a case being appealed on the constitutional issue of whether a rental car agency could lawfully track its customers using a satellite global positioning system. He put down his cup and pushed the End Call button on his phone. His messages stopped. playing. He had his notes with him; frantically, he dug out the number for Pinnacle and dialed.

"Lynette," he said, when he got through to the woman who had helped him, "this is Cliff Knowles again."

"Yes, I recognize your voice," she answered, pleasantly.

"I just heard that some rental car agencies have GPS systems in their cars. Does Pinnacle?"

"Only on the newest ..." she answered evenly, then drew in a sharp breath. "Oh my, you want to know if that Taurus has one. Hold on." Knowles could hear rapid keyboarding in the background. "Yes, it's installed. Oh, I'm so sorry I didn't think of that when I talked to you before. But it's not activated. I don't think it's going to help you. We put that in to keep track of whether people are speeding. There's an extra charge if they do. But our lawyers said there's some lawsuit pending, and they won't let us use it until that's settled. We don't record the information."

"You don't record it, or it's not activated in the car? There's a difference."

"Let me check. No speeding charges showed up on his account when I pulled up the record for you before." There was a long pause. "I just can't tell. You'll need to talk to our engineer in charge of this. I haven't used the GPS yet, and they're still experimenting with it. I'm going to have to find out who that is for you. I'll call you back." She rang off before he could ask her to wait.

Knowles started to go back and listen to the rest of his messages, but he knew that if he did, his phone would ring busy to Lynette when she called. Then it struck him - Lynette had the number in the command post. That might or might not be answered and forwarded back to him. He called that extension, and Matt Nguyen answered. He asked Nguyen to put that extension on forwarding to his desk extension. Nguyen agreed. Knowles could hear that Rothman was making some progress with the credit cards. Someone was talking to him at least. He continued to flip through his mail, but he was unable to concentrate. He just kept staring at his phone, willing it to ring. Eventually, it did.

"Mr. Knowles, this is Lynette again. I have a name and number for you. This is the Vice President of Fleet Maintenance. He's in charge of all service schedules, cleaning, repairs, modifications, everything on a policy level, nationwide. This number is in Texas at our headquarters. It's his home number, actually, and it's two hours time difference. His name is Mr. Lugliani. I don't know his first name, it's just initial V on my emergency contact list."

"Thank you, Lynette. This could be important."

"You're welcome. And good luck to you."

Knowles dialed the number. It rang. A boy, maybe fifteen, answered on the first ring. "Yeah," he said, gum chewing audible.

"May I speak with Mr. Lugliani, please?"

"Not here. Playing golf." More gum chewing.

"This is an emergency. I must speak with him now. Is there a number, a clubhouse number or cell phone where he can be reached."

"He has a cell phone, but we can't give it. It's for emergencies. He gets pissed if his golf game gets interrupted."

"This is an emergency, as I said," Knowles uttered each word slowly and emphatically, trying to keep the tone civil.

"Who is this?" the kid asked.

"My name is Cliff Knowles. I'm an FBI agent in San Jose. We need some information about one of the Pinnacle cars. Your father's the only guy who can help us."

"No shit, you're really FBI?" the boy showed some spark of interest. "Like in the X-Files?"

"The same. I need to talk to your father, really. Can you please give me the cell phone number."

"Hey, I saw a flying saucer once. Honest, we were out drinking beer by the crossover," the boy said, as if Knowles would know what the crossover was, and all about the spaceship. "Should I report it to you, or what? We were pretty wasted, but it was real, I swear. Norma Rae saw it too. I go to school with her..."

"No, I'm not allowed to take reports on those. Those are in a different department. You can call that into the local FBI office there on Monday. Can I get that number for your dad now?"

"Well, I guess. Jeez, I dunno. He gets pissed when he's playing golf. He'll ground me if this is bogus, man, y'know."

"What's your name?"

"Corey."

"Do you want to be on TV, Corey?"

"Naw, you're shittin' me. On TV? Really?"

"Really. The man driving that car is a serial murderer. Your father is the only one who can tell us how to find the car and arrest him. If you get me in touch with your father, I personally guarantee your name will be in the press release we read on TV."

"What the heck. I'll take a chance. That's Corey with an E-Y"

"Corey Lugliani. Got it. Give me the number."

Corey gave Knowles the number, and he wasted no time calling it. It rang four times before anyone answered it.

"This is Vince. Who is this?" The voice sounded just like the son had predicted - pissed.

"Special Agent Cliff Knowles, FBI. We have an emergency, Mr. Lugliani. I'm sorry to interrupt your Saturday morning, but we need some information urgently to save a man's life."

"You're lucky I was between holes. If we'd been playing, I wouldn't have answered."

"Great," Knowles answered, not so sure he was feeling lucky. "Look, we need to know the capability of one of your GPS systems. A kidnapper drove one of your cars, and we're desperately trying to figure out where he took it."

"It only works if the ignition is on, so it won't drain the battery. If it's got the key in the ignition and turned on right now, I can have an engineer go in and query it. It'll respond with exact coordinates, within ten yards. It's not hooked up to our billing yet - some lawsuit thing - but the system is working. We're collecting statistical data for insurance purposes now."

"We know where the car is now. We don't need that. What we need is to find out where it has been for the last week. Does your system record that data?"

"If you know the car number I can call someone and he can look in the data base to see if it registered any speeding transmissions. It only transmits a location to us if we query it, like when it's lost or the driver needs a tow, or when it travels over 70 miles an hour for at least ten minutes. It has to be in a straight line, because if the road's curved or has a corner in it ... well, you probably don't want a geometry lesson, but my point is sometimes even the speeding doesn't get recorded. Anyway, that's the idea, to see if the customers are speeding. Our insurance rates should go way down once we go live."

"I have the VIN and the license plate. I don't know what your company uses for a car number."

"The VIN should do it. I can have somebody look it up. If that car drove over 70 for ten minutes any time since it was rented, it'll be recorded. Give me your number."

Knowles gave him the telephone number and thanked him profusely. He looked at Rothman, who had similarly just hung up. Rothman told him that he, too, had finally gotten through to someone willing to help and would be getting a call back soon. Knowles called Z-man in the command post.

"No luck," Z-man told him. "I've been through every goddam map book in the South Bay Area. No streets starting with Ming, Hing, or Ning. There's the Nimitz Freeway, and a couple of streets like Hines or Mine Road. I didn't think that was possible from the writing, though. That fourth letter looks like a G to me, but it's hard to make out. With these block letters, it could be an E. Have you found an Italian Restaurant yet?"

"No, just going through my messages. I need to get working on that, but I don't even know where to start looking. There's too many phone books. I was hoping you'd give me a region."

"I'm starting to look in San Francisco and East Bay now. I'll let you know."

Knowles didn't want to leave his phone to go to the Internet-connected computer in the high-tech area across the hall. For security reasons the regular computers used for typing 302s and similar investigative work, like the one in his office, were not connected to the Internet. Instead, he decided to try another approach that worked on occasion. He went to Kim's phone next door, to keep his line free for the Pinnacle man, and called the fire dispatch for Santa Clara County. They had more comprehensive maps than were available commercially, including all private roads. He asked if they had any record of any street starting out Ming, Ning, or Hing. The dispatcher was quite confident there were no such street names in the county. Then he did the same for Santa Cruz County, then Monterey County, with the same result.

"Cliff, come in here," Rothman called. "I just got off the phone with the bank. Al-Enwiya's credit card has been used for gas purchases twice within the last week. Once was in San Jose, in the Seventrees shopping center."

"Figures. That doesn't help much. The other?"

"Hollister."

"Hollister. My God, that's San Benito County. We should have considered that. There were no calls from there, so what's he doing there - that's probably the safe house. When was it used?"

"I looked it up. It was about an hour after the ransom call from Aptos. It looks like he drove straight from that call to Hollister. I think we're on to something."

Knowles's phone rang. He answered quickly, "Cliff Knowles."

"Agent Knowles? This is Marty from Pinnacle Rent-a-Car."

"Yes, Marty, I've been waiting for your call."

"My boss said you needed to have the GPS log for a car out of our San Jose office?"

"Yes, yes I do. Go ahead."

"Okay," Marty continued, "We have two entries since the car was last rented. It looks like they're very close together, same day - yesterday. Ready to copy?"

"Yes."

"36:44 North, 121:18 West at 3:15 PM, and 36:48 North, 121:21 West at 5:34 PM."

"What is that, latitude and longitude?" Knowles asked. "Don't you have an address or intersection or something. At least a city?"

"No, that's it. Once we go live it connects to a geoserver that gives a highway name so that in case of dispute, the customer service rep can tell the customer what highway it happened on, but even that is not hooked up yet."

"Okay, I'll figure out where this is. Thanks, Marty, this is very helpful. "

Knowles took down Marty's call back number, and showed Rothman the numerical data. Rothman pulled out an aviation map from his desk.

"South of Hollister, just north of a little town call Paicines," he announced.

Knowles called the information operator for Hollister and got the emergency fire dispatch number for San Benito County. Then he called that number. The man who answered sounded crusty and plain-spoken. He gave his name as Bud. Knowles explained that he was with the FBI and was trying to locate a street or business in the Hollister area, maybe south of there, name Ningimozzo, Hingimozzo, or something similar. Bud knew of nothing by any such name.

"Can you check your maps to see if there's anything starting Ming, Ning or Hing something," Knowles asked.

"Don't need to. There's no such street. Never heard of a family or business like that, but businesses wouldn't be on the map."

"Look, Bud, we know the person we're looking for drove south of there, near a town called Paicines. The writing is really hard to read, so it could be something else. Anything even remotely like that would be a lead."

"Route 25 runs from Hollister to Paicines. Going to Pinnacles, maybe? That's the way to the east entrance." Pinnacles National Monument was a favorite spot of rock climbers due to its striking geological formations. Knowles had been there years ago. "Could that Hingimozzo be Pinnacles or Paicines? Not very close, if ya ask me."

Knowles scrutinized the fax with so much concentration, his eyes began to hurt. What could this be? The first letter was too sharp to be a P. W or V, possibly? "How about Wingi- something or Vingi-.."

"Ving? Ving Ranch Road? That's off of Panoche Road, close to Paicines. But there's no Mozzo or whatever that was at the end. It's just Ving Ranch. Doesn't sound like it."

Knowles adjusted his glasses and stared until he thought his lenses would burn. As he looked at the letters anew, he discerned a slight space after the fourth letter. Everything was run together tightly, but there could be a space intended after the G. VING IMOZZO? It still didn't compute. The V looked right to him now, though. There was a small upstroke, like the beginning of a loop to start the V, rather than the upstroke of an N. "Bud, are there addresses on Ving Ranch that are like 13 or 15 or 73 or 75?"

"Lemme look. We had a fire out there about six years ago. Those are old farm properties where the Ving family used to live in the 1890s, and their farmhands. Big dairy ranch at one time. They called it Moo-Ving. Homes been tore up a few times and redone, but I don't think they ever followed fire codes or nuthin. Yeah, here's the cards. Okay, 3, 4, 9, 10, 15, 16, 21, 22, 27. No addresses higher than 27."

"Do you have a record of who lives at or owns 15 Ving?"

"According to the card, a Luis Hernandez, but this is dated 1985. Unless we get called out there, we don't necessarily get told when people move. Could be anybody by now."

Knowles re-examined the signature line on the receipt. Hernandez was a definite possibility. The final letter below the line was a z, not a g. "Just where is this Ving Ranch Road?"

"Head south on 25, until you get to J1 - that's Panoche Road, go in about three miles, and Ving Ranch's on the right. It's only a quarter mile long or so. It may not even have a sign. A lot of those are just farm roads out there."

"Super. Thanks, Bud."

"Sure." Bud hung up.

Rothman had been listening to one end of the conversation. When Knowles hung up, he stepped over and looked over his shoulder as he wrote. Knowles took a felt pen and wrote on his note pad "**15 VING 1 MO 220**" in block letters, imitating the style of the receipt, but spacing the letters and numbers widely so Rothman could see the interpretation. Then he wrote "Hernandez" in script underneath. He held this notepaper underneath the fax of the receipt Chet Murray had found.

"That's it, Cliff," Rothman declared excitedly. "You've done it. That's a rental receipt for a house. It's got to be their safe house."

"We need to get out there with SWAT. I'm going. Are you with me?"

"Cliff, we can't keep this to ourselves. You and I aren't equipped to make a forced entry to a hostage situation."

"We won't," Knowles replied. "We'll get Hank. But Stroaker's lost in the fog in his chopper again. Do you trust Morales or Rice to organize it?"

"Give this to Ben. He'll get Hank out there."

"I'm not missing this. I've been cut out of too much already." Knowles picked up his phone and dialed into the command post. Within a minute Len Schuler appeared in his office. "Len, something hot." He handed Schuler the page he wrote for Rothman. "This is the safe house. The address was 15 Ving, and the ending was '1 month $220'. He just wrote it all run together, and his 2's look like Z's. It's in San Benito County, south of Hollister. We're going there now. Give us ten minutes head start, then hand this to Ben. He'll know what to do. If I give it to him he'll tell me to stay here, and send SWAT. I just want to be on hand when they do it."

Schuler's jaw fell slightly, and his mouth formed a silent 'oooh' sound. He took the paper daintily with the fingertips of both hands, as if it was a valuable and fragile manuscript from a prior century. "I can't hold this - not long anyway. Every minute counts now."

"I know that. I just want time to get out of here so Olson doesn't hold me here, or wait until he can reach Stroaker. If he knows I'm on my way, he'll move on it immediately. And I've worked too hard on this to sit around on my hands waiting for the three stoo..."

Knowles was tempted to speak his mind as frankly as Schuler had, but thought better of it. He let the sentence hang unfinished.

Schuler nodded, his face in neutral. Then he sat on the corner of Knowles's desk, looked at his watch, and said, "The clock's ticking."

Knowles grabbed his briefcase, threw all his notes into it, and stood to leave. He looked at Rothman. The question was in his eyes, without the need for speaking. Rothman looked over at Schuler, then back at Knowles. He opened up his desk drawer, pulled out his handcuffs, and slipped them into his left coat pocket. In his right hand pocket he dropped a spare magazine for his Sig Sauer 9 millimeter. He closed the drawer, and stood. Schuler gave them both the thumbs up sign, and the two agents walked out together.

They took the stairs two at a time, Knowles leading the way. He told Rothman to bring his car around. As Rothman did so, Knowles raced to his Bucar and got his raid jacket and BPU, or ballistic protective undergarment, from the trunk. News junkies knew them as bulletproof vests, although they were, unfortunately, not really bulletproof. As Rothman pulled up behind him, Knowles tossed the vest into the rear seat and hopped in the front. Rothman drove discreetly out of the parking lot, but as soon as they got out of earshot of the RA, he hit the siren.

They screamed down Interstate 280 as fast as a four-year-old Taurus could take them, Rothman expertly picking his way through the scant traffic that ventured out on a Saturday morning. When they reached U.S. 101, they took it south. They had just come off the ramp when the radio clerk barked out Knowles's call sign. Knowles did nothing but sit stoically, watching Rothman's maneuvers. After the call sign was repeated twice more, Olson's voice came over the air. "Cliff, this is Ben. Get back to the RA. Repeat - return to the RA. I have dispatched another agent to handle that lead."

Knowles knew Olson was telling him the SWAT team was being sent, but didn't want to say so in clear language. The kidnappers could be monitoring the channel. Olson had done a good job of keeping any urgency out of his voice. It sounded like a routine lead. But he knew he couldn't acknowledge the order to return and then defy it. He picked up the mike and punched the channel button with his thumb. The LCD display gaily jumped through the Blue channels, then started with Red. As he had hoped, Red 3 came up in sequence. Rothman's Buradio was equipped with all the SOG

channels because, as a pilot, he had to monitor SOG traffic on his way
to and from the airport. Knowles was able to hear the SWAT and
SOG broadcasts. Morales was on the air trying to raise LaPointe.
LaPointe wasn't answering, for some reason.

Rothman kept his eyes straight ahead, watching traffic keenly,
as he had to in order to drive at that speed. The siren seemed oddly
quiet from inside the car, although they both knew how ear-shattering
it sounded to the motorists directly ahead. Knowles could tell
Rothman was not entirely comfortable with this decision to sneak out
of the RA without Olson's knowledge, but he also knew that Tim
would stick with him. Rothman wanted to be in on the action as much
as he did.

"Tim, I ordered you to drive me, you know," Knowles
declared. "I'm the principal relief supervisor. You're only following
orders."

"And disobeying my squad supervisor's. I'm a big boy. You
don't have to give me cover - as if you could, anyway."

Knowles considered arguing with him, trying to talk him into
feeling he had some protection, but then thought better of it. Rothman
was right. If they got in the way of anything operational, there would
be hell to pay for both of them.

The radio crackled. It was Morales's voice. "Number 1, we're
en route to the supermarket." Supermarket was the code word for the
hideout, wherever Fox was holding the victim.

"Did Fox talk? Is he leading you there?" Stroaker's voice
replied, rotor noise almost drowning it out. So much for the code,
Knowles thought. Anyone listening would be able to figure that one
out.

"Affirmative. He's with us.," Morales answered.

"Good work. I had confidence you'd do it. You won one for
the Gipper. What's the location?"

"It's near QQ24. Do you want the address over the air?"
QQ24 was the map coordinates for a spot south of Hollister, using the
map books that had been chosen for reference for the operation. The
entire division was covered.

"No, we don't want press. I'll find a place to land there, and
you can send a team to pick us up and bring us in."

"10-4."

"That's all we need," Rothman said sarcastically, "the SAC flying his helicopter right into the area. That won't alert the bad guys we're coming."

"Can he land there?" Knowles inquired.

"I think so. The fog doesn't extend that far inland. It's pretty open country. South of Hollister is still mostly agriculture. There'll be some parking lot or open field near a road. Maybe a sheriff's substation. I notice Mo didn't give you credit for coming up with the address. Stroaker probably thinks Morales broke the guy down. If he's cooperating, it's only 'cuz they confronted him with the receipt and your info on Ving Ranch Road."

Knowles grunted in assent. He was more worried about staying out of trouble for showing up uninvited at the raid than getting credit for the break in the case. There would be enough glory to go around if things went well. His stomach was starting to knot up again, anticipating the possibilities before them. There might be nothing but a dead body, or nothing at all. It had been eleven hours since the money was dropped. He checked his seat belt for the fiftieth time, as Rothman zipped past a semi that was splitting lanes around a curve.

The radio again. This time it was Hank LaPointe. The SWAT van just got a flat tire, and it looked like it would put them at least ten minutes behind. That was bad news, Knowles knew. The SWAT van was a full-sized van that carried the whole team, with all their gear. It would probably take awhile for them all to pile out, change the tire and get back in. There was no follow car that could take them all. Even the SOG surveillance vans were too small. Knowles wondered if there was an SOG team or anyone else with Morales.

Stroaker apparently heard the transmission, as he asked, "10-4. Hurry on getting that unit back into action. Mo, who else is with you?"

"Harry's with me and the Fox in this unit. I also had my squad Team 2 coming, but they had to stop to gas up. They're probably ten minutes or more behind, too, with a slower vehicle. Do you want me to wait for them?"

"Don't make entry until you have backup and I'm there. Stay back from the supermarket until you have a team with you."

"10-4."

Knowles looked for a road sign. He was about an hour out of Hollister. He estimated that Morales and Rice would get to the address before he would. They were closer, but their roads coming from the Monterey area were narrow and curvy. Rothman was going over 100 on the freeway, and would be able to keep up that pace for the next half hour or so, assuming the Taurus held up. It would probably be a close race.

Cliff's cell phone rang. He considered not answering it, but figured, why not? He could refuse Olson in private, if not over the radio. "Knowles here," he said.

"Cliff, what the hell are you doing? Get your ass back here. You're no SWAT guy." Olson's tone didn't sound forgiving.

"Ben, I'm the one who called it as real. I'm the one who got the address. I'm still not even assigned the damn case. I want to be there when they find him, and it sounds like they can use all the help they can get. I don't think Stroaker's going to be there unless he intends to land the chopper on the roof of the house. Trust me. I've gotten us this far. You know that interrogation was going nowhere until I came up with address."

Olson hesitated at this. "Okay, I can't make you come back, and I'd feel better with you there, you know that. But Stroaker'll have my butt in a sling if you go charging in there gangbusters trying to do it all. You're a damn good investigator, but I've seen you at firearms; you shoot worse than I do."

That remark hurt, although Knowles knew it was true. He qualified every shoot, but he struggled to score even in the low eighties. The minimum for SWAT agents was 95. "I'm not going to go charging in there, Ben. I know better than that. Those SWAT guys have shields, shotguns and MP5's. I'll leave the heroics to them. Look, if Stroaker asks, you never gave me permission, I just did it on my own. If everything goes well, he won't care anyway."

"Okay, but keep a low profile. And I did NOT give you permission. Understood?"

"Understood," Knowles said, breaking into a grin.

"Z-man is on the phone to the Bureau now, telling them how we broke the case, by the way."

"Let me guess, the SAC personally flew down to Marina and interrogated Al-Enwiya until he gave up the location?"

"Something like that."

"Thanks, Ben."

"Yeah. I may regret this. Be careful."

"Number 1 to any unit in the vicinity. I am about to land at the PG&E substation near grid coordinate QN17. I need to be transported. Please respond." The broadcast came over Red 3.

Knowles looked at the map. The location was right on Highway 156 north of Hollister. They would be passing right by in less than ten minutes. He glanced at Rothman to see if he recognized the coordinates as being near them, but saw no sign of it. After a full minute passed, no one had answered Stroaker.

"I repeat, this is Number 1 to any unit in the vicinity. I need to be transported. I am at QN17. That is near San Juan Bautista on 156. Please respond." Rothman heard it, and this time, because of the town name, realized how close they were. He looked at Knowles, who shook his head.

"We're already past that, boss," Morales finally replied. "I'll have the SOG team pick you up. They should be there in about fifteen minutes."

Knowles did the math. It looked like Morales would be to Ving first, then he and Rothman, then Stroaker with the SOG. Where was the SWAT, before or after the SOG? He reached in the back seat and pulled his vest and raid jacket up front. He unknotted his tie and removed it. Then he shifted his credentials and extra ammo magazine from his suit coat to the raid jacket pockets. He donned the BPU first, tightening all the Velcro attaching straps. Over that he put the raid jacket with its FBI lettering prominently displayed. He was ready. Rothman had his gear, but it was all in the trunk. Rothman had figured he would get it out and put it on when he joined Morales.

Morales turned left onto Panoche Road. The scenery was spectacular all around, with wildflowers blooming in the meadows by the roadsides, and lush green hills rising to either side. A lone redtail hawk soared overhead. Later in the summer the vegetation would turn brown and coarse, but spring was incomparable in this isolated valley. San Benito County was due east of Monterey County, toward the San Joaquin Valley. It was the only county in San Francisco Division that was landlocked. Not quite coastal, and not quite part of the huge central valley that was separated by the Coast Range from the Pacific Ocean, it held a unique place in the sociological and geographic ecosystem. The county had been sparsely populated, and entirely agricultural in its primary economy, until very recently. Silicon Valley's boom had turned the county's sleepy burgs into overflow housing for the blue and pink collar personnel that propped up the dot coms. Craftsmen and secretaries who couldn't afford the $500,000 price tag for a modest home in San Jose were willing to endure the two-and-a-half hour daily one-way drive to work for the ability to own a sprawling house and a couple of acres. There were no military bases or other federal facilities of significance, unless you counted Pinnacles National Monument, and the crime rate was extremely low. The FBI had little occasion to notice this region, and no SAC had visited the county in an official capacity in anybody's memory. Bikers sometimes congregated in the towns, drawn by the winding two-lane roads with speed limits that existed only on the signage, and there were, no doubt, a few methamphetamine labs tucked away in the hills, but the FBI left most of that work to the DEA and the local agencies.

"Slow down," Al-Enwiya said. "It is just about a mile ahead, on the right. Don't pull up to the corner, as Ahmed might see you. If he is standing out front of the house, he can see to the corner. He reduced his speed, and crept up slowly until he could see the small lane on the right. "That's it, that's it," Al-Enwiya said excitedly, "don't go any farther." Morales pulled onto the gravel shoulder.

Morales broadcast in code that they had arrived in the vicinity of the supermarket and were waiting for the SWAT team. Stroaker acknowledged, indicating that he would be there in about another fifteen to twenty minutes. The SWAT team acknowledged as well, but confessed to being at least a half hour away. It seemed the spare tire had been severely underinflated, and with over 2000 pounds of men and equipment in the van, the driver didn't dare go more than forty. They intended to stop at the first gas station they saw that had a tire inflation station.

Rice, Morales, and the Monterey RA agent they had brought to help escort the prisoner got out of the car to get a feel for the lay of the land. One hundred yards ahead of them on the right was the side street Al-Enwiya had identified as Ving Ranch Road. Number 15 was the third house on the left, the far side of the street from where they stood. Their view of the house was blocked by the fences, trees, and houses of the addresses on the even-numbered side of the street. Between them and that row of houses was a grassy pasture with a small collection of black-and-white dairy cows, grazing lazily. Across Panoche Road was a small creek, running full at this time of year. The road curved in gentle S shapes, staying approximately parallel to the creek. The opposite side of the creek was heavily wooded, although there were driveways every few hundred yards off of Panoche where the local ranches' access roads cut in, and crossed the creek on small bridges. Barbed wire fences and heavy metal gates kept the local livestock, and uninvited guests, from wandering off, or onto, the properties. On the far side of Ving beyond the back yards of the odd-numbered houses lay an orchard, according to Al-Enwiya.

The agent from Monterey RA, a former SWAT agent in another division and largely silent up to now, suggested the SWAT assemble in the cow pasture, circle around the end of the street with half their force, creep through the orchard to cover the back of number 15, then move the main entry team directly through the yards from across the street, converge on the house from front and back, and enter through the front. Morales disagreed, arguing that approach was too risky and complicated. He thought the team could be seen, and the occupants might flee while SWAT was getting in position. He recommended a rapid full out charge down the street from the corner, with the team spreading around to the sides and back as they reached the front yard. He called it the swarm method. Rice criticized both plans. He wanted to let Al-Enwiya approach, handcuffed, with a bullhorn after SWAT surrounded the place stealthily, and ask Shaikh to come out peacefully. If that didn't work, Rice would use his hostage negotiating skills to talk them out. The argument grew in intensity as each tried to convince the others of the merits of his plan.

"What the hell?" Rice exclaimed suddenly. He was staring at the intersection, so the other two agents, who had been facing away, turned to look over their shoulders. Right in the middle of the intersection, Al-Enwiya and Shaikh were engaged in a fist fight. Since Al-Enwiya was handcuffed, and was outweighed by about twenty pounds, he was getting much the worst of it. The argument among the agents had gotten so heated that none of them had been paying attention to Al-Enwiya. He had simply gotten out of the car and trotted toward the house to rejoin Shaikh, aka Miguel. Al-Enwiya had been hoping to get their stories straight before Shaikh was captured, and hoping to get some good time credit for helping bring Shaikh into the FBI's hands voluntarily.

As Al-Enwiya had reached the corner, Shaikh had come out of the house, as he had been doing every fifteen minutes, and he had walked down to the corner to check out any signs of his partner, or the law. When he encountered Al-Enwiya there, and saw the handcuffs, he realized the proverbial jig was up, and became enraged at Al-Enwiya for betraying him. After giving him a brief pummeling, Shaikh spotted three overweight FBI agents running toward him, guns in hand.

Shaikh took off down Ving, away from the intersection and out of sight of the agents, the view obscured by houses and foliage. Al-Enwiya, seeing that things were not going as planned, got up, wobbly from the beating, and stood undecided for a moment. When he saw the agents' slow progress, he changed his mind, and decided that escape was his best chance. He waited until the agents got almost to the intersection, then took off eastward on Panoche, in the opposite direction from the Bucar. He was confident he could outrun all three of the agents, even with handcuffs on, and wanted to wait until they got far enough from their car so they couldn't run back and chase him with the vehicle before he put serious distance between them. The country was heavily wooded. He hoped he could find an escape route through the orchard or countryside. He was expert enough with cars to feel he could find something he would be able to steal in one of the neighboring driveways, if he could just avoid immediate capture and find a place to hide.

Harry Rice ran directly to 15 Ving, the third house on the left, and charged inside, with gun drawn. He heard nothing besides his own footsteps. He ran from room to room until he saw a man's legs visible in a bedroom closet. The figure was lying prone on a mattress, his upper body concealed by the double-slider door. Rice made a quick 360 degree survey to make sure no one was concealed, ready to snipe at him, then approached the closet cautiously. Gun drawn, he moved slowly to where he could see the hands of the figure on the mattress. He recognized Fischer from the photos, and kneeled next to him. He holstered his weapon, pulled Fischer's blindfold off, and unlocked the handcuffs with his own handcuff key. When Fischer sat up and looked at him, Rice said, "I'm Harry Rice, FBI."

Fischer stared at him. He saw a heavy-set man wearing plain clothes - slacks, cowboy boots, and a sports coat, no tie. The man was dark and unshaven, and had no badge visible. The man obviously had a gun and handcuff keys, but then, so had Carlos and Miguel. There had been no knocking at the door, no bullhorn, no gunshots or sirens, nothing but a slam of the screen door and footsteps. "I don't believe you," he blurted out. "Let me see your badge."

Rice pulled out his FBI credentials from his inside coat pocket and held them up where Fischer could see them. Fischer dropped his head in his hands and wept. His prayers had been answered.

Morales, overweight by at least 25 pounds but still in better shape than Rice, rounded the corner onto Ving to chase Shaikh huffing heavily. But by the time he made it onto Ving, he could not see his quarry. He lumbered to the end of the street, and still saw no one. To his right were the even-numbered houses and beyond them the cow pasture leading back toward his car. To his left, on the odd side, was the safe house, and beyond that, the orchard, or so he had been told. Directly in front of him the street morphed into a long, rutted driveway that led around a row of trees. He surmised that this was the entrance to the original main farmhouse. He had no idea what lay beyond the trees. He started running from yard to yard, looking behind shrubs, under cars, inside the truck beds of the pickups, any place where Shaikh could have concealed himself. But a one-man search with no organized plan was hopeless, and he gave up after a few minutes.

Morales had realized he was not going to be able to catch either of the fleeing subjects. The nickname Slow Mo applied both mentally and physically. He considered shooting Al-Enwiya before he got out of range. He knew there was something in the law about shooting fleeing felons being okay if they posed an immediate threat, but he wasn't quite sure how it applied to this situation, especially since the felon was supposed to be in his custody, was unarmed, and was still handcuffed. Instead, he decided to call for backup. He jogged back to the car and slipped back into the front seat. He looked at the ignition, and realized the keys were still there. He flushed when he realized that Al-Enwiya could have just climbed over the front seat and driven off in the car while they were arguing. It isn't hard to drive an automatic while handcuffed in front. The key ring hanging from the ignition key even had a handcuff key on it. Al-Enwiya could have unlocked the cuffs as soon as he got away from them. The good news was, with the key in the ignition, Morales could use the radio. He keyed the mike. "This is Morales to all units. The subjects have escaped on foot. There are two Arab males on foot. One is thin build, six feet, and is handcuffed. He was last seen running east on Panoche Road just past Ving. The other is shorter and stockier, wearing a light green print shirt. He was last seen running south on Ving. He may be armed. Approach with caution." Now was not the time for codes. He knew there was nothing to conceal from the kidnappers at this point, and their best hope was to get someone in the area to help them. He was hoping either the SOG van with Stroaker or the SWAT team was close enough to join in the search. He was humiliated to have to broadcast to the world what had happened, but at least he felt confident that there was no press in this remote corner monitoring this channel.

Knowles and Rothman heard the broadcast with amazement bordering on incredulity. How could they have let both subjects escape, one even handcuffed? And what had happened to Fischer? Had anyone even entered the house? Rothman stomped on the gas pedal and switched off the siren. They had already turned left onto Panoche Road from the highway, and knew they had to be within a mile or two of the scene. Knowles kept looking left and right in a studied motion. He spotted a flash of movement to the left. Someone was running across one of the bridges leading across the creek. He was wearing a Hawaiian print shirt with mixed colors, primarily blue. He looked dark, sturdy, and short, like Shaikh. He ordered Rothman to stop, and back up. Rothman did so, skidding onto the gravel shoulder. When the Bucar reached the driveway where Knowles had seen the movement, the man stopped, looked over his shoulder and changed from a jog to a full run. Knowles jumped out, yelling to Rothman as he did so, "You don't have your vest on. I'll take this one." He slammed the door and charged up the driveway.

Rothman could see there was no point in driving up the driveway, since there was a closed metal gate at the other side of the bridge which would prevent any further vehicle pursuit. He watched as Knowles placed one hand on the top of the gate and leapt over the gate in a motion identical to the one Shaikh had used. Rothman decided to go after the other subject. He threw the car back into drive and sped toward the intersection at Ving. After a hundred yards he spotted Morales, emerging from his car, and saw Harry Rice walking Fischer back toward him. Morales spotted Rothman, and his eyes bugged out. He had no idea Rothman was anywhere in the county. He waved Rothman forward, and Rothman could see him mouthing the words, "Go, Go." Rothman whizzed past the intersection of Ving and wheeled around the first big curve, tires squealing. As the road straightened out again, he could see a figure in the distance running full out on the right shoulder. As soon as the figure reached the end of the barbed wire fence that bordered the road, he ducked right, out of sight. Rothman couldn't yet see what lay in that direction. He pulled up to the point where he had seen the figure disappear, and realized that the adjoining property was an immense orchard. He wasn't sure what kind, but his guess was prunes. He jumped out and ran perpendicular to the road, taking what looked like a hard path over the dirt. The trees were planted in rows, over undulating dips and rises of the gentle hills. The rows ran parallel to the road, and the ground had been rototilled between the rows. Rothman figured the escapee would take the path of least resistance, which meant the hardened dirt path at the end of the rows, along the property line where the barbed wire ended.

He ran a few dozen yards and then spotted a footprint in a patch of soft dirt. He was headed the right direction. He picked up the pace and kept running, looking down each row as he did so. Somewhere around row 20 he saw the figure leaning over, winded. The man was behind a low, flat, trailer-like vehicle that was parked between rows. It appeared to be something towed by a truck or tractor and used as a collection or processing table by the pickers. The running figure, now recognizable as Al-Enwiya, was using the vehicle to conceal himself from the direction of the road. He apparently hadn't even realized he was being pursued on foot. Rothman pulled his pistol and ran directly toward him. When Al-Enwiya saw Rothman, he took off in the opposite direction, but winded and handcuffed, he was overmatched. It took him only a few yards to realize this, and he stopped and put his hands up. Rothman called out the usual commands and placed Al-Enwiya under arrest. He took the precaution of proning him out on the ground, unlocking the cuffs, then relocking them behind the back, making sure to double lock them.

A mile away and across the creek, Knowles was chasing Shaikh. The terrain on this side was steeper and more rocky, not pasturage. At the crest of the ridge ran a line of trees, and Shaikh was trying to reach concealment before Knowles caught him from behind. Knowles had the advantage of not having run a half mile before the chase started, but he was older than Shaikh. Shaikh, however, was built for power, not speed, and the climb up the hillside was wearing him down. The gap between them was closing, but very slowly. Knowles judged that Shaikh would make it to the line of trees before he could catch him. He stopped running and shouted, "FBI. Stop or I'll shoot." It sounded so corny in his ears, like a line from an old movie. Shaikh didn't stop, or even slow down. Instead he pulled out his knife and threw it high over his head as he continued to climb toward the ridge. He was smart enough to know that bringing a knife to a gunfight was probably not a good idea, and figured that by making it clear he was unarmed, he reduced the chance of getting shot in the back. As he ran he held his hands out, fingers splayed, to show he had no weapon.

Knowles cursed himself for trying the command, as the delay only served to put more space between him and Shaikh. He saw the knife land, and ran to pick it up, knowing it would be important evidence. It was now clear, though, that Shaikh was going to make the tree line before Knowles could reach him. Still, Knowles had no other choice, so he headed upward in pursuit once more. He still could not be sure Shaikh was unarmed, since throwing the knife away didn't prove that he didn't have a gun, or another weapon. But he knew he couldn't risk shooting Shaikh, even if he was accurate enough to make the shot, which was doubtful. Firearms training had proved to him how difficult it was for even a crack shot to hit a rapidly moving target when the shooter is winded and running himself, and he was no crack shot. He watched as Shaikh disappeared into the trees. Knowles reached the same spot only fifteen or twenty seconds later, but had no idea which way to go. He stopped for a moment, breathing heavily, sweat running down his forehead into his eyes, steaming his glasses, and soaking his shirt under the BPU. His good slacks were already full of burrs and ripped by thorns. He turned to the right, but as he did so, he heard the snap of a broken twig behind him. Reversing his direction, he heard more noise somewhere in the trees ahead. Gasping for breath, he lurched toward the sound, flushing Shaikh out of his hiding place. The weightlifter took off downhill this time, toward the creek and road. Knowles headed after him , trying to intercept the escape route at an angle. This time, when they reached the creek, there was no bridge. Shaikh leapt the stream in one jump, and started to scramble up the other side to the road. Knowles tried to duplicate the stunt, but being not quite as nimble, or as lucky, landed at the edge of the stream. Knowles went down in an ungainly sprawl as his foot slipped on a wet rock. He landed on his right side in the water, but he could tell he hadn't hurt himself badly. He regained his feet quickly and looked up to locate Shaikh. He had no trouble spotting him, since Peter Stroaker and one of the SOG agents were placing cuffs on him by the side of the road.

"Smooth move, Cliff," one of the SOG agents called out to him, laughing.

"I'd give it a six point five," another chimed in. "You didn't stick the landing."

Stroaker looked at him curiously. "What in the world are you doing here, Cliff?" he asked.

"Just trying to help," he answered, wiping mud from his pants. He couldn't think of a better explanation at this moment.

"Well, it looks like you did. Thanks," the SAC commented affably, and hustled Shaikh into the SOG van. The van moved on toward the Ving house, leaving Knowles standing there, muddy and dripping. Slowly, he trudged back up the road.

"Good work," Olson said to Knowles and Rothman as they walked into the San Jose command post two hours later. A few agents and clerical personnel gave them both smiles of admiration and congratulation. "Stroaker and the subjects should be arriving soon. We've called Mountain View P.D. to take custody. This will have to be prosecuted locally; they never left the state. I'm going to need you to tell the officer the whole story when he arrives."

"And what about Los Altos P.D.?"

"It turns out the kidnapping happened in Mountain View, in the parking lot, just like you thought. Los Altos has no jurisdiction."

"So what do I tell Mountain View when they throw a fit over not having been notified earlier?"

"You'll be able to handle it. I have utmost faith in you. Okay, look, you were right, I know. But just tell them we thought it was Los Altos."

"Did you get the whole story from the skinny one?" Rothman asked.

"Most of the basics; Morales called me on his cell phone and filled me in. Once they confronted him with the receipt, and the picture of his brother, he caved. He and his buddy, this goon Shaikh, just decided to get rich. They saw Fischer's picture in the paper and how rich he was, and worked out this plan to kidnap him. Al-Enwiya is a car nut who got sick of all these dot com millionaires coming in and buying fancy cars from him when he was riding around in an old beater. He was planning to buy a Z-3 with his share of the loot."

"Speaking of the loot," Knowles said, "have they found it?"

"No, not yet, and Al-Enwiya isn't talking. He's clammed up since the arrest, uh, the second arrest, and is asking for a lawyer again. Apparently he's hoping to use that last piece of info as a bargaining chip."

"What about the $650,000 number? Where did that come from," Rothman asked.

"They were originally going to ask for a million dollars even, but Fischer told them his family couldn't raise any more than $300,000 cash. Shaikh believed him, and wanted to reduce the demand to that amount. He would have been happy with $150,000. But the other guy didn't buy it. They argued, and Al-Enwiya finally decided just to pretend to agree with Shaikh, but actually ask for $650,000. That would give him his half a mil, and he would just turn $150,000 over to Shaikh without telling him what he'd actually collected. He's a sleaze."

"What about the gun and the underwater thing?" Knowles asked.

"Michael got the gun from his brother Mahmoud, just like Mahmoud said. He says his brother isn't involved, and even Michael's wife didn't know. He was going to escape using the tow. He's a diver and has experienced with them. But when he got to the beach with it, the surf was at ten feet, and he didn't think he could get out past the breakers. Then he saw the Coast Guard Cutter show up, and he abandoned that plan. He saw our SWAT guys forming up, but they weren't in place when the drop was made, and he thought he could make it on foot. He used to run cross country in high school. He grabbed the bag and ran. He didn't think anyone would figure out the car was his so soon. He thought if he got away from the scene immediately he could call someone to pick him up."

"What was he planning to do about Fischer?"

"He says he was going to release him unharmed. Of course, that's pretty self-serving at this point. We don't know if he really would have. Fischer is okay, and is riding up with Rice right now. They're caravanning with Stroaker and the SOG."

Knowles was retying his necktie and straightening his clothes. He had changed from the vest and raid jacket back to his sports coat. He knew press would be here soon. He asked, "Why did they say they had him in Mexico? Didn't he know that would bring in FBI jurisdiction?"

"No clue. They said that because they're often mistaken for Mexicans, with their coloring. They figured they'd imitate a Mexican accent and tell the family he'd been taken to Mexico, that would throw police off the track. That's why they chose that area near Hollister. That street is full of Mexican families, so they used the names Miguel and Carlos, and rented it from a Mexican. They thought that if they were ever followed or traced to that neighborhood later, the cops would be looking for Mexicans."

Stroaker walked in, entourage in tow. The noise level reached rock concert proportions as everybody descended on them. Carl Fischer was led to a quiet corner office. Stroaker told Harry Rice and Cliff to do the debriefing interview, with Knowles the lead interviewer. The Mountain View patrol officer showed up to take a report; he said he'd had some crazy direction from dispatch to drive from Mountain View over to San Jose to pick up two kidnappers on a case on which they didn't even have a report. Reporters began to show up in response to the announcement by the FBI press office that they had just arrested two kidnappers and rescued the victim. Non-essential FBI personnel were told to go home and get some rest; few left.

Pete Stroaker waited patiently until the interview with Fischer was over and Knowles and Rice emerged. When he saw Carl Fischer stand up to walk from the room, he made a signal and all the employees lining the corridor stood and applauded. Fischer was overwhelmed but managed to make a short and gracious speech thanking them for their effort. Stroaker asked him if he wanted to talk to the press, but he declined. He just wanted to get back to his family, so the SAC designated Gina Torres to drive him home. They left out the back exit.

Stroaker next announced to everybody in the halls that because of the necessity of turning the case over to the locals, everybody who had been involved in a search, arrest, or interview, would have to do their 302s before going home. There was a collective groan. Then he announced that he would begin his press conference. He headed to the empty office space used previously for the big briefing. Belinda had converted it to a makeshift press room. The American flag and FBI seal were arranged carefully so the photographers could get shots of them as backdrops during Stroaker's speech. The room was already filled with reporters and photographers, who had been alerted to come for a briefing while everyone was driving up from San Benito County. He walked to the front of the room and launched into his speech.

Olson spotted Knowles and Rothman in the command post. "Come on," he said, "Pete's starting the press conference. Let's hear what he has to say." He gathered up Len Schuler, Belinda, Matt Nguyen, Tobin, and anyone else who had been instrumental in the project, and they filtered in next door to hear the speech. Several other agents were there, or just arriving. The speech, as always, consisted primarily of platitudes and sports analogies. Stroaker kept it mercifully short, probably because his media representative had told him the TV stations were getting very close to deadline for the evening news.

"Can we get a shot of the agents who rescued Mr. Fischer, and the ones who arrested the kidnappers?" one of the television reporters asked.

"Certainly. I arrested the fellow Shaikh myself," Stroaker said. "Al-Enwiya was arrested by our SWAT Commander. Come on up, Hank," he said, waving to LaPointe. LaPointe, caught off guard, blushed a bright pink, but walked up slowly to stand next to Stroaker, fidgeting bashfully. Stroaker looked around, made brief eye contact with Cliff Knowles, then kept scanning. "And as for the agent who rescued the victim, that would be Harry Rice. Come on, Harry. Harry is our kidnap expert and hostage negotiator, trained in Quantico." Rice bounded up to the front, almost glowing with pride, the exact antithesis of LaPointe in demeanor. "And last, the supervisor who assisted me in running the whole operation, Don Zwolinski." The Z-man stepped from the crowd and stood next to Stroaker. He assumed an expression suitably serious. The camera flashes popped, and the cameramen and women moved around to get better angles.

"Mr. Stroaker," another reporter asked. "Can we get shots of the ransom money?"

Stroaker didn't blink. "I'm sorry, but we haven't brought that up from Monterey yet. Next time." Knowles heard one reporter lean over to his photographer and whisper, "They must not have it. They always show the money. I'll bet they lost it."

When Knowles was done with the interview of Fischer he had popped in to hear the SAC briefly, but then had to make the report to the Mountain View police officer. He had to explain the whole series of events from Day 1. The officer, as predicted, was none too pleased that his department had not been notified when the initial report of a kidnapping had come in and excoriated the FBI colorfully and frequently as he jotted page after page of notes. This dragged on for two hours, which really only touched the surface, as both Knowles and the officer realized that the more accurate version would be delivered in the form of the FBI report, i.e. all the 302s reporting investigation from all the agents, to come in due course. It was mid-afternoon before this finished up. Both kidnappers sat silent, in custody in the bowels of the FBI office in San Jose; the FBI had no jail and was waiting for the officer to take custody. The report to the officer finished about the same time the press conference across the hall was finishing up.

There were a few more questions and answers, but then the reporters started hustling out. They were on deadline, and now that the news was in, the radio reporters especially wanted to be the first to get it on the air. Knowles, Olson, and the other agents returned to their office. The Mountain View officer had left with his prisoners in tow, some photographers staying by the entrance to capture that scene. Rice and Morales had grabbed the arms not held by the officer as the Arabs were led from the office, knowing that they would be in the video shot that was shown the most often.

Knowles called Rickie to let her know that he was fine and the case was resolved. She was elated, but not surprised, telling him she knew he could do it, although she had no idea what "it" involved. She hadn't even heard the early news coverage; she just knew Cliff was busy on a kidnapping case and would tell her about his "day at the office" when he got home. He and Rothman flipped a coin to see who would use his computer to do his 302s first. Rothman won, so Knowles moved over to Kim's desk to work. She had gone home right after the press conference. He had massive notes to dictate from, and a lot of events to recall without the benefit of notes. He booted up the system and started to type.

When he next looked up, Tim Rothman was standing next to him. "I'm going home, Cliff," he said. "I've got a date. You can use our computer now if you want. I think we're the last ones here."

Knowles looked at his watch. It was almost 7:00 PM. He had been typing for over three hours. He realized it was getting dark out. "Okay, you take off. I'm almost done here. I'll set the alarm when I go. Good luck with Carlotta." Rothman cast a sly grin, nodded and headed down the hall.

Knowles finished his typing about 7:15 and started to pack up his gear, including his Dictaphone, since he still had more 302s to dictate. Then he heard the switchboard line ring. After hours the switchboard was put on night service, which made the ring go out over the P.A. system so anyone could pick it up if they were expecting a call. He decided it could be important, so he dialed the code to pick up that line.

"My name is Mohamed Shaikh," the caller began. "I just heard on the news that my brother was arrested by the FBI. This cannot be true. He is a devout man. This must be a mistake. Can you tell me what happened?"

"Is your brother Ahmed Shaikh?" Knowles asked.

"Yes, that is right."

"Yes, he was arrested."

"No, no there must be a mistake. Please I must talk to him. Can I come down there and see him?"

Knowles knew this was too important to ignore, but he didn't think he could get another agent to come back for this. If he waited, this guy might have a chance to talk to other relatives and any evidence he had could be lost. "Why don't you come down," Knowles answered. "I can't promise you that you will be able to talk to your brother, but I'll see what I can do." This was literally truthful, although disingenuous to say the least, Knowles knew, but, hey, this wasn't a tea party.

Mohamed Shaikh arrived at the front door to the San Jose Resident Agency within ten minutes. He was alone. Knowles made sure to be armed and have cuffs ready. He opened the door gingerly and made Shaikh walk through the metal detector. There was no alarm, so Knowles felt confident Shaikh was unarmed. Knowles told him he would have to speak to him first before the FBI could tell him anything about his brother. They sat in the interview room off the lobby. Shaikh told him that his brother had gone on a diving trip with a friend of his about a week ago, and wasn't even in the area. He didn't know the friend's name, but he was a car salesman. They were down in Pismo Beach somewhere. Whoever it was that got arrested must have been an imposter using Ahmed's name. Knowles was able to extract more useful details, including the fact that Ahmed liked to carry a knife, and was very skilled with it. He said his brother was traveling with only one friend, not two, and was not active in any Islamic group. Their family was Palestinian, but the car salesman was Iraqi. Ahmed had an old Toyota, he said when asked, with burned paint on the top surfaces. When Knowles got as much as he thought he could from Shaikh, he displayed the knife he had recovered from Ahmed. Shaikh said it looked like the one Ahmed carried. Then he showed a picture of Ahmed, the DMV photo, and announced that this is man they arrested earlier that day, and the victim had been just a few feet away chained to the floor. Mohamed set up a plaintive wail, crying that his brother had disgraced him. Knowles told him he could not visit his brother today, but could contact the county jail tomorrow to find out about visiting hours. Mohamed left, weeping and thoroughly disheartened.

Finally, well after dark, Cliff Knowles closed up the RA and drove   home.

Day 6
Sunday

Chapter 26

At 4:30 AM Hank LaPointe woke to the sound of the telephone ringing. The ASAC was calling to tell him to be at the Marina Beach at 6:00 AM with the dive team ready. They were going to go looking for the money in the water. He had had only six hours sleep after having gone the previous night with none, and very little the night before that. He dragged himself from bed and slipped into his clothes. He began calling the other SWAT members on the dive team.

Nick Lark was the first agent out on the beach that morning. He had flown back from Disneyland Saturday night, and had originally planned to have one day of rest at home before returning to work on Monday. But he had called one of the Monterey RA agents on Saturday morning to see if there was anything going on, only to find that the agent was out on a case. Eventually he tracked down the RA secretary who had filled him in on the whole story. He decided that as case agent he at least had better show up on Sunday.

Over the next hour the SWAT team, one SOG team, one ERT team, and every agent from the Monterey RA arrived. The ERT supervisor, brought down from San Francisco, was in charge. She organized the personnel and assigned them to specific grids. The SWAT was to work in a line, sweeping the beach from one end to the other offshore, in the event the money had been weighted and dumped for later recovery. One agent was assigned the Geiger counter. Others had specific tasks, such as carrying the evidence bags and tags.

LaPointe approached the waterline barefoot, then donned his swim fins there. It was too hard to walk across the sand while wearing them. As he sat in the surf, preparing to go in he noticed a large, black object floating about twenty yards out. He called to the others. One of the men ran out in his wet suit to retrieve it, wanting to get the stat for recovery of the money. When he got there, however, he was in for a surprise. The object turned out to be the head, shoulder and one fin of a sea lion. As he looked around, he noticed several other pieces floating nearby. As another agent came sloshing up next to him, they both realized that they were in the middle of what appeared to be a shark feeding. Quickly they scanned the surface for dorsal fins, but saw none. They high-tailed it back to LaPointe. He checked with the Coast Guard who assured them that there was no shark feeding frenzy - it was killer whales, not sharks. A pod of them had been spotted a couple of hours ago making short work of any sea lions foolish enough to venture into the water. They told LaPointe not to worry, the whales only attacked sea lions, which were black and shiny, about six feet long, and had tail fins in the very back; in other words, they looked just like divers in wet suits.

This fact was brought to the attention of the supervisor, who looked at the water for all of ten seconds and declared that she didn't see any killer whales, so get out there and do your job. LaPointe swallowed hard and led his men into the water.

Lark, as the senior agent in the RA, was the most familiar with the general layout of the area, although several other agents who had been in on the arrest and search the previous day knew this exact beach area better. One them led Lark along the path Al-Enwiya, aka Moussafa, aka Carlos, was believed to have taken. The Geiger counter registered nothing the entire time. The grid search was proceeding slowly and methodically as it should be done.

After four hours, they still hadn't found anything of value. Lark noticed that the marine layer was finally beginning to clear, and the breeze was dropping. He felt optimistic, and as the only agent who had had plenty of sleep, was still going strong. He suggested they talk to the man at the sand company again, so they walked to the factory door. They found a worker driving a forklift. The workman explained that he wasn't the guy who had been on duty when it all happened. That guy was off until Monday night, but he had shown everybody where the crook had gone. Lark told him they were trying to see where the crook had come from, not where he had gone. Lark knew that the money had already been disposed of some time before Al-Enwiya had run into the factory. The worker led him back down the entry path as best he knew it, but they saw nothing. The worker said, sorry, he had to get back to work and left them there.

Lark sat down to think on a weathered driftwood log lying in a mass of rotting seaweed. It was the cleanest surface he could find. He was debating the possibilities with the SOG agent, a fortyish woman who looked more like a soccer mom than an FBI agent, which was why she was so good at surveillance. She felt they should be looking at the other end of the beach reasoning that it was unlikely Fox would carry that much weight that far while being chased. As he sat, Lark noticed something odd. The breeze had died down almost completely, and the sun was breaking through. It was a gorgeous day, the kind that brought vacationers to the Monterey area. But something didn't feel right. There were flies buzzing around the seaweed, as they always did when the sun came out. But some flies seemed interested in a dead bug lying on the log. Then Lark noticed another insect lying on the ground near his foot, with ants crawling all over it. It was a butterfly with striking blue coloration. Within minutes another appeared, then another. They circled the log until Lark moved away, then landed on it and started fluttering madly around the sand next to it. More appeared overhead. Lark looked at the other agent and began to laugh. They lifted the log and began to shovel the sand frantically with their hands. A few inches down they came to bundles of hundred dollar bills. Blue butterflies swarmed into the hole crazily.

Chet Murray and Katie O'Connell led the indoor team at 15 Ving Ranch Road. Other ERT members worked outside. The photographer had already labeled the rooms and taken all the before shots. Methodically, Murray moved through the house identifying items of evidence. O'Connell maintained the log sheet and made up the labels, while Murray did the looking, dusting for prints, and bagging. Carl Fischer's monogrammed briefcase with its insidious inscription "CMF IS DEAD" became item A1. The broken cell phone and the blindfold followed in due course, along with many small and seemingly insignificant items. When they reached the second bedroom, Shaikh's dumbbells were duly labeled and collected. A quick peek in the closet revealed that it was empty, but Murray noticed a square cut in the flooring. He lifted out the panel, realizing it was the access to the crawl space under the house. When he set it on the floor it made a clunking noise like a suitcase being set down. He had read Cliff's 302 before starting the search and remembered Fischer's mentioning hearing a sound like that shortly before being rescued. Miguel had apparently been going down under house and then reemerging every few minutes. Shining a flashlight downward illuminated nothing but loose dirt. Unsatisfied, he lowered himself into the hole and moved on his hands and knees, crablike, in a full circle, turning the flashlight like a lighthouse beam sweeping rocky shoals. Raising his head again, he called for O'Connell to get the photographer back.

When the photographer had finished her work under the house, Murray brought up the only piece of physical evidence being removed from that area: a bright, shiny new shovel. He had found it next to a freshly dug, almost completed, grave. The hole was big enough for a man of six foot two.

Epilogue

Chapter 27

Ben Olson hoisted the pitcher and poured the frothy brew all around. Lifting his mug, he proposed a toast, "To Transitions."

"Hear, hear," Cliff Knowles agreed. They all clinked glasses, mumbling "to transitions" in unison. "Stroaker retiring and Shaikh convicted. Not a bad week, all in all."

Gina Torres nursed her glass of Chardonnay delicately. "Why did he go to trial at all, that's what I don't understand?"

"Well," Knowles answered, "after Michael the mastermind cooperated and pleaded guilty, and got life plus twenty-five years, the light began to dawn in his feeble brain. What did Shaikh have to lose going to trial? A guilty plea would just get him an adjoining cell in Soledad for the next two or three decades."

"He didn't do any better," she pointed out. "Life plus fifteen - plus his whole family humiliated?"

Rothman started chuckling. "He didn't help himself by jumping up in front of the jury and crying out that the trial wasn't fair because what he did wasn't even as bad as murder. Up until that point he still had a long shot on beating the charge on a case of mistaken identity. Michael refused to cooperate after getting screwed on his sentence, so the prosecutor was afraid to call him, not knowing what he would say on the stand. Fischer's identification of him was marginal, Shaikh had changed his appearance so much by trial. He'd shaved and dropped twenty pounds. His scumbag brother got up and testified that Ahmed was with him during the whole time, even after telling Cliff exactly the opposite at the interview in the RA."

Cliff objected, "Yeah, but they still had his fingerprints all over the site and the car, and the neighbor's identification of him and his Toyota casing the Fischer home. All of Al-Enwiya's confession, including everything implicating Shaikh, was admissible, even though it was hearsay, under the co-conspirator's exception. And, best of all, the prosecutor was a genius admitting the briefcase and shovel, covered with Shaikh's fingerprints, into evidence early on, so they could sit there on the prosecution table all throughout the trial, with that crude carving facing the jury, 'CMF IS DEAD.' I think Shaikh had the chances of a pork chop in a hyena pack from the beginning. It's just too bad we couldn't prosecute federally."

"You know, what I do feel bad about, though," Nick Lark said, "is that none of you guys got anything out of it. LaPointe got credit for one arrest, Stroaker took credit for arresting Shaikh himself, and I got the stat for recovery of the money and for the conviction. Shit, I was on holiday the whole time. Z-man's now an ASAC. Rice got the credit for the rescue. You guys solved the damn case. And now Stroaker is a V.P. for Security at some bank, in charge of protecting its whole e-commerce operation"

"He asked me what a hard drive was just last month," Olson said.

"Remind me to cut up my iGlobe credit card when I get home," Cliff said.

"Nick," Olson said, "Don't feel bad about the stats. There was no money given out on the case anyway, because the Bureau was so pissed at Stroaker for disobeying them. That's the first successful rescue in a kidnap case I've ever heard of where there was no incentive award given."

Torres had another question, "Did we ever determine who that Ruben guy was that Fischer told us about?"

Knowles, Rothman, and Olson all looked at each other before Cliff fielded it. "Not 100% for sure. But I think it had to be Al-Enwiya in disguise. He even admitted it at one point, but then retracted it. I think he just got so angry about getting no reduction in his sentence, he decided to throw us into confusion. He was just trying to scare Fischer into thinking they were a bigger operation, like he did when he called the underwater tow a torpedo."

Torres squinched her eyebrows together and formed a sort of pout. "But Fischer said the shoes and the voice were different."

"Yeah," Cliff replied, "I know. But Al-Enwiya said they knew he was peeking out the bottom of the blindfold. He kept tipping his head back when they were around. "Carlos" changed his shoes and his voice. He imitated a Mexican accent pretty convincingly on the phone, you know. We never found physical evidence to indicate a third person."

Matt Nguyen had listened quietly to the senior agents, but finally had to ask, "Why is it Rice and Morales got to be on TV, when their biggest contribution was letting the subjects escape?"

"Let me tell you something about TV," Olson replied. "What you see on TV has no relation to reality. TV news doesn't want reality, they want viewers, and the FBI isn't much better. That video clip of them walking Shaikh out the door will make a nice memento to show their kids, or grandkids. Why spoil that? Let them be heroes in their own houses. They got so eviscerated on cross examination during the preliminary hearing, the prosecutor wouldn't call them at trial. They're the laughing stock of the law enforcement community, and now they can't find retirement jobs."

"Wrong," Knowles said. "I just heard that Stroaker is taking them with him to iGlobe to be the 'crack team' in charge of the personal protection of the CEO. More like the 'crock team' if you ask me." Thinking it a clever remark, he shot a glance at Nguyen, expecting the usual nodding approval from the young FOA, normally a big Knowles fan since the rescue, but saw Nguyen was paying attention only to Torres, who sat next to him. Suddenly he realized why Nguyen had taken to wearing cowboy boots and Torres wore nothing but flats these days. To confirm his suspicions he dropped a napkin and quickly bent under the table to retrieve it. Sure enough, he was just quick enough to see her hand pull away from Matt's knee. He rose, smiling enigmatically.

"Shit," Lark said, giving an involuntary shudder. "Will somebody find out who the insurance company is that insures that CEO's life. I want to sell my stock in it, if I have any."

It was Rothman who spoke up next. "Ben, what have you heard about the new SAC?"

"They're all the same. They come and they go. The first thing he has to do is come down and make kissy face with the chief over at Mountain View P.D. They're still so pissed over not being called in for the kidnapping from day one they won't cooperate on bank robberies or fugitives now. And the other chiefs are backing him up. We need them, and it's about time some SAC realizes that. The arrogance of the executives is what gets us in trouble with the press and the locals every time. The agents work well with the cops on the street level, at least we always have around here. I guess that's not true everywhere."

Nick Lark tossed down the last of his beer, and stood to leave. "Well, it's still just not fair. Stroaker, Z-man, and Morales all moving on to more pay and more recognition for screwing up. You guys save a life, catch two scumbags before they have a chance to kill the victim, and we recover the loot. Even the MVPD detective told me during trial they couldn't have done it. The FBI is the only agency that can mobilize over the west coast, cover leads from Mexico to Seattle on five minutes notice, and mount a rescue operation over nine counties. No local police agency has a Cliff Knowles or a Hank LaPointe. And what do you guys get ..."

Olson interrupted, "We get the chance to stay here and throw more bad guys in jail - and get paid for it, too. Besides, Z-man and Brad Williams both know Cliff solved the case. Cliff's a shoe-in for the new High Tech Squad supervisor slot when it gets funded."

They all looked at each other as Olson's bit of wisdom sunk in. Cliff raised his glass and said, "As Ben said, 'To transitions'." They all clinked glasses once more.

Made in the USA
Charleston, SC
17 May 2012